The Last Gunfighter: Renegades

Also by William W. Johnstone
in Large Print:

Ambush of the Mountain Man
Code Name: Coldfire
Code Name: Death
Code Name: Quickstrike
Cunning of the Mountain Man
Warpath of the Mountain Man
Wrath of the Mountain Man
The Last Gunfighter: Imposter
The Last Gunfighter: Manhunt
The Last Gunfighter: No Man's Land
The Last Gunfighter: Rescue
The Last Gunfighter: Showdown
The Last Gunfighter: The Burning
The Last Gunfighter: Violent Sunday

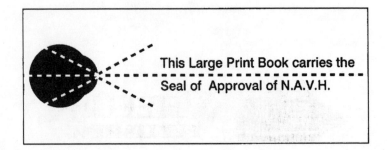

The Last Gunfighter: Renegades

William W. Johnstone

WHEELER PUBLISHING

Published in 2006 by arrangement with Pinnacle Books, an imprint of Kensington Publishing Corp.

Wheeler Large Print Western.

The text of this Large Print edition is unabridged. Other aspects of the book may vary from the original edition.

Set in 16 pt. Plantin by Elena Picard.

Printed in the United States on permanent paper.

Library of Congress Cataloging-in-Publication Data

Johnstone, William W.
    The last gunfighter. : Renegades / by William W. Johnstone.
      p. cm. — (Wheeler Publishing large print westerns)
    ISBN 1-59722-225-9 (lg. print : sc : alk. paper)
    1. Morgan, Frank (Fictitious character) — Fiction.
2. Outlaws — Fiction. 3. Texas — Fiction. 4. Large type
books. I. Title. II. Wheeler large print western series.
PS3560.O415L35535 2006
  813'.54—dc22   2006002246

The Last Gunfighter: Renegades

National Association for Visually Handicapped
·----------------------- *serving the partially seeing*

As the Founder/CEO of NAVH, the only national health agency solely devoted to those who, although not totally blind, have an eye disease which could lead to serious visual impairment, I am pleased to recognize Thorndike Press* as one of the leading publishers in the large print field.

Founded in 1954 in San Francisco to prepare large print textbooks for partially seeing children, NAVH became the pioneer and standard setting agency in the preparation of large type.

Today, those publishers who meet our standards carry the prestigious "Seal of Approval" indicating high quality large print. We are delighted that Thorndike Press is one of the publishers whose titles meet these standards. We are also pleased to recognize the significant contribution Thorndike Press is making in this important and growing field.

Lorraine H. Marchi, L.H.D.
Founder/CEO
NAVH

* Thorndike Press encompasses the following imprints: Thorndike, Wheeler, Walker and Large Print Press.

1

Brown County, Texas, and all the violence that had taken place there were a long way behind Frank Morgan now. The man sometimes known as The Drifter had lived up to his name, riding southward toward the Rio Grande, taking his time, in no hurry to get where he was going . . . wherever that was. Someplace where his past might not catch up to him. A haven where he could go unrecognized.

But as idyllic as that sounded, Frank Morgan knew there wasn't much chance that he would ever find such a sanctuary.

It was hard to blend in when you were the last of the really fast guns.

Some of the others were still alive — Wyatt Earp, Bat Masterson, and Smoke Jensen were three that Frank could think of. Somehow they had managed to settle down. John Wesley Hardin was still alive, too, but he was in prison. Bill Hickok, Ben

Thompson, Doc Holliday, Luke Short . . . They were all dead, along with most of the other shootists and pistoleers who had made names for themselves at one time or another on the frontier.

It was a sad time, in a way. A dying time. But a man couldn't stop the march of progress and so-called civilization. Nor was Frank Morgan the sort of hombre to brood about it and cling to the fading shadows of what once had been. He looked to the future, not the past.

Now the future meant finding a warm, hospitable place to spend the winter. It was November, and up north the snow and the frigid winds were already roaring down out of Canada to sweep across the mountains and the plains, all the way down to the Texas Panhandle. Hundreds of miles south of the Panhandle, however, here in the Rio Grande Valley of south Texas, the sky was blue, the sun was shining, and the temperature was quite pleasant. Frank even had the sleeves of his blue work shirt rolled up a couple of turns on his muscular forearms.

He was a lean, well-built man of middle years, with gray streaking the thick dark hair under his Stetson. His range clothes were of good quality, as was his saddle. A

Colt .45 was holstered on his hip, and the stock of a Winchester stuck up from a saddle sheath under his right leg. He rode a fine-looking Appaloosa called Stormy and led a dun-colored packhorse. The big shaggy cur known as Dog padded alongside him as Frank rode down a trail that cut its way through the thick chaparral covering the mostly flat landscape.

Frank didn't know exactly where he was, but he thought he must be getting close to the Rio Grande. Some sleepy little border village would be a good spot to pass the winter, he mused. Cool beer, some tortillas and beans and chili, maybe a pretty señorita or two to keep him company . . . It sounded fine to Frank. Maybe not heaven, but likely as close as a gunfighter like him would ever get.

Into every heavenly vision, though, a little hell had to intrude. The distant popping of gunfire suddenly came to Frank's ears.

He reined in and frowned. The shots continued, coming fast and furious. They were still a ways off, but they were getting closer, without a doubt. He heard the rumble of hoofbeats, too. Some sort of running gun battle, Frank decided.

And it was running straight toward him.

He had never been one to dodge trouble. There just wasn't any back-up in his nature. Instead he nudged his heels into Stormy's sides and sent the Appaloosa trotting forward. Whatever was coming at him, Frank Morgan would go right out to meet it.

Now he could see dust clouds boiling in the air ahead of him, kicked up by all the horses he heard. A moment later, the trail he was following intersected a road at a sharp angle. The pursuit was on the road itself, which was wide enough for a couple of wagons and a half-dozen or so riders.

Only one wagon came toward Frank, a buckboard that swayed and bounced as it careened along the road. The dust from the hooves of the team pulling it obscured the occupants to a certain extent, but Frank thought he saw two men on the buckboard, one handling the reins while the other twisted around on the seat and fired a rifle back at the men giving chase.

There were more than a dozen of those, Frank saw. He estimated the number at twenty. They rode bunched up, the ones in the lead banging away at the fleeing buckboard with six-guns. The gap between hunter and hunted was about fifty yards, too far for accurate handgun fire, especially from the saddle of a racing horse. But the rifleman on the buckboard didn't seem to be having much better luck. The group of riders surged on without slowing.

Frank had no idea who any of these men were and didn't know which side he ought to take in this fight. But he'd always had a natural sympathy for the underdog, so he didn't like the idea of two against twenty.

He liked it even less when one of the horses in the team suddenly went down, probably the result of stepping in a prairie-dog hole. The horse screamed in pain, a shrill sound that Frank heard even over the rattle of gunfire and the pounding of hoofbeats. Probably a broken leg, he thought in the instant before the fallen horse pulled down the other members of the team and caused the buckboard to overturn violently. The two men who had been in it flew through the air like rag dolls.

Frank sent Stormy surging forward at a gallop. He didn't know if the men had survived the wreck or not, but it was a cinch they were out of the fight, at least for the moment, and wouldn't survive the next few seconds unless somebody helped them. He drew the Winchester and guided Stormy with his knees as he brought the rifle to his shoulder and blazed away, firing as fast as he could work the repeater's lever.

He put the first couple of bullets over the heads of the pursuers to see if they would give up the chase. When they didn't, but kept attacking instead, sending a couple of bullets whizzing past him, Frank had no choice but to lower his aim. Stormy's smooth gait and Frank's years of experience meant that he was a good shot even from the hurricane deck. His bullets laced into the crowd of gunmen in the road.

Frank was close enough now to see that most of the pursuers wore high-crowned, broad-brimmed sombreros. *Bandidos* from below the border, he thought. A few men in American range garb were mixed in the group, but that came as no surprise. Gringo outlaws sometimes crossed the Rio and fell in with gangs of Mexican raiders. A man who was tough enough and ruthless enough — and good enough with a gun — could usually find a home for himself with others of his kind, no matter where he was.

Two of the bandits plunged off their horses as Frank's shots ripped through them, and a couple of others sagged in their saddles and dropped out of the fight, obviously wounded. The other men reined their mounts to skidding, sliding halts that made even more dust billow up from the hard-packed caliche surface of the road. Clearly, they hadn't expected to run into opposition like that which Frank was putting up now.

But the odds were still on their side, and after a moment of hesitation they attacked again, yelling curses and firing as they came toward the overturned wagon.

Both of the men who had been thrown from the wreck staggered to their feet as Frank came closer. He didn't know how badly they were hurt, but at least they were conscious and able to move around. They stumbled toward the shelter of the buckboard as bullets flew around them.

While Stormy was still galloping, Frank swung down from the saddle, as good a running dismount as anyone could make. He had the Winchester in his left hand. With his right, he slapped the Appaloosa on the rump and ordered, "Stormy, get out of here! You, too, Dog!"

The horse veered off into the chaparral at the side of the road, finding an opening in the thorny stuff. The big cur was more reluctant, obviously hesitant to abandon his master in the middle of a fight. Frank didn't want to have to worry about them while he was battling for his life, though, so he added, "Dog, go!"

With a growl, Dog disappeared into the brush.

Frank ran to the wagon and joined the two men who were already crouched behind it, firing revolvers at the charging *bandidos.* The man who had been using the rifle earlier had lost the weapon when the buckboard flipped over. Both of them had managed to hang on to their handguns, though.

The buckboard was on its side, turned crossways in the road. The horses had struggled back to their feet, except for the one with the broken leg, and they lunged and reared in their traces, maddened by the gunfire and the reeking clouds of powder smoke that drifted through the air. A couple of them had been wounded by flying lead.

Frank rested his Winchester on the buckboard and opened fire again, placing his shots carefully now that he had a chance to aim. One of the raiders flipped backward out of the saddle as if he had been swatted by a giant hand, and another fell forward over his mount's neck before slipping off and landing under the horse's slashing hooves.

Bullets pounded into the buckboard like a deadly hailstorm of lead. The thick boards stopped most of them, but a few of the rounds punched through, luckily missing Frank and his two companions. The shots from the men fighting alongside him were taking a toll on the attackers as well. Less than half of the *bandidos* were unscathed so far. The others had been either killed or wounded.

The Winchester ran dry. Frank dropped it and drew his Colt. The range was plenty close enough now for an expert pistol shot like Frank Morgan. He triggered twice and was rewarded by the sight of another rider plummeting from the saddle.

The gang of *bandidos* had had enough. They wheeled their horses, still snapping shots at the buckboard as they did so, and then lit a shuck out of there. Frank and the two men threw a few shots after them to hurry them on their way, but the riders were out of pistol range in a matter of moments.

Frank holstered the Colt and picked up the Winchester, then proceeded to reload the rifle with cartridges from his pocket in case the raiders turned around and tried again. From the looks of it, though, the bandits had no intention of returning. The dust cloud their horses kicked up dwindled in the distance.

"Keep riding, you bastards!" growled the older of the two men from the buckboard as he shook a fist after the *bandidos*. "Don't stop until you get back across the border to hell, as far as I'm concerned!"

The man was stocky and grizzled, with a graying, close-cropped beard. Most of his head was bald. His hands and face had a weathered, leathery look, an indication that he had spent most of his life out-doors.

The second man was younger, taller, and clean-shaven, but he bore a resemblance to the older man that Frank recognized right away. He pegged them as father and son, or perhaps uncle and nephew. Both men were dressed in well-kept range clothes that would have looked better if they hadn't been covered in trail dust. They had the appearance of successful cattlemen about them.

Frank spotted the other rifle lying on the ground about twenty feet away. He nodded toward it and said, "Better pick up that re-peater, just in case they come back."

The older man snorted contemptuously. "They won't be back! Bunch of no-good, cowardly dogs! They travel in a pack and won't attack unless the odds are ten to one in their favor."

"And we cut those odds down in a hurry," the younger man said. He hurried over to retrieve the rifle anyway, Frank noted.

The riders had disappeared in the distance now, without even any dust showing. Deciding that they were truly gone, Frank walked out from behind the buckboard and went to check on the men who had fallen from their horses during the fight. He counted seven of them. Six were already dead, and the seventh was unconscious and badly wounded. Blood bubbled from his mouth in a crimson froth with every ragged breath he took, and Frank heard the air whistling through bullet-punctured lungs. The man dragged in one last breath and then let it out in a shuddery sigh, dying without regaining consciousness.

Frank's expression didn't change as he watched the man pass over the divide. *Any man's death diminishes me,* John Donne had written, and in a philosophical way Frank supposed there might be some truth to that. Donne, however, had never swapped lead with a *bandido.*

Five of the men were Mexicans, typical

south-of-the-border hard cases. The other two were American cousins of the same sort. Frank checked their pockets, found nothing but spare shells for their guns and some coins.

A pistol shot made him look around. The younger man had just put the injured horse out of its misery.

Frank walked back to the buckboard. The younger man began unhitching the team and trying to calm the horses. The older man met Frank with a suspicious look. He asked, "Who are you, mister? Why'd you jump into that fracas on our side?"

"My name's Morgan," Frank said, "and I just thought it looked like you could use a hand. I never have liked an unfair fight."

The man nodded and wiped the back of his hand across his nose, which was bleeding a little. That seemed to be the only injury either of them had suffered in the wreck of the buckboard. They had been mighty lucky.

"Well, the boy an' me are much obliged. My name's Cecil Tolliver. That's my son Ben."

Ben Tolliver paused in what he was doing to look over at Frank and nod. "Howdy." He turned back to the horses, and then paused and looked at Frank again. "Wouldn't be Frank Morgan, would it?"

Frank tried not to sigh. Just once, he thought, he would like to ride in somewhere and not have somebody recognize him almost right away.

And it would have been nice, too, if nobody shot at him.

2

"Yes, I'm Frank Morgan," he admitted.

Cecil Tolliver frowned. "I don't mean to sound ignorant, mister, but I don't reckon I've heard of you."

Ben came over and held out his hand to Frank. "That's because you never read any dime novels," he explained to his father. "Mr. Morgan here is a famous gunfighter."

Tolliver grunted. "I never had time for such foolishness, boy. I was too busy tryin' to build the Rockin' T into a decent spread. You was the one who always had your nose in the *Police Gazette*."

Frank shook hands with both of them and said to Ben, "Most of what's been written about me in those dime novels and the illustrated weeklies was a pack of lies made up by gents who don't know much about the real West."

"You can't deny, though, that you've had your share of gunfights," Ben said.

Frank inclined his head in acknowledgment of that point. "More than my share," he allowed.

"Well, we're much obliged for the help, whether you're famous or not," Tolliver said. "If you hadn't come along when you did, I reckon Almanzar's boys would've done for me and Ben."

"Almanzar," Frank repeated. "I'm not familiar with the name. Is he the leader of that gang of *bandidos?*"

"You could call him that. He runs the rancho where those gunnies work."

Now it was Frank's turn to frown. He waved his left hand toward the sprawled bodies of the raiders and said, "Those don't look like vaqueros or cowhands to me."

"That's because Almanzar's a low-down skunk who hires killers rather than decent hombres."

"Sounds like you don't care for the man."

"I got no use for him," Tolliver said stiffly. "Him and me been feudin' ever since I came to this part of the country, nigh on to thirty years ago. Almanzar specializes in wet cattle, if you know what I mean."

Frank understood the term, all right. It

referred to stock rustled from one side of the river and driven to the other. Down here in this border country, a lot of cattle had gotten their bellies wet over the past few decades, going both directions across the Rio Grande.

Young Ben spoke up. "You don't know that Don Felipe has been rustling our cows, Pa."

"I know all I need to know," Tolliver replied with a disgusted snort. "Almanzar's a thief and a bloody-handed reiver, and this ain't the first time he's tried to have me killed!"

Obviously, there was trouble going on around here, Frank thought. Just as obviously, it was none of his business. But by taking a hand in this gun battle, he had probably dealt himself into the game, whether he wanted that or not. If Cecil Tolliver was correct about Don Felipe Almanzar sending those gunmen after him and his son, then Almanzar would be likely to want vengeance on Frank for killing several of his men.

"Another thing," Tolliver went on angrily to Ben, "I don't want to hear you callin' that bastard by his Christian name again. He ain't our friend and never has been."

"What about when you first settled here, before I was born?" Ben asked. "I've heard you say more than once, Pa, that without Señor Almanzar's help, the Comanches would have lifted your hair back in those days."

"That was a long time ago," Tolliver growled. "Things change."

Frank wasn't really interested in the history of the feud between Tolliver and Don Felipe Almanzar. He said, "Where were you men headed?"

"Back to the Rockin' T," Tolliver replied. "We'd been to San Rosa for supplies." He shook his head in disgust. "All the boxes done bounced out back along the road, when that bunch jumped us and we had to take off so fast. We're lucky the damn buckboard didn't rattle itself to pieces."

"San Rosa's the nearest town?"

"Yep, right on the river about five miles upstream from here. The name's fouled up — it ought to be Santa Rosa — but the fella who stuck the name on it didn't savvy Mex talk. Still a pretty nice place."

"I'll pay it a visit," Frank said. "I was looking for a place to get something to eat and somewhere to stay."

"You don't have to go to San Rosa for that." Tolliver jerked a thumb at the buckboard. "Help us set that wagon up, and then you can ride on to the Rockin' T with us. You'll be our guest for as long as you want to stay, Mr. Morgan."

"Call me Frank. And I wouldn't want to impose —"

"Impose, hell!" Tolliver had picked up his hat, and now he slapped it against his leg to get some of the dust off. As he settled it on his head, he went on. "After what you done to help us, I'll consider it a personal insult if you don't let us feed you and put you up for a spell."

Frank smiled. "In that case, I accept."

He whistled and Stormy came out of the chaparral, followed by Dog. Tolliver and Ben looked with admiration at the big Appaloosa, but were more wary where Dog was concerned. "That critter looks a mite like a cross between a wolf and a grizzly bear," Tolliver commented.

"He's all dog," Frank said with a grin. "Just be sure you've been introduced properly before you go to pet him. Unless you're a little kid," he added. "He'll let kids wool him around like he's still a pup."

Frank took his rope from the saddle and tied one end to the buckboard. Ben saw what he was doing and brought over the surviving three members of the team. The rope was tied to their harness, and the horses did the work as the buckboard was soon pulled upright again. Frank hitched Stormy into the empty spot in the team. The Appaloosa didn't care much for that, but he was willing to tolerate it if that was what Frank wanted him to do. Stormy turned a baleful eye on his master for a moment, though.

"I'd watch out for that horse if I was you, Mr. Morgan," Ben said. "He looks like he might sneak up on you some time and take a nip out of your hide."

"I fully expect that he will," Frank agreed with a chuckle. He grew more sober as he gestured toward the bodies again. "What about them?"

"I'll be damned if I'm gonna get their blood all over my buckboard," Cecil Tolliver said. "When we get to the ranch, I'll send a rider to San Rosa to notify the law. In the meantime, a couple o' my hands can come back out with a work wagon to load up the carcasses. The undertaker can come to the ranch to get 'em for plantin'."

"There's law in San Rosa?"

"Yeah, a town marshal. And there's a company of Rangers that's been usin' the town as their headquarters for a spell, while they try to track down some bandits

25

who've been raisin' hell around here."

Frank's interest perked up at the mention of Texas Rangers. Over the past year or so he had shared several adventures with a young Ranger named Tyler Beaumont. Beaumont was back home with his wife in Weatherford now, recuperating from injuries he had received in that fence-cutting dustup in Brown County. Frank respected the Rangers a great deal as a force for law and order, even though his reputation as a gunfighter sometimes made the Rangers look on him with suspicion.

He wasn't looking for trouble down here along the border, though, so it was unlikely he would clash with the lawmen.

Tolliver and Ben climbed onto the seat of the buckboard. Frank tied his packhorse on at the back of the vehicle, then sat down with his legs dangling off the rear. When he snapped his fingers, Dog jumped onto the buckboard and settled down beside him. Tolliver got the team moving and drove on toward his ranch, the Rocking T.

Frank saw cattle in the chaparral as the buckboard rolled along. They were longhorns, the sort of tough, hardy breed that was required in this brushy country. Longhorns seemed to survive, even to thrive, in it where other breeds had fallen by the wayside. The ugly, dangerous brutes had been the beginning of the cattle industry in Texas, back in the days immediately following the Civil War. Animals that had been valuable only for their hide and tallow had suddenly become beef on the hoof, the source of a small fortune for the men daring enough and tough enough to round them up and make the long drive over the trails to the railhead in Kansas.

As a young cowboy, Frank had ridden along on more than one of those drives, pushing the balky cattle through dust and rain, heat and cold, and danger from Indians and outlaws. Since the railroads had reached Texas, the days of such cattle drives were over. Now a man seldom had to move his herds more than a hundred miles or so before reaching a shipping point. As much as he lamented some things about the settling of the West, Frank didn't miss those cattle drives. They had been long, arduous, perilous work.

With an arm looped around Dog's shaggy neck, he turned his head and asked the Tollivers, "How much stock have you been losing lately?"

"Not that much," Ben said.

His father snorted. "Not that much at one time, you mean. Half a dozen here, a

27

dozen there. But it sure as hell adds up."

Frank knew what Tolliver meant. Rustlers could make a big raid on a ranch, or they could bleed it dry over time. Either method could prove devastating to a cattleman.

"The Rangers haven't been able to get a line on the wide-loopers?"

"They're too busy lookin' for the Black Scorpion."

"The Black Scorpion?" Frank repeated. "What's that?"

"You mean who's that. You recollect what I said about the Rangers huntin' for a gang of owlhoots? Well, the Black Scorpion is the boss outlaw, the son of a bitch who heads up that gang."

Ben laughed. "Now you're talking like the one who's been reading dime novels, Pa."

"The Black Scorpion's real, damn it," Tolliver said with a scowl. "Folks have seen him, dressed all in black and wearin' a mask, leadin' that bloodthirsty bunch o' desperadoes."

That sounded pretty far-fetched to Frank, too, like the creation of one of those ink-stained wretches who made up stories about him. There might be some truth to it, though. The West had seen mysterious masked bandits before, such as Black Bart out in California. Frank was going to have to see this so-called Black Scorpion for himself, though, before he would really believe in such an individual.

Ben was equally skeptical, saying, "I'll believe it when I see it. It seems to me that Captain Wedge and the Rangers are wasting their time looking for phantoms when they ought to be hunting down rustlers."

"Well, I ain't gonna argue about that," his father said. "I wish they'd do something about the damn rustlers, too."

Frank sat in the back of the buckboard and mulled over what he had heard. He had come down here to the border country looking for someplace warm and peaceful. It was warm, all right, but evidently far from peaceful, what with the feud between Cecil Tolliver and Don Felipe Almanzar, the rustlers plaguing the Rocking T, and another gang of bandits led by a mysterious masked figure. With all that going on, it seemed like trouble could crop up from any direction with little or no warning — or from several directions at once.

"Is it possible the Black Scorpion could be responsible for the rustling?" Frank asked.

"Folks have thought about that," Tolliver replied, "but me and some o' the other ranchers around here have lost stock on the same nights that the Black Scorpion's gang was reported to be maraudin' on the other side of the border. The varmint can't be in two places at the same time."

"No, I reckon not," Frank said, but he wasn't completely convinced. His instincts told him that there was even more going on around here than was readily apparent.

His instincts also told him that the smart thing to do would be to unhitch Stormy from the team, mount up, and light a shuck out of here. The troubles had nothing to do with him, and if he stayed around and was drawn deeper into them, his hopes for a quiet, relaxing winter might well be shattered.

On the other hand, he had never turned his back on trouble just to make it easier on himself, and he was a mite too old to start now. A leopard couldn't change its spots, nor a tiger its stripes.

The sun was low in the sky by the time the buckboard reached the headquarters of the Rocking T. Frank saw a large, white-washed house sitting in the shade of several cottonwood trees. Behind it were a couple of barns, several corrals, a bunkhouse, a cookshack, a blacksmith shop, a chicken coop, and some storage buildings. There was a vegetable garden off to one side of the house, and beyond it a small orchard filled with fruit trees. It was a mighty nice layout, Frank thought, the sort of spread that required years of hard work and dedication to build. He admired a man like Cecil Tolliver who could put down roots and create something lasting and worthwhile like this. For all of his accomplishments, Frank had never been able to achieve that. True, he had quite a few business interests scattered across the West, business interests that had made him a wealthy man, at least on paper, but he had inherited those things, not worked for them and built them himself. Most of the time, he felt as if all he truly owned were his guns and not much else. Stormy and Dog were friends, not possessions. And most of the time, that was all right. Frank didn't miss the rest of it except at moments such as this, when he looked at the Rocking T and wondered what his life would have been like if things had been different, if he hadn't been blessed — or cursed — with such blinding speed and uncanny accuracy with a gun.

Tolliver hauled back on the reins and

brought the buckboard to a halt. "This is it," he said. "Welcome to the Rocking T, Mr. Morgan."

3

Their arrival hadn't gone unnoticed. A small black, brown, and tan dog came racing around the house, barking sharply at the buckboard. The dog stopped abruptly, however, when it spotted the big cur sitting next to Frank in the back of the vehicle. A growl rumbled deeply in Dog's throat and was echoed by the smaller animal, even though Dog was more than ten times his size.

"Don't get your back fur in an uproar there, Dobie," Tolliver called to the little dog. "This here's a friend."

"Behave yourself, Dog," Frank said firmly to the cur.

Dog jumped down from the buckboard. He and Dobie sniffed warily at each other, but neither of them snapped. After a moment, Dog strolled over to a clump of grass and hiked his leg to relieve himself on it. Dobie followed suit, establishing himself as the boss around here. Dog seemed to accept that, and if he'd been a human he would have shrugged, Frank thought as he watched the byplay between the two animals.

Dobie wasn't the only one to greet the newcomers. Several men walked out of one of the barns and came toward the buckboard. At the same time, the front door of the ranch house opened and four women emerged. Two of them were fairly young and had the same sandy-colored hair that Ben did. One of the older women had gray hair, while the other was a stunning brunette.

"Come on," Tolliver said as he climbed down from the wagon. "I'll introduce you to the womenfolk."

Frank slid off the back of the buckboard and followed Tolliver and Ben to the house. When he reached the bottom of the three steps that led up to the porch, he took off his hat.

"Ladies, this here is Mr. Frank Morgan," Tolliver said. With rough-hewn gallantry, he went on. "Mr. Morgan, allow me to present my wife Pegeen and our daughters Debra and Jessie. And this is Pegeen's sister Roanne."

Frank held his hat in front of him and

nodded politely. "Ladies," he said. "The honor and the pleasure are mine."

"We're pleased to meet you, Mr. Morgan," Pegeen Tolliver said. She was oldest of the four women, the one with gray hair. She was still a handsome woman, though, and the same lines of timeless beauty to be found in her face were also present in the faces of her sister and her daughters. Roanne, who was around thirty, Frank estimated, was especially lovely. There wasn't that much age difference between her and her nieces, who were both between twenty and twenty-five, fine-looking young frontier women. And both already married, too, judging by the rings on their fingers.

Frank noted that Roanne wore no ring at all, for whatever that was worth.

The men who had come out of the barn reached the house. Two of them stepped up onto the porch and moved next to Debra and Jessie. "My sons-in-law," Cecil Tolliver introduced them. "That's Darrell Forrest with Jessie and Nick Holmes with Debra. They're both top hands."

Frank shook hands with Darrell and Nick and said, "Glad to meet you, boys."

Darrell Forrest looked intently at Frank and said, "Frank Morgan . . . that was the name, sir?"

Before Frank could say anything, Ben Tolliver said, "That's right, Darrell. He's The Drifter."

Pegeen put a hand on her husband's arm and said, "Cecil, you went to town for supplies, but I don't see any in the buckboard. And one of the horses is missing. Does that spotted horse belong to Mr. Morgan?"

"That's right," Tolliver told her. His bearded face grew grim as he continued. "The supplies are scattered up and down the road this side o' San Rosa, where they got jolted out when we had to run from a bunch o' gunmen."

Pegeen's hand tightened on Tolliver's arm. "Are you or Ben hurt?"

"I reckon we'll have some bruises tomorrow. We got throwed off the buckboard when it turned over durin' the chase. But Mr. Morgan come along right about then and helped us fight off those bast— those no-good skunks." Tolliver looked at Nick Holmes. "Nick, send a rider to San Rosa to tell Flem Jarvis that we've got the bodies of seven o' them owlhoots out here waitin' for the undertaker."

"Seven bodies!" Nick exclaimed. "But I don't see —"

"That's because they're still out on the road right now. Once you've sent a man to

36

town, you and Darrell take a couple of hands and a work wagon and go out to get the corpses."

The ladies all looked a little shaken by this casual discussion of corpses and an attack by a gang of outlaws. Being good frontier women, though, they remained calm and didn't waste time with a bunch of chattering questions. It took more than a little trouble to rattle a true woman of the West. And these were Texas women, which meant they had backbone second to none.

Pegeen turned to Frank and said, "Thank you for helping my husband and my son, Mr. Morgan. I hope you plan to stay for supper and spend the night with us. A little hospitality is the least we can do for you."

"Yes, ma'am," Frank said with a smile. "Your husband already told me I'd be staying a while, and I sure appreciate the kindness."

"You're very welcome. Come on inside. I'll bet you could use a cup of coffee."

"Ma'am, coffee is one of my biggest weaknesses," Frank said, his smile widening into a grin. He went into the house with Tolliver, Ben, and the women, while Darrell and Nick hurried off to carry out Tolliver's orders.

The house was well appointed, with thick rugs on the floors and heavy, over-stuffed furniture. A massive stone fireplace dominated one wall of the parlor. A tremendous spread of longhorns adorned the wall above the fireplace. Several sets of deer antlers were attached to the wall as well, and rifles and shotguns hung on pegs. A cavalry saber was also on display, and when Cecil Tolliver noticed Frank's interest in it, the rancher said, "I carried that when I rode with Jeb Stuart, Fitz Lee, and Mac Brannon during the war, Mr. Morgan. That was before I came out here to Texas."

"I thought I detected a hint of Virginia in your voice, sir," Frank said.

"Were you in the war?"

"I was . . . but that was a long time ago."

Tolliver clapped a hand on his shoulder. "Indeed it was. After supper, I'll break out a bottle of brandy I've been savin', and we'll drink to old times. They weren't the best of times, but they made us what we are."

"I reckon that's true enough," Frank agreed. Almost three decades had passed since the end of the war, but it remained the single biggest event in most men's lives.

A man couldn't spend all his time looking backward, though. As the women left Frank, Tolliver, and Ben in the parlor, Frank steered the conversation back to the here and now by saying, "I suppose you've had your hands riding patrol at night, trying to stop the rustling."

Tolliver nodded. "Damn right I have. All it's gotten me is one puncher shot dead and another laid up with a bullet-busted shoulder."

"So the rustlers don't hesitate to shoot?"

"Not at all. Anyway, this is a big spread. It'd take an army to cover all of it at night." The frustration was easy to hear in Tolliver's voice. "But I can't just call in my men and throw the ranch wide open to the damn wide-loopers."

Frank shook his head. "No, you can't do that," he agreed.

"If you have any ideas, Mr. Morgan," Ben said, "we'd be glad to hear 'em."

Tolliver got a cigar from a box on a table next to a heavy divan and jabbed it toward Frank. "What I ought to do is hire some gunmen and ride across the Rio to wipe out Almanzar. I'll bet our rustlin' troubles would stop then!"

Ben frowned darkly, and Frank got the feeling that the young man didn't care for his father's idea at all. Ben wasn't the only one. Pegeen had come back into the room with her sister in time to hear her husband's angry pronouncement, and she said, "You'll do no such thing, Cecil Tolliver! You can't take the law into your own hands, and besides, you don't know that Don Felipe is behind the rustling."

Tolliver stuck the cigar in his mouth and chewed savagely on it for a moment before he said, "When we first come out here, Peg, there wasn't no law but what a man could carry in his own fist. We did all right in those days."

"We all nearly got killed more than once, fighting off Comanches and outlaws," she snapped. "You leave such things to the Rangers."

Tolliver just made a sound of disgust. He took another cigar from the box and offered it to Frank, who slipped it into his shirt pocket. "I'll save it for later, with that brandy," he said.

"Good idea. I got to gnaw on this one now, though, to keep from sayin' things I hadn't ought to say." Tolliver crossed his arms and glared at the world in general.

His wife dared his wrath by saying, "I still need those supplies. Come morning, Cecil, you'll have to go back to town to replace the ones you lost."

"All right, all right," Tolliver muttered around the cigar. "But I'm takin' more of the boys with me next time, and if Almanzar sends his gun wolves after us again, they'll get even more of a fight than they got this time!"

Debra and Jessie came out of the kitchen carrying trays with cups and saucers on them. Steam lifted from the coffee in the cups, and Frank smiled in appreciation of the delicious aroma.

The coffee tasted as good as it smelled. Frank sat in a comfortable armchair and sipped from his cup. A time or two, he caught Roanne watching him with undisguised interest. He wondered if she was married or a widow or had never been hitched. An unmarried woman of her age was considered an old maid out here, but there was nothing old about her. To be honest, the boldness of her gaze wasn't very maidenly, either. Frank returned her looks with an interest of his own. She was a mighty attractive lady.

They hadn't been sitting around the parlor for very long when a sudden rataplan of hoofbeats welled up outside. A large group of riders was approaching the ranch. Tolliver and Ben set their cups aside and stood up quickly. So did Frank. No shouts of alarm had sounded from the ranch hands, but these days, no one was taking a chance. With his hand on the butt of the Colt at his hip, Tolliver strode to the front door. Ben and Frank were right behind him.

As the three men stepped out onto the porch, they saw a group of about twenty-five men entering the ranch yard. The rider in the lead was a big, barrel-chested man with a rawboned, hawklike face and a shock of white hair under a black Stetson. The last of the fading light revealed a badge pinned to his coat. Frank recognized it as a star set inside a circle, the emblem of the Texas Rangers.

"Captain Wedge!" Tolliver called out as the newcomers reined in, confirming the guess Frank had just made. "Good to see you and your boys. Could have used you around a little while ago."

The Ranger captain swung down from his saddle and curtly motioned for his men to dismount as well. "Why's that, Tolliver?" he asked as he turned to face the rancher.

"Because my boy an' me were jumped by a gang o' Almanzar's gunmen from across the border. If it wasn't for Frank Morgan here, Ben an' me would probably be buzzard bait by now."

Captain Wedge turned his dark eyes toward Morgan and repeated the name. "Frank Morgan, eh?"

Frank knew there was no point in denying anything. It came as no surprise to him that a lawman had recognized his name. He said, "That's right."

"Heard of you," Wedge said with a curt nod. "Don't think there's any paper out on you right now, though."

"There never has been except on trumped-up charges that were proven false," Frank said.

Wedge nodded again. "Pretty much what I figured. Heard, too, that you've given the Rangers a hand now and then."

"I'm a law-abiding man," Frank explained. "I do what I can to help, when I'm called on."

"Good to know." Wedge turned back to Cecil Tolliver. "What's this about you and the boy being attacked by Almanzar's riders?"

"They jumped us while we were comin' back to the ranch from San Rosa," Tolliver said. "We'd been to town to pick up some supplies. A whole bunch of 'em came on us suddenlike, yellin' and shootin'. We tried to get away and make a fight of it at the same time, but our buckboard turned over. Then Mr. Morgan rode up and took a hand in the game. We knocked down enough of the bastards so that the rest of 'em turned tail."

"Sounds like you're lucky to be alive," Wedge said.

"That's the way I figure it, too."

The Ranger captain frowned. "How do you know the men who jumped you work for Almanzar?"

"Who else would have it in for me?" Tolliver demanded. "Almanzar and me been crossways with each other for a long time."

"What about the Black Scorpion?"

Tolliver looked surprised at Wedge's question. "What about him?"

"Could the men who attacked you have been part of the Scorpion's gang?"

Ben put in, "That thought crossed my mind, too, even though I'm not sure I believe in the Black Scorpion."

"He's real enough," Wedge said.

Tolliver shook his head stubbornly. "I didn't see no sign of any masked man leadin' the gang. They were just a bunch of border toughs, the sort of hard cases Almanzar hires to make life miserable for me."

"The reason I ask is, the men and I have been trailing the Black Scorpion since yesterday. He and his gang raided a ranch on the other side of San Rosa. They were coming in this direction and it seems logical to me that they could have run into you and your son."

"Nope. Those gunnies worked for Almanzar."

Frank read the skepticism on Captain Wedge's face, and to tell the truth, he was beginning to have his doubts about Tolliver's belief, too. From the looks of things, Tolliver's hatred of Don Felipe Almanzar was so deep-seated that the cattleman was quick to blame Almanzar for everything bad that happened, whether Almanzar had anything to do with it or not.

It appeared that Wedge might have argued the matter further, but at that moment the women came out of the house onto the porch. The light was behind them and shone on their hair. Wedge took his hat off and nodded politely to them, saying, "Ladies. After a long day on the trail, you are sure a sight for sore eyes, if I may be so bold as to say so."

"You may," Pegeen Tolliver told him with a smile. "Hello, Captain. Will you and your men be staying to supper?"

"That sounds mighty nice, ma'am, but we're on the trail of some badmen —"

"You can't follow a trail very well at night," Tolliver put in. "Join us for supper, Captain. Your men can eat in the bunkhouse with the hands."

Wedge chuckled. "That Chinaman who cooks for you probably won't be very happy about having that many extra mouths to feed."

"He'll survive. There's plenty of room for your men to bunk in the barn, too, and we'll find a bed for you in the house."

The captain returned his black Stetson to his head. "I'm much obliged, Tolliver, and on behalf of my men, I accept." He turned and said to his troop of Rangers, "Light for a spell, boys. We're spending the night here on the Rocking T."

A grin creased Tolliver's leathery face. "I'd like to see Almanzar's nighthawks come a-raidin' now, with a couple dozen Rangers on the place! They'd get a mighty warm welcome if they did!"

4

The Rangers dismounted and tended to their mounts, unsaddling the horses and turning them into one of the corrals by the barns. Frank had already noticed that the buckboard was gone, and when he asked about Stormy, Tolliver told him that some of the hands had cared for the Appaloosa when the team was unhitched.

"No offense, but I'll look in on him myself," Frank said.

Tolliver nodded. "Don't blame you a bit. That's a fine horse, and if he was mine, I'd want to be sure that he was properly taken care of, too."

Frank walked out to the barns, trailed by Dog, and one of the ranch hands directed him to the stall where Stormy was. Having assured himself that the Appaloosa had been rubbed down and had plenty of grain and water, Frank headed back to the house.

Before he got there, a big work wagon rattled into the yard, pulled by a team of heavy draft horses. Darrell Forrest and Nick Holmes were on the wagon seat, with Darrell handling the reins. Three punchers on horseback trailed the wagon.

Frank recalled Tolliver's orders to his sons-in-law to go out and recover the bodies of the outlaws who had been killed. Even though the last of the twilight had faded, enough illumination came from the doors and windows of the ranch house for Frank to be able to see that the uncovered back of the wagon was empty.

"What happened?" he asked as he stepped up to the wagon when Darrell had brought it to a stop in front of the house.

"Those bodies weren't there," Darrell said.

That answer took Frank by surprise. He had checked each of the fallen men himself and was certain they had all been dead, including the one who had died while Frank was looking at him. None of them could have gotten up and moseyed off by themselves.

"Pa!" Nick called as he and Darrell climbed down from the wagon.

Tolliver hustled out of the house, along with Ben and Captain Wedge. "What is it?" he asked. His eyes widened as he looked at the empty wagon. "Where the hell are those outlaw carcasses?"

"You'll have to tell us, Pa," Darrell replied grimly. "We drove pert near all the way to San Rosa looking for them, just in case you were a little off target about where they fell, and there's no sign of them anywhere up and down the road!"

Tolliver pounded his right fist into his left palm. "The rest of the skunks came back for 'em!" he said. "That's the only explanation that makes any sense. That damn Almanzar! He must've give orders that if any of his gunnies bit the dust, the rest were to recover the bodies, so they couldn't be traced back to him!"

A frown creased Frank's forehead. Tolliver's theory certainly wasn't impossible, but it struck Frank as a little far-fetched and a good example of Tolliver's determination to blame everything on Almanzar, whether there was any proof for it or not.

On the other hand, *somebody* had spirited those bodies away, and there must have been a reason for it. The most likely explanation was that the rest of the gang had returned for their fallen comrades. Why was a question that Frank couldn't answer at the moment.

His curiosity was aroused, however, and this mystery made him even more inclined to remain in the area until it had been cleared up.

"I was hoping to get a look at those bodies," Wedge said. "Thought there might be some of them I'd recognize."

"We can ride out in the mornin' and I'll show you where the fight happened," Tolliver offered. "Maybe you can pick up the trail of the rest o' the gang."

Wedge nodded, frowning in thought.

The ranch hands took care of the wagon and the team, while Frank, Wedge, and the members of the Tolliver family went inside. As Frank hung up his hat he smelled delicious aromas in the air, to go along with the lingering fragrance of the coffee from earlier.

The women had done quite a job on short notice, perhaps helped out by that Chinese cook Wedge had mentioned. The long hardwood table in the dining room was loaded down with platters of food. Frank saw fried chicken, ham, boiled potatoes, corn on the cob, black-eyed peas, yams, greens, and biscuits. The sight and smell of the food made him acutely aware that it had been a long time since he had eaten lunch, and that had been just a few pieces of jerky gnawed while he was in the saddle. Everyone moved to the table. Tolliver held a chair for Pegeen while Darrell and Nick did likewise for their wives. Roanne didn't have a husband here, though, so being the gentleman he was, Frank moved to perform the gesture for her. Unfortunately, Captain Wedge had had the same idea and started forward, and there was an awkward moment when both men hesitated. Then Wedge stepped back slightly and gave a half wave, indicating to Frank that he should go ahead.

"Thank you," Roanne said graciously as Frank slid the chair under her while she sat down. She looked up at him and added, "Why don't you sit here beside me, Mr. Morgan?"

"Thank you, ma'am," Frank said with a smile. "It would be my pleasure."

"You don't have to call me ma'am," she said as he settled down on the chair next to her.

"Well, I haven't heard your last name. . . ."

"That's right, you haven't. It's Williamson."

"I'll call you Miss Williamson, then."

She didn't correct him on the "Miss"

part, leading Frank to think that he was probably right about her having never been married. But she did say, "Why don't you just call me Roanne?"

"All right. That's a mighty pretty name." Frank didn't add that it went with a mighty pretty lady. He didn't want to be too forward, considering that he had only met her an hour or so earlier. But from the way she smiled, he figured that she got the idea.

"We'll say grace," Tolliver announced gruffly. Frank bowed his head, as did everyone else at the table, and the rancher continued. "Heavenly Father, thank you for this food and all the other blessin's you've bestowed on us. We ask that you watch over us and protect us from the trials and travails o' this world and help us follow your teachin's, so's we'll be prepared for the next world. And if it pleases you, cast your wrath down on any no-good skunks from below the border —"

"Cecil!" Pegeen hissed.

Tolliver drew a deep breath. "Anyway, Lord, bless us and keep us under your watchful eye. Amen."

"Amen," Frank and the others murmured. He tried not to grin as he saw that Pegeen was still glaring at her husband for

52

daring to intrude his own personal grudges into the prayer.

Everyone dug in, passing around the platters of food and eating heartily. Despite the near-tragedy that had occurred earlier in the day, there was a considerable amount of talk and laughter. Frank knew that a similar scene, albeit probably more raucous and profane, would be going on in the bunkhouse as the rest of the Ranger troop broke bread with the Rocking T ranch hands.

Wedge was seated across the table from Frank. The captain said to him, "Not meaning to pry, Morgan, but what brings you to the border country?"

"I'm just drifting, Captain."

"Hence the name by which some people know you?"

Frank shrugged. "I've always been a mite fiddle-footed by inclination, and circumstances have often been such that it was best to ride on."

"You mean that you've run into a lot of trouble over the years because of your reputation." Wedge's words were a statement, not a question.

"As a lawman, you must know there are a lot of hotheads who fancy themselves as fast guns."

"And you probably bump up against them just about everywhere you go."

"It happens more often than I'd like," Frank answered flatly.

"You could hang up your gun," Wedge suggested.

Nick Holmes joined the conversation by saying, "You can't be serious, Captain. If Mr. Morgan did that, he'd probably be dead within a week. There must be dozens of men who'd try to come after him if word ever got out that he'd put away his gun."

"Probably more like hundreds," Ben added.

Frank would have preferred that the conversation hadn't taken this turn, but since it had, he wasn't going to duck the issue. "It wouldn't be safe," he agreed. "I've made more than my share of enemies."

"The West is settling down," Wedge argued. "There's law and order now."

Tolliver snorted. "I didn't see any out on the road this afternoon when those gunnies were doin' their best to ventilate us!"

Wedge flushed, and Frank thought Tolliver had touched a sore spot. "The Rangers can't be everywhere at once," Wedge said, "and it's my judgment that the Black Scorpion and his gang represent the biggest threat around here, not Don Felipe Almanzar. And I'm still not convinced it wasn't the Scorpion's gang that jumped you."

"I'm convinced," Tolliver snapped. "That's all I need to know."

Pegeen eased into the fray. "Gentlemen, please," she said. "Let's just enjoy our supper and leave the wrangling until later."

Wedge inclined his head toward her and said graciously, "You're absolutely right, Mrs. Tolliver. This meal is delicious."

No more was said about Don Felipe Almanzar or the Black Scorpion. The topic shifted to the political situation across the border in Mexico. El Presidente, Porfirio Diaz, had ruled the country for a decade now, after an earlier stint in power as well, and he ran things with an iron fist, enforcing his will by means of his tight control over the Mexican army. But despite — or perhaps because of — Diaz's heavy hand, there was always a certain level of unrest in the country. And the farther away from the capital of Mexico City, the weaker Diaz's control over the population. In northern Mexico, across the Rio Grande from Texas, a frontier police force known as Rurales were in charge, although Diaz sometimes sent in troops from the regular army to quiet things down if too much trouble began cropping up. One thing could be said for Mexican politics: It was always colorful and never boring.

Frank didn't have much interest in any politics, however, having learned from experience that most men who would seek political jobs weren't qualified to hold them. Many were long-winded gasbags with fewer scruples than a coyote. Diaz might be a ruthless dictator, Frank thought, but at least he was more honest about it, ruling with guns rather than slick words and smiles that hid nothing but lies.

When the meal was finished, the men went into the parlor for the brandy and cigars Tolliver had mentioned earlier. The air turned blue with tobacco smoke. Several times during the evening, Frank noticed Captain Wedge giving him an intense, slit-eyed look. He didn't know if Wedge harbored some resentment toward him because he had helped Roanne with her chair, or if the Ranger was just naturally wary because of Frank's reputation as a gunfighter.

Frank had no real interest in winning Wedge's approval. He was what he was, and if that bothered Wedge, it was just too bad. And if the captain was jealous, that was unfortunate, too. Frank wasn't going to pretend that he didn't enjoy Roanne Williamson's company.

After a while the air grew too thick with smoke for Frank's taste. He stood up and said, "I believe I'll walk out to the barn and check on my horse once more before it's time to turn in."

"Go right ahead," Tolliver told him. "You might ought to keep an eye open, though. You never know who might be lurkin' around. Some of Almanzar's men might try to sneak in and raise some hell. Might even be a stray Comanche or two still around."

Frank doubted that. The backbone of Comanche resistance had been broken years earlier at the Battle of Palo Duro Canyon, up in the Panhandle. Indian trouble since then had been sporadic and isolated, mostly occurring in far west Texas where some bronco Apaches still raided across the border from time to time.

With the smoldering butt of a cigar still clenched in his teeth, Frank left the house and strolled toward the barn. On the way he dropped the cigar butt in the dirt and ground it out with his boot heel.

Dog had been waiting on the porch, along with the little dog called Dobie. Both of them walked out to the barn with Frank. They seemed to have become good friends. Dobie jumped up and nipped at Dog's ears every now and then, but the big cur tolerantly ignored the smaller dog.

The bunkhouse was lit up, and Frank heard guitar and fiddle music coming merrily from inside the long structure. The Rangers and the ranch hands were getting along well, from the sound of it.

He went into the barn, where a single lantern was burning with its wick turned low, and looked into Stormy's stall. The Appaloosa seemed fine and nuzzled his nose against Frank's shoulder. Frank scratched the horse's ears for a few moments, talking softly to him, and then turned to go.

He stopped short, his hand moving instinctively toward his gun, when he saw the shadowy figure looming in the doorway of the barn.

5

The figure moved into the light, and Frank edged his hand away from the Colt, hoping that Roanne Williamson hadn't noticed his reaction.

She was too sharp-eyed to have missed it, though. "I'm sorry, Mr. Morgan," she said. "I didn't mean to startle you."

Frank smiled. "If I'm to call you Roanne, then you have to call me Frank. And I didn't mean to be so jumpy. I reckon it's a habit."

Roanne had put on a lace shawl, drawing it around her shoulders against the faint chill in the air. They were far south, but it *was* November, after all. Frank thought the shawl looked nice against her dark hair and the blue dress she wore.

As she came closer, she said, "I imagine the life you've led makes you quite cautious."

"I keep my eyes and ears open," Frank

admitted. "Fact is, I should have heard you coming before you got to the barn."

"I don't make a lot of noise. Even though I live in town now, I was raised on a ranch. When I was a little girl, one of the hands was a 'breed who taught me to be as stealthy as an Indian. It was quite thrilling . . . when it wasn't dangerous."

"I expect so. But you said you live in town? I thought you lived here on the Rocking T with your sister and her family."

"I visit frequently, but my home is in San Rosa. I have a little dress shop there. It won't ever make me rich, but there's enough trade so that I do all right." She hesitated, then said, "At least, I did."

"What do you mean by that?" Frank asked, his curiosity getting the better of his natural politeness.

Roanne shook her head. "Nothing. I'm just tired. It's been a long day. But I like to get a breath of fresh air before I retire for the evening."

"So do I," Frank said. "That's why I came out here."

She smiled. "Yes, the air in the parlor is anything but fresh after Cecil and the boys fire up those cheroots of theirs. Tonight, of course, they have Captain Wedge with them, too."

Frank thought he heard something in her voice when she mentioned the Ranger, a certain coolness. He said, "The captain seems fond of you. I didn't mean to poach on his territory when I went to hold your chair for you."

"Believe me, you didn't. Although I think I should resent being referred to as territory."

"Just a figure of speech," Frank assured her. "I didn't mean any offense."

"None taken."

"Your sister and brother seem to get along well enough with Captain Wedge," Frank commented.

"He commands a troop of Texas Rangers," she said coolly. "What would you have them do when he comes to their home?"

"So you're saying there *is* some friction between them?"

Roanne shrugged eloquently. "Captain Wedge is a lawman. Cecil respects that. Cecil is also a naturally hospitable man. And I really don't want to talk about Captain Wedge anymore."

Frank was still puzzled by her attitude, but he knew that if he pressed her on the matter, she would probably say good night and leave the barn. He didn't want that.

He enjoyed her company.

"Where's this ranch you grew up on?" he asked, changing the subject.

"Over on the Nueces River. Even brushier country than around here. Nothing but longhorns could ever live on it, let alone thrive."

Frank nodded. "I know what you mean. I've seen that *brasada* over there."

"Where are you from, Frank?"

"I grew up in Parker County, up in north Texas. A good long way from here."

Roanne's lips curved in a smile. "Yes, Texas is a big place. They say you can ride for weeks and still not leave the state."

"True enough if you're going in the right direction," Frank said.

"But you've been a lot of other places in your life, haven't you?"

"Pretty much everywhere west of the Mississippi, from the Rio Grande to the Milk River up in Montana." A touch of wistfulness crept into Frank's voice as he answered her question. He hadn't had a real home in so long that he had almost forgotten what it was like before he returned to Parker County a few months earlier. And things had changed so much there that it wasn't really like coming home.

"Do you think you'll ever settle down and stay in one place?"

Frank reached down and scratched Dog's ear for a moment, giving himself a chance to gather his thoughts. As he straightened, he said, "I reckon nearly every man thinks that about himself, even the drifters like me. We believe that the day will come when the urge to always be moving on will leave us. It's just a matter of time and finding the right place. But time runs out and the right place is still somewhere over the next hill, and before you know it, there aren't any more chances."

"That's a sad way to look at it," she said in a half whisper, obviously moved by his answer.

"Sad but realistic," Frank said.

"But what about you?" she pressed. "Your chances haven't run out yet."

"Not so far. But nobody ever promised us tomorrow, either."

She looked at him for a long moment and then said, "You're not at all the sort of man I thought a famous gunfighter would be, Frank."

"I'll take that as a compliment," he said with a smile.

"That's the way I meant it." She drew

the shawl tighter around her shoulders. "I'd better be getting back inside. Good night."

He tugged on the brim of his hat. "Good night, ma'am . . . I mean, Roanne."

She smiled, turned, and walked back to the house. Frank stayed there in the barn for a few minutes, giving her a chance to go up to her room before he went in. Then he returned to the house and found that the brandy-and-cigars session in the parlor had broken up. Cecil Tolliver was waiting for him, sitting alone in a chair in front of the fireplace, rolling a cigar from one corner of his mouth to the other.

"I'll show you to your room," Tolliver said as he got to his feet.

"Everybody else turned in already?" Frank asked.

"That's right. It was a long day, and everybody's tired."

"You seem to get along well with Captain Wedge," Frank commented, wondering what reaction he would draw.

He found out quickly as Tolliver made a face, as if he had just tasted something bitter. "A man's got to get along with the law these days," he said quietly. "Things ain't like they used to be."

So maybe Roanne's hints that there was

some friction between Tolliver and the Ranger captain had some basis in fact, Frank thought. But Tolliver was obviously determined to keep the peace, and again, it was none of Frank's business, so he let it drop.

He was tired, too, and looking forward to spending the night in a real bed after sleeping out on the trail for too many nights in a row.

Dog curled up at the foot of the bed in the upstairs room where Tolliver left Frank. He passed the night in a deep, dreamless slumber. When he woke up in the morning before dawn, as was his habit, he was refreshed, although his muscles were a little stiff from not being accustomed to sleeping on such a soft mattress.

Despite the early hour, the smells of coffee and bacon were in the air when Frank went downstairs. Ranch folk were nearly always up before the sun. He found Captain Wedge sitting at the table with Tolliver, Ben, Darrell, and Nick. Roanne came in from the kitchen, carrying a coffeepot. As she began to fill the cups in front of the men, she nodded toward an empty chair and said, "Have a seat, Frank. The food will be out in a minute."

Frank pulled back the chair and sat down. He was aware that Wedge was watching him closely, but he ignored the Ranger's scrutiny and smiled at Roanne instead. "Good morning," he said to her. "I hope you slept well."

She returned the smile. "Very well, thank you." She finished pouring the coffee and went back to the kitchen.

As the men sipped the strong black brew, Tolliver said, "What are your plans, Frank? You know you're welcome to stay here as long as you want."

Before Frank could reply, Wedge said, "I was hoping Mr. Morgan would agree to come with me and the troop."

Frank's eyebrows lifted in surprise. "Am I under arrest, Captain?" he asked.

Wedge waved a hand. "Hell, no. I thought maybe you'd come with us and help us track down the Black Scorpion and his gang."

"You want me to help the Rangers?" That came as another surprise. Frank had thought that Wedge didn't like him, either because he was a gunfighter or because he was interested in Roanne — or both.

"Word gets around," Wedge said. "I hear tell that you've helped out the Rangers a couple of times before."

66

"That's true," Frank admitted with a shrug. "A young Ranger named Tyler Beaumont befriended me, helped me out when I was in a bad way. I figured it was only fair to return the favor."

"I realize I haven't done you any favors," Wedge said, "but we could use a good man, especially if we catch up to the Black Scorpion. You wouldn't have to be sworn in as a Ranger. We could do it sort of unofficial-like."

Frank pondered the offer. He knew the Rangers were most interested in getting their job done, and they didn't mind cutting a few corners if need be, like recruiting a notorious gunman to give them a hand. He didn't doubt Wedge's sincerity.

However, he was a little leery of accepting because of the uneasy feelings he had gotten about the way Tolliver, Roanne, and perhaps the others regarded the Ranger captain. If they didn't like Wedge, there had to be a reason for their attitude. On the other hand, just because Wedge might rub some folks the wrong way didn't mean that he wasn't a competent lawman and commander.

Those thoughts went through Frank's head in a matter of seconds, along with the admission to himself that he was curious about the so-called Black Scorpion. Wedge seemed convinced that the masked bandit really existed. So did Cecil Tolliver, although Tolliver insisted that it hadn't been the Scorpion's men who had jumped him and Ben the day before. Frank decided that he wouldn't mind finding out the truth of the matter for himself.

He nodded slowly and said, "All right. I reckon I can do that."

"Good," Wedge said with a nod. "I appreciate it, Morgan."

The women came in then with heavily laden platters filled with flapjacks, bacon, eggs, fried potatoes, and biscuits. One thing could certainly be said for the Rocking T, Frank thought: The people here ate well.

After eating a large breakfast washed down with several cups of coffee, the men went outside. The Ranger troop had already eaten in the bunkhouse, and the lawmen were now saddling their horses and getting ready to ride.

Tolliver told Ben, "Saddle my horse, so I can show the captain where those bastards jumped us yesterday."

"I'm going along, too," Ben said.

"No, you ain't. There's work to do here on the ranch, and I'm countin' on you and

Darrell and Nick to see that it gets done."
Tolliver frowned. "There's been too many
times lately, boy, when I've gone lookin' for
you and ain't found you. If you're sneakin'
off to town to have a drink, I'll find out
about it, you know."

Ben flushed, looking angry and embarrassed at the same time. "I haven't been
sneaking off to town, Pa. You know me
better than that."

Tolliver grunted. "I thought I did,
anyway."

"And you can't say that I haven't gotten
my work done, can you?"

"I reckon not," Tolliver admitted grudg-
ingly.

Frank left them talking and went on into
the barn to see about Stormy. Dog and
Dobie were lying in front of the stall where
the Appaloosa moved around restlessly.
Frank smiled and said to the horse,
"You're ready to get out and stretch your
legs, aren't you, old boy?"

Stormy moved his head up and down as
if nodding. Sometimes Frank thought the
horse understood every word that he said.

Within half an hour after breakfast was
finished, the Rangers were ready to ride
out. Frank joined them, leading Stormy
over to the group, and then he swung up

into the saddle. As he did so, the women came out onto the porch. He noticed that Roanne now wore a traveling outfit.

Moving Stormy closer to the porch, Frank asked, "Are you going back to San Rosa this morning, Miss Williamson?"

"That's right. Darrell is bringing my buggy around right now. I'll go part of the way with the Rangers and then on into town."

"By yourself?" Frank asked. "The countryside seems a little troubled for that."

Roanne smiled. "Pegeen and Cecil agree with you. That's why they're sending along a couple of hands to watch over me."

"Be careful anyway," Frank told her. From what he had seen of the Rocking T crew, they seemed like competent cowboys. He wasn't sure two of them would be able to fight off an attack by outlaws, though. For a moment he considered changing his plans and riding on into San Rosa with Roanne.

Then Captain Wedge raised his hand and called, "Move out!" his voice carrying clearly in the early morning air. With the hoofbeats of their horses sounding like rolling thunder, the Rangers rode out of the ranch yard and headed toward the spot of the ambush the day before.

"Go on, Frank," Roanne said as he hesitated. "I'll be fine."

"All right, then," Frank said as he nodded. "But I'll see you again."

"I certainly hope so," she replied with a smile.

Frank put the Appaloosa into an easy lope and followed the Rangers and Cecil Tolliver. Dog padded after him, and Dobie barked a farewell.

6

The large group of men rode northwest toward San Rosa, following the river and raising a large cloud of dust. Frank looked over his shoulder and saw more dust rising behind them. That would be from Roanne's buggy and the mounts of the two men riding with her about a quarter of a mile behind the Rangers. Frank kept alert for the sound of shots. If he heard any, he would turn and gallop back to help make sure Roanne stayed safe.

In the meantime, he moved up alongside Cecil Tolliver and Captain Wedge at the head of the troop. Wedge was saying, ". . . gang looped around San Rosa after they hit that ranch. We lost their trail when we hit a rocky stretch a ways north of here. So you can see why I think it might have been the Scorpion's men who attacked you, Tolliver. They were right here in the area."

Tolliver shook his head. "I don't believe

it. They were Almanzar's men."

Frank said, "What if Don Felipe Almanzar *is* the Black Scorpion?"

The question had been an idle one, but both Tolliver and Wedge looked sharply at him. "Damn it!" Tolliver exclaimed. "That might be the answer. I wouldn't put anything past Almanzar!"

"Well, maybe," Wedge said. He didn't sound convinced, though. He went on. "Why would Almanzar turn owlhoot? He's got a pretty good ranch on the other side of the Rio, from what I hear."

"It's in his nature," Tolliver insisted. "He was born no good."

Once again, Frank thought Tolliver was reaching pretty far in his attempt to blame everything on his old enemy. Tolliver would seize on any idea that made Don Felipe Almanzar look bad.

They reached the site of the gun battle a short time later. Landmarks were sparse in this flat, brushy country, but Frank recognized the place from a small clump of scrubby live oaks nearby. He saw the marks in the road where the buckboard had overturned, too.

Tolliver pointed out the same marks to Captain Wedge. "Right there," he said. "That's where the buckboard wound up when it crashed. Ben and I got behind it and started bangin' away at the sons o' bitches with our Colts, and a second later Frank came gallopin' up and joined in on the fracas."

"If you'll look there in the road," Frank said, "you'll probably find bloodstains where the wounded men fell. Cecil's men probably didn't see the blood when they came out to recover the bodies because the light was already bad."

Wedge nodded. "Let's take a look."

True to Morgan's prediction, the bloodstains were easily found in the clear light of an autumn morning, even though someone had kicked dirt and gravel over them. Whoever had taken the bodies had tried to conceal the evidence that there was a fight here, but they had been in too much of a hurry to do a good job.

Roanne's buggy rolled up, trailed by the two Rocking T hands. She hauled back on the reins and brought the buggy horse to a stop. "Was this where you were attacked, Cecil?" she asked her brother-in-law.

"It sure is." Tolliver pointed to the ground. "And there's some of the blood the polecats spilled when we ventilated 'em!"

Roanne glanced down at the dark

splashes on the road and then looked away, paling a little. She was a frontier woman and not easily spooked, but the sight of that much blood was still a little unnerving to her, Frank thought.

She lifted the reins and said, "Well, since you gentlemen don't need me here, I'll go on to town."

Frank and Wedge touched their hat brims and nodded politely to her as she flapped the reins and got the horse moving again. The buggy started off up the road. Frank watched it dwindle.

"You can see the tracks that bunch left," Tolliver said, pointing at the road again.

"There are a lot of tracks," Wedge said. "This is a well-traveled route."

"Yeah, but look how they're all together," Tolliver insisted.

Frank wasn't as talented a tracker as the old mountain men, such as Jim Bridger and Preacher, had been, but he could read signs well enough to see that Tolliver was right. The profusion of hoofprints on the road made it more difficult, but he thought they could track the gunmen.

Wedge seemed more dubious. "We'll give it a try," he said. He lifted a hand and waved for the troop to follow him.

A few hundred yards farther on, the

tracks left the road and cut north. With Frank, Wedge, and Tolliver in the lead, the Rangers followed them. The brush made for slow going, but in a way it helped with the tracking because from time to time the men spotted a broken branch that indicated a man on horseback had forced his way past.

The morning stretched out, and the sun grew warmer as it rose higher in the sky. If this had been June or July instead of November, they would have been baking by now, Frank thought. The Rangers pushed on, with only an occasional stop to rest their horses.

Toward noon, Wedge reined in and grated, "Damn it."

"What's wrong?" Frank asked as he brought Stormy to a halt.

"I recognize these parts," the captain explained. "We're just about back to the place where we lost the Black Scorpion's trail yesterday."

That seemed like too much to be a coincidence. Maybe there *was* something to the idea that Almanzar's men and the Black Scorpion's gang were one and the same. Either that, or Almanzar had had nothing to do with the attack on Tolliver and Ben and the Black Scorpion had really been to blame for it.

A frown creased Frank's forehead. This situation was anything but clear-cut.

The Rangers rode on, and a few minutes later they came to a dry creek bed that marked the border of a wide area of barren, rocky ground. "This is it, all right," Wedge said bitterly.

The tracks they had been following disappeared onto the rocks. "How big is this stretch?" asked Frank.

"Half a mile wide, three or four miles long," Wedge replied.

"The raiders had to go somewhere," Frank pointed out. "If we ride along the edge, we're bound to find their tracks."

"Unless they split up and left one by one at different spots. One man can cover up his trail pretty well. Then they could rendezvous somewhere else and regroup."

Frank nodded. Wedge's theory sounded reasonable, but the only way to prove it was to check the edges of the rocky area. He was about to point that out when the captain went on. "But we'll check it out. That's about all we can do."

"You'll have to do it without me," Tolliver said. "I got a ranch to run, so I'll leave you to this chore. Frank, are you goin' with Captain Wedge or comin' back to the Rockin' T with me?"

"I think I'll stick with the captain a while longer," Frank said, making his decision without any hesitation. "I've gotten a mite interested in this Black Scorpion fella."

"I wish you luck, then." Tolliver raised a hand in farewell and wheeled his horse to ride back the way they had come.

Quickly, Wedge issued commands, dividing his troop into two forces. They would circle the rocks in either direction, meeting up again on the far side. That would cut in half the time required to check all the way around the area.

"If you find any tracks, fire three shots," Wedge instructed the Ranger sergeant in charge of the second group. "We'll come a-runnin'."

"Sure, Cap'n," the man said. "You do the same."

The party split up and resumed the search. Frank went with the group led by Wedge.

They searched slowly and carefully, and it took until mid-afternoon before the Rangers rendezvoused on the far side of the rocks. Wedge's group hadn't found anything, and Frank could tell from the glum looks on the faces of the second group that their search had been equally futile.

When the sergeant had said as much, Wedge cuffed his black Stetson to the back of his head and looked disgusted. "Whoever they are, they've given us the slip again," he declared. "They must've done like I said and snuck out of here one at a time."

Wedge didn't look to Frank for agreement, but Frank nodded anyway. "Are you going back to San Rosa?"

"I reckon. Not much else we can do except wait for the Black Scorpion to hit somewhere else and hope we can get on his trail again."

"I'll ride with you, if that's all right." Frank found himself eager to see the settlement of San Rosa. The fact that Roanne Williamson would be there had nothing to do with it, he thought.

But he wasn't sure if he believed that.

Wedge said curtly, "Suit yourself." Whether his brusque attitude came from his disappointment at losing the trail or his dislike of the idea of Frank visiting San Rosa, Frank couldn't have said. Nor did he particularly care.

The riders made their way back to the road. They had been out all day, eating a cold lunch of jerky and biscuits from their saddlebags, and it would be late in the afternoon before they reached the settlement. Frank was looking forward to supper, although he doubted if it would be as good as the meals he had gotten at the Tolliver ranch.

They were still several miles from San Rosa when the crackle of gunfire suddenly sounded to the south. Frank and Wedge reined in sharply, and the members of the Ranger troop followed suit.

"What in blazes?" Wedge exclaimed. "Sounds like a small war going on down there."

"Is that shooting on this side of the river," Frank asked, "or the Mexican side?"

Wedge shook his head. "Hard to say. The Rio's a couple of miles in that direction. We'll go check it out."

The brush wasn't quite as thick here, so the Rangers were able to move through it easier than they had earlier. The shooting didn't last long before it died away into an ominous silence. Frank glanced over at Wedge and saw that the captain's face was set in grim lines.

Smoke began to rise in the sky ahead of them.

Wedge grated a curse. "There's a little farm down there, I recollect. The Black Scorpion must have raided it!"

"Why would an outlaw raid a farm?" Frank asked. "There wouldn't be enough loot there to make it worth the bullets."

"That's the sort of bloodthirsty mongrel the Scorpion is. He wants everybody on both sides of the border to be scared of him, so that he can come and go without anybody helping the law track him down. Every so often he raids some farm or small ranch just as an example of his power, to keep all the other settlers in line."

Frank's jaw tightened. Such wanton destruction rubbed him the wrong way. He found himself hoping that the Black Scorpion was real and that he himself would be with the Rangers when they caught up to the bandit leader and his gang.

The Rangers pushed on quickly, and after a few minutes of riding toward the smoke they came in sight of its source: an adobe house that was blazing brightly inside. The thick earthen walls wouldn't burn, but the roof and the interior would, and that was what was happening. Off to one side of the burning building were several sheds and corrals that seemed to be untouched.

Frank expected to find the bodies of women and kids, perhaps, and he wasn't looking forward to what he might see. As the Rangers galloped up and reined in, however, Frank spotted only the sprawled shapes of a couple of men. That was bad enough. Maybe worse, in fact, because if a family had lived here, the other members might still be inside that burning house.

Wedge put that worry to rest by saying, "Looks like the Hernandez brothers tried to fight back and got wiped out. It's a damned good thing they didn't have wives and kids, or it would have been really bad."

"They're the only ones who lived here?" Frank asked.

"Yeah. Just a couple of harmless pepperbellies."

The dead men were lying facedown, with the rifles they had dropped on the ground nearby. Wedge and Frank dismounted. The captain used the toe of his boot to roll the Hernandez brothers onto their backs. Both had lean, wolflike features that were distorted by the grimaces of pain that death had frozen onto their faces. Judging by the bloodstains on their clothes, each man had been shot once.

Wedge brushed back the tails of his black coat and shifted his gun belt a little. Staring toward the south, he muttered, "The Scorpion thinks that running back across the border will keep the Rangers from coming after him. Well, he's wrong."

"You don't have any jurisdiction in Mexico," Frank pointed out.

"If you're worried about that, you can turn that spotted horse around and ride out, mister," Wedge snapped, scorn dripping from his voice. He looked at the Rangers and added, "As for us, we're going after the men who did this!"

A cheer of agreement went up from the troop.

Wedge swung up into the saddle and kicked his horse into a run toward the Rio Grande, which was only a few hundred yards away. The Rangers followed him. Frank watched them go, then looked at Stormy and Dog and sighed.

"Sometimes I'm a damned fool," he said. With that, he mounted up and rode after the Rangers, thinking that neither the Appaloosa nor the big cur had disagreed with him.

7

A few minutes later, Stormy splashed up out of the waters of the Rio Grande and The Drifter was in Mexico. Dog emerged from the river, too, and paused to shake the water violently off his muscular, thick-furred body.

Frank put the Appaloosa into a fast lope that quickly brought them up even with the Rangers. He made his way to the head of the group, next to Wedge.

The captain glanced at Frank and said over the noise of the hoofbeats, "I thought you weren't coming."

"I've got just as much right to be over here as you do," Frank said. "In Mexico you're a civilian just like me."

Wedge grinned humorlessly. "The way I figure it, this badge gives me the right to go wherever I need to, to defend the State of Texas."

Frank wasn't going to waste any breath

arguing with him. Instead, he kept his eyes on the tracks that the raiders had left after wiping out the Hernandez brothers and torching their jacal.

The vegetation was sparser on this side of the river, the ground sandier and more likely to take a print. Frank and the Rangers had no trouble following the trail. It looked as if Wedge was right about the outlaws being confident of their escape. Frank wondered what would happen, though, if the Rangers ran into a troop of Rurales. The Mexicans probably wouldn't be happy about finding a group of armed Texans on this side of the river.

The trail led south from the Rio Grande for a mile or two and then swung back to the west. The sun sank toward the horizon and was swallowed by a bank of clouds, meaning that night would fall earlier than usual. Wedge had been setting a fast pace, but now he reined in and settled his horse into a deliberate walk.

"We don't want to ride right up their backsides before we know what's going on," he said by way of explanation. "They can't be too far ahead of us."

That made sense to Frank. He matched Stormy's pace to that of the captain's mount.

The clouds continued to move in, and a cool breeze freshened from the north. It was too early in the year for one of the blue northers that whistled into the Texas Panhandle seemingly straight from Canada, and besides, Frank doubted such a cold snap would penetrate this far south. It was certainly possible, though, for some chilly weather to move in here in northern Mexico, and it looked like that was what they were in for. Not a freeze by any means, but air cool enough so that a man's breath would fog in the morning.

The advancing clouds brought the shadows of dusk with them. Beside Frank, Wedge muttered, "Will they push on in the dark, or make camp somewhere?"

Frank didn't know if Wedge was directing the question at him or just thinking out loud, so he didn't attempt to answer. Anyway, he had no idea what the raiders would do.

The terrain was a bit more rugged on this side of the border, as it sloped gradually upward toward a mountain range that rose in the west. The landscape was cut with arroyos that were dry nearly year-round, except during the infrequent rainstorms when they were prone to flooding. It was also dotted with occasional mesas and other upthrusts of stone. From time to time a spiny ridge wound its way across the countryside.

The Rangers were climbing one of those ridges when Frank said sharply, "Wait a minute."

Wedge lifted a hand to signal a halt and then, sounding irritated that Frank had issued a command, asked, "What the hell is it?"

Frank sniffed. "Smell that?"

Wedge took a deep breath. "Yeah," he said after a second. "Smoke. Somebody up ahead of us has built a fire."

"That sounds to me like the men we're after have decided to camp for the night."

"I think you're right. Probably not more than half a mile in front of us, either." Wedge hipped around in the saddle and called a low-voiced order for his men to dismount. The Rangers in the front of the group passed along the order to those farther back. They began to swing down from their horses.

Frank dismounted as well. Wedge detailed a couple of men to hold the horses. Frank handed over Stormy's reins somewhat reluctantly.

"Will that animal behave himself?" Wedge asked, gesturing curtly toward Dog.

"Or will he start barking and give us away?"

"He'll behave if I tell him to," Frank assured the captain. He bent to rub a hand on Dog's neck and said, "Quiet now, Dog, you hear?"

Wedge grunted. "You talk to him almost like he was human."

"I prefer his company to that of a lot of humans I've run into," Frank said.

Wedge didn't ask him what he meant by that.

Now on foot, the Ranger troop slipped stealthily toward the top of the ridge. When they reached the crest, Frank and Wedge knelt to take a look. Both men had keen eyesight, and it took them only a moment to spot the orange glow in the sky, emanating from a spot about a quarter of a mile ahead of them.

"What did I tell you about those bastards feeling like they're safe because they're on this side of the river?" Wedge said.

"That's a good-sized fire, all right," Frank agreed. "They must not think anybody is on their trail."

"They're about to find out how wrong they are," Wedge said grimly.

He passed the word for the men to advance on foot. It wasn't necessary to tell them to check their guns as they moved forward. They did that anyway. Frank slipped the thong off his Colt and slid the revolver up and down slightly in its holster, even though he knew it would move smoothly.

Darkness fell quickly and completely as the Rangers cat-footed toward the source of the smoke that all of them could now smell. They passed several clumps of yucca plants and slid down a shallow bank into an arroyo. Sand and gravel grated under their boots.

"Quiet!" Wedge hissed, and once again the command was passed through the group. The men walked more carefully.

They climbed out of the arroyo and up another hogback ridge. When they reached the top, they could look down the far side of the ridge into a shallow depression where a large campfire had been built. Frank and Wedge went to their knees to study the camp. The troop of Rangers waited patiently behind them.

A wild pig, one of the vicious breed called *javelina,* roasted on a spit over the flames. Several men stood around the fire, warming themselves as they talked and laughed. Others were sitting on rocks or on the ground itself. Frank counted fourteen of them in all. Each man wore a sombrero, a short jacket, and tight trousers. The clothing was functional, not fancy. These men could have been mistaken for typical vaqueros instead of murderous border raiders.

For a second Frank considered the idea that maybe they *were* just vaqueros and didn't have anything to do with the attack on the Hernandez farm, or the raid north of San Rosa, or the running gun battle with Cecil and Ben Tolliver in which Frank had taken part. The trail had led the Rangers straight here, however, and it wasn't really reasonable to think there might be two armed gangs practically on top of each other.

What Frank saw a moment later was conclusive proof that the trail had led the Rangers to the right bunch. A man strolled up to the fire, holding himself somewhat apart from the others. He stood there stiffly, with no one speaking to him, and Frank recognized the loneliness of command. This was the boss.

And he wore a black mask. What appeared to be a silk scarf the color of midnight was tied around the lower half of his face. Instead of a tall sombrero, he sported a flat-crowned black hat that was tipped forward to conceal even more of his features. His jacket, trousers, and boots were black as well.

"The Black Scorpion!" Wedge whispered.

Frank had come to the same conclusion.

Wedge turned and gave low-voiced orders that the horses were to be brought up as quietly as possible.

"What are you going to do?" Frank asked.

"If we attack them on foot, they'll jump on their horses and take off. I don't want any of them getting away. That's why I'm going to split the troop and leave just enough men up here to throw a good volley into them. That'll make them run down that barranca on the other side of the camp. But the rest of us will be mounted and waiting for them when they come roaring down there."

That sounded like a reasonable plan, although Frank wasn't sure about the wisdom of splitting their force. As it was, they outnumbered the raiders. Once the Rangers were divided, the odds would be more even.

It was Wedge's decision to make, however, and Frank thought the plan stood a good chance of succeeding. He said, "I want to be on horseback."

"Come on, then," Wedge told him. They began slipping quietly back down the slope.

The captain picked out the men who were to remain on the ridge. "Give us fifteen minutes to get into position," he instructed them. "Then open fire on those murdering bastards."

The Rangers nodded in understanding.

Wedge, Frank, and fourteen other Texans moved farther back and reclaimed their horses from the men holding the mounts. Dog whined a greeting to Frank, and Stormy tossed his head. Frank took the reins, put his left foot in the stirrup, and stepped up, settling into the saddle. He turned Stormy and walked the Appaloosa after Wedge.

Again, they had to move slowly, quietly, and carefully, slipping around the raiders' camp until they reached the wide, dry wash that led toward the mountains. The clouds obscured the moon and stars, and even though the hour was relatively early, it was already as dark as midnight. One way the Texans could tell that they had reached the barranca was the sound of its gravelly surface under the horses' hooves.

Frank could see the campfire at the head of the wash, maybe three hundred yards away. The men moving around it cast wavering shadows in the night. They had no idea that flaming hell was about to descend upon them. Frank frowned slightly. He felt no sympathy for the raiders — they had chosen the *bandido*'s life and all the perils that went with it — but at the same time, ambushes rubbed him the wrong way, even when they were carried out by lawmen.

But there was nothing he could do about it now. He wasn't just about to warn those bandits.

"Ought to be nigh on to the time," Wedge said softly. There was no point in looking at a watch; the night was too dark for that. The timing of the attack had to be strictly guesswork.

But Wedge's guess was pretty close to being right on the money. Less than a minute after he had spoken, gunfire blasted from the top of the ridge overlooking the bandit camp. Loud reports broke the nighttime stillness, and spurts of flame split the darkness.

Everything was suddenly chaos in the camp. Men shouted curses and ran back and forth and blazed away with handguns, firing blindly toward the ridge. Most of the men leaped for their horses, just as Wedge expected. A couple of them fell, cut down by Ranger lead, before they could ever reach their mounts.

These men were superb natural riders, though, and they had left their horses saddled. In a matter of seconds, even as they fought back against the ambush, the raiders were mounted up. With a thunder of hoofbeats, they charged straight down the barranca toward Frank and the waiting Rangers. Captain Wedge's plan was working perfectly so far.

"Hold your fire!" Wedge hissed. "Let them get closer . . . wait, wait . . ."

The fleeing *bandidos* were almost on top of them.

"Now!" Wedge bellowed.

Every Ranger's hand was filled with iron. On Wedge's command, a volley roared out, the storm of lead scything into the onrushing raiders at close range. Some men cried out in pain as bullets ripped through them. Others toppled silently from their saddles.

Frank held his fire, though he had the Colt ready in his hand. He couldn't have said why he didn't shoot. It was just that suddenly something about this entire situation seemed wrong to him. He pulled

Stormy to the side as one of the sombrero-wearing bandits galloped past him, the high-crowned hat visible even in the poor light. Frank reversed the revolver in his hand and lashed out, slamming the butt of the Colt down hard on the bandit's head. The man groaned and fell off his horse. That was at least one they could take prisoner, Frank thought.

There might not be any more prisoners, though. The fighting was fierce in the barranca as guns spouted flame and lead. The muzzle flashes lit up the wash like the constant flickering of lightning. In that uncertain light, Frank saw another of the bandits race past him. This man was dressed completely in black and wore a flat-crowned hat.

The Black Scorpion!

Frank wheeled Stormy and jammed his heels into the Appaloosa's flanks as he called, "Dog!" Stormy lunged into a gallop, and Frank leaned forward in the saddle as he gave chase after the leader of the bandit gang.

8

Instantly, Frank knew this was better. If he caught up to the Black Scorpion, the showdown between them would be man-to-man, not an ambush out of the darkness. He wanted to capture the bandit chief, but if it came down to a hook-and-draw, each man would have to take his chances. That was the way it ought to be, the way Frank Morgan had always lived his life ever since he had discovered his skill with a gun. If a fight wasn't fair, it wasn't worth fighting.

Stormy thundered along the barranca, leaving the battle between the Rangers and the *bandidos* behind. Frank had to listen closely to hear the hoofbeats of the Scorpion's horse, but hear them he did, and he knew his quarry was still in front of him.

He was a little surprised that the Scorpion would cut and run like this, abandoning his men. Usually the sort of man who ascended to leadership wasn't the type to turn tail. Yet every man was different, and Frank could understand how suddenly being surrounded by death coming out of the darkness could unnerve a fella. *He* wouldn't have run, but that was just him.

The hoofbeats of the Scorpion's horse were closer now. Stormy was cutting the gap between them. After a few more minutes, Frank realized he could actually *see* the Black Scorpion now, a slightly deeper shade of darkness moving against the lighter-colored terrain. The *bandido* was only about ten yards ahead of him.

Suddenly the Black Scorpion twisted in the saddle. Frank saw the move and ducked as the Scorpion fired. The bullet whistled over Frank's head. He knew he couldn't afford to give the Scorpion many more chances like that. "Take him, Stormy!" he urged the big Appaloosa.

Stormy poured on the speed as the Black Scorpion fired again. Frank didn't know where the bullet went, but he and Stormy weren't hit, and that was all that mattered. With a final lunge, Stormy drew even with the Black Scorpion's horse.

Frank lashed out as the bandit tried to bring his revolver to bear for another shot. He hit the Scorpion's arm and knocked it up. The gun blasted, but the bullet went harmlessly into the sky. Frank veered Stormy even closer, until the two horses' shoulders were touching as they galloped along. Kicking his feet free from the stirrups, Frank tackled the Black Scorpion, knocking him out of his saddle and off the horse.

Both men fell, landing heavily and coming apart as the impact of landing made them roll over and over on the sandy ground. Even though the breath had been knocked out of him, Frank was able to get to his feet first. He lunged at the Scorpion, swinging a fist as the bandit tried to get up. The blow landed solidly on the masked face and knocked the Scorpion backward. Frank went after him.

The Black Scorpion wasn't out of the fight yet. His foot came up and his boot thudded into Frank's midsection. Frank grunted as still more air was driven from his lungs. The Black Scorpion grabbed him and heaved, pivoting Frank over him on that upthrust leg. Frank flew through the air and slammed to the ground on his back.

Now the momentum had shifted to the Scorpion as Frank tried to catch his breath and get out of the way of the man's rush.

He rolled over and threw himself to the side, sweeping a leg out to knock the Scorpion's feet out from under him. The Scorpion tumbled to the ground again.

Frank pushed himself to his hands and knees, shook his head, and dragged a deep breath into his body. That helped clear his brain a little, and he surged back to his feet. His hand went to the holster at his hip. He intended to draw his Colt and get the drop on the Black Scorpion.

But the gun was gone, having slipped out of its sheath sometime during the rough-and-tumble fight. Frank didn't have a chance to look for it because the Black Scorpion tackled him, driving him back several feet. The two men grappled desperately.

Frank had every confidence that he would win this brawl, until his foot came down on a fist-sized rock and it rolled under him. Pain shot through Frank's ankle as it bent far to the side. More agony shot up his leg as it collapsed underneath him, unable to support his weight.

The Black Scorpion took instant advantage of this unexpected opportunity. As Frank fell, the Scorpion brought up his knee sharply. The blow caught Frank on the jaw and stunned him, stretching him out. The Scorpion pounced on him, slamming fists to his face and driving a knee into his stomach. Frank knew he had to turn the tide of this fight quickly, or he was going to lose.

He never got the chance. The Black Scorpion snatched up a rock and crashed it against Frank's head. The terrible impact sent Frank spiraling down, down, down . . . into a darkness even deeper than the shrouded night.

Something rough scraped against his face, again and again, until it felt as if the skin itself was being stripped away from the flesh underneath.

Frank didn't know what kind of torture this was, but it was effective at bringing him out of his unconsciousness. He groaned against the pain that filled his head, but at the same time the discomfort was welcome in a way. It told him that he was still alive. The dead felt no pain.

Something jolted his shoulder. He jerked away from whatever it was, and the movement made his skull throb with renewed agony. He tried to open his eyes, but a red glare struck him like a physical blow and forced him to squeeze his eyelids shut again.

Maybe he was dead after all, he thought, and that glare came from the fires of hell. . . .

Something whined in his ear and started licking his face again. Frank forced his muscles to work and rolled onto his side. This time he was able to open his eyes, and he found himself staring into Dog's furry face.

Above him, Stormy leaned down and nudged Frank's shoulder again.

Frank rolled all the way over onto his belly. Sand and gravel pressed into his cheek, but for a long time he was too weak to move. Gradually he got his arms underneath himself and forced his head up. He saw Stormy's reins dangling in front of him as the big Appaloosa stood steadfastly beside him. Dog sat down a few feet away and watched Frank curiously, evidently satisfied by the fact that his master was still alive, if not well.

Propping himself on an elbow, Frank reached out with his other hand and closed his fingers around the trailing reins. He twisted his hand, wrapping the leather straps around it so that he couldn't let go. Then he got hold of the reins with his other hand and grated, "Back . . . Stormy . . . back!"

The horse took a couple of steps backward, following Frank's command. At the same time, Frank held tightly to the reins and pulled himself up with all his meager strength. He got a foot under him and pushed. The combination of efforts brought him shakily to his feet. His right ankle felt as if someone had jabbed a knife in it, but it supported him enough so that he didn't fall.

"Stand still . . . boy," he told Stormy. The Appaloosa didn't budge as Frank leaned against him. Frank moved one hand from the reins to the saddle horn. With that to steady him, he stood there waiting for the trembling in his muscles to stop and the pounding in his head to go away.

Eventually he felt a lot steadier, although the anvil chorus inside his skull continued with a shattering crescendo each time his pulse beat. His ankle hurt like blazes, too. Still leaning on Stormy, he took his hand off the saddle horn and gingerly touched the side of his head above his left ear. He winced as his fingertips prodded a big goose egg coated with dried blood from the gash in his scalp.

Frank remembered the fight with the Black Scorpion. The bandit chief had had him down and was pummeling him. That was the last thing Frank recalled. The Scorpion must have really walloped him with a rock or a gun butt, something like that.

And then, obviously, the Black Scorpion had escaped, leaving Frank lying senseless on the ground. The bandit must have believed him to be dead; otherwise he would have finished him off.

Blinking bleary eyes, Frank peered around. It was daylight; early in the morning, he guessed. The sky was still mostly overcast and the air was cold and dry. There were a few breaks in the clouds, however, and it was through one of those gaps that the sun had shined directly into Frank's eyes when he tried to open them.

He estimated that at least twelve hours had passed since the Rangers had attacked the Black Scorpion's camp. What had happened since that time? Had the Rangers wiped out the *bandidos,* except for the leader who had gotten away? Frank recalled that he had knocked out one man during the fight. Maybe that man was a prisoner . . . or maybe the Rangers had killed him, too.

And why hadn't Wedge and the others come to look for him?

Maybe they had, Frank told himself, and

just hadn't found him yet. They might be riding through the semiarid Mexican landscape right now, searching for him.

Or they might figure that he had been killed in the fight. They could have turned around and ridden back to the Rio Grande, leaving him here.

Even though he hurt like hell and had a bad ankle, Frank wasn't too worried now about his survival. He had Stormy and Dog to keep him company and help him, he had a Winchester and plenty of rounds for it in his saddlebags, he even had some jerky and biscuits he had brought with him from the Rocking T. And as he looked around some more, he discovered that he still had his Colt, too. He spotted it lying on the ground about twenty feet away.

Holding tightly to the reins, he hobbled over to pick up the revolver. After checking the barrel to make sure it wasn't fouled, he slid the weapon back into leather. He found his hat, too, not far off, and hung it on the saddle horn for now. As bad as his head hurt, he didn't want to even think about putting a hat on it.

Now it was just a matter of getting back to the border. Once he did, he thought he could find his way to the Rocking T. They would welcome him there, and he could spend a few days recuperating from the banging around he had received.

It bothered him that the Black Scorpion had gotten away. Even if his gang had been wiped out by the Rangers, the bandit might be able to recruit more followers, and his reign of terror along both sides of the border would continue. Frank wondered if he might be able to trail the Scorpion from this spot.

He knew he was in no shape to be trying to track down the bandit leader, but once the thought was in his head, he couldn't shake it. He began to look around, searching for tracks.

It didn't take him long to find them: the hoofprints of one horse leading toward the mountains. Grimly, Frank considered the tracks for a long moment. His ankle was sprained but not broken, he decided, and he was able to stand on it long enough to get his left foot in the stirrup and swing up onto Stormy's back. Then he hitched the Appaloosa into a walk, following a course that paralleled the tracks left behind by the fleeing Black Scorpion.

Frank's stomach was empty, but he was a little queasy and thought it probably wouldn't be a very good idea to try to eat. He took a sip from his canteen, though, as

Stormy rocked along at an easy pace. Dog walked alongside.

The water made Frank even more nauseous at first, but then his stomach settled down and he seemed to draw some strength from the liquid. He tried another sip and found that it didn't bother him. With that he realized just how thirsty and hungry he really was, but he still proceeded with caution, taking a strip of jerky from his saddlebag and gnawing off just a small piece. He chewed it slowly for a long time and finally swallowed it, then took another drink of water.

The life he had led had blessed Frank with a hardy constitution. His recuperative powers came into play during that morning as he followed the Black Scorpion's trail into the foothills of the mountains. While he was still far from being at top strength, he no longer felt as weak as a kitten. The pain in his head had receded into a dull ache that was bearable, though still annoying. He wouldn't be able to move very fast on foot because of that bad ankle, but as long as he was on horseback, he thought he could handle most trouble that might come his way.

The landscape had changed when he entered the foothills. There was more grass on the ground, and some of the hills were dotted with pine trees. He saw a few cattle here and there, but when he came close enough to one of the animals to be able to make out the brand on its hip, he couldn't read it. The brand was the usual "skillet of snakes" sort preferred by Mexican ranchers. They could make sense of the markings even when no one else could. Frank wondered if he was on Don Felipe Almanzar's range and if those were Almanzar's cows.

The trail grew harder to follow as the ground became rockier and less sandy. Frank thought about turning around and heading for the border, but he was too stubborn to give up on his quest. He wanted to find the Black Scorpion. Of course, he reminded himself, he was a civilian, and a gringo to boot. If he captured the bandit and took him back across the Rio Grande, it would be tantamount to kidnapping in the eyes of the Mexican authorities.

On the other hand, the Rurales would probably be glad to get their hands on the Black Scorpion, too. If he captured the Scorpion and then ran into a troop of the Mexican frontier police, he would just have to turn his prisoner over to them — that was all there was to it.

But maybe he wouldn't run into the Rurales, he thought as he rode along a canyon between two of the hills. Maybe he wouldn't even find the Black Scorpion. This whole thing might be crazy, just a wild-goose chase. . . .

Somewhere up ahead, somebody screamed.

No, Frank thought a second later, not somebody. Some *thing*. Unless he was badly mistaken, that had been the screech of a mountain lion. He knew such creatures were to be found here in these Mexican sierras.

Stormy tossed his head, no doubt agreeing that the unnerving noise had been the cry of a mountain lion. Horses had a natural aversion to the big cats, and Stormy hesitated, not wanting to go on down the canyon toward the sound. Alongside, Dog curled his lip and snarled as the thick fur on his back ruffled up.

The scream of the mountain lion came again, followed by another cry. Frank stiffened in the saddle as he realized that the terrified shriek had come from a human throat. A woman's throat.

"I know you don't like it, boy, but let's go!" Frank said as he sent Stormy galloping along the canyon.

9

The trail went around a bend up ahead. Frank drew his Winchester from the saddle sheath as Stormy rounded the turn at top speed. The gunfighter's eyes took in the scene before him instantly. About fifty yards ahead of him, a huge, tawny mountain lion crouched atop a rock outcropping that loomed over the trail. The big cat's tail swished back and forth rapidly as it poised to leap on its prey. The only thing holding back the mountain lion was its indecision as it tried to choose between two victims.

A black horse danced around skittishly, trying to pull free from where its reins were caught in some brush. That was the only thing that kept it from bolting in terror. A few yards away lay a young woman in a riding outfit: boots, split skirt, a leather vest over a blousy white shirt, and a hat with its neck strap tight under her chin. She had pushed herself into a half-sitting position and was staring in horror at the mountain lion. Frank knew that she must have been riding along the trail when the big cat leaped to the top of the rocks and screamed. That had caused her mount to shy and rear up, throwing her. Then the horse had tried to run but had gotten snagged in the brush alongside the trail. Frank knew it as well as if he had seen it happen.

Just as he knew that within a second or two at most, the mountain lion would spring.

He yanked Stormy to a halt and brought the rifle to his shoulder in one smooth motion. His aches and pains were all forgotten as muscles and nerves trained by long years of danger galvanized into action. The big cat leaped from the top of the rocks like a tawny lightning bolt. Frank tracked it with the barrel of the Winchester and squeezed the trigger, knowing he had time for only one shot.

The rifle kicked hard against his shoulder as it blasted. The mountain lion jerked and yowled and twisted in midair as the bullet caught it. Falling short of the young woman, the cat rolled and flailed with its paws as its blood pumped out onto the dirt of the trail.

"Get away from there!" Frank shouted at the woman, not knowing if she understood English but knowing that one of those slashing paws might still reach her. If it did, the claws would rip vicious wounds in her flesh. Thankfully, she was able to overcome the fear that had nearly paralyzed her a moment earlier. She scrambled to her feet and ran away from the wounded mountain lion.

Frank levered another round into the Winchester's chamber, lifted the rifle again, drew a bead, and fired a second shot. This one struck the big cat in the head, bored through its brain, and put the animal out of its misery. The mountain lion stretched out, quivered and trembled for a moment, and then lay still.

Frank lowered the rifle but didn't replace it in the saddle sheath. He heeled Stormy into a walk that carried them toward the young woman. She stood beside the trail with her hands pressed to her mouth, her gaze jerking back and forth between Frank and the dead mountain lion.

He reined Stormy to a halt again and asked, "Are you all right, Señorita?" He imagined he looked a little frightening, too, a gun-wielding gringo with streaks of dried blood on his face.

She gave him a shaky nod. *"S-sí, señor,"* she said. She was around twenty years old, Frank thought, and definitely lovely with long black hair, dark eyes, and smooth olive skin.

As pretty as she was, though, he had other things to worry about at the moment. He turned and studied the hillside, making sure that the big cat didn't have a mate somewhere close by ready to avenge him. When he didn't see any sign of another mountain lion, he finally slid the Winchester back in its scabbard.

"What's your name?" he asked. *"Su nombre?"*

"I speak English, Señor," she said. "My name is Carmen Maria Luisa Almanzar."

That came as a surprise to Frank, although not much of one. He hadn't known that Don Felipe had a daughter, but there was no reason for him to have thought that the man had no children. Almanzar could have a dozen kids for all Frank knew.

She stepped closer to him, lifting a hand. "You are hurt, Señor."

Frank started to tell her that he'd had a run-in with the Black Scorpion, but then he stopped before the words could come out of his mouth. Running across Señorita Almanzar might be a lucky break for him.

112

For the moment, he would play his cards close to the vest.

"Yes, I was attacked," he said, "but I'll be all right."

"Who assaulted you, Señor? Bandits?"

Frank shook his head. "I don't know. I never got a look at them. I assume they intended to rob me. They creased my head with a bullet. . . ." He pointed to the bloody knot on his head, which Carmen Almanzar had already seen. "I was knocked unconscious. When I came to, whoever shot me was gone."

"Perhaps your . . . wolf . . . frightened them away."

Frank glanced around and saw Dog sniffing at the carcass of the mountain lion. "Get away from there," he called, and Dog obediently abandoned the body to come trotting over to Frank. Carmen shrank back a little at the big cur's approach.

"You don't have to worry about him," Frank told her. "He's a dog, and he's friendly when I tell him to be."

"*Sí, señor.* I will take your word for it." She paused and then went on. "Who are you, Señor? What are you doing on Almanzar land?" She caught her breath and lifted a hand to her mouth. "Oh! That's sounds rude, and so ungrateful. I would not be alive now if you had not killed that . . . that awful beast."

Frank smiled. "You're welcome as you can be, Señorita Almanzar. I'm just glad I came along in time to help. As for me, my name is Frank Morgan."

There was no recognition in Carmen's lustrous dark eyes. It was nice for a change, Frank thought, to run into somebody who *hadn't* heard of him.

"I'm just drifting," he went on. "I never stay in one place for too long, and I was looking for a nice warm place to spend the winter." That wasn't exactly a lie. He *was* a drifter, hence the nickname, and he had come to south Texas hoping to find a good spot to hunker down until the next spring.

"But Señor, you are in Mexico," Carmen protested.

"A warm, friendly country, from everything I've heard," Frank said with a grin.

"Not that friendly. Not now. Not for gringos . . . or anyone else."

Carmen's face was solemn, even grim, as she spoke. Frank wondered if the reason she felt that way had anything to do with the Black Scorpion.

He lightly touched the swollen lump on the side of his head and said, "I reckon I'm beginning to see what you mean. You have a bandit problem down here, don't you?"

"Bandits . . . and others," she said enigmatically. Before he could question her any further, she went on. "You must come with me to my father's hacienda. His rancho is the biggest one in this part of Mexico, and once he hears how you saved my life, he will welcome you, Señor Morgan. To be honest, he has little use for gringos, but in your case I am sure he will make an exception."

"I could use a place to rest up for a spell," Frank said with a grateful nod. "I twisted my ankle, too, so I'm a mite hobbled right now."

"Let me get my horse, and I will take you to the hacienda." She went over to the black mare, which had settled down some once the big cat was dead. The horse still seemed fairly nervous, though. It took Carmen a moment to free the reins from the brush. She spoke softly, calmingly, in Spanish to the mare as she did so.

"What about the mountain lion?" Frank asked. "You want me to throw a rope on it and haul it in, so you can have the hide?"

A shudder went through Carmen as she settled down in the saddle. "Not at all. If my brother killed a cat like that, he would want to mount the head as a trophy. A barbaric custom, if you ask me."

They rode side by side along the canyon, Carmen indicating the way they should go. Frank said, "If I'm not being too forward, what were you doing, out riding around by yourself like that?"

She sniffed and gave a defiant little toss of her head that made her long black hair swirl around her shoulders. "This is my father's rancho," she said. "I ride where and when I please."

So she was more than a little spoiled, Frank thought. Probably the apple of her daddy's eye and used to getting her own way. A girl as pretty as her couldn't hardly help but be spoiled, because there would always be some man around, falling all over himself to do whatever she wanted. Frank was old enough to be immune to such feminine charms, however.

Well, maybe not completely immune, he corrected himself as he thought about Roanne Williamson.

They came to a better-traveled trail that led through the foothills. From a high spot on the trail Frank looked to the northeast and saw rangeland stretching into the distance toward the Rio Grande. Here along the edge of the mountains the pastures were fairly lush with grass, or at least they would be during the spring and summer, he judged. The advancing season had made the vegetation die down a bit. Farther out on the flat, the land was drier and it would take more acres to support a cow. Or did they measure land in hectares on this side of the border? Frank couldn't remember, and he knew it didn't really matter what they called it. The Almanzar ranch appeared to be a good spread, better probably than the Rocking T across the border.

"My father's hacienda is only a few miles away," Carmen was saying when Frank noticed dust rising from the trail a few hundred yards ahead of them. He reined in, causing Carmen to do likewise.

"Somebody's coming," he said with a nod toward the spiral of dust.

Carmen took a deep breath and paled. "Is it more than one rider?" she asked tautly.

"I don't think so," Frank replied, "but I can't be sure about that just yet."

Carmen reached for her saddlebag, opened it, and drew out a small pistol. She handled it like she was used to the weapon.

"You reckon it might be bandits?" Frank asked.

"Perhaps."

Again, he was struck by the feeling that in Carmen's opinion, there were worse things than bandits on the loose in these parts. She didn't volunteer an explanation, though, and he didn't press her on the matter. He might learn more just by keeping his eyes and ears open.

Anyway, he was pretty sure now that only one rider was kicking up that dust, and Frank was confident in his ability to handle one man, whoever he was.

The man came in sight, riding swiftly toward them on a big gray. Carmen relaxed and heaved a sigh of relief. "I know that horse," she said. "That is my brother riding it."

Frank had been ready to draw the Winchester from the saddle boot. He took his hand away from the rifle. Surely he wouldn't have anything to fear from Carmen's brother, especially once he heard how Frank had saved the young woman from the mountain lion.

Carmen lifted a hand over her head and began to wave as the rider came closer. "Antonio! Antonio!" she called.

The young man wore a fine suit of brown cloth decorated with embroidered gold threads. His flat-crowned hat was a darker brown. The tight trousers were tucked into high-topped boots, and strapped onto the boots were spurs with the big rowels that Mexican horsemen usually preferred. His saddle and the gray's harness were worked with silver trappings. He was a fine young grandee, Frank thought, the very picture of a wealthy *hacendado*'s son.

"Carmen!" he called as he came closer, and then suddenly his dark, handsome face contorted with anger as he looked over at Frank. He jabbed those spurs into the gray's flanks and sent the horse leaping forward. At the same time his hand flashed toward the butt of the revolver holstered on his hip.

10

"Antonio!" Carmen cried as she desperately spurred her own mount forward, getting between Frank and her brother. "No!"

Instinct had made Frank reach for his own gun. The Colt had come out of the holster in less than the blink of an eye. It was already up and leveled, but Frank held off on the trigger as the girl got in the way.

She twisted in the saddle and looked wide-eyed at him. *"Por favor, Señor Morgan!"* she pleaded. "Do not kill my brother!"

"Carmen!" Antonio Almanzar shouted. "Get back! Get away from the bandit!"

Antonio hadn't drawn his gun. Carmen's action had startled him and kept him from completing the hook-and-draw he had started. Frank lowered his Colt slightly and called, "Take it easy, Señor. I'm not a bandit."

Antonio glared at him. "You are a

gringo!" the young man practically spat, as if that was enough of a condemnation by itself. "You must be down here to rob us. Look at you! You have your gun out like a common killer!"

"You went for your iron first, son," Frank said tautly as anger welled up in him. He kept it under control as he holstered the Colt. "There. That ought to make you feel better."

Antonio would have responded hotly, but before he could speak, Carmen said, "Antonio, Señor Morgan saved my life. And this is the way you greet him?"

Antonio frowned at her. "Saved your life?" he repeated.

"Yes, my horse had thrown me, and a mountain lion sprang at me." A touch of awe could be heard in Carmen's voice as she went on. "Señor Morgan shot the beast out of the air, even as it leaped. Never have I seen such a shot."

"That is . . . incredible," Antonio muttered. He still didn't look pleased to see Frank, but at least he wasn't reaching for his gun. He said, "I thank you for saving my sister's life, Señor. My foolish sister," he added, "who should not have been out riding alone."

"Foolish, am I?" Carmen flared.

Antonio jerked his head in a nod. "Indeed. When our father realized that you were gone, he sent me to look for you. You defy his wishes all too often, Carmen."

She did that head-tossing thing again, Frank saw. "My life is my own, to lead as I see fit!"

Frank knew her brother saw that differently, and he would have been willing to bet that her father did, too. Carmen was more outspoken, more defiant, than most young Mexican women. Again, it went back to her beauty, he supposed. That and the fact that her father's wealth had no doubt shielded her from many of the harsh realities of life.

With a surly glare, Antonio turned his horse. "Come," he snapped. "I will accompany you back to the hacienda."

"What about Señor Morgan?" Carmen said.

Antonio looked over his shoulder at Frank, still with no friendliness. "It seems my family owes you a debt," he said. "Come with us so that we can repay you."

Frank had no interest in being repaid, but he did want to see the Almanzar hacienda and meet Don Felipe. So he nodded and said simply, *"Gracias."*

The three of them rode on, with Antonio

looking a little askance at Dog as the big cur trotted along with them. After a few minutes, he said, "That is an ugly brute."

"Yep, that he is," Frank agreed. "But he's the best dog I ever ran into."

"I will take your word for it, Señor." Antonio lifted a hand and gestured vaguely toward Frank's head. "What happened to you?"

"Señor Morgan was shot by bandits, or perhaps by someone else," Carmen said before Frank could answer. *"Es verdad?"*

Frank shrugged. "It's just a graze. I'm lucky it wasn't a whole lot worse."

"Sí," Antonio said. "Lucky."

Frank wondered what in blazes the young man meant by that. Antonio must have reasons to dislike all gringos, or at least he thought he did.

A short time later they came within sight of the Almanzar hacienda. It was a sprawling, two-story structure of whitewashed adobe with a red tile roof. Frank could tell that it was built Spanish-style, around an open central plaza. Nearby were several large barns and corrals, along with a long bunkhouse made of logs and other adobe outbuildings. Like the Rocking T, there was an air of prosperity and success

123

about the place. If anything, the Almanzar hacienda was even more impressive than Cecil Tolliver's spread.

Frank asked himself why a man who owned a place like this would send gunmen across the border to attack a Texas rancher. That idea made no sense to him. From the looks of the Almanzar hacienda, Don Felipe would have plenty to do just keeping it running smoothly.

Of course, Tolliver had mentioned a feud, Frank recalled. Old grudges didn't always have to make sense in order to cause trouble.

The hacienda was cupped in a shallow bowl on the side of a hill. A creek ran down from above, at one point sparkling in a short waterfall before winding its way past the house and the barns and then running on out toward the flats, where it disappeared. Pine trees grew on the hill and around the house. It was as pretty a spot as Frank had seen in quite a while. Damn near a paradise, in fact.

Sometimes serpents lurked in paradises, he thought, recalling the story of the Garden of Eden. He wondered whether any snakes waited for him here.

Frank, Carmen, and Antonio rode down the slope toward the big house. A man stepped out of the log bunkhouse, looked up and saw them coming, and began ringing a bell that hung beside the door on a post. The pealing of the bell had a strident sound to it, as if it were not so much an announcement of Carmen's return as a warning about something.

About *him,* Frank thought with a quirk of his mouth.

A good-sized group of men had assembled in response to the bell by the time Frank and his two companions reached the hacienda. All of them except one were typical vaqueros. They all carried pistols, and each man had his hand close to the butt of his gun.

The lone exception carried no weapon that Frank could see. He was tall, broad-shouldered, wore high boots, tight trousers, and a white shirt. A crimson bandanna was tied around his throat. His dark hair was long and a fierce mustache drooped over his mouth. His darkly tanned face resembled a hatchet. Frank had no doubt the man was Don Felipe Almanzar, and even though he was an aristocrat, there was Indian blood somewhere in his lineage. The high, sharply planed cheekbones were proof enough of that.

He stalked forward as the three riders

reined in. "Carmen!" he said. "Where were you?"

The young woman's defiance and haughty attitude slipped somewhat in the face of that harsh demand. But then she recovered and said with a lift of her chin, "I went for a ride. You should know by now that is my habit, Papa."

"I know your habit is to take foolish chances with your own life and the lives of those I send to look for you, including your own brother. You know it is no longer safe for a young woman to ride alone in these hills!"

Now that they were closer, Frank could see that Don Felipe's face was lined and weathered. From a distance, the man's vitality made him seem younger than he really was. Even up close, he was still an impressive figure. Frank could see how such a man could carve an empire out of the wilderness in northern Mexico.

"It was not my wish to endanger anyone," Carmen began. "I did not think that —"

"You can stop when you say that you did not think," her father cut in.

Carmen flushed but didn't say anything else.

Frank's gaze played quickly over the

group of vaqueros. He didn't see any *norteamericanos* among them. Tolliver had insisted that the gunmen who had jumped him and Ben had been sent by Almanzar, but based on what he saw here, and on Antonio's attitude toward gringos, Frank thought it was unlikely any such men worked for Almanzar. So the identity of those raiders remained one more question without an answer, at least for the time being.

Almanzar turned his dark eyes toward Frank. "Who is this injured gringo?"

Even though the query hadn't been addressed directly to him, Frank answered. "My name is Frank Morgan, Don Felipe. My apologies for trespassing on your land. I did not mean to cause trouble."

Almanzar grunted. "It looks as if trouble has found you despite your intentions, Señor Morgan. What happened to you?"

Frank stuck with the story he had told Carmen and Antonio. "I was bushwhacked. A shot grazed me, knocked me out."

"Whoever attacked you did not cut your throat or steal your horse?"

"Nope. I reckon something must have spooked them."

Almanzar nodded slowly. "My apologies

to you, Señor. I admit that I care little for your kind. You are a Texan, are you not?"

"That's right," Frank said, "although I've traveled around a lot over the years."

"I have no trust or affection for Texans," Almanzar said curtly, "but I would not have a stranger come to harm on my land. Please accept the hospitality of my house."

"Gracias, Don Felipe."

Carmen said, "You have reason to feel grateful to Señor Morgan, Papa. He saved me from a mountain lion."

Almanzar's eyebrows lifted in surprise. "Come inside, Señor Morgan. I would hear of this encounter with the lion of the mountains."

Some of the vaqueros had drifted off when it became obvious there wasn't going to be any trouble, but several had stayed behind. They stepped forward now to take charge of the horses as Frank, Carmen, and Antonio dismounted. Stormy blew air through his nostrils and bared his teeth as one of the men reached for his reins. The vaquero drew back.

"It's all right, Stormy," Frank said as he patted the big Appaloosa's shoulder. "You can go with this hombre. He'll take care of you."

Stormy looked dubious about that, but

he allowed the vaquero to take the reins and lead him toward one of the barns.

"Go with Stormy, Dog," Frank said to the cur. "These are friends, you hear?"

Dog padded after Stormy, his tongue lolling from his mouth, his eyes watching the vaqueros suspiciously.

"A one-man horse and a one-man dog," Almanzar said. "And impressive animals they are. My respect for you grows, Señor."

He ushered Frank toward a wrought-iron gate in the outer wall of the house. Carmen and Antonio followed. Frank carried his hat and limped on his injured ankle.

Once they entered a cool, shadowy interior of the house, a *mozo* appeared to take the hat. Frank gave it to the servant, who hung it carefully on a peg set in the adobe wall.

It was chilly inside the house. At Almanzar's command, the *mozo* hurried to light a fire in the big fireplace on the other side of the room. For a moment, as Frank looked around, he almost thought he was back at the Rocking T. This parlor had the same sort of fireplace, the same heavy, overstuffed furniture. There were no mounted animal heads, however, and instead of a cavalry saber, a pair of thin-bladed rapiers hung on the wall.

"Do you require medical attention, Señor Morgan?" Don Felipe asked. "I can have one of the Indian women tend to your wound."

Frank shook his head. "Perhaps later. There's really not much that can be done for it, other than washing off some of this dried blood."

"You might be surprised. There are compresses and other such things. . . . These Indians can sometimes work wonders with their cures and remedies."

"I know. I'm all right for now, though."

"What about your leg? I notice that you limp rather badly."

Frank shrugged. "The ankle's just twisted. I'm not going to be running any races any time soon, but I think it'll be all right."

Almanzar shrugged. "As you wish. Can I offer you a glass of brandy?"

"Actually, right now a cup of coffee sounds mighty good. And maybe something to eat." Ever since Frank's head had settled down, his stomach had been reminding him incessantly of how long it had been since he'd had any real food.

"Of course." In rapid Spanish, Almanzar

issued orders to his majordomo, and the old man scurried out of the room to carry them out.

Almanzar gestured for Frank to have a seat on a cowhide-covered divan and said, "Now, about this mountain lion . . ."

"The cat frightened my horse, Papa," Carmen began, "and I was thrown off —"

Almanzar held up a hand to stop her. "Please allow our guest to tell the story, Carmencita."

She subsided with a pout on her lips. Whether she was angry at being interrupted or at being called by the diminutive, as if she were a child, Frank couldn't tell.

"Your daughter has the straight of it, Señor," Frank said. "I was riding along after I came to from being knocked out, and I heard the mountain lion scream ahead of me. I might have tried to avoid it, but then the señorita screamed, too, and I knew I had to go lend a hand."

"Carmen claims this man shot the lion out of the air," Antonio put in, sounding like he thought such a thing was utterly impossible.

"He did!" Carmen said.

"It was a lucky shot, I reckon," Frank said. "I didn't have time for anything else.

That big cat had to choose between going after the señorita or the horse, and he'd made up his mind."

"You are obviously a man who has much skill with guns," Don Felipe said. "I am in your debt, Señor. I owe you for my daughter's life."

Before Frank could respond, Antonio said, "This man Morgan should be a good shot, Papa. I recognize his name now. He is the infamous gringo gunfighter known as The Drifter, and I would not be surprised if he had been sent here by Cecil Tolliver to assassinate you!"

11

Almanzar's face flushed even darker than normal as he listened to his son's accusation. Glaring intently at Frank, he demanded, "Is this true, Señor?"

"Which part?" Frank asked dryly. "Am I sometimes called The Drifter? I reckon I am. And some folks regard me as a gunfighter. I guess the description fits. But I'm not an assassin and never have been. Nobody sent me here, either. I came on my own."

"To kill me?"

Frank bit back the frustration he felt. "Not hardly. I don't have a thing in the world against you, Don Felipe."

That was true enough. Frank didn't know who was right and who was wrong in the feud between Almanzar and Cecil Tolliver, whatever it was based on, but he was convinced that it hadn't been Almanzar's men who had attacked Cecil and Ben on the road from San Rosa to the Rocking T. He didn't think it was likely that Almanzar had anything to do with the Black Scorpion, either. The owner of a successful rancho had no reason to turn *bandido.*

"Do not listen to him, Papa," Antonio advised. "You know that no gringo can be trusted. No matter what he says, he must be Tolliver's man."

"I'm nobody's man but my own," Frank snapped, unable to completely contain his irritation at Antonio's continued accusations.

"All right," Almanzar said, motioning for his son to be quiet. He faced Frank and went on. "As a guest in my house, you will be treated with respect, Señor Morgan. But I warn you, if you seek to harm me or my family, you will regret it."

"I told you, I didn't come down here looking for trouble." That was stretching the truth a mite, Frank thought. When he had crossed the Rio Grande with Captain Wedge and the Texas Rangers, on the trail of the Black Scorpion's gang, he had indeed been looking for trouble. And he had found it, in spades.

The tense atmosphere in the room eased a bit as the *mozo* came in carrying a tray with a coffeepot and cups. A couple of heavyset Indian women followed him with platters containing tortillas, strips of meat, peppers, and beans. They set the food on a table to one side. The old man placed the coffee on the table as well and began filling the cups from the pot.

Don Felipe waved a hand, inviting Frank to help himself. He and his two children — the only ones Frank had seen so far, at least — joined him.

The coffee was thick and sweet, though it held a hint of bitterness from the chocolate that had been melted in it. Frank used some of the tortillas to scoop up the beans while he rolled meat and peppers in the others. The food was excellent, though heavy enough that he began to get a little sleepy. He knew he needed to stay awake. A doctor had once told him that it could be dangerous to go to sleep too soon after a hard crack on the head. Something about a bruise on the brain. Frank figured his skull was too thick and hard for that to have happened, but he didn't want to take the chance. He drank several cups of the thick coffee to help keep him alert.

Antonio Almanzar was still sullen, but Carmen chattered happily as the four of them sat around the table. She seemed to have gotten over the scolding her father had given her. Don Felipe appeared to have forgotten about being angry with her, as well.

Like a dog with a bone, Antonio wasn't ready to let go of his resentment. He said bluntly to Frank, "Do you know the man Tolliver?"

"I know who he is," Frank said obliquely. "Rancher who has a spread on the other side of the border. The Rocking T, isn't it?"

"Once he was just a simple rancher, perhaps," Don Felipe said. "When he first came, I took him to be an honest man. But he has shown his true colors over the years. He is a thief and a scoundrel."

"What's he stolen?" Frank asked.

"He has stocked his ranch with our cattle," Antonio said hotly.

"Rustler, eh?"

"And our vaqueros have been attacked," Almanzar said, his voice grim. "Some have been killed."

"How long has this been going on?"

"For years," Almanzar said. "Many long years."

Carmen took Frank by surprise by saying, "That is not true, Papa, and you know it!"

Don Felipe glared at her. "Do not dispute your elders, child," he said sternly. "You know nothing of this."

"I know that until recent months, we lost only a few cows, and they were probably taken by the Yaquis who live high in the mountains. And when our men were attacked, it was by *bandidos*."

Don Felipe slapped a palm on the table. "Perhaps once, but no longer!" he said. "Now it is Tolliver's men who plague us!"

"You don't know that," Carmen shot back at him.

Frank listened to the exchange with great interest. Don Felipe Almanzar was saying the same sort of things about Cecil Tolliver that Tolliver had said about Almanzar. That had to mean something.

"You only hate Señor Tolliver," Carmen went on, disregarding the obvious fury building up on her father's face, "because of what happened with Mama."

"Enough!" Almanzar exploded. "I will listen to no more! Carmen, leave us! Go to your room and stay there!"

"No! You are not being fair —"

"Go!" Don Felipe bellowed, rising to his great height to loom over his daughter.

Mama? Frank thought. Was Carmen talking about her mother, about Don

Felipe's wife? What connection did the doña have with Cecil Tolliver?

And for that matter, where *was* Doña Almanzar?

More mysteries seemed to crop up every time he turned around, Frank mused.

Sullenly, Carmen left the table and disappeared through an arched doorway. Don Felipe turned to Frank and said stiffly, "My apologies for my daughter's disrespectful behavior, Señor. Since her mother's unfortunate passing, Carmen has grown even more headstrong." The man sighed, and for a second Frank saw his façade of iron self-control slip. "My late wife, may El Señor Dios rest her soul, knew better than I how to deal with the whims of a young woman."

"The best way is with a strap and a strong arm," Antonio said.

His father glared at him. "Silence! I will not hear of such things." Almanzar nodded to Frank. "Again, my apologies, Señor Morgan."

"No apologies necessary, Señor Almanzar," Frank assured him. "I don't know from personal experience, but I imagine that raising children is a tricky business."

For a moment, the conversation made wistful memories of Victoria Monfore race through Frank's mind. Victoria might or might not be his daughter; he would probably never be one hundred percent certain about that, but she was far away, up in Parker County, safely married to Tyler Beaumont now. An injury had confined her to a wheelchair, perhaps for the rest of her life, but Frank could rest easy knowing that Beaumont was there to care for her. And then there was Frank's son Conrad, back East somewhere, still estranged from his father, although when they had last parted, Conrad no longer seemed to bear any hatred for his father. Frank hadn't been around while Victoria and Conrad were growing up. In fact, he hadn't even known about them until they were grown, but he could imagine what it was like trying to bring up youngsters so that they followed the right path in life.

Almanzar sighed. "Of all the travails that may befall a man, Señor, none is heavier than the weight of trying to do the right thing."

Frank nodded, fully understanding what Don Felipe meant.

A few moments of silence went by, and during that time Frank mused that at least one of his questions had been answered. Almanzar's wife was dead. But was there a connection between her death and Cecil Tolliver? Every answer brought with it a new question.

When the meal was finished, Don Felipe asked, "Will you stay with us for a few days, Señor Morgan, or do you prefer to move on?"

Frank had been pondering the same question. He thought they might be getting worried about him at the Tolliver ranch, especially if the Rangers had returned to the Rocking T and said that Frank had been lost in the battle with the Black Scorpion's gang. He didn't like the idea of causing needless concern.

On the other hand, he might come closer to finding the cause of all the trouble plaguing the border country if he remained on this side of the Rio Grande for a while.

It wasn't his problem, he reminded himself. He could ride on any time he wanted to. But he liked the Tollivers, he was intrigued by Roanne Williamson, and he found himself respecting this savage old aristocrat at whose table he sat. It sounded to him as if someone might be playing both ends against the middle, setting Tolliver and Almanzar at each other's throats for some unknown purpose. Nothing good could come of that.

Besides, when you came right down to it, he was curious about what was going on around here, Frank decided, and he was at a stage in his life where he could afford to indulge his curiosity.

"If that's an offer, Don Felipe, then I accept," he said. "I appreciate your hospitality, and I appreciate the opportunity to let this banged-up head and ankle of mine heal a mite before I move on."

Almanzar nodded. "It is done, then. You will remain here as my guest as long as you wish, Señor Morgan." He silenced any protests Antonio might make with a fierce glare at his son. "It is the least I can do to repay you for my daughter's life. She is at times a vexation, but still precious to me."

"I reckon that's probably the way most folks feel about their youngsters, Don Felipe," Frank said.

They drank the last of the coffee, and then Almanzar summoned the elderly servant again and instructed him to show Frank to his quarters. Before Frank followed the old *mozo* out of the room, Almanzar took a heavy walking stick carved out of some sort of dark, heavy wood from a stand in a corner and presented it to him.

"This was my father's, Señor Morgan,"

141

Don Felipe said. "May it ease your steps while you are with us."

"Thank you, Don Felipe," Frank said formally. "I'm much obliged."

He followed the servant through a door and along a walkway with pillared openings to the central plaza along one side. On the other side were arched doorways that led into sleeping quarters. With each step the walking stick thumped against the tile floor and the servant's slippers whispered on the stone as well.

The old man opened one of the heavy doors, grunting with effort as he did so, and ushered Frank into a room with thick adobe walls, a single narrow window with its shutters closed, and a bed with a straw mattress. One chair sat in a corner. The room was a little larger and a bit better furnished than a monk's cell, but that was what it reminded Frank of.

It also occurred to him that if the door and the shutters were locked from the outside, this room truly would be a cell, for he would be unable to get out.

No one had tried to take his gun, though, so he didn't think it was likely Almanzar would treat him like a prisoner in other respects. He nodded his thanks to the *mozo,* who lit a candle in a wall sconce, then shuffled out and closed the door behind him.

Frank dropped his hat on the bed and sat down beside it. The past thirty-six hours had been filled with action and violence, and weariness gripped him. Almost without thinking about it, he stretched out on the soft mattress, and despite all his intentions, he was asleep within moments.

12

Frank felt some alarm when he woke up and realized that he had dozed off. He pushed himself into a sitting position and swung his legs off the bed, waiting to see how his head was going to react to this movement. He could tell from the way the candle had burned down that several hours had passed.

Somewhat to his surprise, he didn't feel dizzy. And the throbbing inside his skull had gone away, too. He took several deep breaths and felt fine. Clearly, some good food and a nice long rest had been just what he needed. His brain hadn't been injured after all, thanks to that thick skull of his, he thought with a smile.

His ankle still hurt, though, as he discovered when he tried to stand up. With a gasp, he sat back down and got his weight off it. He reached down and worked his boot off. His ankle was swollen, and it might have been a mistake to remove the boot, Frank thought. He might have a hard time getting it back on.

He took a bandanna from one of the hip pockets of his jeans and used it to bind up the injured ankle, tying it tightly. When he stood up, the ankle still twinged painfully, but it didn't hurt as much as it had before.

A frown creased his forehead as he noticed that his saddlebags were draped over the back of the chair. They hadn't been there earlier. That meant someone had brought them in while he was asleep and left them there without disturbing him. That shouldn't have happened. No one should have been able to come into the room without alerting him. If the intruder had meant him harm, he might be lying there in the bed with a slit throat right now, or a stab wound in his heart.

Getting older was one thing, Frank told himself sternly. Getting careless was another. Given the life he led, a moment, even a single second, of carelessness might be enough to mean death.

He gave a little shake of his head. Brooding about it now wasn't going to help. He resolved not to let it happen again.

Not wanting to try to pull his boot back

on, Frank took the other one off instead, and in his stocking feet he went to the window. The shutters swung open when he unlatched them, so he definitely wasn't a prisoner here. A cool breeze blew into the room. Outside, the sky was dark blue and purple as the light of day faded. As Frank stood there, the stars overhead began to wink into existence. The overcast was gone and the sky was clear.

The breeze made the candle flame flicker behind him and then go out. The room was plunged into darkness relieved only by the faint glow from outside. The view from the window was toward the hill behind the house. There were mountains beyond those foothills, but Frank couldn't see them from here. He could see the top of the hill, though, silhouetted against the last vestiges of the sunset, a dark mass against a sweep of fading rose.

That fleeting illumination was the only reason he was able to see the rider coming over the hill, skylighted for only a moment before disappearing.

Frank rested his hands on the thick adobe sill of the window and leaned forward. A frown etched lines on his forehead as he listened intently. He couldn't hear any hoofbeats. Had he imagined the rider?

Or had the rider swung down from the saddle so that he could approach the hacienda on foot? If that was the case, there was something unsettling about it. No one would be skulking around the Almanzar rancho unless he was up to no good.

Something else about what he had seen bothered Frank, and it took him several minutes of hard thought before he realized what it was. Though the image of that rider had been glimpsed only for a second, something was wrong about it, and when Frank finally succeeded in recreating the picture in his mind's eye, he knew what it was.

All of Almanzar's vaqueros had worn sombreros with very wide brims and short, dimpled crowns. The rider Frank had seen had worn a high-crowned hat, and the brim had been all wrong, too. That was the sort of hat a gringo might wear, and given the hostility toward *norteamericanos* Frank had seen displayed on the Almanzar rancho, why would such a man be sneaking up on the hacienda as night fell?

This was a mystery that Frank couldn't ignore.

He didn't want to raise an alarm, though, until he was sure that there was really a threat. He eased the shutter closed

147

and then, still in his stocking feet, turned toward the door of the room. He picked up the walking stick, then put it down again. With the bandanna bound tightly around his ankle, he thought he could walk well enough without the stick. The sound it made as it thumped on the tiles would be bound to give him away if he tried to move silently. He just had to be careful and not put too much weight on the bad ankle.

Frank limped to the door and paused there long enough to touch the butt of his Peacemaker for a moment, moving it a little in the holster to make sure it wouldn't hang on anything. Then he pulled the latch string and put his shoulder to the door, easing it open. Thankfully, the hinges were well oiled and didn't squeal.

He stepped out into the night and pulled the door closed behind him. The tiles of the walkway were cold through his socks, and that chill climbed to his ankle and made it throb slightly. Frank ignored the discomfort. He walked silently to his left, away from the main part of the hacienda. The blue was gone from the sky he saw above the enclosed courtyard. Now the heavens held only swathes of purple and black, dotted with the pinpricks of the stars.

He came to a dark, tunnel-like passage through the ground floor of the hacienda. The far end of it was closed off by a wrought-iron gate. Frank didn't know if the gate was locked. He slipped along the passage, tried the latch, and found that it lifted freely. When he opened the gate, it swung easily and made no noise. He would have stepped through it without hesitation if a faint, almost indistinguishable smell had not caught his attention. He leaned closer to the hinges on which the gate hung and touched a fingertip to the top hinge. His finger came away slick. He rubbed it with his thumb and held it to his nose. Oil of some sort, and freshly applied.

Someone had gone through this gate a short time earlier, but only after applying oil to the hinges so that they wouldn't make any noise. Frank would have been willing to bet that the gate was normally kept locked. Someone inside the house had unlocked it and used it to slip out into the night. Either that, or they had unlocked it to allow someone else to slip in.

The rider on the hill?

The hillside loomed above Frank. There would be rocks and cactus and Lord knows what else up there, and he wasn't going to try to climb it without his boots. Besides, if anything was about to happen, it would have to come right through this gate. The rider hadn't had time to get down here yet, so he was still out there somewhere in the darkness. He might try to sneak into the hacienda. If someone had gone out to meet him, that person would probably come back this way . . . that is, unless he wasn't coming back at all. If that was it, then there was nothing Frank could do about it. If either of the other two possibilities were correct, he could wait right here and let the mystery come to him.

With a twisted ankle and no boots, that sounded like the best idea to The Drifter. He eased the gate closed again and moved back in the corridor that ran from the courtyard to the hacienda's outer wall. The darkness around him was as thick and impenetrable as ink as he leaned back against the adobe wall to wait.

As he stood there, he listened. The night might seem quiet, but it seldom ever was. Horses moved in their stalls in the barn, stamping and blowing in their restlessness. Men talked and laughed in the bunkhouse, their voices like music as the liquid Spanish flowed from their tongues. From time to time someone plucked at the strings of a guitar. High in the hills, a coyote howled, greeting the stars as they emerged from their daylong slumber.

Or *was* that a coyote? Frank asked himself. Did the Indians in these Mexican mountains use animal cries as signals, like the Comanches and the Apaches north of the border did?

He waited and listened, letting the sounds of the night wash over him, instinctively separating them and assessing them, listening for anything that would warn him of the approach of danger or impart information that might help him figure out the answers to the questions that nagged at him.

Time didn't mean much in a case like this. If Frank had been forced to guess, he would say that he had been standing there in the darkness for about half an hour when he finally heard the scuff of leather against the ground on the other side of the gate. His muscles tensed. The sounds increased and came closer. The stars shone faintly on the ground outside the gate, providing just enough light for him to be able to make out a vaguely human shape as it came up to the gate. Whoever it was opened the gate, but only narrowly, slipped through, and then eased it closed behind them. Frank heard the rattle of a chain and the sharp click of a padlock being snapped shut. The gate was locked again.

Frank didn't move as the person who had just come in walked quietly toward him. The steps were light. He heard the rustle of cloth. The folds of a skirt? Had the figure Frank had seen been that of a woman? He thought it was possible, but he hadn't gotten a good enough look to be sure.

The next moment he was certain, as he caught a whiff of a flower-scented fragrance and then heard a little snatch of a song as the woman sang to herself in Spanish. Frank recognized the words and the tune. It was a Mexican love song.

He recognized the voice of the young woman singing it, too.

The voice belonged to Carmen Almanzar.

Frank didn't move, didn't even breathe as Carmen went past him. He was sure she had no idea he was there. She thought she had gotten away to her evening rendezvous without anyone being the wiser. Clearly, given her attitude and the song she sang, she had slipped out of the hacienda to meet a lover. One of her father's vaqueros?

Frank thought that was unlikely. He believed that Carmen had gone out to meet the man he had seen riding over the hill behind the hacienda. A man who wore the hat of a gringo. Don Felipe, by his own admission, had no use for men from north of the border. Antonio hated them. Would Carmen dare the wrath of her father and brother to carry on a secret romance with such a man?

The answer to that was pretty obvious, Frank told himself. Carmen was a headstrong young woman who was accustomed to getting her own way, getting whatever she wanted. If that was a young man from the other side of the Rio Grande, of course she would dare.

Frank waited until she was gone. Then he went back to his room, still moving quietly, turning over in his mind everything he had just seen and heard. The question remained: If Carmen was in love with a gringo, then who was he?

Frank thought he might have the answer to that one, too. It would certainly explain some things if his theory was right.

He had only been back in his room a few minutes, just long enough to scratch a lucifer to life and relight the candle on the wall, when a knock sounded on the door. Frank opened it and found the *mozo* standing there. The servant said, "Don

Felipe awaits you in the dining room, Señor."

"Dinner time, is it?" Frank asked innocently.

"Sí, Señor."

"Good. It's been long enough since that snack that I'm hungry again." Frank looked down at his feet. "I don't know if I can get a boot back on my right foot, though."

"Wait here a moment, *por favor*."

Frank waited, and a couple of minutes later the servant returned carrying a pair of finely worked moccasins with fringed tops that would come as high on the calf as most boots.

"Try these, Señor," the *mozo* suggested.

Frank sat on the bed and pulled on the moccasins. The soft leather had enough give to it so that he was able to get the right one over his swollen ankle. At the same time the moccasin was tight enough to give the injury even more support. When Frank stood up, his ankle still hurt some, but not nearly as much as it had earlier.

"What's your name?" he asked the servant.

The old man looked down at the floor, as if afraid that he was about to be chastised. "Esteban, Señor."

"Well, Esteban, you did a fine job by finding these moccasins for me. *Muchas gracias.*"

Esteban smiled slightly, pleased by the unexpected praise. *"De nada, Señor,"* he said.

Frank left his Stetson in the room. He was recovering more rapidly than most men would from the injuries he had received the previous night, but he still wasn't ready to wear a hat. The tender lump was still there, above his left ear.

He followed the old-timer to a dining room with a vaulted ceiling and a long, highly polished table. Don Felipe and Antonio were already there, but Frank didn't see any sign of Carmen. He nodded politely to Almanzar and asked, "Will your daughter not be joining us for dinner?"

"Carmen has sent her regrets, Señor Morgan," Almanzar said. "Her experiences today . . . the mountain lion, you know . . . have tired her and she wishes to rest."

"I hope she feels better tomorrow," Frank said. He wondered if Carmen's nocturnal rendezvous had anything to do with her not coming down for dinner. She hadn't sounded tired when he heard her singing to herself.

The Indian servant women began bringing in platters of food and placing them on the table. The air filled with spicy, intriguing aromas.

Before the three men could sit down to eat, however, a bell suddenly began to ring outside. Looks of alarm appeared on the faces of both Don Felipe and Antonio. They turned toward the entrance as a rumble of hoofbeats drifted in from the night. From the sound of it, a large group of horsemen had just ridden up to the hacienda.

Don Felipe and Antonio started toward the door. Frank was right behind them. Almanzar glanced over his shoulder and said, "This does not concern you, Señor Morgan."

"You've most generously offered me your hospitality, Don Felipe," Frank said. "If trouble's come to call, I'd be honored to help you answer."

Almanzar only considered the offer for a second before nodding curtly. "Come, then," he said. "Let us see who pays us a visit this night."

13

A moment later, the three men stepped through a wrought-iron gate into the courtyard in front of the hacienda. As Frank had thought, the area was filled with milling horses. A couple of servants, including Esteban, hurried out of the house carrying blazing torches, and the light from the burning brands revealed that the newcomers were not *bandidos*. Instead they wore the gray wool jackets and trousers of the Rurales, the Mexican police force responsible for law and order in the far-flung rural areas of the country. Sombreros with slightly smaller brims and slightly higher crowns than those worn by the vaqueros were on their heads, giving them a distinctive appearance.

A man dressed in similar but more expensive fashion sat his horse in front of the others. He had a red bandanna around his throat, and the buttons of the jacket were silver instead of the more ordinary wood or brass to be found on the uniforms of the other men. The buttons shone in the torchlight, as did the scabbard of the saber he wore at his hip. The outfit would have been resplendent, even garish, if its bright colors hadn't been dulled by the thick coating of trail dust that lay on the uniform. The officer removed his gray sombrero, brushed dust from it rather ostentatiously, and settled it back on his mostly bald head before he said in Spanish, "Good evening, Don Felipe. I trust you are well."

"I am fine, Captain," Don Felipe replied stiffly. Frank instantly sensed the dislike between these two men. "Please, avail yourself of the comfort of my home."

The Rurale captain swung down from his horse and barked a command at his sergeant for the men to dismount. He handed the reins of his horse to the sergeant and turned back to Almanzar, Antonio, and Frank.

The officer was tall and lean, with a narrow face and a neatly trimmed mustache. He smiled, but his dark eyes were cold as he glanced at Antonio. They warmed slightly with a spark of interest as his gaze turned toward Frank.

"A visitor from north of the border," he murmured.

Don Felipe gestured toward Frank. "Señor Frank Morgan, of Texas," he said. "Señor Morgan, this is Capitán Estancia of the Rurales."

The captain actually clicked his boot heels together as he nodded to the American, and Frank thought that somewhere along the way the man must have been drilled by a Prussian mercenary. Frank knew that El Presidente, the dictator Porfirio Diaz, had hired professional soldiers from all over the world to help train his army.

"Captain Domingo Estancia of the Gendarmeria Fiscal, at your service, Señor Morgan," the officer said in English. "What brings you below the Rio Bravo?"

"Nothing in particular," Frank lied. "Don Felipe was kind enough to extend his hospitality when I found myself on his land."

Almanzar said, "Señor Morgan is too modest. He was responsible for saving the life of my daughter when she was attacked by a mountain lion."

Estancia's thin eyebrows arched. "Indeed?"

"I was in the right place at the right time

to lend the young lady a hand," Frank said with a shrug.

Don Felipe added, "And before that, he was attacked by bandits."

Estancia was even more interested in that. He leaned forward as he asked sharply, "The *ladrones* who ride with the Black Scorpion?"

"I don't know who they were," Frank said. "I never got a look at them."

Captain Estancia waved a hand toward his men, who had all dismounted and were being taken into the bunkhouse, probably to be fed by Don Felipe's cooks. "My men and I have been in pursuit of the Black Scorpion for days now. Anything you can tell me that might help us will be greatly appreciated, Señor Morgan."

"Sorry," Frank said. "Like I told you, I never saw whoever it was who took a potshot at me."

Estancia took a deep breath, the nostrils of his high-bridged nose flaring. "Very well. On behalf of El Presidente Diaz, I apologize for what happened to you, Señor. Such disgraceful things are a shame on our beautiful country."

"I'm all right. Nothing to worry about, Captain."

Estancia looked around. "I do not see

Señorita Carmen, Don Felipe. I trust she was not injured in her encounter with the mountain lion."

"My daughter is fine," Almanzar replied, the chilly stiffness in his voice again. Obviously he didn't want to discuss Carmen with the Rurale captain. "She is resting."

"Ah. Perhaps I will be blessed with the beauty and graciousness of her presence at a later time."

"Perhaps," Don Felipe said curtly. "For now, Señor Morgan, Antonio, and I were about to sit down to dinner. You will join us, of course?"

"Of course," Estancia said.

The four men went into the hacienda, trailed by Esteban and the other servant carrying torches, which were extinguished once the men were back in the soft yellow glow of the lamps.

At an order snapped by Don Felipe, the Indian women hurried to set an extra place at the table. Unlike the simple meal earlier in the day in the parlor, this one was more elaborate, served on the gleaming hardwood table. At each place setting were fine china, silver, and crystal.

"After many days on the trail, this reminds me of El Presidente's palace," Captain Estancia remarked as he sat down. He had given his sombrero to one of the servants to hang up on a peg, and the light from the chandelier above the table shone on his scalp. Frank thought it looked a little like a skull. Estancia went on. "I appreciate your hospitality, Don Felipe."

"As always, it is my pleasure to host the representative of El Presidente." Don Felipe didn't sound all that pleased, though, Frank thought.

The women brought out platters of thick steaks, tortillas, and corn on the cob, bowls of beans and peppers and thick sauces. There were enchiladas and tamales, pots of stew, bowls of cut-up squash and tomatoes and peppers, pork ribs, rice, and fried chicken. Maybe not quite enough food for an army, Frank mused, but nobody was going to leave this table hungry.

The men dug in, eating heartily, washing down the food with wine from glasses that never seemed to empty. Frank just sipped his, knowing that he wanted to keep a clear head.

After some time had gone by in relative silence, Antonio asked, "What deviltry has the Black Scorpion been up to this time, Captain?"

Frank saw Estancia's fingers clench harder on the silverware he held, as if the mere mention of the Black Scorpion angered him. "The damned bandit and his rabble blew up a railroad bridge south of here. When a train came along and was forced to stop, they boarded it and looted it, robbing all the innocent men and women who traveled on it."

"When was this?" Don Felipe asked.

"A little over a week ago. We were able to get on their trail quickly, but despite that, the devils have eluded us."

Frank took a sip of his wine and then said, "I heard something about this so-called Black Scorpion on the other side of the border. Folks up there are blaming him for a raid on a ranch northwest of San Rosa several days ago. How could the same gang be operating on both sides of the border with such a short amount of time in between?"

"Nothing seems to be beyond the capabilities of the Black Scorpion, Señor Morgan," Estancia replied solemnly. "He crosses the Rio Bravo with impunity, daring both the Gendarmeria Fiscal and the Texas Rangers to capture him. He seems to know all the trails, all the . . . what do you call them? . . . shortcuts." The captain gave an eloquent Latin shrug. "So far, the Black Scorpion has had things all his own way. But the time is coming when justice has its day."

"That is all one can pray for," Don Felipe said. "That justice will triumph."

Estancia cleared his throat. "Yes. Of course."

Once more Frank sensed some byplay under the surface in the comments by both men, especially Don Felipe Almanzar. He wondered what the chances were that the man might open up to him and reveal what was really going on here. Pretty small, Frank decided, at least for the time being. It would take a while to build up some trust between them. The fact that Frank was a gringo wasn't going to help.

Antonio took a drink of his wine and then said, "I'm not sure anyone will ever catch the Black Scorpion, Captain. It is said that he can disappear like a shadow in the night or a puff of wind."

Estancia scowled. "Any man who is human can be caught, and the Black Scorpion, despite being in league with Satan, is human."

"Are you so sure?" Antonio smiled.

"We have no need of such talk, Antonio," Don Felipe snapped. He must have known, as well as Frank did, that Antonio was goading the captain. The dislike in the air was palpable.

Estancia narrowed his eyes as he studied Antonio over the rim of his wine glass. "The task of capturing the bandit would be less difficult if he had not terrorized all the peasants and small landholders into helping him. They fear his wrath too much to cooperate with the authorities. Perhaps one day they will realize there are others whose wrath they should fear even more."

"Perhaps," Antonio said. "But perhaps they already know this and consider the Black Scorpion the lesser of two evils."

Don Felipe changed the subject by saying, "While your troop is here, your men should feel free to fill their canteens and replenish the supply of grain for their horses, Captain."

Estancia inclined his head. *"Gracias, Don Felipe."*

"And as late as it is, you are welcome to spend the night, of course."

"Your hospitality is much appreciated."

"I suspect, though, that your quest will force you to leave on the morrow."

"Unfortunately true. Our scouts are out now, seeking the trail we will follow." Estancia turned his head to look at Frank. "Señor Morgan, I would know more of you. Your name . . . It is familiar to me for some reason."

Before Frank could answer, Antonio said, "North of the border Señor Morgan is a famous gunfighter, Captain. Perhaps you have heard of the man called The Drifter?"

Recognition flickered in Estancia's eyes. "Of a certainty. You are very well known in your country, are you not, Señor Morgan?"

"Too well known, sometimes," Frank said. "Trouble seems to find me whether I'm looking for it or not."

"To one degree or another, that is the way of the world, is it not?"

Frank nodded. "Seems to be."

He didn't care for the sort of verbal fencing that was going on at the table. Don Felipe and Antonio didn't like Captain Estancia, and it seemed like the Rurale officer didn't care much for them, either. Antonio was still suspicious of Frank, and now Estancia was, too. And over it all, somehow, loomed the shadow of the Black Scorpion.

"Father," Carmen said reproachfully from a balcony overlooking the dining room. "No one informed me that we had visitors."

The four men came quickly to their feet. Captain Estancia did that heel-clicking thing again, and this time he bowed all the

166

way to the waist. "Señorita Almanzar," he said as he straightened. "You are as beautiful as ever."

"Carmen, I thought you were resting," Don Felipe said as Carmen walked over to the staircase that led down to the dining room.

"I was," she said, "but I feel much better now."

Estancia was right about one thing, Frank thought: Carmen was beautiful. She wore a long, light blue gown that left her shoulders and throat bare down to the top of the cleft between her breasts. Her arms were bare, too, and Frank thought she must have been a little chilly in that getup. The servants had started a fire in the fireplace in the parlor — Frank could hear the crackling of the wood through the open door — but the warmth of it hadn't spread very far into the dining room.

Looking elegantly lovely, Carmen came down the stairs. Captain Estancia was the closest to her and might have stepped forward to take her hand, but Frank saw the fires of anger burning in Don Felipe's eyes and moved quickly, sliding around Estancia to reach Carmen first. He ignored the pain that the hasty action caused in his sore ankle. He took Carmen's hand and found it smooth and cool.

"Allow me, Señorita," he murmured. Holding her hand, he turned to escort her back to the table.

When he did, he saw the dark glower on Captain Estancia's face. He had sensed before that the officer disliked him; now he was certain of it.

Frank didn't care. A young woman like Carmen didn't need the attentions of a man such as Estancia.

Don Felipe was about to call the servants to set a place for Carmen when she stopped him.

"I am not really hungry," she said. "But I would like a glass of wine."

Don Felipe frowned. "I do not like to see you drink wine, Carmen."

"I am old enough," she shot back. "I am old enough for many things now, Father."

At that, a smile appeared on Estancia's face that was just short of a leer. Frank saw it and thought that he didn't like Estancia, so the feeling was mutual now.

Don Felipe flicked a hand at Esteban, who poured a glass of wine for Carmen. She sipped it and smiled and laughed and flirted with Captain Estancia as he made small talk with her. The faces of Don Felipe and Antonio grew darker.

Frank asked himself what in blazes Carmen was up to. Was she just feeling giddy because earlier tonight she had been with her mysterious lover?

There was no telling what sort of blowup the strained atmosphere in the dining room might have culminated in, because the sounds of a disturbance came abruptly from outside. Men shouted angrily in Spanish. The commotion sounded like it might turn into a brawl.

But then a shot rang out and an even more ominous silence fell, the sort of quiet that could usually be heard just before all hell broke loose.

14

The four men started up from their chairs. Even Carmen tensed and leaned forward. "The Black Scorpion!" Estancia said.

"I doubt that," Antonio said. "The Black Scorpion has never bothered us."

"Raiders sent by Cecil Tolliver!" Don Felipe said. "That is more likely."

Frank didn't think the ruckus was caused by either of those things. It had sounded to him more like an argument between two groups of men. Almanzar's vaqueros and the captain's Rurale troops, most likely.

Don Felipe and Captain Estancia started to stalk toward the door at the same time. Ever the polite host, Don Felipe stopped and let Estancia precede him. He and Antonio were right behind the officer, though. So was Frank.

When they reached the courtyard in front of the hacienda, they found about what Frank expected. Don Felipe's vaqueros were bunched up on one side, muttering and casting dark, furious glares toward the Rurales on the other side of the courtyard. While the vaqueros all wore six-guns, none of them had drawn a weapon. That was probably because the Rurales had rifles leveled at them. It must have been one of the Rurales who had fired that warning shot a moment earlier, Frank decided.

The subject of the disagreement was in the front ranks of the Mexican police. One of Don Felipe's men was held tightly in the grasp of two of the Rurales. He struggled to get loose, but they hung on. Blood dripped from a cut on the captive's forehead.

"What is going on here?" Almanzar demanded in a loud voice.

Captain Estancia strode forward and barked at his sergeant, "Explain yourself, Cabo!" The Spanish words flew quickly, but Frank understood them.

The sergeant, a swarthy, heavy-mustached man who looked more like a bandit than any of the men Frank had seen in the camp of the Black Scorpion the previous night, gestured toward the prisoner and said in a guttural voice, "This man spoke against El Presidente! He said the people would be better off without his foot on their neck! And then he called us Diaz's dogs!"

An angry murmur went though the ranks of the Rurales at that.

Don Felipe stepped forward and said to the captive, "Is this true?"

The vaquero being held by the Rurales blinked blood out of his eyes and said, "I only spoke what all of us feel, Don Felipe. These men come swaggering in here and eat our food and lust after our women, and when one of them demanded that I give him my tobacco, I told him that I do not share with dogs!"

The sergeant turned and rammed the butt of his rifle into the vaquero's belly. The man gasped in pain, then bent over and retched. He would have fallen if not for the cruelly tight grip of the men holding him.

"See?" the sergeant said as he turned back to Estancia. "Sure disrespect cannot be permitted, *mi capitán*."

Frank glanced over at Antonio and saw that the young man was trembling from the depths of the outrage he felt as he looked at the prisoner. "Father," he said quietly to Don Felipe, "are we to stand by and watch one of our men being treated this way?"

Don Felipe looked furious, too, but he had his emotions under control. He kept a tight rein on them as he said, "Captain Estancia, I must protest. This is my land, and my men have the right to speak as they please."

Estancia sighed. "Unfortunately, this is not the case, Don Felipe. You know it is against the law to foment rebellion against the rule of El Presidente."

"Rebellion!" Don Felipe flung a hand toward the prisoner. "He just didn't want to give up his tobacco to one of your men!"

"The Gendarmeria Fiscal is empowered to commandeer anything we may need to fulfill our mission," Estancia said.

"But tobacco!"

"It is not for refusing to give up his tobacco that this man must taste the whip," Estancia said. "It is because his disrespect is an affront to our president."

Don Felipe drew himself up, and Frank could tell that his self-control was fraying. "The whip?" he said in a disbelieving voice.

"Five lashes." Estancia shrugged. "It is a serious offense, but since I have such great respect for you, Don Felipe, I will levy only a minor punishment."

Five lashes with a whip didn't sound like such a minor punishment to Frank. Judging by the angry mutters that came from the crowd of vaqueros, they didn't care for it, either. But if they tried anything, those Rurales would fire the leveled rifles, and the volley would be deadly at this range. In a matter of seconds, the courtyard would turn into the scene of a bloody massacre.

Don Felipe had to know that, too. He drew a deep breath and then said, "Five lashes. It is . . . just." The words sounded like they tasted as bitter as wormwood in his mouth.

Captain Estancia smiled, snapped his fingers, and gestured for the prisoner to be brought over to a hitching post. The rest of the Rurales covered the vaqueros while the sergeant drove the butt of his rifle into the small of the prisoner's back and knocked him to his knees. His hands were jerked above his head and bound with rawhide thongs to the hitching post. The man who tied the knots drew them cruelly tight.

Then the prisoner's shirt was ripped off him, leaving his back bare. Knowing what was to come, he whimpered a little even though he had not yet been struck. The sergeant went to his horse and came back holding a coiled whip. He shook the coils loose, and the whip fell loosely around his feet, slithering in the dust of the courtyard like a snake.

Frank glanced at Don Felipe. The man's face might have been carved out of mahogany for all the emotion it displayed at this moment. The same couldn't be said of Antonio, who stood there horror-stricken with his hands clenching and unclenching into fists at his sides. The vaqueros looked much the same way. They wanted to come to the aid of their comrade, but there was nothing they could do as long as they were menaced by those rifles.

Frank heard soft crying and looked over his shoulder. Carmen Almanzar stood at the entrance to the hacienda, tears running down her face as she watched this display of cruelty, violence, and arrogant power. Frank thought about going to her and trying to convince her to return to the house, but before he could start toward her, she turned and half-ran, half-stumbled back inside.

"Carry out the punishment, Cabo," Captain Estancia said to his sergeant.

Frank heard the hiss of indrawn breaths in dozens of throats as the burly sergeant raised his arm and drew back the whip. His arm fell and the whip lashed out, striking the prisoner's back diagonally and curling almost lovingly over his shoulder. The prisoner lunged forward against the hitching post but didn't cry out.

When the sergeant pulled the whip back, it left a narrow wound that oozed blood. Taking his time about it, the sergeant got ready and then struck again, this time flicking his wrist so that the lash crossed the prisoner's back in the opposite direction. The wounds formed a large, crimson X on the unlucky vaquero's skin. Blood began to trickle down his back.

Frank had felt rage stirring inside him even before the first blow was struck. This wasn't right, and his sense of justice cried out for him to do something about it. But there was nothing he could do, not without the risk of starting a bloodbath. Like Don Felipe and Antonio and the others, he had to just stand there and watch this atrocity.

But the day would come, he vowed right then and there, when he would settle the score with Estancia and that brutal sergeant.

Again the whip flashed and peeled flesh from the prisoner's back. The man had remained silent on the first two lashes, but the third one brought a choked cry of agony from his throat. He sagged against the post and twisted pitifully, trying futilely to escape the whip as it rose and fell yet again. After four lashes, the vaquero's back was awash with blood, and crimson droplets splattered through the air as the sergeant drew the whip back. The prisoner cried and shuddered and writhed, but he couldn't escape the pain.

The sergeant poised his arm for the fifth and final blow. He took a step forward as he struck, putting all the strength in his muscular body behind the whip. More blood and little gobbets of flesh flew through the air as the stroke landed. The vaquero gave a gurgling scream.

And once more the sergeant pulled his arm back, lifting the whip to strike yet again.

Without thinking about what he was doing, Frank stepped forward. With the same speed that had saved his life in many a showdown, his hand shot out. Not reaching for his gun this time, but for the sergeant's wrist instead. His fingers clamped like iron bands around that wrist before the sixth stroke of the whip could fall.

The sergeant was taken by surprise. To tell the truth, Frank was, too, at least a little bit. He hadn't planned this. He had acted purely on instinct. He jerked down on the sergeant's wrist, and at the same time, his left foot hooked around the man's right ankle and tugged hard. Already off balance, the sergeant fell backward and landed heavily. Frank plucked the bloody whip out of his hand and threw it on his chest. The sergeant recoiled from it as if it really were the snake that it resembled.

"Señor Morgan!" Captain Estancia shouted. "You dare to interfere —"

"You said five lashes," Frank said coldly as he turned to face Estancia. Now his hand hung near the butt of his Colt, ready to hook and draw if he had to. "That hombre was about to hit him for the sixth time."

"You miscounted," Estancia snapped.

A faint smile tugged at the corners of Frank's mouth. "I don't think so," he said. "I've been able to count up to six for a long time." His finger tapped the walnut grip of the Peacemaker as he spoke.

For a long, tense moment, the two men stood there, their gazes locked. Then Estancia's shoulders rose and fell in a slight shrug and he said, "I suppose it could have been five." To the sergeant, he snapped, "On your feet!"

The sergeant climbed to his feet, and the

look on his dark Indio face that he gave to Frank was full of murder and hatred. Frank knew that he had made a couple of enemies tonight, but he didn't care. The whole thing had been unjust to start with, and there was only so much of that he could swallow before it stuck in his craw and he had to do something about it.

Antonio started forward, toward the prisoner. Estancia said, "What are you doing?"

"Cutting him loose," Antonio said. He paused and looked back. "With your permission, Captain." The scorn in his voice made it clear that he wasn't really asking Estancia's permission at all.

The officer nodded and flicked a hand anyway, and Antonio went to the hitching post. He drew a knife from a sheath at his waist and sawed through the rawhide thongs. When they parted, the prisoner groaned and started to topple over. Antonio caught him and supported him, obviously not caring that he was getting blood on his fine clothes.

Don Felipe signaled to his men, and several of them hurried forward to help Antonio with the whipped man. The Rurales made no move to stop them. The bloodied vaquero was taken off to the bunkhouse to be cared for by his compadres.

Estancia turned to Don Felipe. "I apologize for this unpleasantness. It is necessary, however, to maintain order and respect for the authorities, and for El Presidente."

"As you say," Almanzar replied stiffly.

"As for you, Señor Morgan," Estancia said, "I forgive you for your interruption. This is not your land, and you do not know our ways."

"I know right from wrong," Frank said.

Estancia's lips tightened. "You will find that on this side of the border, Señor, the meaning of those words sometimes differs from your American conception of them."

"I don't think so."

Estancia glared, but he didn't say anything else to Frank. Instead he turned to the sergeant and ordered, "Cabo, have the men withdraw a short distance and pitch their tents. We will remain here tonight."

"Sí, mi capitán."

Before turning away to carry out the command, the sergeant stared for a long moment at Frank, who had no trouble reading the threat in the man's dark eyes. Then, as his lips drew back in a snarl he could no longer contain, the sergeant turned away. A second later he began to spit orders at the Rurales.

"Once again I apologize for this unpleasantness, Don Felipe," Estancia said to Almanzar. "Now, if you wish, we can resume our meal. . . ."

"I no longer have much of an appetite," Don Felipe said. "Dinner is over."

Even though Frank had known the man only a short time, he realized how uncharacteristic this lack of hospitality was in Don Felipe. That showed just how upset he really was.

"I will have Esteban show you to your quarters," Don Felipe continued.

"You will tell Señorita Carmen that I said good night?"

Don Felipe just grunted, not promising anything. Estancia's face darkened a little more at this insult, but he didn't press the issue.

The vaqueros had all gone into the bunkhouse, and Antonio had gone with them. Esteban led Captain Estancia into the hacienda to escort him to his room. That left Frank and Don Felipe standing alone in the courtyard, where the dark splatters in the dust bore mute testimony to the violence that had occurred here.

"You must think that we are a barbaric people," Don Felipe said abruptly.

"There are barbarians among every

181

race," Frank said, "and some believe that ultimately, they're bound to triumph over the civilized men."

"And is this what you believe, Señor Morgan?"

Frank looked at the splashes of blood on the ground and said, "I'd like to think otherwise, Don Felipe, but sometimes I don't know. I just don't know."

15

The rest of the night passed quietly. Frank didn't see either Carmen or Antonio before he went to his cell-like chamber and climbed into bed, leaving the bandanna tied around his tender ankle. He slept soundly.

By the next morning, when he untied the bandanna, the swelling had gone down some. Likewise, the knot on his head was smaller and less painful to the touch. Another day or two and both injuries would be almost healed, he thought. For today, though, he left his Stetson in the room and pulled on the moccasins instead of his boots.

As was his habit, he had risen early, not long after dawn, but of course the inhabitants of the rancho were already up and about, getting a fair start on a good day's work. Vaqueros rode here and there, and the ringing of hammer against anvil came from the blacksmith shop. The sound reminded Frank of his friend Reuben Craddock, the blacksmith in the little settlement of Nemo, Texas, far to the north. The burly Reuben shared Frank's love of reading, and that thought reminded Frank that he needed to find another book for his saddlebags before too much longer. Nothing passed the time like a good book.

No one challenged him as he walked into the main part of the sprawling hacienda. When he came into the dining room, he found Carmen sitting at the table, the remains of her breakfast still in front of her as she sipped on a cup of coffee. She greeted him with a smile.

"Buenos dias, Señor Morgan," she said. "How did you sleep?"

"Passable," Frank said. "And you, Señorita?"

She put her coffee cup on its saucer and a delicate shudder ran through her. "Not well. I kept hearing the crack of the whip and those cries of pain, even in my dreams."

Frank sat down and gazed solemnly across the table at her. "Do you know how that man is doing this morning?"

"As well as can be expected, I suppose. The Indian women cleaned his wounds and dressed them with an ointment they make from plants that grow in the hills. My father checked on him this morning and said that he will recover, but I think it will take a long time. And the poor man's spirit may never be the same again." Carmen sighed and shook her head. "It was a dreadful thing. I could not watch it. Hearing it was bad enough."

Frank nodded in agreement. "It's probably good that you went back inside, Señorita," he told her. "There was nothing you could do to stop it."

She tilted her head a little to the side as she regarded him intently. "Antonio tells me that *you* stepped in to stop it, Señor Morgan, when the sergeant tried to exceed the five lashes Captain Estancia ordered."

"The fella must have lost count," Frank said, as he had the night before.

Carmen shook her head. "I do not think so. Many of the Rurales are brutal men. They like to inflict pain." She paused. "Did you notice their sombreros?"

"I suppose," Frank said with a puzzled frown. "What about them?"

"Did you see how some of the sombreros were gray, to match the uniforms, but many of them were black?"

Frank thought back to the night before

and then nodded. "I reckon you're right. What does that mean?"

"Most of the men who serve in the Rurales were recruited from prisons in Mexico City and elsewhere. They are given the choice of serving the sentences they have received for their crimes either behind bars or in the Gendarmeria Fiscal, which is the official name for the Rurales. It is said that any such prisoner who has been convicted of murder receives a black sombrero when he joins the Rurales."

Frank felt a chill along his spine. "Then more than half of the men in that troop are murderers."

"*Sí,*" Carmen said softly. "And those are the men who are supposed to bring law and order to our land."

"What about Captain Estancia?"

"Rurale officers are first officers in the Regular Army. They are often aristocrats, not at all the same class as the cutthroats and brigands who make up the men they command." Carmen hesitated. "But that does not mean they cannot be every bit as brutal and ruthless."

The young woman was speaking freely, probably because she and Frank were the only ones around at the moment. He decided to take advantage of that and hoped that she would keep talking.

"Last night at dinner you seemed to be playing up to Captain Estancia," he said bluntly. "Why would you do that if you don't like him?"

"The captain wields great power in this region. Great power," she said again. "It is best not to anger or defy him. A pleasant smile, and he rides on without seeking to humble us." She added bitterly, "At least, not too much."

"Did the Rurales leave this morning?"

Carmen nodded. "Yes, they are off on their . . . How do you *norteamericanos* say it? Their wild-goose chase?"

"After the Black Scorpion?"

"*Sí.*" She gave a little scornful laugh. "As if they would ever stand a chance of catching the Black Scorpion."

"Pretty slick bandit, is he?"

"Pretty slick, yes. A bandit?" Carmen shrugged. "Who knows?"

That was intriguing, but before Frank could say anything more about it, footsteps sounded nearby, and a moment later Don Felipe Almanzar strode into the dining room. He was dressed for riding the range, much like his vaqueros.

"Ah, *buenos dias,* Señor Morgan," he said. "I trust you are well this morning?"

"Not bad," Frank said. "I hear the Rurales are gone."

The affable expression on Almanzar's face disappeared, to be replaced by a look of anger that seemed more natural somehow on his hawklike features.

"*Sí,* Capitán Estancia and his men rode out a short time ago."

"And you were happy to see them go?"

"As any honest man would be."

"That's about the way I feel, too," Frank agreed with a smile that didn't reach his cold gray eyes. "The captain seemed like a first-class son of a —" With a glance at Carmen, he stopped before he could finish the epithet.

"Indeed," Don Felipe said. "Have you had breakfast, Señor Morgan?"

"Not yet."

Carmen got to her feet, since she was finished with her meal. "I will tell Esteban to see to it, Papa," she offered.

Don Felipe nodded. *"Gracias."* He turned back to Frank as Carmen left the room. "And after you have eaten, Señor, would you feel like riding?"

"You want me to leave?" Frank asked, a little surprised.

Don Felipe looked shocked. "On the contrary. I wish to show you my rancho, if

188

you will indulge an old man's pride."

Don Felipe might be getting along in years, but Frank had a hard time thinking of anyone so vital as old. He smiled again, more warmly this time, and said, "I'd be pleased to see your ranch, Don Felipe."

Almanzar took a quirt from behind his belt and flicked it against his leg. "Meet me at the main corral, then, in thirty minutes."

"I'll be there," Frank said with a nod.

Esteban bustled in with eggs scrambled with ham and peppers, along with the inevitable tortillas and some sweet rolls. Frank enjoyed the meal, washing it down with a couple of cups of strong coffee. When he was finished, he went back to his room and picked up his hat. Carefully, he settled the Stetson on his head and found that it didn't hurt the lump above his ear. He wasn't going riding without a hat on. He would have felt naked. He kept the moccasins on, preferring not to trade them for his boots just yet.

When he reached the corral he found Don Felipe waiting for him, as promised. Almanzar stood beside a huge black stallion, and as Frank looked from man to horse and back again, he decided that they were a good match. They had the same sort of primitive wildness about them, despite the civilized clothes on the man and the silver-studded saddle and harness on the stallion.

Stormy was hitched to the corral fence, too, already saddled and ready to ride. The Appaloosa tossed his head when he saw Frank. Dog sat nearby, his tongue lolling from his mouth and his tail swishing back and forth in the dust.

"I hope it is all right that I took the liberty of having one of my vaqueros saddle your horse," Don Felipe said.

Frank nodded. "That's fine, as long as he didn't get a finger or two nipped off in the process. Stormy can be a mite feisty at times."

"I think my man emerged uninjured." Don Felipe smiled. "A Mexican can handle any horse, Señor Morgan. The talent is in our blood."

Frank might have argued about that, and he probably could have demonstrated that he was right by offering to let Don Felipe ride Stormy and then giving the Appaloosa a single sharp-voiced command. But Frank had no desire to see his host or anybody else go flying through the air after being thrown from Stormy's back, so he didn't say anything.

Instead he untied the reins, grasped them loosely in his hands, and swung up into the saddle. Don Felipe mounted the black stallion, and the two men turned the horses away from the fence. Dog trotted along behind them.

The morning passed very pleasantly. The sky was almost clear now, a deep blue with only a few puffy white clouds floating in its vastness. The snow-mantled mountains that loomed to the west seemed so close in the crystal-clear air, it was like Frank could have reached out and touched them. Frank and Don Felipe rode through high pastures, alongside cold, sparkling streams, and through stands of dark green, aromatic pine. The cattle had already been moved down to the flatland for the winter, so the hills seemed strangely deserted, as if this morning was the very morning of their existence.

The hills weren't completely empty, however. Frank saw birds flitting from branch to branch in the trees, and once he and Don Felipe startled a pair of deer drinking at a creek. Dog flushed a few long-legged jackrabbits from the brush. Don Felipe pointed out light-colored shapes moving around the lower reaches of the peaks and explained that they were mountain goats. There were wolves up there, too, he told Frank, although the two men didn't see any this morning. Once a coyote loped across a pasture a couple of hundred yards in front of them, though.

Don Felipe had brought tortillas and a small pot of beans with him in his saddlebags. At midday he and Frank stopped beside a stream and had a cold but satisfying lunch. When they were done, Don Felipe brought out a bottle of pulque. He and Frank sat on rocks and passed it back and forth, taking swigs of the fiery liquor. Almanzar filled a pipe while Frank took out the makin's and rolled a quirly. They drank and smoked in silence, content with the beauty of the day.

Eventually, though, Frank felt the urge to break that silence. He said, "You have a fine rancho here, Don Felipe. I'm honored that I was able to visit it."

"I wish your visit had not been marred by such unpleasantness, Señor Morgan. First the attack on you, then the encounter with the mountain lion —"

"I don't mind that, because it meant I got to meet Señorita Carmen," Frank put in with a smile.

"And then the business with Captain Estancia and the Rurales," Don Felipe finished heavily. He took a drink of the pulque.

Frank dropped the butt of the quirly at his feet and stepped on it. The thick sole of the moccasin ground it out with no problem. He said, "From what I saw, and from what Carmen told me, folks around here don't like the Rurales."

"Carmen should not speak of such things," Almanzar said sharply.

"Many of the men who ride for Estancia are convicts. Murderers, judging by their black sombreros."

Don Felipe sighed. "It is true. Most of the Rurales are worse scum than the bandits from which they are supposed to protect us. But what can we do? El Presidente has sent them up here to police the frontier."

"I reckon all you can do is try to stay on their good side."

Don Felipe's back stiffened. "You think I allowed Estancia to have that vaquero whipped because I was afraid?"

"You weren't afraid for yourself," Frank said, "but you were concerned about the men who ride for you, and their families, as any good *patrón* would be."

Slowly, Don Felipe relaxed and nodded. "*Sí*. I knew that if Estancia was challenged

193

too strongly, he would order his men to attack. My vaqueros would have fought bravely, but in the end they would have been killed. That would have left the women and children at the mercy of those . . . those dogs!" He took a deep breath. "It is the only word for them, as poor Pablo Benavides found out to his great suffering."

"It looks like there ought to be something that could be done about this," Frank said.

Don Felipe smiled sadly. "That is your American nature, Señor Morgan. You *norteamericanos* always think that any time there is injustice or cruelty, something can be done about it. But here, south of the border, we are an older people. We know that sometimes there is nothing that can be done."

Frank wanted to argue — as Don Felipe said, simply accepting evil went against his nature — but he knew he wouldn't convince the older man. Instead he changed the subject slightly by saying, "This Black Scorpion is a pretty notorious fella, on both sides of the border."

"Yes, he is known far and wide as a daring bandit. But sometimes I think he is not as bad as he has been painted. Consider the one who damns him."

Frank knew Don Felipe was talking about Captain Estancia. If Estancia wanted so strongly to capture the bandit, then maybe the Black Scorpion wasn't such a bad hombre after all. It would have made sense, and Frank might have accepted the theory, if not for the fact that the Texas Rangers wanted to catch the Black Scorpion as much as the Rurales did.

When he commented on that, Don Felipe shook his head and said, "I mean no offense, Señor Morgan, but I put no faith in the word of the Texas Rangers, or in men like Cecil Tolliver."

Since Don Felipe had been the one to bring up the owner of the Rocking T, Frank took advantage of the opening. "You know, everything I've heard about Tolliver tells me that he's a pretty good fella. Got a nice family and a successful ranch."

"A ranch built on cattle stolen from me!"

"I hear he says the same about you," Frank prodded.

"Lies! The man is incapable of telling the truth!" Don Felipe's hand clenched tightly around the neck of the pulque bottle. "Why, once he even dared to say —"

The words were choked off. Almanzar

muttered a savage oath and took another drink.

"What did he say?" Frank asked quietly.

For a moment he thought Don Felipe wasn't going to answer. But then, without looking at Frank but gazing out over the spectacular landscape instead, he said in hushed tones, "That the evidence I saw with my own eyes was wrong. That there was nothing — nothing! — between him and my wife!"

16

Well, now, thought Frank, that was interesting. Not totally unexpected, considering what Carmen had said the night before, but still mighty interesting.

"Don Felipe," he said, "you don't really know me, but it sounds to me like you want to talk about this. I'd be glad to listen."

"There are some things a man does not speak of."

"And sometimes when he doesn't, they gnaw away at his insides until it feels like there's a hole all the way through to his soul."

Again there was a moment of silence. Don Felipe handed the bottle to Frank and sat there stolidly, smoking his pipe. At last he said, "You saved my daughter from the mountain lion, proving your prowess and your courage. You stood up to the Rurale sergeant, proving your honor and my lack of same."

"Not hardly on that last one," Frank said. "I just happened to get to him before you did."

"I would like to think this is true, but I doubt it. I would have let him strike poor Pablo again, to protect the rest of my people. If he had beaten Pablo to death . . ."

Don Felipe left the thought unfinished and stood up, pacing over to the edge of the creek. He gave the bowl of his pipe a sharp smack, knocking the dottle from it into the water. When he turned back toward Frank, he looked older than Frank had seen him so far. His face still resembled a wooden carving, but now it showed the ravages of time.

"You think me a man of honor, Señor Morgan, but I failed that test many years ago when I found my wife in the arms of Cecil Tolliver and did not kill him."

Frank had figured that was what Don Felipe was leading up to, but he found it a little difficult to reconcile what he was hearing with what he had seen of Cecil Tolliver. The rancher was an impressive man, but he was hardly the type to sweep a doña off her feet and make love to her.

"I'm listening," Frank said.

For a moment he thought Don Felipe

wasn't going to say anything else, but then the words began to pour out of the man.

"It was not long after Tolliver came to Texas and established his rancho. A few years, perhaps. Long enough so that our families had met. The river stood between his land and mine, and cows . . . Well, cows stray."

Frank nodded but didn't say anything. He didn't want to interrupt now that Don Felipe was talking.

"There was friction at first between his cowboys and my vaqueros, whenever men from either ranch would cross the Rio Bravo to round up the cattle that had gotten on the wrong side. Shots were fired, though no one was killed. I thought it best that Señor Tolliver and I should meet, so that we could discuss the situation peacefully and perhaps arrive at a solution."

"You were a peacemaker," Frank said, taking a chance and commenting. "That doesn't surprise me."

Don Felipe nodded. "Yes. My people are a fierce race, a race of warriors, but I do not believe in fighting when it is not necessary. I sent word to Cecil Tolliver, promising him safe passage to my hacienda, and he agreed to meet me there. When he came to talk, he was well armed, as were the men with him. But they put away their guns, and Tolliver and I drank and talked and realized that we were . . . much the same sort of man."

That was the conclusion Frank had arrived at after meeting both of them. Despite the differences in nationality and language, they had a lot more in common.

"We struck a truce, Señor Tolliver and I," Almanzar went on. "When his cattle crossed the river onto my land, my vaqueros turned them back. His riders did the same when my cattle strayed. And if any of the other man's stock was rounded up and sold, the one who sold them paid the other man immediately. It was a satisfactory arrangement. It was more than that. Tolliver and I, we became amigos."

Frank wasn't surprised by that at all. From the start, they had seemed the sort of men who would be friends.

"Not only that, but our families were friendly as well. We visited each other's rancho, and our children played together. My Antonio and Tolliver's son Benjamin raced horses like the wild young things they were. Tolliver's daughters were older than Carmen, but they took her under their wing and were kind to her. Twice a year, at least, the families gathered, and this went on for several years."

"Sounds mighty fine," Frank said. "There's always been trouble along the border, but you and Tolliver put that aside and forged your own peace."

"Yes, a separate peace from the rest of the border country. We celebrated together when my son Matteo was born. . . ."

That was the first Frank had heard of another Almanzar son. A moment later, he knew why.

"And we mourned together when the fever took him, shortly before his second birthday," Don Felipe said heavily. "This is a hot land, a land where such a fever can strike with no warning and tear a man's loved one from his bosom before he can do anything about it."

"I'm sorry," Frank said, and meant it.

Don Felipe looked at him. "Do you have sons, Señor Morgan?"

"One son," Frank replied, thinking of Conrad.

"Are you close to him?"

"No. Never have been."

"That is regrettable. Still, you know what it is like to look on the face of a child and be aware that he sprang from your loins. You know the mingled joy and pain such awareness can bring."

"Yes." Now Frank thought of Victoria. He knew what Don Felipe meant.

"Trust me, Señor Morgan, when I tell you that if you have never suffered the loss of a child, you have never known the very worst pain a man can endure."

"I'll take your word for that, Don Felipe, and I wouldn't wish that on anybody."

Don Felipe looked away. "It is even worse for the mother. A man has his work, his responsibilities. There are always cattle to brand, to round up, and drive to market and ship. Things that must be done. While a woman has nothing but her grief. There is no knowing what she may do. . . ." His face hardened even more, though Frank might have said that was impossible. "It was less than a year later when I caught them together, my Maria and Tolliver. He claimed she was merely upset by some memory of Matteo that had taken her by surprise, and he attempted to comfort her as a friend. But his arms were around her, and hers around him, and I knew better."

Why, you stupid, stiff-necked son of a bitch, Frank thought, because it sounded to him as if the explanation offered by Cecil Tolliver was perfectly believable. But he didn't say anything, preferring to let Almanzar finish the story in his own way.

"Maria denied it, too, saying that there was nothing between them other than friendship. But I knew the truth and was outraged. I sent Tolliver and his family away. They were no longer welcome on my rancho. This upset the children, but it was unavoidable. Later, when Antonio was older and knew the truth, he shared my anger and knew that I had done the right thing. He quickly grew to hate the gringos as much or more than I did."

A look of amazement came over Don Felipe's face then, as he turned to look at Frank.

"And yet now I spill all the pain in my heart to a gringo," he said. "Why is this, Señor Morgan?"

"Maybe you can tell that you and I have shared some of the same sort of pain, Don Felipe, even though I never lost a child. Tell me," Frank said, "what happened to your wife?"

"She died." The words came out flat and hard, like a piece of granite. "I believe she mourned herself into the grave."

"I've been married twice," Frank said. "Both of my wives were killed by evil men."

An indrawn breath hissed between Don Felipe's teeth. "You hunted down these men and took your vengeance on them? Surely you must have. I see it in your eyes."

Frank nodded slowly. "I took my vengeance, all right. It had to be done. But it didn't bring back either of the women I loved."

"No. There is no bringing back those who are gone from us."

Again there was silence between the two men. Finally, Frank said, "What happened between you and Tolliver?"

Almanzar shrugged. "Once I saw him for the sort of man he really was, I realized he had been stealing from me. My hatred for him grew, and I suppose his for me did as well."

Frank knew that was true. Feeling betrayed by his friend, Cecil Tolliver had looked for any excuse to hate Don Felipe Almanzar, and he had found them. The spirit of cooperation between the two ranches had disintegrated, and over the years the friction had grown into outright hostility. It might even turn into open warfare if it went on long enough. And all because of a probable misunderstanding born only of compassion and sympathy.

Mighty oaks from little acorns grow, the old saying went. And trouble and hate were often the same way, Frank mused.

"Now, Señor Morgan, you know my story," Don Felipe went on. "I would ask that we say nothing more about it, and that you do not discuss it with anyone else. A man's pride is a private thing, and so are his wounds."

"Of course," Frank murmured. "I won't say anything."

Don Felipe stepped over to his horse and gathered up the reins, getting ready to ride again. But he paused long enough to say to Frank, "You are an uncommon man, Señor Morgan. I have not spoken of these things in years. I thought I would never speak of them again."

Frank took hold of Stormy's reins and gestured with his other hand, calling Dog to him. He thought for a moment and then said, "You're a cattleman, so you must have seen sore places that you have to take a hot knife to, places you have to cut open no matter how much it hurts, so that all the festering can come out."

Don Felipe nodded. "*Sí,* of course."

"Sometimes I think the human heart is the same way."

Don Felipe didn't say anything to that. He mounted the black stallion, and Frank swung up onto Stormy's back. The two men rode toward the hacienda in a companionable silence. For the moment, there was nothing left for them to say.

Even though Frank knew he ought to get back north of the Rio Grande, he allowed inertia to overtake him and spent the next three days at the Almanzar hacienda, resting his injured ankle and letting the sore lump on his head go away completely. Life was pleasant here, and the slow-paced way of life was seductive. He ate well, drank fine wine, and grew fond of the afternoon siesta. After all, there was nothing that absolutely *had* to be done during that time each day.

He grew friendly with the vaqueros, too, and sometimes sat with them of an evening, listening to their guitar music and the soft, liquid sounds of their songs that flowed like water in a peaceful stream. These bold riders were puzzled at first, knowing the animosity their *patrón* felt toward all gringos. All but this quiet-spoken but deadly man Frank Morgan, who seemed the sort who was able to make himself at home wherever he went. If Don Felipe accepted him, then so did Don Felipe's vaqueros.

Frank's ankle was healed and he could

wear his boots again, though Don Felipe insisted that he keep the fine moccasins of soft leather. His head no longer ached. The injuries suffered in his fight with the Black Scorpion were gone. And so his thoughts turned at last toward returning to the Rocking T, so that he could let his friends north of the border know that he was all right. He found himself wanting to see Roanne Williamson again, as well.

On the third night, he left the bunkhouse where he had been visiting with the vaqueros, telling them stories of his life. Even down here below the Rio Grande they had heard of Frank Morgan, and they wanted to know if, *es verdad,* he had killed a thousand men in his long career as a gunfighter. Frank had tried to set them straight without disappointing them too much. He had learned over the years that most folks preferred the legend to the truth.

As he strolled across the courtyard toward the hacienda with Dog at his heels, the big cur suddenly growled deep in his throat. Frank stopped and looked down at the animal, asking quietly, "What is it, fella?"

Dog was gazing intently at the hacienda, and as Frank looked in the same direction, he saw a shadowy shape dart around a corner of the sprawling adobe building. He didn't get a good enough look to tell if the lurker was male or female, but he remembered how Carmen had snuck out to meet someone a few nights earlier. Maybe this was Carmen again trying to make some clandestine rendezvous.

Or maybe whoever she had been meeting had grown bolder and come all the way down to the hacienda tonight.

Either way, Frank was curious enough to investigate. For that matter, he told himself as he started toward the spot where he had glimpsed the mysterious figure, the Black Scorpion might be around somewhere, too. There was no telling what mischief that elusive *bandido* might be up to.

After a whispered command for Dog to be quiet, Frank moved forward with silent grace. He reached the hacienda and edged along the outer wall with his back to the adobe. When he reached the corner, he heard the soft murmur of voices nearby. Although he couldn't make out the words, after listening for a few moments he was sure that one of the voices belonged to a man, and the other to a woman.

Carmen and her lover . . . It had to be them, Frank told himself.

He took off his hat and risked a careful look around the corner. Halfway along the outer wall, near one of the gated entrances, a dark shape was visible against the lighter-colored adobe. After a moment, the shape parted, became two, and Frank realized that he had been watching them embrace. Feeling a little ashamed at spying on them like this, he drew back. Carmen's romance was none of his business, he told himself. He wasn't the girl's father, and it was obvious that the intruder he had spotted a few minutes earlier meant no harm. The youngster was just here to spark a while. Frank smiled tolerantly in the darkness, remembering when he himself had been young . . . and not so young, as far as that went. What he ought to do was just go away and leave them alone. . . .

And he might have done that, too, if he hadn't suddenly heard the swift rataplan of hoofbeats approaching the hacienda. That many riders didn't come galloping out of the night without it meaning trouble.

So he slapped his hat back on his head, whipped around the corner, and called in a low, urgent voice, "Carmen! Ben Tolliver! Better hustle, there's trouble coming!"

17

Gasping in surprise, the two young people leaped apart, putting some distance between them. Carmen said, "¿Qué . . . Señor Morgan?"

"Morgan!" the young man with her repeated in a shocked voice. "Frank Morgan?"

"That's right, Ben," Frank said. He stepped forward and grasped Ben Tolliver's arm. "You'd better light a shuck back to wherever you left your horse if you don't want to get caught here. I've got a feeling hell's about to pop."

As if to prove him right, gunshots blasted out, shattering the peacefulness of the night.

Carmen clutched at Frank's sleeve. "Señor Morgan, you mustn't tell my father about this!" she pleaded. "He must not know that Ben and I —"

"You've got more to worry about than

that," Frank snapped as the shooting continued. "But I won't say anything." He gave Ben's shoulder a shove. "Now vamoose!"

Ben grabbed Carmen, gave her a hurried kiss on the mouth, and then turned to run into the darkness. Over toward the bunkhouse, the battle continued as the raiders swept in from the night and slammed bullets into the sturdy walls of the structure. The vaqueros tried to return the fire, but the storm of lead that came their way forced them to duck for cover.

Frank took hold of Carmen's arm and hustled her toward the nearby gate, assuming that was where she had slipped out of the hacienda. If he was wrong and the gate was locked, they were about to be caught between a rock and a hard place.

But the gate swung open under his touch, and he pushed Carmen inside. "Get to your room and stay there!" he told her as he slammed the gate shut behind her. "Where's the blasted lock?"

A second later he found the open padlock hanging on the gate. He slipped it through the hasp and snapped it closed. Carmen reached out toward him through the wrought-iron bars and asked, "Señor Morgan, what will you do?"

"Don't worry about me," Frank assured her, even as a stray bullet passed well over his head and slammed into the wall above him. "Go!"

She turned and ran across the interior courtyard, heading for the main part of the hacienda. Frank darted along the wall toward the front of the compound, calling over his shoulder, "Come on, Dog!"

With the shaggy creature bounding after him, Frank ran around the corner and saw the scene of battle laid out before him, illuminated by muzzle flashes and lamplight from the hacienda and the bunkhouse. He halfway expected the raiders to be Captain Estancia's Rurales, but instead of uniforms the men wore the garb of vaqueros — or bandits. Frank wondered if they rode for the Black Scorpion.

Some of the raiders had the ranch's vaqueros pinned down in the bunkhouse. Others rode toward the hacienda itself, whooping and firing their guns into the air. Bullets whined over Frank's head. He drew his Colt and was about to join in the fight, when the front gate of the compound was thrown open and someone raced out brandishing a rifle.

It was Antonio Almanzar, Frank saw, and he knew the young man's passion had gotten the best of his common sense. He had left the cover of the thick adobe walls to carry the battle to the raiders. Unfortunately, he was outnumbered by more than ten to one, and he would probably be cut down by gunfire in a matter of seconds.

One of the bandits had other ideas, though. A big man with a floppy-brimmed sombrero and a poncho reined his horse toward Antonio. He had a rifle in one hand and appeared to be large enough and strong enough to fire it that way.

Instead of gunning down Antonio, the big man raised his rifle to strike a blow. Frank snapped a shot at him, but the man's horse reared at that exact moment, causing the bullet to miss. Frank yelled, "Antonio! Look out!" but the warning came too late. The rifle barrel slashed down viciously and caught Antonio across the shoulders, staggering him and making him drop his own rifle. The big man guided his horse with his knees as he reached down and plucked Antonio from the ground as if the young man weighed nothing at all.

Frank ran toward them, but then some of the other raiders saw him coming and opened fire on him. Bullets pounded into the ground in front of him and made him retreat. As he ducked around the corner, he saw the big man wheel his horse and gallop off into the darkness, taking Antonio Almanzar with him. A smaller man rode up to the wall and tossed something over it, then jerked his mount around and raced away.

Thinking that the thing the man had thrown into the hacienda's inner courtyard might be a bundle of dynamite, Frank dropped to the ground to wait for the explosion. When it didn't come after a few moments, and when he realized that the gunfire was slacking off, he pushed himself to his feet and darted out into the open again.

He saw that all the raiders were escaping, throwing a few shots at the bunkhouse as they did so to keep the vaqueros inside from rushing out and giving chase. Frank ran to the spot where Antonio had been captured. The young man's rifle lay there where he had dropped it.

"Señor Morgan! Señor Morgan!"

The alarmed shout came from inside the wall. Frank looked over and saw Don Felipe running toward the gate, clutching a shotgun.

"Señor Morgan, you are all right?"

"I'm fine," Frank said, "but they got Antonio."

"Aaiii! Antonio!" Don Felipe flung the gate back and ran outside. The hooves of the raiders' horses had stirred up a cloud of dust that mixed with the haze of powder smoke. The acrid mixture filled the night air. Don Felipe stared through it in the direction of the retreating hoofbeats, which could still be heard over the angry shouts of the vaqueros. "My son!"

Frank holstered his Colt. There was nothing to shoot at now. He put a hand on Don Felipe's shoulder and said, "One of them threw something over the wall. We'd better go see what it was."

Don Felipe was furious and agitated, of course, but Frank's words made sense. With a head jerk of a nod, Almanzar turned toward the gate.

As he and Frank went into the inner courtyard, old Esteban came scurrying out of the house carrying a torch. The *mozo* looked frightened, but he hurried forward as if he knew that his place was at his master's side.

"Over here, Esteban!" Don Felipe snapped. When the servant came up, Almanzar snatched the torch out of his hand and thrust it forward boldly, lighting up the courtyard. Frank saw the rock, about twice the size of a man's fist, lying on the paving stones. It had a piece of paper wrapped around it and tied in place.

"Dios mio!" Don Felipe exclaimed. "A note!"

Frank stepped forward and bent to pick up the rock. His fingers plucked at the rawhide thong that held the paper around the irregular chunk of stone. When he had it loose, he dropped the rock. Smoothing out the paper with his hands, he turned so that the light from the torch fell over the words scrawled on it in Spanish.

Frank didn't read the language as well as he spoke it, since he'd never had much occasion to read things written in Spanish. He understood enough of it, though, so that he wasn't surprised when Don Felipe said grimly, "Ransom! They have stolen my son and seek to exchange him for ransom!"

"How much are they asking for him?"

"Two million pesos!" The words came out of Don Felipe's mouth in a near-groan.

Frank did some quick ciphering in his head. He was no expert on such things, but he was pretty sure that was about the same as ten thousand dollars, American. A nice chunk of change, any way you looked at it.

"Do you have that much money?" he asked.

"Not here on the rancho, no. I might have half that, perhaps a little less. I could raise the other, though." Don Felipe took the ransom note from Frank and brandished it angrily. "They give me a week, the dogs!"

"Can you get the cash together in that time?"

Don Felipe nodded. "*Sí,* I think so. I will have to ride to Nuevo Laredo, where there is a telegraph, and send a wire to my bank in Mexico City." In a fit of anger, he crumpled the paper. "Damn the Black Scorpion! Damn his eyes!"

"You're sure the Black Scorpion is responsible for this?"

Don Felipe straightened out the note again. "There is his signature! Until now he and his men have left us alone, but now that he has struck at last, he has pierced straight to my heart!"

Frank hadn't seen the black-clad figure during the brief flurry of gunfire. The big hombre who had grabbed Antonio had seemed to be in charge. But that didn't really mean anything. The Black Scorpion could have planned the raid and could have been with the men who had kept the vaqueros trapped in the bunkhouse.

Something seemed wrong about the

whole thing, though. Frank couldn't put his finger on what it was, but he knew that something about the raid didn't completely make sense. He would have to ponder it later, however. He had come to consider Don Felipe Almanzar a friend, and right now his friend needed help. That came first with Frank.

"Don't worry about the money," he said. "I'll go with you to Nuevo Laredo and send a wire to one of my lawyers in Denver. He can arrange a transfer of funds from one of my accounts."

Don Felipe frowned at him. "You have that kind of money, Señor Morgan? I do not wish to pry into another man's business affairs, but this is very important to me."

"Of course it is. And to answer your question, yes, I've got it. My first wife was a very wealthy woman, and when she died she made sure that I inherited a great deal of money, even though I never particularly wanted it. I have lawyers in Denver and San Francisco who look after it for me, and darned if it doesn't just keep growing."

"I am surprised. I thought —"

"That I was just a down-at-heels, drifting gunman?" Despite the solemn circumstances, Frank had to grin. "I've found that things are more peaceful if that's what most folks think about me. I already run into enough trouble without people knowing that I'm rich."

"And you would share this with me?"

"I consider you a friend, Don Felipe. If there's anything I can do for you, I'm going to do it."

Almanzar stuffed the ransom note in his pocket, then reached out and clasped Frank's shoulder. "*Muchas gracias, mi amigo.* I will never forget this, Señor Morgan . . . Frank."

The two men met each other's gaze squarely for a moment, and then both nodded. Nothing more needed to be said. The century might be lurching toward a new, more modern era, but there were still some true frontiersmen around. Frank Morgan and Don Felipe Almanzar were cut from the same cloth.

"Papa?" The plaintive voice belonged to Carmen. Both men turned toward her as she came from the hacienda with lines of fright on her lovely face. "Papa, what has happened?"

"The Black Scorpion has kidnapped Antonio and demands two million pesos ransom for him," Don Felipe said heavily.

Carmen cried out as if she had been struck. "No! No!"

Her father went to her and slid an arm around her shoulders. "Do not worry, Carmencita. We will get him back. The Black Scorpion would not dare to harm him."

She shook her head and said, "The Black Scorpion strikes at us here, in our own home! He will dare anything!"

There was nothing Don Felipe could say to that. Clearly, the bandit chief had become more audacious than ever. "Go back inside," Almanzar growled. "There is nothing you can do."

"Will you go after them? Or will you pay the ransom?" Carmen clutched his sleeve. "You must not risk Antonio's life!"

"We will get him back safely. That is all I can promise."

Carmen put her hands over her face and ran sobbing into the hacienda. Don Felipe looked after her and sighed.

"I reckon you'd better post some guards for the rest of the night," Frank suggested. "I don't know of any reason why the bandits would come back, but it's hard to say what gents like that might do. They can be almost as notional as Indians."

Don Felipe nodded. "Yes, I will set out sentries. And then in the morning you and

I will start for Nuevo Laredo, Frank. We can reach it in a day's hard ride."

"Sounds good to me," Frank agreed. "Since we'll be in the saddle all day tomorrow, we'd better get some rest tonight."

"You are right," Don Felipe said with a sigh. "I fear sleep will not come easy on this night, however."

He was probably right about that, Frank thought.

Don Felipe went to the bunkhouse to see about posting some of the vaqueros on guard. Frank circled through one of the gardens to reach the central plaza. His room was located just off that innermost courtyard. Dog was at his heels, and once again the big cur growled to warn him of something not being right. This time, however, Frank had already spotted the shadowy figure waiting for him in the covered walkway in front of his door.

"You shouldn't be here, Carmen," he said. "It's not what you'd call proper."

She stepped forward enough so that the moonlight touched her tear-streaked face as she gazed up at him. She said quietly, "I am in love with the son of my father's greatest enemy, Señor Morgan. I have long since stopped worrying about what is proper, and what is not."

18

Frank stepped forward and opened the door to his room. "Might as well get in out of the night air," he said. "I get the feeling that you want to talk, Señorita."

Carmen followed him inside and stood there nervously as he flicked a lucifer to life and lit the wall lamp. The yellow glow filled the room. Frank eased the door closed and turned toward her.

"What is it you want to talk about, Señorita? Your brother being kidnapped by the Black Scorpion, or the fact that you're in love with Ben Tolliver?"

"How did you know? We have been so careful!"

Frank shook his head. "Not really. I spotted Ben riding over the hill in back of the house a few evenings ago. That same night I saw you sneaking back into the hacienda after you met him. The way you were singing to yourself, I could tell you were a woman in love."

"But how did you know it is Ben who has captured my heart?"

Frank shrugged. "That was sort of a guess. When I saw him ride over the hill, I got a look at his hat and could tell it wasn't a sombrero, but rather the kind that gringos wear. That started me thinking about who might be able to ride across the border to see you. The Rocking T is the closest ranch on the other side of the river, and Ben is Cecil Tolliver's only son. Of course, it could have been one of the Rocking T cowboys who's been courting you, but I remembered how Tolliver made some comment about Ben dropping out of sight at times. I figured that was when he came over here."

Accusingly, Carmen said, "You told my father that you knew of Cecil Tolliver, but not that you had been to his ranch."

"I shaded the truth a little," Frank admitted. "I suppose when you mentioned to Ben that I was staying here, he told you I'd been to the Rocking T, too."

"He did."

"But you couldn't say anything to Don Felipe about it," Frank guessed, "because that would have meant explaining where you got the information, and you sure didn't want to do that, did you?"

Carmen frowned at him but didn't say anything, and he knew his theory was correct. He hadn't told Don Felipe the complete truth . . . but Carmen had even bigger secrets to hide.

"Just because I'm acquainted with the Tolliver family doesn't mean that I intend any harm to your family," Frank went on. "But I knew of the bad blood between your father and Cecil Tolliver, even though I didn't know the cause of it, and I figured it would be better not to mention certain things."

"Better for whom, Señor Morgan? What is your true purpose here?"

That was a good question. Frank was here partially because of his curiosity, and partially because the trouble on both sides of the border offended his sense of justice. After a moment of thought, he said, "I want to find out who's really responsible for all the problems going on now between your father and Cecil Tolliver."

"Tolliver is a rustler —"

"He says the same thing about your father," Frank pointed out.

Carmen's chin lifted defiantly. "Don Felipe Almanzar would *never* steal another man's cattle!"

"Well, somebody is wide-looping Tolliver's stock, and a bunch of gunmen attacked him and Ben the other day and nearly killed them."

A solemn expression appeared on Carmen's face. "Ben told me of this. He said you saved their lives, Señor Morgan. I must thank you for that."

"Cecil Tolliver believes those gunnies who jumped them worked for your father."

"A lie! It is Tolliver who sends armed men down here to ambush our vaqueros."

"Now tell me," Frank said, "do you really believe that the father of the man you love would do a thing like that?"

"Well . . ." Anger and doubt warred on Carmen's face. "I remember what Señor Tolliver was like when Ben and I were young. I thought he was a good man, and a good friend to my father. It is hard to believe that he has become so evil. . . . But Papa is so sure. . . ."

"Just like he was sure something was going on between Tolliver and your mother?"

Carmen shook her head emphatically. "You must not speak of such things! I am surprised my father even told you about what happened."

"But he did tell me," Frank said, "and

everything goes back to that, doesn't it, Carmen? Before that, the Tollivers and the Almanzars were friends. Good friends. You and Ben were young, but maybe you already felt something for each other."

"*Sí,*" she said in a half whisper. "Even as children, I think we knew how we felt about each other. I . . . I always wanted to be with him."

"But then it all went wrong, and when the two of you finally did get together again, you had to meet on the sly, didn't you?"

Carmen clenched her hands into fists and pressed them against her mouth. "It has been so hard," she said in what was almost a moan. "So hard . . ."

"And now on top of everything else, your brother's been kidnapped by the Black Scorpion."

"Antonio will be all right. I am sure of it."

"How can you be so certain?" Frank asked.

"It is just . . . a feeling. I know the Black Scorpion would not harm my brother."

"Uh-huh," Frank said, not convinced.

"It is important, though, that my father pay the ransom, just to be sure nothing happens to 'Tonio."

"He plans to pay," Frank told her. "In fact, I'm going to loan him the money. We're going to Nuevo Laredo in the morning to arrange it."

Carmen's eyebrows arched in surprise. "You, Señor Morgan? I had no idea you were a rich man."

"I don't make a lot of noise about it. I figure if a man has a good horse, a good dog, and a good gun, what else does he need?"

"A good woman, perhaps?"

"Well, maybe, at the right place and time." Frank didn't want to go into that with Carmen, so he went on. "You know, even if your father pays the ransom, that's no guarantee the Black Scorpion will go through with his part of the deal."

"You mean you think he might not release Antonio . . . or that he might . . . might kill him?" Carmen went pale at that thought.

"I just think the smart thing to do is to be ready for any possibility," Frank said. "If the Black Scorpion tries to double-cross us, we've got to be prepared to take Antonio away from him."

Carmen crossed herself. "I pray that it does not come to that."

Frank nodded and said, "You and me both, Señorita."

* * *

Frank and Carmen reached an understanding before she slipped out of his room: He wouldn't say anything to Don Felipe about her relationship with Ben Tolliver, and she wouldn't mention that he had been a guest at the Rocking T and had become friends with the Tolliver family.

Sleep didn't come easily to Frank that night. Something was still nagging at him, but try as he might he couldn't put his finger on what it was. He tried sifting through everything that he had seen and heard since riding into the border country a week or so earlier, but that didn't yield any results. He resolved not to think about it instead, in hopes that whatever it was that was bothering him would pop into his head.

All through the long night, that didn't happen. And when he finally dozed off, it seemed as if he had barely closed his eyes when the strident ringing of a bell and the sound of men shouting jerked him out of his slumber.

He sat up sharply, swung his legs out of bed, and reached for his trousers. It took him only a moment to pull them on, stamp his feet down into his boots, and thrust his arms through the sleeves of his shirt. With the shirt still unbuttoned, he was buckling on his gun belt as he went out the door of the room.

The hour was early, with the rosy flush of dawn on the eastern horizon. Frank followed the sound of the ringing bell, fastening the buttons on his shirt as he hurried toward the front of the hacienda. When he reached the outer wall of the compound, he saw that the gate was open. Horses milled around in the open space between the hacienda and the barns. The gray uniforms of the riders tended to blur into the dawn shadows.

The Rurales had returned.

Frank strode up and saw Don Felipe Almanzar standing next to one of the horses, talking to Captain Domingo Estancia. Their words were low and angry. Estancia spotted Frank approaching and glared at him. "You are still here, Señor Morgan?"

"That's right," Frank said. "And I reckon you're still on the trail of the Black Scorpion, Capitán."

Don Felipe turned toward Frank. "I have told Captain Estancia that the Black Scorpion is holding my son for ransom."

"And I have explained to Don Felipe," Estancia said coldly, "that although his son's captivity is regrettable, it can have no effect on the way my men and I carry out our mission, which is to hunt down the *bandidos* and destroy them."

"I suppose the trail of the Black Scorpion's gang led you back here?" Frank said.

Estancia jerked his head in a nod. "That is correct. We are closing in on them, and we expect to have them at bay within another day or two."

Don Felipe said tightly, "If you engage them in battle, Captain, it is likely that they will kill Antonio."

"As I said, any danger to your son is regrettable. But I *will* smash that band of lawbreakers!"

For a moment Frank thought Don Felipe was going to reach up and grab Estancia to drag him out of the saddle. If that happened, the Rurales would swarm them, and there might be another whipping carried out, this time on Don Felipe himself. The vaqueros wouldn't stand for that and would try to fight. Once again, the threat of a bloody massacre was imminent.

Frank put a hand on Don Felipe's arm, knowing that he was being bold in doing so but figuring it was worth the risk to the don's honor.

"Don Felipe, if I could talk with you for a moment . . ." Frank said as he thought swiftly, trying to determine the best course of action.

Don Felipe continued to stare daggers up at Captain Estancia for a couple of seconds, but then he turned away with a muttered curse. "What is it, Señor Morgan?" At the moment, he was too angry to be informal.

Frank drew him aside, out of earshot of Estancia and the other Rurales. Speaking quietly, Frank said, "You can't stop him from going after the Black Scorpion, Don Felipe. He has too many men, and you have your vaqueros and their families to think about."

"But Antonio —"

"I know," Frank said. "Estancia's just going to put him in more danger by chasing the *bandidos.* What we have to do is find the Black Scorpion's gang *first* and get Antonio away from them before Estancia can hit them. Or I reckon I should say that's what *I* have to do."

Don Felipe had started to get a hopeful expression on his face as Frank spoke, but now he said doubtfully, "You? But you are injured —"

"I'm pretty much healed up now. I can

231

ride, and I can get to Antonio first. That's what I'm counting on, anyway."

Don Felipe shook his head dolefully. "Such an attempt might stand a chance of success, but you cannot go alone. I should send some of my men with you."

"I can move faster by myself," Frank argued. "And if I do locate the bandit camp, one man would have a better chance of slipping in and out of there than a group."

Don Felipe scrubbed a hand over his face as he agonized over the decision facing him. Over at the creek, the Rurales were watering their horses and filling their canteens, which was evidently the reason they had stopped at the rancho in the first place. Captain Estancia still sat his horse, his back stiff, his face set in stubbornly arrogant lines.

Finally, Don Felipe said, "I know your reputation as a fighter, Frank, but this is not your land. It is unlikely you would be able to find the Black Scorpion before the Rurales do."

Frank had thought of that, but he intended to try, anyway.

"However," Don Felipe went on, "if I sent one man with you, one man who knows this part of Mexico better than any other, that would increase the chances of success, no?"

"Well, maybe," Frank said with a frown. "Somebody to help me find the gang, and then I could snatch Antonio away from them."

"*Sí,* that is what I mean." Don Felipe's excitement was growing as he realized that there might still be a way to free his son. "I have just such a man, one who can guide you, one who knows the hills and the mountains and the plains better than anyone."

Frank nodded. "All right. Send him to me, and as soon as Estancia and his men pull out, we'll leave, too, and ride around them to get on the trail first. But while we're doing that, you go on to Nuevo Laredo as planned. I'll write out the message for you to send to my lawyers in Denver. They'll know it's from me. Go ahead and prepare the ransom just in case we need it. If we don't, there's no harm done."

"Yes, we must be prepared. That is wise." Don Felipe clasped Frank's hand. "Bring my son back to me, amigo."

"If I can," Frank promised. "You have my word on that."

19

The Rurales stayed at the Almanzar rancho only a short time before riding out again. That was long enough, however, for Frank to see to it that Stormy was saddled and ready to ride. He left the Appaloosa in the barn and went back to the house to gather some provisions. The mission he had chosen for himself might take several days to accomplish.

He found that the Indian women in charge of Don Felipe's kitchen had already packed a bundle of food, including tortillas, jerky, and fruit from the Almanzar orchard. Frank took the supplies and thanked them.

As he was about to leave the hacienda and return to the barn, he heard, "Señor Morgan!" and turned to see Carmen hurrying toward him. Her hair was tousled and she had a robe wrapped around her, clear indications that she had not been out of bed for long. She came up to Frank and said, "Señor Morgan, my father has told me what you are about to do. Thank you, Señor. I know that if anyone can save my brother, it is you."

"I'll do my best," Frank said.

"And you and I, we will keep our secrets?"

"Of course."

Carmen put her hands on his arms, came up on her toes, and leaned forward to kiss him on the cheek. He hadn't taken the time to shave and he knew his beard stubble must be rough, but she didn't seem to mind. *"Vaya con Dios, Señor Morgan,"* she whispered.

Frank left her there and walked out to the barn where Stormy and Dog waited. As he approached, he saw Don Felipe standing there with a short, poncho-draped figure wearing a sombrero that seemed almost as big as he was. When the second man turned toward him, Frank was surprised to see the wizened face of old Esteban.

"Here is your guide," Don Felipe said as he rested a hand on Esteban's bony shoulder.

Frank couldn't help but frown. "Are you sure about this, Don Felipe?"

"This rancho was given to my family by a land grant from the King of Spain more than a century ago, Señor Morgan. Esteban's father worked for my great-grandfather and my grandfather. Esteban himself worked for my grandfather and my father. He has lived with the Yaquis, and he knows every hectare in the region."

"Can he stand up to a long hard ride?"

Esteban lifted his head, straightened his back, and answered for himself this time. "I can keep up, Señor," he declared. "Do not concern yourself with that."

Frank hadn't paid that much attention to the old *mozo,* and now, as he looked into Esteban's eyes, he saw that that had been a mistake. The fires of pride burned fiercely there, and something else as well: A spark that showed the soul of a warrior still resided inside the old man's body.

"All right," Frank said. "I'm honored to have your help, Esteban."

The *mozo* nodded, his grim features unbending.

Don Felipe snapped his fingers, and one of the vaqueros brought out the big black stallion. The horse was Don Felipe's personal mount, but he said, "Esteban, you will take El Rey."

"Sí, patrón." Esteban's head bobbed up

and down. He took the stallion's reins from the vaquero and scrambled up into the saddle like a monkey. He looked a little like a monkey, too, Frank thought, perched there on the big horse's back. The King was a fitting name for the stallion, and somebody who didn't know better might think Esteban was the court jester.

Frank knew better, though.

He hung the bag of supplies on his saddle and then swung up onto Stormy's back. Don Felipe reached up, and Frank took his hand and shook with him, a firm grip from both men. *"Vaya con Dios,"* Don Felipe said, echoing what Carmen had told him a few minutes earlier.

Frank nodded and lifted a hand to the brim of his Stetson in farewell. Then he pulled the Appaloosa's head around and heeled him into a trot that carried them away from the hacienda. Esteban fell in alongside on El Rey. Neither man looked back.

Frank let Esteban take the lead and set the pace. The old-timer knew what he was doing. He had seen the way the Rurales had ridden when they left the ranch, heading northwest through the foothills that paralleled the mountain range.

Esteban took an even more westerly direction, which brought them into more rugged terrain.

"We could pass them quickly if we rode east and traveled on the flat," Esteban explained, even though Frank hadn't asked him why they were going this way. "But if we did that, we would run the risk of being seen. Once we are above them, we can pass the Rurales more easily without the risk of being observed."

"It'll be slower this way, though, I imagine," Frank commented.

"If our forces were of the same size, then yes, our path would be slower. But they are many and we are few. What would be a disadvantage in battle we must turn to our advantage in speed and stealth."

That made sense to Frank. He nodded and concentrated on keeping up with the little old man on the big horse . . . just the opposite of what he had been worried about when Don Felipe told him that Esteban was going with him.

The sun rose higher in the sky, but cast only feeble warmth as the morning wore on. The winds were brisk and chilly and helped to keep Frank revitalized after his night of poor sleep. The thing that had bothered him on the previous night was still elusive, but it seemed to be closer now, almost teasing him as it stood just outside the light of understanding.

Since the ground was rocky, the hooves of Stormy and El Rey raised little dust. The same could not be said of the Rurales' mounts. As Frank looked to his right, he could see the haze of dust that rose to mark the passage of the larger group. He was surprised to see how much lower the Rurales were, compared to him and Esteban. He had known that they were climbing quite a bit, but he hadn't been aware they were that much higher.

Don Felipe had been right: Esteban knew every trail. Some led through deep slashes in the sides of the mountains so that rock rose sheer for a hundred feet or more on each side of the riders, the walls so close at hand that Frank could have reached out and touched them. Other trails were little more than narrow ledges that crawled along the sides of the peaks with rock to the left and a dizzying drop to the right. In those cases, Frank let Stormy have his head and trusted the Appaloosa to find his way. Stormy was surefooted and negotiated those perilous paths with the seeming ease of the mountain goats that frolicked even higher in the great gray stone monoliths.

By midday Esteban judged that they were well ahead of Captain Estancia's troop of Rurales. "We start down now," the old man announced. "We must find the trail of the Black Scorpion."

"You could have tracked him down any time you wanted to, couldn't you?" Frank asked.

Esteban's narrow shoulders rose and fell eloquently. "*Quién sabe?* I had no need to until now."

That made perfect sense, too. Frank grinned and rode on, following the old man.

As they worked their way down to a lower altitude, the air grew a bit warmer. Frank rolled each of his shirt sleeves up a couple of turns. When they made one of their infrequent stops to rest the horses and let them crop at one of the sparse clumps of hardy grass, Frank took a swig of water from his canteen, ate a tortilla, and then gnawed a bite off one of the strips of jerky. Esteban managed to chew some of the tough, dried meat, too, even though he didn't have all of his teeth. The ones he still had were strong.

"When we catch up to the gang," Frank said, "we'll follow them until they make camp for the night. Then you'll wait with the horses while I slip in and get Antonio."

"The *bandidos* may have already reached their camp," Esteban pointed out.

"Then we'll wait until dark anyway. I can't just waltz in there."

"I could," Esteban said.

Frank's forehead creased in a frown as he stared at the old man. "What do you mean?"

"I could walk into the *bandidos'* camp," Esteban said calmly. "It is doubtful that any of them would know that I work for Don Felipe. I could pretend to be a crazed old goat herder who has lost his way. Tell me, Señor . . ." Esteban spread his hands. "Would anyone really be suspicious of an old man like me?"

Frank thought about it, and he had to admit that Esteban was probably right. There would be risks involved, though.

"What if somebody did recognize you?" he asked. "If the Black Scorpion knew that you worked for Don Felipe, he might have you shot."

"Not if I told him that I had come to arrange for the payment of the ransom."

The cagy old-timer had an answer for everything, Frank thought. And it was certainly true that some advance reconnaissance might come in handy.

Esteban pointed out the same thing. "If I visited the *bandido* camp, I could find out exactly where they are holding Antonio and how he is guarded. That would make your task much easier, would it not?"

Frank nodded. "Yeah, you're right. I just hate to see you taking such chances, Esteban."

The old man smiled. Frank couldn't remember if he had seen such an expression on Esteban's face before or not.

"At my age, Señor, when I close my eyes to sleep at night I risk never waking again."

"I reckon that's true of all of us, amigo." Frank clasped a hand on Esteban's shoulder. "All right. That's the plan, then. When we find the Black Scorpion's camp, you'll scout it out for us first."

With that settled, they mounted up again and rode on. Frank looked over his shoulder and saw the dust from the Rurales' horses. It was more than a mile behind them. That wasn't far enough, though. They didn't want Estancia's men coming up and ruining everything just as they were about to snatch Antonio away from the Black Scorpion.

When Frank mentioned that to Esteban, the old man nodded and pushed on at a faster pace. Stormy and El Rey still had plenty of stamina left, so they didn't mind.

By mid-afternoon, they had begun to spot the occasional telltale marks that told them a large group of riders had passed this way recently: stones chipped by horseshoes, branches bent back and sometimes broken, a welter of hoofprints here and there, piles of horse droppings. Esteban nodded in satisfaction.

"This trail was left by the Black Scorpion and his men," he told Frank. "I am sure of it."

"So am I," Frank agreed. "Looks like they're only a couple of hours ahead of us, too."

The two men increased the pace even more, trying to catch up to the *bandidos* and at the same time put more distance between them and the Rurales. The sparsely wooded foothills and the shallow valleys between them made for fairly easy riding.

It was late in the afternoon when Esteban held up a hand to call a halt. "Look there," he said to Frank, pointing with a gnarled finger. Frank looked in the direction Esteban indicated and saw several thin columns of smoke rising into the air.

"That looks like a settlement of some kind," Frank said.

Esteban nodded. "It is. A small farming community. I have been there before, but it has been many years. I doubt that anyone there would remember me, but we will go around the village anyway. If the people there saw us, they might try to warn the Black Scorpion."

"Because they're afraid of him?"

Esteban snorted at that idea. "That is what that pig of a Rurale *capitán* would have you believe. In truth, from what I know, the Black Scorpion has never given the people of the village any reason to fear him."

"I thought he raided on this side of the border just like he does on the Texas side."

"He does, Señor, he does," Esteban said cryptically.

Frank wanted to know what he meant by that, but questioning the old *mozo* would have to wait. Right now they had to concentrate on finding the Black Scorpion's hideout. With Esteban still leading the way, they circled to the west around the little farming village nestled in the foothills. From a distance it looked like a charming place, Frank thought, with a church and a scattering of adobe buildings around a plaza.

As Esteban pointed out in the fading

light, the trail left by the Black Scorpion's gang went around the village, too. It led onto a ridge and then up a hill. They weren't yet at the top of the slope when Esteban reined in suddenly. He turned to Frank, who nodded.

"I smell it, too," Frank said quietly. "Wood smoke, and meat roasting. Must be a good-sized campfire somewhere close by."

"*Sí,*" Esteban said. "We will leave the horses here and go on up the hill on foot."

They dismounted and tied their reins to small pine trees. All day long, Dog had kept up without complaint, but now the big cur growled as Frank told him to stay with Stormy and El Rey.

"I know you're disappointed, Dog," Frank said with a quick grin. "We're just scouting right now, though."

"Some men would think you a fool for talking to a dog as if he understood your words, Señor," Esteban commented.

"Not you, though."

Esteban gave one of his usual shrugs. "A good horse and a good dog speak the same language of the heart as a good man."

That pretty much summed it up, Frank thought.

He and Esteban cat-footed their way to

the top of the hill, using the scattered pines as cover. When they reached the crest, they crouched behind some bushes and peered out into the narrow valley on the other side of the hill. The sun was low enough so that the valley was in shadow, but enough light remained for the two men to be able to see the wide, dark mouth of the cave that opened into the slope on the far side of the valley. A fire had been built in the cave mouth, and the smoke that rose from it was broken up by the overhang above it. Men moved around, dark silhouettes against the garish glare of the leaping flames.

"Señor," Esteban said, "I think we have found the stronghold of the Black Scorpion."

20

Frank knew Esteban was right, even though he hadn't yet spotted the black-clad figure of the *bandido* chief himself. The Black Scorpion was probably farther inside the cave, and perhaps Antonio Almanzar was being held there as well.

"You still want to walk in there and see what happens?" Frank asked quietly.

Esteban nodded. "That is our best course of action. I will take a look around the camp, and then if no one recognizes me, I will slip out and come back here to tell you what I have discovered."

For a moment, Frank considered what Esteban had just said. It still wasn't too late to overrule the old man and change the plan. But like it or not, what Esteban had proposed made the most sense. Frank took a deep breath and said, "Be careful."

"Do not worry, Señor. I am too old to take extra chances."

Esteban stood up and walked over the top of the hill. He started making his way down the other side. Frank watched him go, wondering how long it would be before the *bandidos* spotted him. The Black Scorpion would have sentries posted. He was too careful not to have taken that precaution.

Just as Frank expected, Esteban was less than halfway across the valley when he stopped suddenly and waited as men carrying rifles stepped out from behind some trees and covered him. Frank couldn't hear what was being said, but Esteban talked to the guards for several minutes, gesturing emphatically as he spoke. He was probably telling them that he was looking for some goats that had wandered off, as goats had a tendency to do. The *bandidos* laughed, probably finding the old man to be an amusing figure. Esteban was a mite humorous, Frank thought, with that big sombrero dwarfing him.

Finally, the guards must have told Esteban to go on up to the cave, because the old man started toward the camp and the sentries disappeared back into the trees. Frank watched as Esteban climbed to the cave.

Some of the *bandidos* met him at the

top of the slope and waved their arms around as if to say that there were no missing goats there. Esteban talked to them for a moment and then walked past the fire and deeper into the cave. The shadows were thick enough so that his slight figure was soon swallowed up. Frank frowned. He didn't care for the fact that Esteban was now out of his sight. He was pretty sure, though, that the old man was looking for Antonio. Frank hoped that Antonio had his wits about him enough not to show any reaction if he saw Esteban.

The minutes dragged by. Part of Frank wanted to go down there and find out what was going on, but he knew he had to wait right where he was. He couldn't help Esteban by barging in. It was up to Esteban to pull off this masquerade.

At last, Esteban appeared again, shuffling out of the cave. He laughed with some of the *bandidos* and started down the hill. No one stopped him. His ruse had been successful, at least as far as getting in and out of the bandit camp. Whether or not he had located Antonio was a question that would have to wait for an answer.

Frank glanced over his shoulder and wondered how close the Rurales were. It was almost dark now, so he hoped that

Estancia would order a halt and not push on until morning. That would give Frank a chance to rescue Antonio before the Rurales could attack the *bandidos*.

By the time Esteban got back, full night had fallen, and although Frank could still see the campfire in the cave mouth, the valley between him and the camp was cloaked in darkness. He heard Esteban coming, though, and the old man called out softly, "It is only me, Señor Morgan."

"Come ahead, Esteban," Frank told him, and a moment later Esteban walked up to him. Frank didn't waste any time in asking, "Did you locate Antonio?"

"*Sí, señor.* He is in the cave."

"Is he all right?"

"He appeared unharmed."

"Did he see you?"

"Yes, but he said nothing to give me away."

Relief went through Frank, but it didn't last long. "Getting to him through that bunch and getting him out of there isn't going to be easy."

Esteban gave a dry chuckle. "Easier than you think, Señor. I know something about that cave that the Black Scorpion does not. There is a back way in and out of it from the other side of the hill."

"It's not guarded?" Frank asked sharply.

"No, because as I said, the Black Scorpion knows it not."

Frank nodded. "All right. If you can take me to the other entrance, I'll slip in once the camp is asleep and take Antonio out of there. Did you see the Black Scorpion?"

"Sí, the man is there."

"Is he guarding Antonio personally?"

"The Black Scorpion is never far away, but even he must sleep."

"Where exactly is Antonio?"

"When you come out of the passage, he will be very close," Esteban explained. "Turn to your left and you will see him."

"Is he tied up?"

"No. The bandits have no fear of him escaping."

"That confidence is going to backfire on them," Frank said with a tight smile. "Let's go. I imagine it'll take us quite a while to work our way around behind their camp. By the time we get there, maybe most of them will be asleep."

"I think that is likely, Señor," Esteban said. "There will be much drinking of tequila and pulque and mescal tonight. Many worms will be eaten."

They slipped back down the slope to where they had left the horses. Dog whined a greeting to Frank, and Stormy tossed his head. Taking the reins, Frank and Esteban led their mounts until they were well away from the camp. Only then did they ride, as Esteban led the way in a circuitous route that would eventually take them to the other side of the hill where the cave was located.

"How do you happen to know that there's a back door in that cave?" Frank asked.

"Don Felipe told you that for a time I lived with the Yaquis. They used it as a camp when they hunted in this region."

"How'd you wind up staying with them, if you don't mind my asking?"

Esteban shrugged. "I was a young man with more *cojones* than sense, and like many such, I sought adventure. I was lucky that the Yaquis befriended me instead of simply killing me. Worse yet, they could have entertained themselves by torturing me for a long time. No people are more skilled at the art of torture than the Yaquis."

"So I've heard. I've never run into any of them myself, though."

"If you ever do, Señor, pray for a quick death."

The night was dark, the moon, when it

rose, only a pale sliver in the ebon sky. The thin, dry air quickly lost the warmth of the day and Frank's breath fogged a little in front of his face. The horses' breath formed plumes of steam, too. Frank took a lightweight denim jacket from his saddlebags and slipped it on. Esteban seemed unaffected by the cold, just as he didn't seem to feel heat, either. He had been too long in the world for much of it to touch him.

"You went back to work for Don Felipe eventually, though," Frank said.

"*Sí*. The wild life, sooner or later it pales. The young man may eat danger for breakfast, but as he grows older he begins to hunger for something more nourishing." Esteban chuckled again. "I have had four wives, you know."

"Nope, I didn't know that," Frank said.

"*Sí*, three of them I have buried, but the fourth yet lives. She is nineteen years of age and will soon give birth to my twelfth child. I have seven sons and four daughters. My life has nourished me, Señor Morgan. I am filled."

Frank just grunted, not knowing what to say. He might have never seen Esteban as anything but a servant. Despite the perilous errand they were on, he was glad he had gotten the chance to know Esteban the man.

Finally, when it seemed like they had been riding for hours, Esteban reined in and said, "We will leave the horses here. The rest of the way we must go on foot."

"I thought you were staying with the horses."

"I must show you the entrance to the passage."

Frank couldn't argue with that. They dismounted, and once again he ordered a disappointed Dog to stay there with Stormy and El Rey.

Within moments, Frank saw why they'd had to leave the horses behind. They came to an almost sheer wall of rock rising blackly in front of them. Esteban gestured toward it and said, "From here we climb. It is not far, though."

Esteban went first and Frank didn't argue the matter, figuring that he could find handholds and footholds better by watching the old man. Esteban climbed with an agility belying his age. Frank followed, making sure with each move that he had a good grip before trusting his weight to it. A hard fall now could ruin everything and spell doom for Antonio Almanzar.

When Esteban was about fifty feet up

the rock wall, he stopped and motioned for Frank to come up even with him. Frank could barely see the gesture in the shadows. Carefully, he finished the ascent, and when he pulled himself up beside Esteban, he saw the narrow black slash in the rock.

"There is room for only one man," Esteban said in a voice that was little more than a whisper. "And a tall man such as yourself must bend over to keep from hitting your head. The passage makes two turns, but you cannot get lost since there are no other openings between here and the cave. When you reach the other end, you must slide around a rock that blocks the passage from view and climb down a short distance, perhaps eight feet."

"All right, I understand," Frank said. He took off his hat and handed it to Esteban. Then he reached out to explore the opening by feel. The narrowness of the passage made a feeling of coldness go down his spine. Frank had heard of folks who couldn't stand to be in tight, enclosed places. That had never been a problem for him, but at this moment he could certainly understand the feeling. The idea of so many tons of rock and dirt pressing in so closely on both sides was enough to give any hombre the fantods, even one who wasn't normally bothered by such things.

"I'll be back with Antonio as quick as I can," he told Esteban.

"Take great care, Señor."

Frank clasped Esteban's shoulder for a second, then turned toward the rock wall and insinuated himself into the opening. His broad shoulders brushed lightly against both sides of the passage. He checked the height and found that he had to stoop only slightly at this point. He would have to be careful, though, not to bump his head if the ceiling dropped any more.

Awkwardly, because of the way he was bent over, Frank shuffled forward into the darkness. He kept his left hand stretched out in front of him while the right hovered near the butt of his gun. He wouldn't use the Peacemaker unless it was absolutely necessary. For one thing, in these close confines the noise of a shot would deafen him at least temporarily and might do permanent damage to his hearing. For another, such loud reports sometimes caused rockfalls and cave-ins. He didn't think that was likely here, but he didn't want to take the chance.

When he glanced over his shoulder he

could see a tiny patch of light that marked the entrance to the hidden passage. It wasn't so much light, he thought, as it was darkness that wasn't quite as deep as the surrounding stygian gloom. But when he reached a bend in the passage and moved around it, even that miniscule bit of illumination was gone. Utter darkness surrounded him. It was darker than the inside of a sack full of black cats.

Frank paused for a moment and took a deep breath to steady his nerves. He smelled dust and dirt and rock. His fingers touched the wall, trailed through a slick, slimy seepage. This was living stone, still growing and changing, although at such a slow pace that any major movement might take eons. The vastness of time pressed in on Frank like the rock walls.

But on a more personal level, time seemed to have little or no meaning. Frank couldn't have said how long he had been inside the hill. It seemed like mere seconds, and then with the next heartbeat it felt more like hours or even days. Frank couldn't see anything, could hear only a faint trickle of water and the whispered scuffing of his boot leather on the rocky surface of the passage. This almost total lack of sensation was something he had

never experienced before. It was suffo-
cating, and he had to force himself to keep
breathing at a regular rate.

He wondered suddenly if he had been
struck blind. That was crazy, he knew, but
the thought passed through his brain
anyway.

To take his mind off the situation, he
thought back over everything that had happened since he crossed the border into
Mexico. It had been an eventful few days,
culminating in the raid by the Black Scorpion's gang on the rancho of Don Felipe
Almanzar. . . .

And just like that, he had the answer to
the question that had been eluding him.
He wasn't sure he was right — there were
other, less likely explanations, and the answer that had burst with stunning force in
his brain just raised more questions — but
at least he knew now what had been
plaguing him. The theory that formed in
his head, though still nebulous, was an intriguing one.

And the only way to find out for sure if
he was right was to keep going.

The passageway bent again, and Frank's
head brushed the ceiling. He stooped
lower and moved on, but now he could see
his goal. A narrow slit of reddish light hov-

ered in front of him in the blackness, looking almost like a wound. He knew the light came from the campfire in the mouth of the cave. The glare flickered and shifted, and the opening changed from a wound to an aperture into hell. Frank's lips pulled back from his teeth in a savage grin.

He reached the end of the passage and saw the large rock that jutted up in front of it, blocking direct sight into the cave. The light from the fire reflected around it. Frank slipped out, put his back against the rock, and slid around the spire. He found himself some eight feet above the floor of the cave, just as Esteban had told him he would. The wall of the cave was rough enough, though, so that Frank had no trouble finding handholds to lower himself down.

His boots touched the floor and he stepped away from the wall. He hadn't seen Antonio or anyone else. In fact, the camp appeared to be deserted. The fire in the cave mouth, about a hundred feet away, was still burning, but none of the *bandidos* moved around it.

Then cloth rustled and boot leather scraped on the floor and men stepped out of the shadows behind Frank. He knew even before he heard the metallic sounds of guns being cocked that he was covered. He didn't move, and he kept his right hand well away from his gun.

"Stand very still, Señor Morgan," a voice said from behind him. "I would not want to see you die, but my men will shoot if you make any threatening moves."

"Take it easy," Frank said. "It's your play, Antonio . . . or would you rather I call you the Black Scorpion?"

21

"Madre de Dios!" Antonio Almanzar exclaimed. He stepped around Frank and pointed a revolver at him. "How did you know?"

"It was a guess of sorts," Frank said, "but it explained how come those *bandidos* already had a ransom note written out and ready to toss over the wall into the hacienda. They knew you'd come running out, so they could pretend to kidnap you. That bothered me for a while. What I don't know is why you'd do such a thing. Just to get money from your father?"

Antonio wore the sable shirt and trousers of the Black Scorpion, but not the hat or the mask. He said, "It takes a great deal of money to fight a war, Señor Morgan. And that is what we are doing, you know: fighting a war. A revolution."

Several of the men behind Frank muttered, *"Viva la revolución."*

"What you're saying is that you're not a gang of bandits?"

A small figure appeared near the front of the cave and strode toward Frank. Esteban said, "That is right, Señor Morgan. We are not *bandidos*."

Frank looked at the old man and nodded slowly. "So you were in on it, too. I halfway thought as much, but I wasn't sure."

Esteban shrugged. "It was perhaps a more elaborate ruse than it really needed to be, but we have learned to take no chances. We wanted you here where you could do no harm to our cause, but at the same time we have no wish to do you any harm, either, Señor Morgan."

"You could have told me what was going on," Frank snapped.

Esteban handed him his Stetson, which he had brought into the cave with him. "You have come to consider Don Felipe a friend," the old man said. "Would you have willingly gone along with our plan?"

"That depends on what it is."

Antonio said, "My father will pay two million pesos for my safe release. Then the Black Scorpion and his men will use that money to buy guns and supplies so that we may continue fighting against the oppression of Capitán Estancia and the Rurales."

"So Don Felipe knows nothing of this?" Frank asked, gesturing around him at the cave. The gesture took in Antonio's garb as well.

Antonio shook his head. "No. Nothing."

"He doesn't wonder where you've gotten off to when you're leading your gang on its raids?"

"My men are not a *gang*," Antonio said with a scowl. "They are a band of courageous fighters for liberty. And as for my absences . . . The Almanzar rancho is quite large. My father thinks little or nothing about it when I and some of our vaqueros are gone for several days tending to the stock. Besides, I have quite a capable lieutenant and do not always need to be on hand." He crooked his hand, calling one of the men forward.

The bearded giant who had grabbed up Antonio during the raid on the ranch strolled around so that Frank could see him. "This is Lupe, my *segundo*," Antonio went on. "He was once a soldier in El Presidente's army."

"Until my spineless coward of a commander broke under fire and I was forced to strike him down," Lupe growled. "For that he would have had me in front of a firing squad, had I not escaped. Bah! The army is no life for a real man, at least not that army."

"So you became a rebel," Frank said. "I imagine all the rest of your group has their own stories, their own reasons. That doesn't give you the right to prey on innocent people."

"Innocent!" Antonio spat on the stone floor. "Never have we preyed on any innocents, Señor Morgan."

"What about that ranch you raided on the other side of the border, or those two peasants you killed when the Rangers were chasing you?"

"That so-called ranch was the headquarters of smugglers who work with Capitán Estancia and the Rurales."

Frank's forehead creased. "Wait a minute. The Rurales are supposed to stop smugglers, not work with them."

Antonio gave a humorless laugh and said, "That shows how little you know about what is really going on along the border, Señor. Gold, guns, cheap opium, Chinese laborers who are little more than slaves . . . All of these and more are smuggled regularly across the Rio Grande. The profits go into the pockets of the thrice-damned Domingo Estancia and his American partners."

"You're saying the Rurales have turned outlaw?"

"That is exactly what I am saying." Antonio lowered his gun and looked intently at Frank. "El Presidente is bad enough and will someday be overthrown. Now, though, along this stretch of the border, Estancia is the true dictator. Perhaps he shares his ill-gotten gains with Diaz . . . but I doubt it. I do not think El Presidente truly knows what is going on here."

Frank lifted a hand and rubbed his jaw as he thought. What Antonio Almanzar was telling him was fantastic, but it wasn't beyond belief. This part of the country was a long way from Mexico City. Estancia would have pretty much a free hand to operate however he wanted to. If he wanted to ride roughshod over the people and take part in smuggling operations and generally line his own pockets with loot, there was nothing to stop him, no one to oppose him.

No one, perhaps, except for a band of men branded as outlaws themselves, led by the son of a rich rancher . . .

Frank wasn't satisfied yet that Antonio was telling the truth. He said, "What about those two men, the brothers . . . I don't remember their name. . . ."

"Hernandez," Antonio said tautly. "They pretended to be farmers, but their place was really a way station for the smugglers. They acted as informers for Estancia, too."

"So you murdered them," Frank said, his voice flat.

Lupe answered this time, his voice rumbling in his barrel chest. "We wanted only to question them, to find out Estancia's plans. But they fought back before we had a chance to ask them anything. When they opened fire on us, we had no choice but to defend ourselves."

"Then you burned their jacal."

Esteban wasn't the only one capable of an eloquent Latin shrug. Lupe did it, too, as he said, "Call it a warning to others who would lie down with Estancia and his bloodthirsty dogs."

"We do not cloak ourselves in robes of purity, Señor Morgan," Antonio said. "It is bloody work we do, but it is work that must be done if Estancia's grip on our land is ever to be broken."

"If your cause is so noble, why don't you just ask Don Felipe for the money you need?" Frank wanted to know.

Esteban answered this time. "Don Felipe believes in the rule of law, even when that law is unjust and its purveyors are evil men. His great-grandfather bowed to the king of Spain, and Don Felipe bows to El Presidente, whether he likes it or not. Estancia is the representative of Diaz."

"I got the feeling Don Felipe doesn't care for Estancia at all," Frank commented.

"Disliking a man and taking action against the government are two different things," Antonio pointed out. "Perhaps someday my father will see things in the same light that we do. But in the meantime we need guns and ammunition and supplies, and I will not allow us to descend to the level of actual banditry!"

"Like train robbing?" Frank asked pointedly.

"That train was supposed to be carrying a shipment of rifles. That is the only reason we stopped it. When we saw that there were no rifles, we rode away without molesting or robbing any of the passengers." Antonio's mouth quirked bitterly. "Estancia tells the story differently in order to justify his pursuit of us. In truth, what he really wants is to see all of us standing in front of a wall with a firing squad aiming at us."

"You, especially, amigo," Lupe rumbled.

"Yes, me especially," Antonio agreed. He

smiled wearily. "I have been a great thorn in Capitán Estancia's side. He is tired of being pricked."

Antonio certainly seemed sincere, Frank thought, and while some of what he said might be a little far-fetched, none of it was impossible. But even if Frank decided to believe what Antonio, Esteban, and Lupe had told him, the question remained: What was he going to do about it?

For that matter, what *could* he do about it? Although he still had his Colt, he was surrounded by rifle-toting revolutionaries.

"What happens next?" he asked.

Antonio holstered his gun. "You remain here with us for a few days —"

"As a prisoner?"

"As our guest," Antonio said with a cold smile. "My father pays the ransom and is reunited with his kidnapped son. And our battle against Estancia and the Rurales continues."

"What's to stop me from telling him later about your little masquerade?"

Antonio's smile disappeared. "Do not mock me, Señor Morgan! The people need someone to rally them, to give them hope. For now, the Black Scorpion is that figure. Perhaps someday I will be able to lead them openly." He stopped and took a deep breath. "As for you, it is our hope that after a few days among us, you will see the justice of our cause and will agree not to reveal our secrets."

"And if I don't agree?"

Lupe smiled and drew a heavy-bladed knife from a sheath at his waist. He began cleaning his fingernails with the tip of the blade as he looked squarely at Frank.

"Stop it," Antonio snapped at him. "As we have already told Señor Morgan, we are not murderers." He looked at Frank and went on. "You will have to follow your own conscience, Señor."

"I'll think about it," Frank said. "For now, though, it doesn't look like I'm going anywhere."

"No." Antonio shook his head. "For now, you will stay right here."

Being a revolutionary didn't pay very well, Frank thought, and the food wasn't very good, either. He sat with his back propped against the rock wall of the cave and looked at the single tortilla and the small spoonful of beans that Esteban had brought to him on a battered tin plate.

Esteban had a similar plate. He sat down cross-legged next to Frank and said, "You see now why Antonio needs money for supplies. He will not steal from the people."

"But he'll steal from his own father," Frank said. He rolled the tortilla and scooped up some of the beans with it.

Esteban's shoulders lifted and fell. "Don Felipe can afford it."

"It's *his* money," Frank argued. "It doesn't matter whether the government takes it away from him in the form of unjust taxes, or if a band of so-called revolutionaries extorts it from him to support their cause. It's not right either way."

"Perhaps not. Do you believe in the lesser of two evils, Señor Morgan?"

Frank hesitated. "Maybe not in principle, but in real life I reckon it does work out that way sometimes."

"Then consider us the lesser of the two evils now at large in the border country," Esteban said.

"I only have your word for that."

"No," Esteban said flatly. "You have seen Estancia with your own eyes. You saw what he had done to Pablo. You are a man who recognizes true evil when you see it, Señor Morgan."

Frank couldn't argue with that. Estancia was a cold-blooded bastard who wouldn't hesitate to destroy anyone who got in his way. Frank also had no trouble believing that he was a criminal as well, just like the Rurales that he led. The only difference was that Estancia had never gotten caught.

Yet.

Frank had already started weighing his options. He knew that Porfirio Diaz, Mexico's El Presidente, was an iron-fisted dictator in his own right. But it was unlikely that Diaz would tolerate one of his Rurale captains setting up an outlaw empire of his own along the Rio Grande. If Diaz knew what Estancia was doing, there was at least a possibility that he would move in with the Mexican army and clean up the situation.

Antonio and his cohorts weren't going to turn to Diaz for help, though. They hated and distrusted Diaz almost as much as they did Estancia. So that wasn't likely to come about. On the other side of the river were the Texas Rangers, but they had no jurisdiction over here. The Rangers were good Texans, which meant that if there was no legal and proper way to do the right thing, they'd just do it illegally and improperly. But even they would balk at crossing the border and going to war against a troop of Rurales, Frank thought. That would cause too big of an international incident even for Texas.

Like it or not, that sort of left Antonio, in his guise of the Black Scorpion, and his men to oppose the true *bandidos*. Frank couldn't see any other way.

"What about Stormy and Dog?" he asked Esteban.

"Your horse is with ours and is being cared for," the old man replied. "I was the only one he would allow near him."

That came as no surprise to Frank. Stormy would consider Esteban to be a friend, or at least acceptable, after Frank had ridden with the old man all day.

"The dog, he ran away," Esteban went on. "But he is nearby. Some of the men have seen him, lurking on the edge of the darkness like a wolf. One man wanted to shoot him, but Antonio forbade it."

"Good," Frank grunted. If anybody started taking potshots at Dog, he might have to forget about his promise to behave himself. That pledge was the only reason he still had his gun and Antonio didn't have armed guards surrounding him even now.

The two men ate in silence for a moment, and then Esteban said, "You have thought about everything you were told, Señor Morgan?"

"I've thought about it," Frank admitted. "I still don't think it's right to put Don Felipe and Señorita Carmen through all the worry they're going through while they think Antonio has been kidnapped. I don't like lying and trickery."

"You are a simple man, in the best sense of the word, Señor."

"Thanks, I think," Frank said. "Anyway, I can understand why you think you have to fight back against Estancia. I knew from the start Don Felipe didn't like him. I didn't care for him, either."

"And you have seen only the smallest part of his wickedness," Esteban said. "*He* is the one feared by the common people, not the Black Scorpion. That is why no one will help the Rurales. So he tries to force them to aid him by whipping them and burning their crops and sometimes killing them."

"Damn it," Frank growled. "Somebody's got to put a stop to that."

"*Sí*. We are trying."

Again silence fell. Esteban hadn't pressed Frank for an answer about what he was going to do, and Frank hadn't offered one. He didn't have an answer.

The fire died down to embers and the cave darkened. Esteban brought Frank a

273

threadbare blanket. "It is not much," the old man said, "but it is all we can spare."

Frank took the blanket and patted the rock floor beside him. "Not much of a mattress, either. But it won't be the first time I've slept between a rock and a hard place."

He wadded up his hat for a pillow and stretched out, rolling in the blanket's meager protection from the chilly night. It took Frank a long time to get to sleep, but he finally did.

When he awoke, it was to startled shouts from the Black Scorpion's men, and the snarling crackle of gunshots in the distance.

22

Frank rolled over and came to his feet, snatching up his hat as he did so. Carrying the Stetson in his left hand, he joined the men he saw hurrying toward the mouth of the cave. Some of them seemed to think that the group was under attack, but despite being groggy from sleep, Frank had already figured out that the shots were too far away for that to be true.

He spotted Esteban, stepped up beside the old man, and asked, "What's going on?"

Esteban shook his head. "I do not know, Señor Morgan. The shooting started a few moments ago, with no warning."

A knot of men gathered in the cave mouth, holding rifles and pistols ready in case they had to fight. Frank and Esteban joined them, and a moment later Antonio Almanzar pushed his way to the front of the group. He wore the flat-crowned black hat and was tying the black bandanna around his neck so that all he would have to do to complete his disguise as the Black Scorpion was to pull it up.

"What is it?" Antonio asked. "Does anyone know?"

Esteban leveled his arm and pointed with a gnarled finger. "The shooting seems to be coming from the village," he said. "Something is burning there, too."

Frank's jaw tightened as he gazed in the direction of the small farming community Esteban had pointed out to him the day before. As the old man said, a column of smoke was rising into the early morning air, stark black against the pale blue sky. The sun was not quite up.

Death had come to call in the dawn.

"Esteban, ride with me!" Antonio snapped. "Lupe, you and the rest of the men stay here until we find out what is going on."

"But 'Tonio —" the giant Lupe started to protest.

"Do as I have ordered!" Antonio said, clearly not caring that his lieutenant was nearly twice his size.

Lupe nodded. *"Sí, jefe,"* he said.

"I'm going with you, too," Frank said to Antonio.

The young man shrugged. "You are not one of my men to command, Señor Morgan. There may be danger."

"That's never stopped me from doing what I want to do."

Antonio nodded curtly and headed down the slope. Esteban and Frank followed. A few moments later, Frank saw a rope corral hidden in the trees. The group's horses were kept there. He spotted Stormy among them and was glad to see the big Appaloosa.

Dog had seen Frank and came bounding forward. Frank paused long enough to grab the big cur and rub his ears for a second, as pleased by the reunion as Dog was. Then Frank strode on to see about getting his saddle on Stormy.

Quickly, the three men prepared to ride. As they did so, the gunfire in the distance tapered off and finally died away completely, leaving an ominous silence in its wake. Frank exchanged a grim look with Antonio and Esteban as they swung up into their saddles. They knew what that silence might mean.

They rode down the valley, through shadows that faded as the eastern sky lightened even more. With Esteban leading the way, they topped a couple of hills, galloped along a rocky ridge, and finally came to a point where they could gaze down at the village below them, at the edge of the foothills where the plains started that ran all the way to the Rio Grande.

Although there had been no doubt in Frank's mind about the source of the smoke, his jaw tightened as he saw with his own eyes the house that was burning in the village below. Flames leaped from the windows as the adobe dwelling was gutted by fire. A couple of huddled shapes lay in the dirt just outside the entrance. A man and a woman, Frank thought, no doubt the couple who had lived there, cut down by gunfire as they fled from the inferno that their home had become.

Those weren't the only bodies he saw. Several others lay sprawled around the village. Most of the little settlement's inhabitants still seemed to be alive, though. They were being herded into the plaza by armed men on horseback, men who wore the gray uniforms of the Gendarmeria Fiscal, the Rurales.

A lot of black sombreros down there, Frank thought. They had swept into the village at daybreak, shooting up the place and torching that house, terrifying the people so that they wouldn't put up much of a fight. The villagers couldn't make a stand against a gang of such cold-blooded killers.

And the most cold-blooded of them all sat on his horse at the edge of the plaza and watched the villagers being rounded up. Frank didn't need a spyglass to tell him that the stiff, erect figure was Captain Domingo Estancia, the man who was trying to make himself lord and master of this entire region.

Antonio began to curse in a low, shaken voice. "Why is Estancia doing this?" he wanted to know. "Those villagers are no threat to him!"

"No doubt he seeks to use them against you," Esteban said. "Perhaps his men lost your trail, but he knows that your hiding place is around here somewhere. Or at least he thinks it may be. He seeks to force the villagers to betray you." Esteban looked over at Antonio. "Do any of them know where you and your men may be found?"

Antonio's head jerked in a nod. "A few of them share our secret. They bring us supplies from time to time, when the people of the village can spare them."

Frank rested his hands on the saddle horn and said, "There's a good chance

Estancia will find out what he wants to know from them."

"No! The people will not betray us!"

"A man's mouth cannot stay closed when he is being tortured," Esteban said sadly. "He will talk even sooner if it is his loved ones who are being threatened."

Frank nodded toward the village. "Looks like that's what's about to happen."

The Rurales on horseback formed a half circle around the group of frightened villagers in the middle of the plaza. They kept their rifles trained on the prisoners as Captain Estancia and his sergeant slowly rode forward. Estancia pulled his horse to a stop when he was facing the villagers. He spoke in a loud voice, and although the sound of it carried in the thin air to the hilltop where Frank, Antonio, and Esteban watched, they couldn't make out the words.

They didn't really have to understand what Estancia was saying to know what was going on. "He is asking them where to find the Black Scorpion," Antonio guessed.

Esteban nodded. "No one wants to speak up. No one wants to be the first to break."

The Rurale officer fell silent. The crackling of flames from the burning building could be heard. After a moment, Estancia snapped an order, and the burly sergeant at his side rode forward. Frank recognized the man who had carried out the brutal whipping at the Almanzar rancho.

The sergeant trotted his horse up to the group of villagers and dismounted. Those in the front cringed away from him as he walked back and forth, studying them. Abruptly, he stepped forward, pulling a revolver from a holster at his waist. One of the women screamed, a terrified wail. The revolver rose and fell. Its barrel slammed against the head of one of the male villagers, knocking him to his knees. The sergeant kicked him aside and reached past him for the smaller figure that had been cowering behind him. It was a young woman in a nightdress, Frank saw. The sergeant clamped the fingers of his free hand around her and jerked her out of the group, dragging her with him as he started back toward Estancia.

The man who had been knocked down scrambled to his feet, blood running from the cut on his forehead that had been opened up by the slashing gun barrel. He ran after the sergeant, yelling angrily. The woman was either his wife or daughter, Frank guessed, and the villager's fear for her had overcome his common sense.

The sergeant stopped, half-turned, lifted the revolver, and shot the man in the face.

The villager went over backward, his head seeming to crumple like a deflated ball as the bullet tore out the back of his skull and sprayed brains and blood in the dirt. He landed on his back, arms and legs outflung, and spasmed a couple of times as his muscles caught up to the fact that he was dead. The young woman shrieked as she stared horrified over her shoulder at the body.

"Madre de Dios," Antonio breathed.

"It will only get worse," Esteban said.

The old man was right. As they watched, the sergeant dragged the young woman in front of Estancia. The captain gestured sharply. The sergeant took hold of the neck of the young woman's nightdress and ripped it open. He yanked the ruined garment off of her, making her stumble. She stood there naked, shaking and sobbing as she tried to cover her breasts.

The Rurales laughed and hooted as the sergeant pulled the young woman's hands down and began to paw her, running his rough, callused hands all over her body. Estancia watched the degrading display impassively. The villagers just stood there, numb, afraid to move. A large pool of blood had formed around the head of the man the sergeant had shot. From this distance, Frank couldn't see, but he figured flies had already begun to buzz around the crimson puddle.

Estancia said something else, and the sergeant forced the young woman to her knees. She tried to lower her head, but he wrapped his fingers in her long black hair and cruelly jerked her head so that she had to look up at him. With his other hand, he began to fumble with the buttons of his uniform trousers.

"That's just about enough," Frank said as he pulled his Winchester from the sheath strapped to Stormy's saddle. "Hell, it's more than enough."

He levered a round into the rifle's chamber and brought it to his shoulder in one smooth motion. Below in the village, the sergeant had his stiff penis out and was trying to force it into the young woman's mouth. Laughter rolled from his lips as he twisted her hair.

The Winchester cracked sharply. The shot was a long one, somewhere between four and five hundred yards, but instinct and experience guided Frank's aim. The sergeant jerked and stopped laughing as the bullet slammed into the back of his head, bored on through his upper spine, tore out the front of his throat in a shower of gore, and passed over the young woman's head to bury itself in the dirt behind her. Covered in the man's blood, she screamed and tore loose from his suddenly nerveless grip. She scuttled away on hands and knees, still screaming, as the echoes of the single shot rolled across the plains and finally faded. The sergeant stood there for a second as if he still lived, and then he pitched forward onto his face.

Antonio said to Esteban, "Ride back and tell the men to prepare for battle. I think Señor Morgan has just — how do the gringos say it? — opened the ball."

23

As the hoofbeats of Esteban's racing horse drummed behind him, Frank worked the Winchester's lever and shifted his aim. If he could drop Estancia, the Rurales would be leaderless and a lot less likely to mount an effective pursuit. But just as Frank pressed the trigger and the rifle cracked and bucked, one of the other Rurales lunged his horse forward. It wasn't a deliberate move; the previous shot and the sergeant's unexpected death had plunged the plaza into chaos and men and horses were jumping around all over the place. In this case, though, fate protected Estancia, because the Rurale trooper's body shielded him. Frank's bullet struck the other man and tumbled him from the saddle. The Rurale's black sombrero went sailing through the air.

"Kill them! Kill them all!" Estancia shrieked. The furious, bloodthirsty command was so loud Frank could make it out even at a distance.

The Rurales were going to have a hard time carrying it out, however. Already one of the villagers had broken out of his terrified stupor and snatched up the sergeant's pistol. He emptied it into the milling, uniformed men, knocking down a couple of them. Others of the villagers were fighting back with their bare hands, grabbing the Rurales and dragging them out of their saddles.

Taking careful aim, Frank sent several more slugs into the plaza. With each shot, another Rurale was wounded, and either fell or sagged in his saddle. Some of the men lost their nerve and fled, galloping out of the village as if the hounds of hell were on their heels.

Frank looked for Estancia but couldn't see him anymore. Blinding clouds of dust, kicked up by the hooves of the frantic horses, began to billow in the air. Men, women, and children ran for their homes, guns roared, and the plaza was now utter confusion.

It wouldn't take long, though, for Estancia to rally his men, Frank thought. Then the captain would come looking for whoever had killed his sergeant and caused all hell to break loose.

Frank slid the Winchester back in its sheath. "Maybe I shouldn't have done that," he said as he looked over at Antonio.

"I thank El Señor Dios that you did," Antonio said. "You were the only one among the three of us who could stop that devil." A bleak smile played over the young man's lips. "I take it you are now with us, Señor Morgan, rather than against us?"

"I reckon I was always on your side. I just didn't know it yet."

They wheeled their horses and rode back toward the cave that was the Black Scorpion's stronghold.

Frank knew he had forced a showdown. That hadn't really been his intention. He had simply been unable to stand by any longer and watch the sort of evil that he was witnessing go unpunished. His act had been impulsive, a matter of sheer instinct.

And yet he didn't regret it for an instant. Left alone, Captain Estancia might well have slaughtered everyone in that village. No doubt some of the people had died in the fighting, but at least they had died standing up for themselves, not like sheep meekly having their throats cut.

Side by side, Frank and Antonio galloped into the valley where the cave was located. They saw that the other men were already mounted and ready to ride. Their hands bristled with guns. Esteban and Lupe urged their mounts out ahead of the others, and Lupe said, "What are your orders, Don Antonio? Do we flee . . . or do we fight?"

Antonio clenched his right hand into a fist and thrust it over his head. "We fight!"

A cheer burst out from the men.

They were caught up in the emotion of the moment, and to a certain extent, so was Frank. He wanted nothing more than another chance to get Estancia in his gun sights.

But he also knew that in spite of the damage he and the villagers had inflicted on Estancia's men, the Rurales still outnumbered Antonio and his friends. They had better rifles and more of them. No matter what the emotions involved or the rightness or wrongness of the cause, battles were usually won with firepower.

"It might be better to split up and sort of fade away," Frank said to Antonio. "Regroup again later to strike at the Rurales."

Antonio stared at him. "You would say this, Señor Morgan, after you were the one who fired the opening round?"

"I'm just saying you boys are outnumbered. You need to be sure this is what you want to do."

"I have never been more sure of anything in my life." Antonio swept a hand toward Esteban, Lupe, and the other men. "Look at their faces, Señor. This is the chance they have been waiting for, the chance to finally join in battle with a hated foe. Would you deny them this?"

Frank looked at the men and saw the anticipation on their faces. Sure, they were scared. But more than that, they were eager to have this showdown with the Rurales and perhaps end the reign of terror that had held the border country in its grip.

"All right," Frank said, nodding slowly. "We fight."

Again the men cheered. They thrust their rifles over their heads and shook them. They were ready for whatever might come.

"We will strike them before they can strike us," Antonio said. "The element of surprise will be on our side."

Frank, Esteban, and Lupe all nodded their agreement with the tactic. That would give them their best chance of success. They were outnumbered perhaps two to one, so they had to try to even up those odds as quickly as they could.

Antonio pulled the mask up over his face so that only his eyes were visible. Then he spurred his horse ahead. Frank and Esteban rode beside him. Lupe was right behind them, and the rest of the men were close on his heels. The band of revolutionaries galloped down the valley, as to the east the sun rose and the sky began to change from pale blue to a darker shade.

The rolling thunder of hoofbeats rose into the sky as well. Frank knew that as soon as Estancia was able to regroup his men, the Rurales would charge up into the foothills to find whoever had fired on them. Estancia was no fool, however; not knowing how many men he would be facing, he wouldn't attack blindly. He would probably send out scouts to gauge the opposition.

Sure enough, a few minutes later as the riders topped a hill, Frank spotted a couple of black-hatted Rurales coming toward them. The Rurales saw the Black Scorpion and his men at the same time and frantically reined in. They turned their horses to gallop away.

Frank spurred ahead, thinking it might be good to stop those scouts from reporting back to Estancia. He didn't want the Rurales digging in along a defensive position. They already had the advantage in numbers. They didn't need to be forted up, too.

Stormy's long legs stretched out, muscles working smoothly under the sleek hide. Frank leaned forward over the Appaloosa's neck as he urged more speed. Surprisingly, from the corner of his eye he saw another rider draw even with him. The big black stallion, El Rey, was running just as easily as Stormy, and if anything, his stride was longer. Esteban looked over and gave Frank a gnomelike grin as he and El Rey pulled slightly ahead of Morgan and Stormy.

"Damn it, it's not a race!" Frank called over the pounding of hoofbeats.

"*Sí, Señor!*" Esteban replied, but he didn't slacken his pace any.

They had pulled out well in front of the rest of the group and were closing in on the two fleeing Rurales. The trail curved around a large boulder. The Rurales swept around the big rock and disappeared. Seconds later, Frank and Esteban flashed around the boulder as well.

A hundred yards away, the rest of the Rurales under Captain Estancia emerged from a stand of pine trees. They saw their two scouts between them and the pursuers on the Appaloosa and the black stallion. Instead of waiting to hear the scouts' report, Estancia shouted a command to charge. The company of Rurales surged forward, whooping and shooting.

Frank hauled back on the reins as bullets whipped around his head. "The damn fools think there's only two of us!" he shouted.

"Let them think that!" Esteban replied as he wheeled El Rey back in the direction they had come from.

Frank and Esteban suddenly found themselves in the position of being bait as they raced back along the trail. The Rurales came after them, howling furiously. If Estancia had changed his mind and tried to stop them so that they could proceed more cautiously, he had failed. The Rurales might have had discipline imposed on them, but at heart they were a bunch of thugs and criminals, given to impulsiveness.

This time that recklessness might just backfire on them.

Frank glanced over his shoulder and saw that the Rurales were coming on at a gallop. They were still firing, too, but only a few of their shots came very close. One bullet ripped through the high crown of

Esteban's sombrero and tipped it forward so that it fell down over his eyes. He cuffed it back off his head and let it dangle on his back, held there by its chin strap. From time to time a slug would kick up dirt and rocks in the trail alongside the running horses. Frank grinned. The shots were coming close enough to keep the Rurales excited and careless.

As they neared the boulder, Frank called, "We'll slow them down a little!" Esteban nodded his understanding.

As they rounded the boulder, Frank pulled back on the reins and slowed Stormy. Drawing the Winchester from its sheath, he dropped out of the saddle while the Appaloosa was still moving, and a slap on the rump sent Stormy galloping ahead. Likewise, Esteban performed a running dismount from El Rey, looking like a young man as he did so. As the horses continued running, the two men hurried into the shelter of the boulder. Frank crouched at the edge of the big, rugged rock next to the trail, while Esteban scrambled up the hillside a short distance to a place where he could fire his revolver over the top of the boulder.

"Let 'em have it!" Frank ordered.

He opened fire with the rifle, picking his

shots carefully. He hadn't had a chance to reload, so there were only seven or eight rounds left in the Winchester. Above him and to the right, Esteban's pistol began to roar. Frank hadn't really paid much attention to the weapon before, but now he realized from the sound of it that it was an old cap-and-ball revolver. Guns like that might not have the same muzzle velocity as newer weapons, but they fired a heavy ball that packed an incredible amount of punch when it hit something.

Like the Rurale's head that seemed almost to explode on his shoulders when one of Esteban's shots crashed into the middle of his forehead. The corpse flew backward out of the saddle and caused men behind him to shy away from the spray of blood and brains.

Frank dropped a couple of the Rurales with the Winchester. He wanted a shot at Captain Estancia, but he couldn't see the officer. Probably hanging back where there wouldn't be as much danger, Frank thought. Brutal, evil men like Domingo Estancia were often physical cowards, needing flunkies to carry out their ruthless orders.

The charge faltered. Frank didn't want the Rurales to stop and turn back. He glanced over his shoulder, searching for any sign of Antonio, Lupe, and the others. He didn't see them yet. He and Esteban had gotten quite a ways out in front when they gave chase to the Rurale scouts. But the others had to be coming along soon.

"Hold your fire!" he called to Esteban. "Let them think they have us!"

"A few more minutes, Señor, and I think they will!" the old man replied with a fighting laugh. As Frank had ordered, though, he stopped shooting.

The Rurales slowed down for a moment, and then they came on, charging with renewed enthusiasm. They must have thought that their quarry was running low on ammunition or had been wounded. They didn't anticipate much of a fight; that much was obvious.

"Hold on," Frank muttered under his breath. "Hold on."

The Rurales were less than fifty yards away now. When they came sweeping around the boulder, Frank and Esteban would be overrun. The Rurales would either shoot them down — or draw their sabers and hack the two men into bloody little pieces.

"Any time now, Antonio," Frank said quietly.

Suddenly, over the top of a hill twenty yards away, a horse leaped into view. The man in the saddle was dressed all in black, with a black hat pulled low on his head and a black silk bandanna over the lower half of his face. He had a silver-plated, ivory-handled revolver in each hand, and Lupe and the rest of the revolutionaries were right behind him. Colt flame spurted from the muzzles of the guns as Antonio Almanzar galloped past the boulder and charged right into the faces of the Rurales.

The Black Scorpion had arrived, and the battle was joined.

24

Frank let out a whoop of excitement as the revolutionaries thundered past the boulder. The roar of gunshots was deafening. Clouds of powder smoke billowed up over the trail.

As the last of the riders galloped past, Frank spotted Stormy and El Rey bringing up the rear of the charge. The two riderless horses had fallen in with the others. Frank put his fingers to his mouth and gave a loud, shrill whistle. Stormy veered toward him.

As the Appaloosa came up, Frank grabbed the reins and the saddle horn and swung up onto Stormy's back. He rammed the empty Winchester in its sheath. He saw movement from the corner of his eye, and looked over to see Esteban leap from the side of the hill into El Rey's saddle. The old man gave Frank a grin to indicate that he was all right.

With a touch of Frank's heels, Stormy leaped forward, carrying him toward the battle. Frank had lost track of Dog, but he figured the big cur was around somewhere, probably close by. Dog could take care of himself.

Frank drew his Colt. The two groups of riders had slammed together in the trail and were now firing at each other at close range, and in some cases men who had been knocked off their horses were fighting hand to hand. The dust and smoke made it difficult to see, but as Frank charged into the ruckus, one of the Rurales suddenly loomed up to his right. The man fired his rifle, the shot coming close enough so that Frank heard the wind-rip of the bullet beside his ear. The Rurale lunged his horse toward Stormy and thrust the bayonet attached to the barrel of his rifle at Frank.

Frank twisted in the saddle, making himself a smaller target. The move almost came too late. The tip of the bayonet caught the side of his denim jacket and ripped a gash in it. The Rurale didn't have a chance to pull the rifle back and try again, because Frank shot him in the chest. Rocking back, the Rurale dropped his rifle and clutched at his saddle, trying to hold himself on his horse. He failed. His fingers slipped off, and he fell, screaming as he landed under the slashing hooves of his half-crazed mount.

Another horse slammed into Stormy from the left. The Appaloosa stayed upright somehow, but the impact slewed Frank far over. His left foot came out of the stirrup, and he would have fallen if he hadn't used his left hand to grab the saddle horn at the last instant. Hanging on Stormy's side like a Comanche on the side of a war pony, Frank thrust the Peacemaker under the Appaloosa's neck and fired at a sharp upward angle at the Rurale who had nearly unhorsed him. The bullet caught the man under the chin and tore through his throat, angling on up into his brain. He toppled off his horse, dead before he hit the ground.

With a grunt of effort, Frank's muscles strained against his weight and pulled him back up into the saddle. His left foot found the stirrup again. He pulled on the reins and Stormy reared up on his hind legs, turning around and around as Frank searched for another enemy.

One of the Rurales charged screaming at him, waving a saber. As Stormy came down on all four legs again, Frank ducked under the bloodstained blade and reached out to jam the muzzle of his Colt against the man's chest. The Rurale's eyes widened in horror as he realized what was about to happen, but he didn't have time to do anything else before Frank pressed the trigger and blew his heart right out of the gaping hole the .45 slug left in his back when it exited.

"Señor Morgan! Señor Morgan!"

Even over all the tumult and the roar of gunshots, Frank heard his name being shouted. He twisted around in the saddle and saw Esteban flash past him, motioning for him to follow. Frank sent Stormy racing after El Rey. As he looked past Esteban, he saw what had prompted the shouts of alarm from the old man. Four Rurales had the Black Scorpion surrounded.

One of the men fired and blood spurted from Antonio Almanzar's side. Antonio tumbled off his horse. Esteban yelled, "'Tonio!" and rammed the big black stallion into the Rurales' mounts. El Rey and a couple of the other horses went down in a welter of flailing hooves. Frank saw Esteban go sailing through the air.

The old *mozo* managed to land nimbly and use his momentum to roll over a couple of times and come to his feet. One leg appeared to have been injured, however, because he dragged it behind him as he hurried toward Antonio. Esteban had dropped his revolver, too, but he snatched a knife from his belt and plunged it into the body of one of the Rurales. Wrenching the blade free, Esteban stumbled on until he was standing over the body of the fallen Antonio. A couple of Rurales lunged at him, but he just snarled and brandished the knife.

From horseback, Frank snapped a couple of shots at the men attacking Esteban. One of the Rurales spun off his feet, killed by Frank's bullets. But the other one reached Esteban, used his rifle to knock the knife aside, and rammed the bayonet on the end of it into the old man's belly.

The hammer of Frank's Colt clicked on an empty chamber. The gun was empty, and there was no time to reload. Frank holstered the Peacemaker, kicked his feet out of the stirrups, and launched himself from the saddle in a diving tackle as Stormy raced past the Rurale, who had pulled his bayonet out of Esteban's body and poised it to strike again.

Frank crashed into the man, wrapping his arms around the Rurale's shoulders and knocking him off his feet. They rolled over a couple of times, locked together by Frank's iron grip. Frank got an arm around the man's throat and pressed his forearm against it like a steel bar. The Rurale flopped and writhed and made gagging noises, but Frank kept up the pressure. The muscles in The Drifter's shoulders bunched as he squeezed and heaved even harder, and a sudden sharp cracking sound, along with the way the Rurale's body went limp, told Frank that he had just broken the man's neck.

Breathing hard, his eyes stinging from powder smoke, Frank let go of the dead Rurale and pushed himself to his feet. A few yards away, Esteban still huddled over Antonio's sprawled form, protecting the young man with his own body. Esteban's white cotton shirt was crimson now with blood. He had been hit several times, and as one of the Rurales rushed up to him, triggering a pistol, several more rounds ripped through the old man's body. He collapsed on top of Antonio.

Frank leaped forward, grabbing up a fallen rifle. He flung it like a spear, and the bayonet buried itself in the throat of the man who had just shot Esteban. The Rurale gave a gurgling scream as blood flooded down his chest from his ravaged throat. He stumbled and fell on his face to kick out the few remaining seconds of his life.

His face grim, Frank dropped to a knee beside Esteban and Antonio. He rolled the old man over and was surprised to see a smile on the wrinkled, nut-brown face. "Señor Morgan!" Esteban gasped. "It was . . . a good fight . . . no?"

"It was a good fight," Frank told him. "Hang on, Esteban, and I'll get you out of here." The fighting seemed to be dying down around them. Frank thought that if he could get Esteban on a horse . . .

The old man's fingers clawed at Frank's arm. "No! You must . . . leave me! Save Antonio!"

Frank looked at the young man. Antonio's hat had fallen off, and the mask had slipped down so that most of his face was visible. He was pale, but he was still breathing, Frank saw. The side of his black shirt was wet with blood, but he might have a chance. Esteban, on the other hand, was shot to pieces, and he and Frank both knew it.

The savage smile of battle had disappeared from Esteban's face, to be replaced by a look of mute appeal. Frank nodded and promised, "I'll do everything I can for him."

"*Gracias, Señor,*" Esteban gasped. "My life means nothing . . . save perhaps to . . . my wife and children . . . but the Black Scorpion must live . . . so that one day our people will be . . . free . . ."

"Your life means a lot more than that, *mi amigo,*" Frank told him. He saw a flicker of understanding and gratitude in Esteban's eyes, and then they glazed over in death. Gently, Frank closed the lids over that empty stare.

He came to his feet and looked around. Gunfire still blared here and there. The battle had spread out over a wide area, and bodies of both the revolutionaries and the Rurales were sprawled everywhere he looked. In the area right around Frank and Antonio, however, there was a lull in the battle.

Frank spotted Stormy about fifty yards away, and El Rey was with him. The big black stallion had survived the collision with the other horses and seemed to be all right. Frank whistled, and Stormy trotted toward him. El Rey followed.

That was good, Frank thought. He would put Antonio on the stallion and tie him into the saddle. Frank's only thought now was to get Antonio back to the Almanzar hacienda. Once he was there, his father and sister and the servants could care for him and perhaps nurse him back to health.

As the horses came up and stopped, Frank bent and grasped Antonio under the arms. He lifted the young man, gritting his teeth with the effort required. As long as he was unconscious, Antonio was so much deadweight.

El Rey shied a little when Frank began to lift Antonio into the saddle. No doubt the stallion was spooked by the smell of blood, as well as the reeking clouds of smoke. "Take it easy," Frank said quietly, trying to calm the horse. He strained until Antonio was on El Rey's back, and was then slumped forward in the saddle.

Suddenly, a savage yell came from behind Frank. He jerked his head around to see that one of the wounded Rurales had struggled to his feet and was lurching toward him, ready to run him through with a bayonet. Frank's Colt was empty, and the Rurale was almost on top of him, too close for him to avoid the lethal thrust of cold steel.

Before the bayonet could rip into Frank's belly, a brown and gray streak flew through the air and smashed into the Rurale from the side, knocking him off his feet. Dog landed on top of the man, and with one lunge, his razor-sharp teeth ripped out the Rurale's throat. The man's heels drummed against the ground as he died.

Snarling, Dog backed away from the body toward Frank. "Thanks, partner," Frank said wearily. "I'd have been a goner if it wasn't for you."

Frank called Stormy over, and with rawhide thongs that he took from his saddlebags, he lashed Antonio's ankles together under El Rey's belly. Then he tied the young man's hands to the saddle horn to keep him from slipping under the horse. Antonio would stay on El Rey now until somebody either untied him or cut the thongs.

Frank glanced around for his hat, which had come off during the fighting, but he didn't see it. There wasn't time to look for it, either. He mounted up quickly, caught hold of El Rey's reins, and said to Stormy and Dog, "Let's get out of here." He rode to the south, away from the scene of the battle.

He hadn't gone fifty yards when he heard shouting behind him and a volley of rifle fire rang out. Bullets whined around him. A look back over his shoulder showed him Captain Estancia screaming at several mounted Rurales.

"Stop them! Kill them!"

Frank dug his heels into Stormy's sides and sent the Appaloosa leaping forward into a gallop. He held El Rey's reins tightly, and the black stallion fell into a racing stride beside and just behind him.

It was a race now. Frank knew that he and Antonio were mounted on better horses than the Rurales were, but not even Stormy and El Rey could outrun a bullet. At least Antonio was still unconscious and slumped far forward over the stallion's neck, unwittingly making a smaller target of himself. Frank did likewise, bending over in the saddle as he urged Stormy on. Guiding the Appaloosa with his knees, he zigzagged back and forth a little to throw off the Rurales' aim.

Frank headed for the flats. If he could get out of the foothills and down there on more level ground, the superior speed of Stormy and El Rey would give him even more of an advantage over his pursuers. The Rurales hung in steadily behind them, though, banging away at him and Antonio. Luckily, the back of a racing horse wasn't very conducive to accurate shooting.

Although Frank's attention was focused on getting away from the Rurales, a part of him was sick at heart. Esteban was dead, and from what Frank had seen, so were many of the Black Scorpion's band. Even though many of the Rurales had been killed, Estancia had survived along with quite a few of his men. The ones he had lost could be replaced, although it might take a while to get reinforcements up here. His grip on power in this region had been shaken, but in the end he was going to emerge victorious, or at least not defeated.

For now, Frank told himself. But it wasn't over, not by a long shot.

What felt like a finger of fire touched him on the upper left arm. He gritted his teeth against the yell of pain that tried to come up his throat. When he looked down, he saw the rip in the sleeve of his jacket and shirt. A bullet had come close enough to rip the clothes and burn his flesh without breaking the skin. Luck was still smiling on Frank Morgan.

They came down out of the hills, two men on fine horses moving at breakneck speeds, and then Stormy and El Rey lunged forward in great, ground-eating strides across the flatland. When Frank looked over his shoulder he saw the Rurales falling farther and farther behind. Puffs of smoke still came from their rifles, but Frank and Antonio were nearly out of range. Most of the slugs were dropping short now.

The Rurales gave up, reining in and dropping back. They dwindled rapidly in Frank's sight until they were gone. The horses continued to run freely, flashing across the brush-dotted landscape. Frank didn't slow down until he was sure that no one could catch them now.

A short time later, he stopped to check on Antonio. The young man was still unconscious, but he groaned and his eyelids flickered a little. Frank took hold of a wrist and found his pulse. It was rapid and irregular, but fairly strong. Without taking Antonio down from El Rey's back, Frank tore his shirt away to have a look at the wound in his side. From the looks of it, the bullet had gone in the front and out the back, plowing a channel through Antonio's body. The wound was fairly shallow, though, and Frank hoped the slug had missed anything vital. It might have broken a rib or two, but when Frank put his ear close to Antonio's mouth and listened to his breathing, he was confident that the young man didn't have a punctured lung. Although the bullet holes were covered with black, dried blood, they weren't bleeding anymore. He thought that Antonio stood a good chance of recovering from this injury if the wound didn't fester and if he didn't get blood poisoning. Frank wished he had some whiskey or tequila. If he could have poured a bottle of liquor through those holes to clean them, Antonio's chances would be even better.

But he didn't have anything like that, so all he could do was push on toward the Almanzar hacienda and hope that Antonio was strong enough to hang on. Frank mounted up and heeled the Appaloosa into a lope, leading El Rey behind him. Dog padded along with them, bringing up the rear.

25

Difficult though it was to believe, considering everything that had happened, the hour was still pretty early in the day. Frank looked at the sun and estimated that it was around mid-morning. He couldn't make it back to the hacienda before nightfall. Rummaging around in his saddlebags, he found some jerky and bit off a piece of it. He chewed the tough, dried meat for a long time before he swallowed it. It seemed to give him a little strength. He washed the jerky down with some water from his canteen.

A short time later Frank stopped and managed to get Antonio to swallow a little water. The young man still wasn't awake enough to eat anything, although he mumbled incoherently. Frank rested a hand on his forehead and thought the skin was warmer than normal. Antonio might be developing a fever, and that wasn't a good sign.

They pushed on, with Frank stopping only occasionally to let the horses rest and to give Antonio more water. Stormy and El Rey might seem tireless, but Frank knew they really weren't. He had to be careful not to wear them out too much.

By midday clouds had begun to appear in the sky to the north. The wind at their backs freshened. Frank sniffed the air and thought he smelled rain. Sure enough, the clouds continued pushing south and swallowed up the sun, and less than an hour later, the first drops pattered down around them. The rain was light, hardly more than a drizzle, but it was cold and Antonio didn't need to be chilled.

Maybe the rain was really a blessing in disguise, though, Frank thought when he checked on the young man in the middle of the afternoon. Antonio's face was hot and he was definitely running a fever. He might have been burning up even worse if not for the rain.

Eventually they were both soaked. The drizzle became thicker. No one would be able to track them very easily in this, Frank told himself, and that was something else to be thankful for. But at the same time, the weather was liable to make it more difficult for him to locate the Almanzar hacienda. He didn't know this country well at all, and had been steering his course by keeping the mountains on his right hand. By late afternoon, with the rain and the overcast skies, everything was gray everywhere he looked, and he couldn't even see the mountains anymore. All he could do was hope that he had Stormy and El Rey plodding in the right direction and that he wouldn't ride past the hacienda without ever seeing it.

Frank reined in as Antonio cried out abruptly. He dismounted and stepped back to find that the young man was sitting up in the saddle and staring wildly around him. "Esteban!" Antonio called. "Lupe!"

"They're not here, 'Tonio," Frank said, using the familiar form of the name in hopes it would help him get through to Antonio. "I'm Frank Morgan. I'm taking you home."

"Carmen!"

"That's right, I'm taking you home to Carmen," Frank told him in a soothing voice.

Antonio stared at him with no recognition in his dark, burning eyes. "Mama," he croaked. Then he groaned and fell forward. Frank reached up to grab his shoulder and steady him. Antonio started muttering again as he closed his eyes, but none of the words made any sense to Frank. He was out of his head from fever and loss of blood. His black hair, soaked from the rain, fell down over his eyes. Frank pushed it back and then shook his head. There was nothing he could do for Antonio except what he was already doing.

Back in the saddle, he rode on. After a while he began to wonder if he was out of his head, too, because he could have sworn that he heard music in the rain.

He tugged on the reins, bringing Stormy to a halt. A frown corrugated his forehead. He blinked rainwater out of his eyes and looked around, searching for any sign of life other than that half-heard music. After a moment he thought he saw a tiny scrap of light in the gloom. Frank pointed the horses toward it and walked them forward.

The light vanished and the music stopped, and for a bad minute Frank believed he had imagined them both. But then the faint glow reappeared. Not only that, but he could see it better now, too, and he recognized its square shape. It was coming through a window. The rain had grown hard enough to obscure it momentarily, but now Frank knew it was real. "Come on, hoss," he said to Stormy, and his voice had such an exhausted croak to it that it sounded strange to his ears.

A few minutes later, he reined Stormy to a halt in front of a squalid little adobe hut that might as well have been the fanciest mansion in Philadelphia or New York to Frank Morgan's eyes. The hut had only one oilcloth-covered window, but the light in that window had served as a beacon, leading Frank here. He dismounted, so tired that he had to grab hold of the saddle horn for a second to steady himself when his feet hit the ground. Hanging onto the reins of both horses, he stumbled over to the door of the jacal and banged a fist on it.

"Help!" he called. "*Por favor!* I've got a wounded man out here, and I need help!"

"Step away from the door, Señor," a man's voice replied in English, "or I will shoot through it!"

"Damn it, I'm not looking for trouble!"

"Step back!" the voice ordered again.

Frank moved away from the door. "All right," he said. "I did what you told me."

The door swung inward, letting light spill out into the thickening gloom. Frank saw the twin barrels of a shotgun poke through the opening. "Who are you?" the hut's inhabitant demanded.

"My name is Frank Morgan. I have a wounded man with me. His name is Antonio Almanzar —"

"*Dios mio!*" the man exclaimed. "Don Antonio?" He appeared in the doorway, caution forgotten for the moment in his surprise. "I am one of Don Felipe's vaqueros. I have heard that you were a guest at the hacienda, Señor Morgan. What happened?"

Frank sighed with relief. This jacal had to be the Mexican equivalent of a line shack, and this man was one of Don Felipe's riders. "Give me a hand with him," Frank said. "He's been shot through the side."

The vaquero set his shotgun aside and hurried out into the rain. He was a short, stocky man wearing a poncho. He hadn't bothered to put on his sombrero, so the hard drizzle streamed off his black hair. Together, he and Frank untied the bindings that held Antonio on the black stallion and lowered the young man from the saddle. Antonio was unconscious again.

They carried him inside and the vaquero said, "Put him on my bunk, Señor."

"He's soaking wet, just like me," Frank pointed out.

"That matters not. He is the son of my *patrón*."

They lowered Antonio onto a rope bunk in the corner. As they straightened, the vaquero stared down at the young man. "*Madre de Dios,* is he going to die?"

Frank said, "Not if I can help it. Do you have any tequila here?"

"*Sí, Señor.*" The vaquero went over to a crate that served as a cabinet of sorts and he brought back a bottle. He drew the cork from the neck with his teeth and offered the bottle to Frank, evidently thinking that his visitor wanted a drink.

Instead, Frank knelt beside the bunk and pulled Antonio's torn shirt aside to expose the bullet holes in the young man's torso. During the long afternoon, the rain had gradually washed away most of the dried blood, leaving the raw, red-rimmed holes visible. Frank poured the tequila into the entrance wound, taking his time about it, letting the fiery liquor run all the way through and trickle out the exit wound, mixed with fresh blood. Antonio gasped and arched his back off the bunk.

"Hold him down!" Frank snapped at the vaquero.

Clumsily, the man did his best to help. Frank poured the tequila into the wound until he felt like it had been cleaned out as best he could manage under the circumstances. Antonio lay back on the bunk as the pain subsided a little. Frank handed the bottle to the vaquero and said, "You wouldn't happen to have any coffee, would you?"

"For Don Antonio, you mean, Señor?"

Frank smiled. "For me, amigo, because without it I think I might just go to sleep right here on your floor."

The vaquero's name was Hermando. He had been working for Don Felipe for several years and had a wife and three children and a cottage near the hacienda, where he would have been on this cold, rainy night if it had not been his turn to stay for a few days in this jacal. The hut was located near the boundary line of the Almanzar rancho, and Hermando's job was to push back any cattle that had strayed too close to or even over the line.

Frank sat at the rough-hewn table in the center of the jacal's single room, sipped coffee, and ate some goat stew that Hermando had warmed up for him over the flames in the tiny fireplace. The food made Frank feel a lot better. The fact that Antonio seemed to be sleeping fairly peacefully helped ease his mind, too.

Dog lay by the door, resting, his head on

his paws. Hermando hunkered in a corner near the fireplace and strummed the strings of the mandolin that Frank had heard him playing earlier. Frank said, "I'm glad you were feeling musical tonight, amigo. The music helped lead me to this place."

"A song is a good companion, Señor. It does not make me miss my wife and my little ones any less, but it makes being away from them more bearable." Hermando looked over at Antonio. "Everyone on the rancho knows that the Black Scorpion kidnapped Don Antonio. Did you snatch him from the clutches of that hombre, Señor Morgan? Was that how he came to be wounded?"

"Something like that," Frank said noncommittally. He had spent part of the long ride debating with himself whether or not to reveal the fact that Antonio was really the Black Scorpion. He had decided that for the time being he would play his cards close to the vest and keep that knowledge to himself. Esteban had known Antonio's secret, of course, but Frank had no idea if anyone else on the rancho was aware of it.

"The Rurales had gone after him, too. What happened to them?"

"They shot it out with the Black Scorpion's gang," Frank replied grimly. "I didn't see the end of the fracas, so I'm not sure what happened." That much, at least, was pretty much true.

"It would be too much to hope for that Capitán Estancia and his Rurales were all killed," Hermando muttered. "It is said that the Black Scorpion is an outlaw, but I have never seen any proof of it. At least, not until he raided Don Felipe's hacienda and stole Don Antonio. And even then, Señor, did you know that no one was killed or even wounded?"

That was because the raid had been staged, Frank thought. Antonio's followers had fired their shots high, creating a lot of sound and fury but not much real danger. In fact, the raiders had been in more danger than the hacienda's defenders, because the defenders hadn't known that it wasn't a real raid and had been trying to fight back. The lightning quickness of the foray had prevented any of Antonio's men from being killed, however.

"The Rurales, though," Hermando went on, "I *know* they are bad. Everyone around here lives in fear of them."

"That won't go on forever," Frank said. "Sooner or later somebody will put a stop to it."

"From your mouth to the ear of El Señor Dios, amigo."

Hermando had enough blankets to make pallets on the floor for himself and Frank. Earlier, Frank had put Stormy and El Rey in the little shed behind the hut with Hermando's horse. They had water and grain and Frank was confident they would be all right for the rest of the night. Having finished his food, he stood up and walked over to the bunk, carrying his tin cup of coffee. He sipped the last of it as he looked down at Antonio's pale, drawn face. Underneath the blanket that was spread over him, his chest rose and fell regularly. Frank had bandaged the wounds, and that was all he could do for Antonio now.

"In the morning, you can ride to the hacienda and fetch help," Frank said to Hermando. "Antonio might be able to ride the rest of the way, but it would be better if Don Felipe brought a wagon for him."

"*Sí, Señor.* If you prefer, I can stay with Don Antonio and you can go to the hacienda."

Frank shook his head. "You know the way better than I do, so you can make better time. The sooner this boy is back in his own bed, being cared for by somebody who knows what they're doing, the more likely it is that he'll recover."

"Of course, Señor. You must remember, though, that without you, he would already be dead. If he lives, it is you who have saved his life."

Frank drank the last of his coffee and stood there for a moment longer. He didn't care who got the credit for saving Antonio's life. Such things meant nothing to him. What was important was that the young man pull through and recover from his wounds.

And that somebody, somehow, should put a stop to the reign of terror being carried out by Captain Domingo Estancia and the Rurales, so that no more innocent men would be cut down by the ruthless bullets of bastards whose only goal was to steal freedom from those who deserved it.

26

Several times during the night, Antonio thrashed around and cried out and babbled nonsense without really waking up. Frank checked on him during those times and found that his fever was high. But in the morning, Antonio's face was covered with sweat despite the fact that the room was chilly. Frank knew that the fever had broken.

The rain had stopped but the sky was still overcast. Hermando left before dawn, setting out for the hacienda. Frank boiled a pot of coffee and made a skimpy breakfast on tortillas and beans. He was sitting at the table finishing up the meal when Antonio said weakly from the bunk, "Señor . . . Señor Morgan?"

Frank stood and walked over to him. Antonio tried to push himself up on an elbow. Frank rested a hand on his shoulder and eased him back down. "You're all right, Antonio," he said. "Just lie there and rest.

I'll get you some water if you want it."

"What . . . what happened? Am I shot?"

"You sure as hell are," Frank told him with a smile. "Bullet went right through your side. You're going to be all right, though. Probably have to be laid up for a while, but you'll get over that."

"Wh-where are we?"

"A jacal on your father's rancho. A vaquero named Hermando was staying here. He's gone back to the hacienda to fetch help. I imagine your father will be along later in the day with a wagon to take you home."

Antonio closed his eyes and sighed. "When I was hit, I thought surely I would die. That is the last thing I remember." He gasped and his eyes snapped open. "Esteban! Lupe! Where are they?"

Frank had hoped that Antonio wouldn't think of that right now. The shape he was in, the young man didn't need to get worked up about anything. Frank wasn't going to lie to him, though.

"I don't know where Lupe is. I lost track of him during the fight with Estancia's Rurales."

"Then he may still be alive!"

"He may be," Frank agreed.

"And Esteban?"

"Esteban . . . didn't make it."

Antonio groaned as if in mortal pain. Frank supposed that, in a way, he was.

"How . . . how did he die?"

This might just make it worse, Frank thought, but again, he wasn't going to lie. "When you were wounded, Esteban jumped right in the middle of those Rurales who had you surrounded. He fought them off and protected you with his own body. I got there as fast as I could to help him, but he'd already taken a bayonet thrust and been shot a few times. He kept you alive, Antonio."

"At the cost of his own life."

Frank nodded slowly. "It was a price he was willing to pay."

Antonio turned his head to the side and closed his eyes again. He drew a ragged breath. *"Dios mio,"* he murmured. *"Dios mio . . ."*

Frank brought the room's single chair over, reversed it, and straddled it. After a few minutes of silence, Antonio looked at him again and asked, "The other men with me . . . what happened to them?"

"A lot of them were killed. I don't know how many got away, if any. But they gave as good as they got before they went down. They probably wiped out half of Estancia's command."

"At the cost of *all* my command," Antonio said.

"They knew they were outnumbered and outgunned. The fight was of their choosing. And they struck a heavy blow against the Rurales. My guess is that Estancia will be licking his wounds for a while, instead of running roughshod over the countryside and terrorizing folks."

"But Estancia himself, he lives?"

Frank shrugged. "He was alive the last time I saw him, when I was riding away from there with you."

"That bastard. The fires of Hell are too good for him."

"You won't get any argument from me," Frank said.

Antonio fell silent again. After a few more minutes went by, he said, "When my father gets here, will you tell him that I am the Black Scorpion?"

"What's the point in that?" Frank asked. Until this moment, he still hadn't made up his mind what he would do, but now his course seemed clear. "It would only hurt Don Felipe to know that you staged your own kidnapping to finagle that ransom out of him. It just doesn't seem to matter anymore, does it?"

Antonio shook his head. "No. As you

said, it will be a long time before I recover from these wounds." With a shaking hand, Antonio pulled the bandanna from around his neck, wadded it up, and held it out to Frank. "The Black Scorpion might as well have died in battle."

"Might as well," Frank said as he took the bandanna and stuffed it in his pocket. "There's just one more thing I want to know before we lay the Black Scorpion to rest. Was it your men who jumped Cecil and Ben Tolliver a while back between San Rosa and the Rocking T and tried to kill them?"

Again, Antonio shook his head. "We have never done anything to harm any of the Tollivers, despite how my father feels about them."

That jibed with Frank's hunch, but it left unexplained the real identity of the raiders who had ambushed Tolliver and Ben. It had been a mixed bunch, both Mexicans and gringos, and so far in his adventures, Frank hadn't come across anything to indicate who those gun wolves had been working for.

Late in the morning, Frank heard the rattle of wagon wheels outside. Antonio had dozed off again, and Frank was letting him sleep. The young man needed the rest.

But he awoke as Dog barked at the wagon and riders who were approaching the jacal.

Frank stepped outside. Hermando had ridden to the hacienda on El Rey, and now Don Felipe was on the black stallion, riding alongside the covered wagon. Carmen sat on the wagon seat next to the vaquero who was handling the reins. Hermando and several other vaqueros trailed the vehicle.

When Don Felipe saw Frank, he spurred ahead. "My son," he said anxiously as he brought El Rey to a halt in front of the hut. "Does he still live?"

"He lives," Frank said with a smile and a nod. "The fever has broken. He still needs a lot of care, but I think he's going to be all right."

Don Felipe made the sign of the cross before dismounting. He closed his eyes and murmured thanks to the Blessed Virgin. Then he swung down from the saddle and strode to the doorway. Frank stepped aside to let him enter the jacal.

While Don Felipe was inside being reunited with his son, Frank went over to the wagon to help Carmen down from the seat. "He is truly all right?" she asked as soon as her feet were on the ground.

"As good as can be expected with a

bullet wound through his side," Frank told her.

"What of old Esteban?"

Frank shook his head. "He didn't make it."

Tears glittered in Carmen's dark eyes. "He was a good man. He was almost like a grandfather to me."

"He was quite a fighter, too."

For a moment, Carmen's face twisted in lines of hate. She spat, "Estancia! He is to blame for this. Esteban's blood is on his hands, as is the blood of my brother!"

"That's right. There was a showdown between the Rurales and the Black Scorpion's men, and that was when Antonio was wounded."

"But you saved his life, Señor Morgan. You brought him back from the threshold of death."

Frank shook his head. "I wouldn't go so far as to say that. I just put him on a horse and got him out of there. Hermando helped me patch him up when we got here last night."

Carmen took Frank's right hand in both of hers and said, "I cannot thank you, Señor. There are no words."

Frank leaned a little closer to her, lowered his voice, and asked, "You hear anything from Ben Tolliver?"

Carmen gave a quick shake of her head. "Nothing. But I know he told his family that you were all right and at our hacienda."

Frank was glad to hear that. He hadn't wanted the Tollivers — and Roanne Williamson — to be too worried about him when he didn't come back from below the border with the Rangers.

It seemed like months had passed since he rode across the Rio Grande, rather than just a couple of weeks. A little less than that, actually. His time in Mexico had been eventful.

Don Felipe appeared in the doorway. "Carmen, your brother wishes to see you."

Carmen hurried inside. Don Felipe came over to Frank and extended his hand. "I owe you more than I can ever repay you, Señor Morgan."

"You were calling me Frank, remember?" Frank said as he took Almanzar's hand.

"Of course. You will always be a friend to the Almanzar family, Frank. Anything that is within my power to do for you, you have only to ask."

"How about giving some thought to mending fences with Cecil Tolliver?"

The suggestion came out before Frank really thought about it, and yet he knew instinctively it was a good one. With all the problems going on in the border country, neither Don Felipe nor Cecil Tolliver needed the added distraction of their long, senseless feud.

A frown appeared on Don Felipe's face. "You do not know what you ask, *mi amigo.* I said I would do anything in my power . . . but some fences cannot be mended."

"How do you know if you don't try? Tell me the truth, Don Felipe: Since the trouble cropped up between you and Tolliver, have the two of you ever sat down and just tried to hash it all out?"

"I have not set foot on his land, nor he on mine," Don Felipe said stiffly.

"Well, there you go. If the two of you would talk, you might find that you could reach an understanding."

Almanzar shook his head. "No. Tolliver would never agree to such a meeting."

"Even if you were willing to go to his place?"

"Never! I would not trust him not to try to ambush me."

"And I reckon he'd feel the same way if you asked him to come to your hacienda," Frank said.

Don Felipe gave a snort of contempt. "No doubt! A man so unworthy of trust himself would never agree to trust another —" He stopped short and his frown darkened as he glowered at Frank. "A neat trap you have laid for me, Señor. Very neat indeed."

"I don't reckon I know what you're talking about, Don Felipe," Frank said. "But it sounds to me like what you two need is some neutral ground for your meeting."

"I never said there would be a meeting."

"But if there was, and if it was held someplace like, say, San Rosa, you and Tolliver could trust each other not to cause any trouble."

"San Rosa is on the Texas side of the river," Don Felipe pointed out.

"True enough, but it's not part of the Tolliver ranch."

"He has friends there."

"I don't think they'd stand for any sort of ambush, though." Frank shrugged. "It's up to you. I'd be glad to ride up to the Rocking T and carry a message to Tolliver for you. I could give you my word that I'd do my best to see that there's not any sort of double cross."

"Your guarantee?"

"That's right."

"And if there was trouble, you would stand at my side?"

Now Don Felipe was the one who had done a neat bit of boxing in. Frank had no choice but to go along with him. "I'll stand at your side," he said.

"Then it is a bargain. I will write a message for Cecil Tolliver, and you will carry it to him."

Frank nodded. He would be taking a chance, but it would be worth it to arrange a truce between the two ranchers, so that they could turn their attention to more pressing problems than an unnecessary feud.

A thick pallet was set up in the back of the wagon for Antonio. The vaqueros went into the jacal and carried him out, bunk and all, and then carefully lifted him into the wagon. Carmen stayed at his side all during the ride back to the hacienda. Once they were there, the vaqueros carried Antonio to his room, where the Indian women waited to clean his wounds, apply their healing ointments, and cover the wounds with fresh bandages.

Don Felipe took Frank into the parlor and poured glasses of brandy for both of them. "It will not seem the same around here without old Esteban," the don said with a sigh. "He seemed as unchanging, as eternal, as the mountains themselves."

"There's a good chance your son wouldn't be alive if not for Esteban," Frank said. "I trust you'll provide for his wife and children?"

"Of course." Don Felipe chuckled. "Some of Esteban's children are grown, with children and grandchildren of their own. And yet his wife's belly is heavy with a new child. An amazing man, Esteban."

Frank lifted his glass. "I'll drink to that."

They drank their brandy in a silent, solemn memorial to Esteban's passing.

After a moment went by, Don Felipe said, "You must tell me what happened, Frank. Who shot my son? The Black Scorpion's *bandidos* — or Estancia's Rurales?"

"It was Estancia's men. With Esteban's help, I had gotten into the Black Scorpion's camp. I'm not sure they were really what you'd call *bandidos*. I think mostly they were just interested in fighting the Rurales."

Don Felipe nodded slowly. "From everything I have heard about them, I am not surprised. They never attacked the common people, only those who worked with Estancia."

"From what I heard while I was there,

334

Estancia is closer to a bandit than the Black Scorpion was. He's mixed up with all the smuggling that goes on along this part of the border, and he's got regular folks living in terror of him." Frank's voice hardened as he went on. "I saw again for myself how he treats people. He took over a village not far from the Scorpion's hideout and was about to torture the villagers into betraying what they knew about the revolutionaries."

"Revolutionaries?" Don Felipe repeated. "That is what the Black Scorpion and his men call themselves?"

"That's right."

Almanzar poured more brandy. "As good a name as any, perhaps. Go on, Frank."

"The Black Scorpion and his men attacked the Rurales rather than let them kill more of the villagers." That wasn't exactly the way it had happened, Frank thought, but close enough. "Antonio was still with them when the showdown came, and he was wounded in the fighting. Esteban was killed defending him. I was able to get him on El Rey and get out of there. We made it back to that jacal where Hermando was staying, and you know the rest."

"What of the Black Scorpion?"

Frank shook his head. "Gone. Whether he's dead or not, I don't know. Most of his men were wiped out, though, so I wouldn't expect to see him around any time soon, if ever again."

"And the Rurales?"

"Estancia was alive the last I saw. He suffered heavy losses. But he can get replacements up here, I reckon. Nobody in Mexico City knows that he's more interested in setting up his own outlaw empire than he is in carrying out El Presidente's orders."

"If someone was to get in touch with the authorities and tell them the truth . . ." Don Felipe mused.

"It might do some good, eventually," Frank said, "but it might not. I imagine Estancia is paying off some of his superiors to keep his activities covered up."

Don Felipe jerked his head in a nod. "Unfortunately, you are probably correct about that. It may be that the Rurales are a problem the people will have to deal with on their own."

"Most of the time the people are to be trusted more than the government, anyway."

Don Felipe sighed. "This is certainly true in my country." He took a deep breath. "But for now, at least, Estancia's plans have been damaged. Perhaps by the time he rebuilds his forces, things will have changed."

"We can hope so." Frank knew better than to count on that, however. Change usually came slowly.

"In the meantime, I have a son to nurse back to health, and — perhaps — fences to mend."

"I'll drink to that, too," Frank said.

27

Frank took a couple of days to rest up from all the excitement and danger before he rode back across the Rio Grande. Though still vital and healthier than most men twenty years younger than him, he wasn't as young as he had once been. Good food and plenty of sleep, coupled with his own hardy constitution, put him back at full strength pretty quickly, though.

Before he left, Don Felipe summoned him to the parlor and made a presentation to him. "You mentioned that you lost your hat during the fight with the Rurales," Don Felipe said as he held out a brown felt sombrero, its band studded with conchos and its brim decorated by crimson and gold needlework. Carmen stood to one side, watching. "Allow me to replace it, amigo."

Frank grinned as he took the hat. "*Muchas gracias,* Don Felipe. I don't reckon I've ever seen a finer sombrero." He set it on his head and tightened the bead on the chin strap.

Carmen clapped her hands and laughed. "You look like a vaquero now, Señor Morgan. Surely at least a drop of Mexican blood flows in your veins."

"Well, maybe so," Frank said. "I don't rightly know."

Don Felipe gave him an envelope as well. "This is the letter I have written to Cecil Tolliver, suggesting that we meet in San Rosa one week from today. If he is agreeable, I will see him there. If not . . ." The don shrugged. "At least I tried, as you asked of me, Frank."

"And I appreciate that," Frank said as he tucked the envelope in his shirt pocket. He shook hands with Don Felipe and gave Carmen a hug and a kiss on the cheek. He told her, "Say good-bye to your brother for me."

"I will, Señor Morgan," she promised. "Antonio will be upset that you left while he was sleeping."

"He needs his rest, and I need to be riding. Besides, I reckon I'll probably see him again one of these days."

Antonio was still flat on his back in his bed, resting and recovering from his wound. He had lost a lot of blood, and Frank figured it would be at least a week before the young man was up and around again.

Don Felipe and Carmen followed Frank outside. Stormy and Dog waited for him in front of the wrought-iron gate in the outer wall. Frank swung up into the saddle and lifted a hand in farewell as he rode away from the Almanzar hacienda.

Stormy had had more than enough rest, and the big Appaloosa was obviously glad to be on the move again. He stretched his legs out into an easy lope that ate up the miles. Dog kept up easily, venturing off to the sides of the trail in hopes of scaring up a rabbit or a lizard.

As he rode, Frank thought about everything that had happened. Since the ransom hadn't been needed, Don Felipe had returned to Nuevo Laredo and sent wires arranging for the money's return to Frank's accounts, where it had come from to start with. He had also brought back to the hacienda the stories he had heard in the border city about how Captain Domingo Estancia's Rurale company had suffered grievous losses in a battle with *bandidos*. Captain Estancia had appealed to Mexico City for new men to replace those he had lost. In the meantime, the Rurales who were left would continue their regular patrols as best they could. As for the *bandidos,* Estancia's report stated that they had been wiped out to the last man. Frank knew that wasn't the case. He knew at least one man — Antonio — had escaped, and he wouldn't have been surprised if a few of the others had as well. Estancia just didn't want to admit that.

Late in the day, Frank forded the Rio Grande at a shallow crossing and sent Stormy up the northern bank. He was back on Texas soil at last, and that felt mighty good. He wasn't sure exactly where he was, but he knew that if he kept going, sooner or later he would strike the main trail between San Rosa and the Rocking T.

The sun was just about down when he did so. Judging the Tolliver ranch to be to his right, Frank turned Stormy in that direction.

He had ridden less than half a mile when he spotted a small adobe ranch house off to the side of the road, with a barn and a large corral behind it. It appeared to be a well-kept layout, and Frank knew it must belong to one of Cecil Tolliver's neighbors. He would have ridden on past without giving the place a second thought, if a gunshot had not suddenly rung out from somewhere over by the house.

That made Frank rein in for a moment. He was curious but not worried. This was Texas, after all. There could be all sorts of innocent explanations for a single shot: The rancher could have killed a snake or tried to run off a coyote, or something else like that.

The woman's scream that followed on the heels of the gunshot was what made Frank stiffen in the saddle and stare toward the little spread.

Something was wrong over there, no doubt about that, he thought. He heeled Stormy into motion again, turning the Appaloosa so that he was trotting toward the ranch house.

As he came closer, Frank saw three men on horseback in front of the house. One of them held a revolver with a thin curl of smoke rising from the barrel. A man lay on the ground just in front of the doorway, writhing in pain as he used his good hand to clutch at a bullet-shattered shoulder. A woman knelt beside him, sobbing as she tried to comfort him. She lifted her head as she cried out, "You didn't have to shoot him!"

"I thought he was goin' for a gun,"

drawled the man holding the smoking Colt. He slid the weapon back in the holster on his hip.

"He isn't even carrying a gun!" the distraught woman accused.

"Maybe he ought to start," one of the other mounted men said. "If he's goin' to be a troublemaker, he better be ready when it comes to call."

"Nobody's trying to start any trouble," the woman insisted.

"That ain't the way it looks to us."

Frank was close enough to hear the exchange, which meant that the men could hear Stormy's hoofbeats. One of them said to the others, "Somebody's comin'," and they all swung their horses around so that they were facing Frank. In the thickening shadows, he couldn't see their faces very well. They were just shapes on horseback.

But that meant they couldn't see him very well, either, and that was confirmed as one of the men snorted in contempt and said, "Hell, it's just some damned greaser."

They saw the sombrero, Frank thought. It was hard to miss, even in bad light. He pulled Stormy back to a walk and then halted at the edge of the small yard in front of the ranch house. His head was tipped forward a bit so that the broad brim of the sombrero obscured his face even more.

"What do you want, Pancho?" one of the men snapped. Frank had heard the voices of all three and knew that they were Texans.

"I heard a shot, Señor," he said. "I thought perhaps something was wrong."

"Something's wrong, all right. What's wrong is that you're messin' in something that's none o' your business, pepperbelly. Why don't you just ride on outta here?"

"Wait a minute," one of the others said. "Look at that horse he's ridin'. Where'd a Mex get a fine-lookin' horse like that? Most of 'em ride donkeys, don't they?"

"I'll bet he stole it," the third man said.

Frank said, "No, Señor, this is my horse. I am not a thief."

"Well, if you don't want to be strung up as one anyway, light a shuck, Pancho," the first man said. "This don't concern you."

Frank gestured toward the wounded man on the ground. "What did he do?"

"Gave us some lip, that's what he did. And if you don't want what he got in return for it, you'll turn around and get your Meskin ass outta here."

"Wait a minute, Dewey," one of the other men said. "Don't you reckon the greaser ought to leave that horse here with us, until we find out for sure whether he's lyin' about stealin' it?"

"Yeah," Dewey said. "That's a right fine idea, Terrall." He moved his hand closer to the butt of his gun. "Get down off that horse, Mex. It's too good an animal for the likes of you."

"You would take my horse, Señor?" Frank said.

"Damn right! Now do what I told you."

Frank had looked the men over in the fading light as best he could, and he had them pegged as drifting hard cases, the sort of scum who would shoot down an unarmed man. They probably planned to rob this place, and there was no telling what they would do to the rancher's wife. Frank remembered a time when a decent woman would have been safe from even the most hardened, ruthless owlhoot. But the West was changing, and not necessarily for the better. That was "progress" for you.

"It seems to me, Señor, that if there is a horse thief here, it is you," Frank said.

"Why, you dirty pepperbelly!" the one called Terrall exclaimed.

"But if you're bound and determined to try to take my horse," Frank went on, "then you've got it to do." With his left hand, he pushed the sombrero back off his head so that it hung by its chin strap.

"Dewey," the third man said nervously, "he ain't a greaser! He's a white man, ridin' an Appaloosa, and he's got a big dog with him —"

"Son of a bitch!" Terrall burst out. "He's —"

"I don't give a damn who he is!" Dewey yelled. His hand stabbed toward his gun. "Hook and draw, you bastard!"

Facing odds of three to one and not knowing how fast on the draw these men were, Frank couldn't afford to waste any time. He drew smoothly and swiftly, in less time than it would take a man to blink his eyes. Stormy stood absolutely still, having experienced many moments like this before. Frank fired without seeming to aim, the Colt in his hand bucking and crashing twice, the shots so close together they sounded almost like one. He put the first two slugs in Dewey's chest, since Dewey was the first one to get his gun out. The hard case went backward out of the saddle like a giant hand had slapped him down.

The third shot came hard on the heels of the first two and slammed into the chest of the man whose name Frank hadn't heard yet. And he might never know it, because the man toppled from his saddle and was dead before he hit the ground. That left the one called Terrall, and Terrall managed to get one wild shot off before Frank's fourth bullet punched through his sternum. Terrall's shot had gone harmlessly into the ground between Stormy and the other horses. He dropped his gun and clutched the saddle horn with his right hand as he swayed backward. Shakily, he lifted his left hand and pressed it to his chest. Blood welled between his fingers.

"You've killed me!" he gasped.

"Your choice," Frank told him coldly. "It wasn't my idea."

"You . . . you're Frank . . . Morgan!"

A line of crimson leaked from the corner of Terrall's mouth as he gasped the name. With a groan, he swayed back and forth and then toppled out of the saddle, falling heavily to the ground like a cut-down tree going over. He flopped in the dust and didn't move.

Dog padded forward and sniffed at all three of the men. When he didn't growl at any of them, Frank knew they were all dead. Trusting Dog's senses, Frank holstered his Peacemaker and swung down from the saddle. He stepped over to the wounded rancher and knelt beside him. The man's wife was on his other side, and she looked at Frank with something like amazement in her stunned eyes.

"You . . . you killed all three of them," she said in awed tones.

"They slapped leather first," Frank told her. "I wouldn't lose much sleep over the likes of them, ma'am." He bent his head to take a look at her husband's wound. "Let's see about patching up this bullet hole, friend."

"I . . . I'm much obliged, mister," the rancher said through teeth gritted against the pain. "I reckon they would've killed me, and no tellin' what they would have done . . . to Doris . . ."

"Well, you don't have to worry about that," Frank assured him. "Those hard cases won't ever bother anybody else." He slipped an arm around the man's shoulders and another under his knees. "Let's get you inside."

Grunting a little from the effort, Frank lifted the wounded man and carried him into the ranch house. The man's wife hurried ahead and indicated the room where Frank should take him. "Put him down there on the bed," she said as Frank carried the man into a small bedroom.

"Dang it, Doris," the rancher said, "I'll get . . . blood on the sheets."

"If you think I'm worried about a little thing like that, then you don't know me very well, Howard Longwell," she told him.

"I'd listen to her if I was you, Howard," Frank said with a smile as he lowered the man onto the bed.

Longwell's wife fetched a basin of water and a clean cloth and began washing the blood away from his wounded shoulder. Frank thought there was probably a broken bone or two in there, but if the doctor came out from San Rosa and set them properly, they might knit up all right. Longwell might not ever get the full use of his arm back, though, and Frank felt anger burning inside him as he watched the woman minister to her husband. Those bastards outside had sure enough had it coming, he thought.

Longwell appeared to have lost consciousness, either from loss of blood or the shock of being shot, or both. Without looking up from what she was doing, the woman said quietly, "You'd better get back on your horse and ride, mister. Don't stop until you've covered a lot of miles."

"I was thinking I ought to ride into San Rosa to find a doctor for your husband, ma'am."

"You don't want to do that. You've done enough. You saved Howard's life, and probably mine, too. They wouldn't have wanted to leave any witnesses behind. But that's no reason for you to throw away your own life."

Frank frowned. "Are you saying those fellas had kinfolk or partners or something like that who might come after me?"

She looked up at him then, her face startled in the light from the lamp on the table beside the bed. "You don't know, do you?" she said. "You really don't know who those men were."

"Drifting owlhoots, from the look of them," Frank said.

The woman began to laugh, but there was no humor in the sound. "Go take another look," she told him, "and then ride out, as far and as fast as you can."

Frank didn't intend to run, no matter who the men had been. When the Good Lord was putting him together, he hadn't put in much back-up. But Frank was curious, and he stepped outside the little ranch house to satisfy that curiosity.

Only a faint red glow remained in the western sky, all that was left of the daylight. Frank reached into his pocket, dug out a lucifer, and snapped the match to life with a thumbnail. He held it down so that the glare from the flame washed over the men he had killed.

Terrall and the man whose name Frank didn't know lay on their sides, facing away from him. But Dewey had landed flat on his back and lay that way still, with his arms flung out to the sides. He stared up sightlessly into the deep blue sky where stars were beginning to be visible. His vest had fallen open so that the light from the lucifer shone clearly on the breast of his shirt.

And on the five-pointed silver star set inside a silver circle carved from a Mexican five-peso piece. Frank recognized it with a shock that went through him all the way to the bone.

Pinned to the dead man's chest was the badge of the Texas Rangers.

28

Frank stood there stiffly for a long moment, trying to figure out how it had come about that he had shot and killed three Texas Rangers. He had always considered himself a law-abiding man, even when peace officers who were distrustful of his reputation had tried to run him out of their jurisdictions. His closest friend in recent years was a Ranger, and Frank Morgan had helped that famous organization on more than one occasion, even to the point of risking his own life.

But now, in the blink of an eye and the flash of six-guns, everything had changed. Even though Dewey and the other two had wounded the rancher, Howard Longwell, and had drawn first on Frank, in the eyes of the Rangers, Frank would be considered a murderer. They would add him to their Doomsday Book and hunt him down. . . .

The flame reached Frank's fingers. He

shook out the lucifer and dropped it at his feet, only to take another one from his pocket and light it. He stepped over to the other two men and used the toe of his boot to roll them onto their backs. He wanted to make sure they wore Ranger badges, too.

They did. Frank hadn't seen the badges during the confrontation because what little daylight had been left was at the backs of the three men, throwing their fronts into even deeper shadow. Frank cursed silently anyway, telling himself that he should have noticed the silver stars.

The dead men's horses, spooked by the shooting, had wandered off a short distance. Frank walked over and rounded them up, taking the reins of all three animals and leading them back to the corral, where he tied them to the top rail. Stormy was all right where he was and would stay there in front of the house, ground-hitched, until Frank told him otherwise. "Guard," Frank said to Dog, and then went back inside. If anyone approached the ranch house, the big cur would let him know.

Doris Longwell must have heard his footsteps in the front room, because she appeared in the doorway to the bedroom and asked, "What are you doing still here?

You have to get away before anybody comes to look for those men."

"They're Rangers," Frank said sharply. "Texas Rangers."

The woman gave that same hollow laugh. "I know."

"What were they doing here? Why did they shoot your husband?"

She didn't answer the question. Instead she said, "I heard one of them call you Frank Morgan. Is that your name?"

"It is."

"The one they call The Drifter?"

"Some do," Frank said with a nod.

"I heard about how you helped Cecil Tolliver a while back. You even rode with the Rangers when they were chasing that Black Scorpion fella."

"That's right."

"But you don't know what the Rangers are really like around here," Doris Longwell said. "They don't really care about the law. They just run things to suit themselves."

A frown creased Frank's forehead again. He recalled Cecil Tolliver saying something about how the Ranger company under Nathan Wedge operated in a sort of heavy-handed manner. He could understand how some folks might see it that way, even if it wasn't actually the case. The Rangers were accustomed to being pretty much a law unto themselves. They didn't have to answer to local authorities, only to the governor back in Austin.

It suddenly reminded Frank a little of the way the Rurales operated across the line in Mexico.

But that was crazy, he told himself. Estancia and the Rurales had turned renegade and were working for themselves now, not for El Presidente Diaz. The same couldn't be true of Wedge and the other Rangers.

But Howard Longwell, apparently an honest rancher, was lying in the other room with a bullet-shattered shoulder, having been gunned down by a Texas Ranger. Longwell hadn't even been packing iron when he was shot. And Dewey and the others had tried to steal Stormy, Frank reminded himself. True, they had believed him to be a Mexican at the time, but that was no excuse for stealing a horse.

"How's your husband?"

"Sleeping right now," Doris Longwell said. "He needs a doctor, but I reckon it'll be tomorrow before I can get one out here from town."

"You don't have any ranch hands you

can send to San Rosa?"

She shook her head. "There are a couple of boys who work here during the day, but they go home at night. That's all Howard and I can afford."

"I'll fetch a sawbones, then," Frank said. "But first, I want to know what happened before I rode up. The whole story."

Doris Longwell sighed. "I reckon I owe you that much. We raise horses here, Mr. Morgan, not longhorns. Mighty good horses, if I do say so myself. A couple of days ago Howard was in the settlement, and that Captain Wedge came up to him and told him he wanted to buy some of our riding stock for the Rangers. But the price he offered Howard wasn't even half of what the horses are really worth. When Howard told Captain Wedge he couldn't sell them for that price, Wedge got upset and said that since it was for the Rangers, he could just take the horses if he wanted to and not pay Howard a dime." She smiled sadly and shook her head. "Howard, bless his heart, isn't much of one for arguing. He just shook his head and told Wedge he couldn't do that. Wedge went on his way and Howard figured it was all over. But today those men showed up and said they'd come for the horses. When

Howard said they couldn't take them, that man . . . the first one you shot . . . he pulled his gun and . . . and shot Howard. He didn't warn him or anything, just . . . shot him."

Tears were rolling down her cheeks by this time, and she was trembling. Frank stepped closer to her and said, "Don't worry, ma'am. I'll ride on to San Rosa tonight and see to it that the doctor comes out to tend Howard."

"What about . . . what about those men?" she asked, rolling her eyes toward the door.

Instead of answering her directly, Frank said, "Does Howard have a pistol?"

"What? A pistol? Yes, but . . . why do you want to know?"

"Better let me have it for a minute," Frank told her.

She went into the bedroom and came back with a coiled shell belt and holstered Colt. "He usually wears it when he's out working on the ranch, but he'd already taken it off for the evening. We were . . . we were going to be eating supper soon."

Frank took the revolver out of the holster and checked to see that it was loaded. It was, with five rounds in the cylinder and the hammer resting on an empty. He carried the gun outside, cocked it, and fired one round into the ground. Then he put it back in the holster with the hammer still on the spent cartridge.

"Howard's not much of a hand with a gun, is he?" Frank asked when he came inside and gave the Colt and the gun belt back to the woman.

Doris smiled again, this time with genuine fondness. "Bless his heart, no. He's a hard worker and a fair shot with a rifle, but nobody would ever mistake him for a gunfighter."

"Good. If anybody asks, he was about to start cleaning this pistol when it went off and accidentally shot him in the shoulder." Frank looked at her intently. "You understand that, Mrs. Longwell?"

She took a deep breath and nodded. "Yes. Yes, I think I do."

"You never saw those three outside. They never rode up here."

"That's right. Howard and I haven't had any visitors this evening until you rode up."

"And that was after Howard accidentally plugged himself," Frank went on. "So when I saw that he was hurt, I offered to ride to San Rosa and fetch the doc."

"And that was very kind of you," Doris Longwell said.

Frank nodded and went out, taking up Stormy's reins and leading the Appaloosa toward the corral and the Rangers' horses. He didn't know if the woman would be able to stick to the story or not, but he thought she might. He untied the other horses and led them away from the corral.

Doris Longwell stepped into the doorway with the light behind her as Frank bent and hefted each corpse in turn, throwing the bodies over their saddles. Frank said to her, "You might ought to get a broom and brush out all these hoofprints once I'm gone."

"You're taking a big chance, Mr. Morgan."

"No reason for this trouble to come back on you and your husband. I'm the one who shot these men."

"To save us."

"Well, that was part of it," Frank admitted with a smile. "But they threatened to take *my* horse, too, and I'm a mite touchy about things like that."

"Be careful, Mr. Morgan," she said quietly.

"I intend to," Frank said.

He lashed the bodies in place and then mounted up himself. Saying, "Come on, Dog," he rode out, leading the other horses with their grisly burdens and putting the Longwell spread behind them.

Frank rode toward the Rio Grande, steering by the stars and his own reliable sense of direction. He reached the river a short time later. The moon had not yet risen, so it was a dark night.

One by one, he lifted the bodies from the horses. He unpinned the badges from their shirts and threw them out into the river as far as he could. Then he rolled the dead men off the bank into the water. The Rio Grande was a slow-moving stream, but it had enough of a current to carry the corpses downriver for quite a way. They might travel for miles if they didn't hang up on some sort of snag. Then Frank led the now-riderless horses across the river to Mexico. He removed the saddles and hid them in some thick chaparral. Then he used the sombrero Don Felipe had given him to swat the horses' rumps and send them trotting off to the south. Somebody would probably find the animals and claim them. At the very least, he had delayed the discovery of what had happened at the Longwell ranch, hopefully for several days.

But it had been hard, he mused as he rode Stormy back across the river to Texas. Each big splash as a body landed in the

Rio had been like an accusation to Frank. Even though he had killed the three men in a fair fight, and even though they had been trying to steal the Longwells' horses and might have even killed the couple, they were still Texas Rangers. Killing them rubbed Frank the wrong way, no matter how much he told himself that it shouldn't. Concealing what had happened bothered him, too. He had always been the sort of man to carry out his actions in the open, where everyone could see them. Sneaking around just wasn't in his nature.

It was necessary, though, to protect the Longwells. Once he got that through his head, he felt better. When you got right down to it, Dewey, Terrall, and the other man had been acting like outlaws, not Rangers, and as Frank had told Mrs. Longwell, he wasn't going to lose any sleep over ventilating them. They had deserved it.

He made his way back to the road and turned left this time, toward San Rosa. The moon rose, providing enough light so that he could push Stormy at a faster pace. It wasn't long before he spotted a small clump of twinkling lights up ahead. The lights grew larger, and he knew he was approaching the settlement.

A few minutes later he got his first look at San Rosa as he walked the Appaloosa down the main street. It was a typical Texas cow town, with a main street lined with businesses for several blocks, a few cross streets, and a scattering of houses and churches around the downtown district. The Spanish influence from nearby Mexico could be seen in the large open plaza in the center of town and in the architecture of the buildings made of adobe. There were frame buildings, too, including a couple of false-fronted saloons. Quite a few horses were tied up at the hitch rails in front of each oasis, and a few people strolled along the boardwalks in spite of the relative lateness of the hour. A lot of the citizens of San Rosa probably went to bed with the chickens, but not everybody.

Frank hailed one of the men on the boardwalk and asked him, "Is there a doctor in town?"

"There are three," the townie replied with a touch of pride in his voice. But then he added, "You don't want Doc Caldwell tendin' to you unless you just have to, though, mister. I don't reckon he's been completely sober since '85 or '86. And Doc Kuykendall's gone down to Laredo. That leaves Doc Ervin, I reckon."

"Where can I find him?" Frank asked, trying to contain his impatience.

The citizen pointed. "Right on down the street a couple of blocks. Look for a white house on the left side of the road. The doc lives there with his wife and son, got his office there, too."

"Much obliged," Frank said and started to turn Stormy away.

"Hey, mister," the local called. "You ain't a Mexican, are you?"

"No," Frank said.

"Then how come you're wearin' a Mexican hat?"

"To keep the sun off my head," Frank said, and he heeled Stormy into a trot before the man could ask any more questions.

He found the doctor's house without any trouble. Doc Ervin was a tall, spare man in late middle age with a wife and a half-grown son. Frank explained that he had ridden up to the Longwell ranch right after Howard Longwell had accidentally shot himself in the shoulder.

"I'll get my buggy and ride out there right away," the physician promised as he stood on the front porch of the neat white house. "I know the Longwells. Good people." He turned and called into the house to his son. "Bob, go out back and hitch up the buggy. We're going on a call."

Frank thanked the man and then walked back out to untie Stormy's reins from the neat picket fence around the yard. He mounted up and rode along the street toward one of the saloons. San Rosa's only café appeared to be closed for the night, but Frank hoped he could get a cup of coffee and maybe something to eat at the saloon. It was called the Border Palace, according to the sign on its false front. The border wasn't too far away, Frank reflected with a wry smile, but it would be stretching things to call this drinking establishment palatial.

He tied Stormy to the hitch rail, told Dog to stay, and stepped up onto the boardwalk. The night was cool, so the doors of the saloon were closed. They opened just as Frank reached them, and he stopped so that the man leaving the saloon would have room to get by.

Instead the man who stepped onto the boardwalk stopped short, grunted in surprise, and said, "Morgan?"

In the light that spilled out through the open door, Frank found himself looking at Captain Nathan Wedge of the Texas Rangers.

29

Frank stared at Wedge for a second and then nodded curtly. "Captain," he said. "I didn't expect to see you again so soon after I rode in."

"I didn't expect to see you at all," Wedge said. "I thought you'd been killed down there in Mexico, when we had that ruckus with the Black Scorpion's gang."

"Hung around to look for me, did you?" Frank asked coolly.

In the light from the saloon, he saw Wedge's face flush angrily. "Nobody knew where you'd gotten off to, and I had wounded men to get back across the border and take care of. I'm sorry if that rankles you, Morgan, but my first duty is to my men."

"I reckon I can understand that," Frank said. "Anyway, I'm all right."

"And I'm glad to hear it." Wedge inclined his head toward the door of the saloon. "We're letting the night air in. Come inside and have a drink with me."

"You weren't about to leave?"

"It was nothing that can't wait. Come on."

It wouldn't do any harm to have a drink with Wedge, Frank decided. Even though he harbored some suspicions about the man after what had happened out at the Longwell ranch, he wasn't ready just yet to assume that Wedge had crossed over to the wrong side of the law. It was possible that Dewey, Terrall, and the other man had been acting on their own, rather than following Wedge's orders. Most of the Rangers were fine, upstanding frontiersmen, but a few rotten apples could work their way into any organization.

Frank followed Wedge into the Border Palace. The Ranger captain closed the door behind them. He walked to the bar. Frank moseyed along behind him, taking advantage of the opportunity to see how the citizens of San Rosa regarded Wedge. Some of the men in the room lowered their eyes and didn't look at the Ranger. Others glared at him and then looked away. A few seemed nervous and afraid, and a few more stared at Wedge with what looked to Frank like outright hatred in their eyes.

But out of the couple of dozen men in the saloon, not a one of them seemed to actually like Wedge.

Being a lawman didn't automatically make a fella popular, Frank reminded himself. In fact, often just the opposite was true. But Frank had seldom seen a situation such as this, where everyone seemed either to be afraid of Wedge, or to hate him, or both.

"Couple of beers, barkeep," Wedge said as he rested his left hand on the polished hardwood bar. With a surly expression on his face, the bartender drew the beers and slid them over in front of Wedge. The captain tossed a coin onto the bar.

The apron stared at the coin and said, "What's that, Captain?"

Wedge frowned and flipped his hand. "For the beers."

"You know I can't charge you, Captain."

"Nonsense. I always pay my way." Wedge's face was getting red again.

Stubbornly, the bartender shook his head. "No, sir. You know your money's no good here, Captain Wedge."

"Well, I'm damned if I'm going to stand here all night arguing with you." Wedge picked up the coin and put it back in his pocket. "Drink up, Morgan."

Frank picked up one of the mugs of beer and drank from it. He said to the bartender, "You have any coffee on the stove, maybe something to eat?"

"Are you one of the Rangers, sir?" the man asked.

"Nope."

The bartender seemed to warm up to him a little. "Got a pot of stew in the back, and coffee, too."

"Bring it on," Frank said. "And I'll be paying for it."

"Sure, mister."

Wedge glowered as he drank some of the beer. "Man's got a burr up his butt about something," he muttered after the bartender had stepped through a door behind the bar.

"Seemed pleasant enough to me," Frank commented.

Wedge changed the subject by asking sharply, "Where have you been, Morgan? It's been almost two weeks since you disappeared."

"I was a guest at the rancho of Don Felipe Almanzar."

Wedge grunted. "Almanzar, eh? I don't know the man, but I hear he's a troublemaker and hates gringos. Especially Cecil Tolliver."

"He was hospitable enough to me," Frank said. His instincts told him not to say anything about the effort he was making to patch things up between Don Felipe and Cecil Tolliver.

"Well, you're lucky he didn't kill you." Wedge looked over at him. "One of my men said he thought he saw you chasing after the Black Scorpion. Is that right?"

"I went after him, but I didn't get him," Frank replied truthfully.

"Did you get a good look at him?"

"Not really. He always had his mask on. But it wouldn't have mattered if I did. I wouldn't have known who he was, now would I?"

"No, I reckon not," Wedge admitted. "I just thought you might be able to describe him. A good description might help us catch up to him one of these days." He took another drink of the beer and then added, "I could pass it on to the Rurales, too. They'd like to catch that son of a bitch."

Since Wedge had given him the opening, Frank took advantage of it. "I don't know that I'd be too helpful to the Rurales if I was you, Captain. From what I heard over there, they've gone bad. Turned renegade."

Wedge set his mug on the bar with a

thump. "That can't be!" he said. "I know the commander of the local company, Captain Estancia. He's a fine officer."

"Is that so?"

"That's right." Wedge's eyes narrowed angrily. "You don't know what you're talking about, Morgan."

Frank shrugged and appeared to take no offense, despite the anger he felt inside. "I'm just going by what I heard."

"Well, you heard wrong," Wedge snapped. A moment of tense silence went by. Wedge broke it by saying, "Are you going back out to the Rocking T?"

"Thought I would tomorrow."

"What brings you to town tonight?"

Frank decided it was time to take a chance. He said, "I was looking for a doctor."

"A doctor?" Wedge repeated with a frown. "You don't look hurt to me."

"Wasn't for me. I rode up to a little ranch outside of town where a fella had accidentally shot himself in the shoulder while he was cleaning his six-gun. When I saw how bad he was hurt I offered to fetch a sawbones for him. Doc Ervin's on his way out there now."

"Hombre shot himself, did he? You get his name?"

"Longwell, I think," Frank said. "Harry, Howard, something like that."

Wedge had a good poker face, but not quite good enough. Frank saw the way the Ranger's eyes flashed for an instant, saw as well how Wedge's muscles stiffened. The captain said, "Howard Longwell is his name. I know the man. Raises horses. You say he shot himself?"

"That's right." Frank took a sip of his beer.

"You didn't see anybody else around the place?"

"No, I don't think so," Frank said with an innocent shake of his head. "Nobody but his wife. Should I have?"

"No, I was just curious. Maybe I'll ride out there and see if he's all right, find out if there's anything he needs."

"That's neighborly of you."

"Just doing my job," Wedge said gruffly. "Protecting the people along the border."

The bartender came out of the kitchen with a cup of coffee and a bowl of stew for Frank. Both were steaming. Frank grinned in anticipation as the apron set the food and drink on the bar.

"I'm much obliged," Frank said. "What do I owe you?"

"Four bits'll cover it," the bartender said.

Frank slid a fifty-cent piece across the bar and dug in. Wedge pushed his empty mug aside and said, "I'll be seeing you, Morgan. You plan on staying in these parts long?"

"For a while," Frank said.

Wedge grunted and left the saloon. The atmosphere inside the room eased as soon as he was gone. Men began to talk louder, and a few of them even laughed. That made Frank aware of just how subdued the place had been while Wedge was there.

The bartender leaned over the hardwood and said quietly, "Pardon me, mister, but . . . are you and Captain Wedge friends?"

"I wouldn't say that. We're acquainted." Frank lowered his voice, too. "From the looks of it, the captain's not a very popular hombre around here."

"Nobody said that," the bartender replied hastily. Worry sprang up in his eyes, as if he was afraid that he had said too much.

Frank shook his head and said, "Take it easy, amigo. Like I told you, Wedge and I aren't friends. Fact of the matter is, I don't care much for him."

"Well, I ain't sayin' anything against him. Nobody is."

"Because you're all afraid to?"

The bartender didn't answer. He didn't have to. The look in his eyes was answer enough. Instead he said, "How's that stew?"

"Mighty good," Frank said with a smile. "Just what I needed."

He had gotten what he needed in the saloon, all right. Wedge's reaction to the mention of Howard Longwell being shot had told Frank that Dewey and the other two hadn't gone out to the Longwell ranch on their own initiative. Wedge had sent them out there. Whether or not he had ordered them to gun Longwell down if he didn't cooperate was still unknown, but Frank would have been willing to bet that those had been Wedge's orders.

Difficult though it was to believe, it was beginning to look as if the Rangers under Wedge had turned renegade, just like the Rurales on the other side of the border.

As Frank continued eating the stew and sipping from the cup of hot, black coffee, he thought about the situation and told himself that he didn't have the full story yet. There was still more to learn.

He wasn't likely to learn it tonight,

though. Instead, when he finished his meal, he asked the bartender, "Do you know Miss Roanne Williamson? She has a dress shop or something like that here in town."

The man smiled. "Sure, I know Miss Williamson. Fine lady. Her shop is down the street a block, on the other side. It'll be closed at this time of night, though."

"Do you happen to know where Miss Williamson lives?"

"She's got quarters in the back of her shop, I think." The bartender looked a little embarrassed. "I ain't rightly sure about that."

"I'm obliged for the food and the information." Frank gave the man a friendly nod and went out of the saloon.

The night air was cool but pleasant. Frank untied Stormy from the hitch rail and led him down the street. Dog padded along beside them. Frank's keen eyes searched the businesses along the boardwalk, looking for Roanne's dress shop.

A sudden, deep-throated growl from Dog warned him. Frank stopped short as Colt flame bloomed in the darkness of a nearby alley. He heard the wind-rip of a bullet as it passed right in front of his face. Another step and the slug would have blown a hole in his head.

He threw himself forward, diving and rolling behind a water trough as the bushwhacker's gun blasted again. This time the bullet sizzled right behind Frank. He had known the ambusher would try to correct his aim; that was why he had flung himself forward. His Peacemaker was in his hand as he came up on one knee behind the water trough. He triggered twice, flame lancing from the barrel of the Colt as the two fast shots thundered.

Dog ran into the alley, growling and snarling furiously. Frank heard a man scream. Dog had the bushwhacker cornered. Another shot roared, and instantly, Dog yelped in pain.

"Dog!" Frank shouted as he vaulted over the water trough and sprinted toward the alley. If that son-of-a-bitch drygulcher had hurt Dog — !

Footsteps thudded rapidly farther along the alley. Another muzzle flash split the darkness, and Frank felt the sombrero fly off his head as a bullet tore through it. He fired twice more, but didn't know if he hit the gunman or not.

His foot struck something soft and yielding. He went to a knee and thrust out a hand, feeling the coarse hair of the big cur. "Dog," Frank grated.

To his relief, Dog whimpered and moved around on the floor of the alley. He wasn't dead.

Frank heard a swift, sudden rataplan of hoofbeats that faded into the distance. The bushwhacker had reached his horse and gotten away. Frank holstered his Colt and ran both hands over Dog's big, muscular body, searching for a wound. He found a bloody gash on the animal's flank. Thankfully, that seemed to be Dog's only injury.

Dog struggled to get to his feet. Frank helped him and thought that the shock of being shot might have numbed Dog's nerves for a few minutes and knocked his legs out from under him. Dog was still unsteady, but seemed to be generally all right. "Come on, boy," Frank told him. "Let's see about getting you patched up."

He slid his arms under Dog's belly and picked him up. Dog was a big creature, weighing close to a hundred pounds, maybe a little more than that. Frank carried him like a baby, though, cradling the big animal against him. When he reached the street, he turned in the same direction he'd been going before somebody tried to kill him. Stormy trailed along behind without being led.

Frank noticed that no one had emerged from any of the buildings to see what all the shooting was about. That realization brought a frown to his face. Gunshots *always* brought people out. The fact that these hadn't told Frank something.

San Rosa was a frightened town.

A moment later Frank spotted a sign on the front of one of the frame buildings that read WILLIAMSON'S DRESS SHOP. The front of the building was dark, but he thought he saw a faint glow in the back. Roanne might still be up. He climbed to the building's little porch and kicked on the door. "Miss Williamson!" he called. "Roanne!"

A moment later the glow he had glimpsed through the window got brighter as someone approached the front door from inside with a lamp. A nervous voice that he recognized as belonging to Roanne called, "Who's out there? We're closed."

"It's Frank Morgan, Roanne," he replied.

Instantly, a key rattled in the lock, and a second later the door swung open. "Frank!" Roanne exclaimed. The light from the lamp in her hand revealed that she wore a thick robe belted tightly around her waist. "Is it really you? What in the world?"

"It's me, all right," Frank told her. "I need a little help. Dog's been shot."

"Oh, my God. Is he hurt bad?"

"I don't think so."

She stepped back. "Come in, come in. I was afraid I was never going to see you again, Frank."

"And here I turn up on your doorstep with a dog in my arms."

"I'll take you any way I can get you, Frank Morgan." She blushed as she said it, but she said it anyway. Frank carried Dog inside, and Roanne closed the door behind them.

30

Dog rested comfortably on the floor of Roanne's kitchen. Frank had cleaned the gash in his side and tied a bandage in place over it. Dog would be sore for a few days, but Frank was confident that the animal would be back to normal quickly.

Frank and Roanne sat at the kitchen table, sipping from cups of coffee Roanne had poured from the pot on the stove. While he was tending to Dog, Frank had told her a little about what had happened. Now she asked, "Who would want to kill you like that, Frank?"

"I'm not sure, but it seems to me that the most likely hombre is Nathan Wedge."

Roanne frowned. "I don't like Captain Wedge, but he *is* a Texas Ranger. He swore an oath to uphold law and order, and lurking in an alley to try to kill someone isn't what I'd call enforcing the law."

"To some men, an oath is just words,"

Frank said. "It doesn't mean anything. They don't realize that words are what men live by. You can't go changing them to mean something they don't."

"You're saying that Wedge and his men have become outlaws?"

"Three of the Rangers gunned down a rancher named Howard Longwell this evening, just because he wouldn't let them steal some of his horses."

"Oh, my God!" Roanne gasped. "I know the Longwells. Is Howard dead?"

Frank shook his head. "No, just wounded. I sent Doc Ervin out there to patch him up. But as far as Doc or anyone else in town knows, Longwell accidentally shot himself while he was cleaning his gun."

"Is Doris all right?"

"She's fine, just shaken up."

"What happened to the men who shot Howard?"

"They won't shoot anybody else," Frank said flatly.

Roanne looked at him for a long moment without saying anything. Then she sighed and said, "I'm going to pretend I didn't hear that, Frank. In fact, I didn't hear anything you just told me about the Longwells or Captain Wedge and the Rangers."

Frank nodded and said solemnly, "I reckon that would be the smartest thing you could do, Roanne."

"I'm touched, though, that you trusted me."

"You strike me as a trustworthy sort of woman."

A pleased smile tugged at her lips. "I'm glad to hear that," she said.

"Good, because I'm going to ask you to look after Dog for me while I'm gone."

"Of course. I'd be happy to. But where are you going?"

"I can't stay here tonight. That wouldn't be proper."

Roanne laughed. "When a lady gets to be my age, Frank, she places less value on propriety than she might have when she was younger."

Frank was tempted, but he wasn't going to take her up on the invitation that was implied in her words. His instincts told him that all hell could break loose at any time, and he wanted to be able to move quickly without having to worry about Roanne's safety.

"I think I'll ride on down to the Rocking T," he said. "There's enough moonlight so that I can follow the trail with no trouble."

"Oh." She sounded a little disappointed.

"All right. I'll take good care of Dog."

"Before I go, though . . . tell me what's been going on around here while I was gone."

Roanne hesitated before she answered, sipping her coffee in an apparent effort to put her thoughts together before she spoke. Finally, she said, "Things have gotten worse, no doubt about that. Captain Wedge seemed furious when he came back without catching the Black Scorpion. He seemed to think that the gang has supporters and informers around here, and he began interrogating people that he suspected of being connected in some way with the Black Scorpion. The questioning got pretty rough at times, from what I heard. But he never found out anything."

"Reckon that made him that much more angry and frustrated," Frank commented.

Roanne nodded. "That's right. He hasn't actually declared martial law yet, but things are heading in that direction. He relieved our town marshal, Walt Duncan, of his duties and said that the Rangers were completely responsible for maintaining law and order now. He told Heck Carmichael, the operator at the telegraph office, that no messages could be sent or delivered unless they were cleared through the Rangers first. So nobody's been able to get in touch with the county sheriff, and there's no deputy on duty up here. But everybody has sort of gone along with that. After all . . . Captain Wedge and his men are Rangers."

Frank nodded slowly. He knew what Roanne meant. The Rangers had such a long record of sterling public service, dating back to the days when Texas had been an independent republic, and they were so well respected that no one really wanted to believe the worst of them. Folks were willing to give them the benefit of the doubt, just because they were Rangers.

That was probably the very thing that Wedge had counted on when he decided to go his own way.

If not for the incident at the Longwell ranch, Frank might have thought that Wedge was just being overly aggressive in enforcing the law. The shooting of Howard Longwell, though, was a definite step over the line into outlawry. Once that step was taken, there was no going back.

"Even if Captain Wedge has . . . has turned renegade, why would he want to kill you?" Roanne asked with a puzzled frown. "Why would he think that you represent a threat to him?"

"Other than the fact that he just doesn't

like me, I reckon he knows I've got a reputation for sticking my nose in wherever
there's trouble. He knows that I've worked
with the Rangers — the *honest* Rangers —
before. And I'm called The Drifter for a
reason. I usually don't stay in one place for
very long. Could be he's afraid that if I ride
on, word of what he's doing here will get
out and the governor might send in some
other Rangers to investigate."

"Well, it sounds to me like you'd better
be very careful."

Frank nodded. "I intend to be."

He finished his coffee, scratched Dog's
ears for a minute, and told the big cur to
stay there with Roanne. As he straightened
and started toward the back door, she
stepped closer to him and put a hand on
his arm to stop him.

"Frank," she said softly, "I meant what I
said about being careful."

"So did I," he told her. And then, with
her standing so close to him like that with
her face tilted up to his, he did the natural
thing.

He kissed her.

It was a sweet, warm kiss that grew in ur-
gency. Frank stepped back before things
got too hot and heavy. With a regretful
sigh, Roanne let him go.

He slipped out the back door of the building that housed both her business and her home. The night seemed to be peaceful and quiet, but Frank knew that danger could lurk anywhere in the darkness. Whoever had tried to bushwhack him earlier, whether it was Wedge or someone else, might make another attempt on his life. Judging by the way the man had run off so nimbly, none of Frank's shots had wounded him.

Frank whistled quietly and Stormy came around the building to him. Taking the reins, Frank led the Appaloosa behind the other buildings along San Rosa's main street until he came to the one where the bushwhacker had lurked. He lit a match and looked for anything that might give him a clue to the gunman's identity, but he didn't see anything. Too many people moved along this alley during the day for any footprints to stand out among the welter of prints on the ground.

He did find the sombrero Don Felipe had given him, still lying where it had fallen after being shot off his head. He shook his head ruefully as he saw the neat hole drilled all the way through the high crown. A few inches lower and he'd be a candidate for the undertaker now.

After slapping the sombrero back on his head, Frank mounted up and turned Stormy to the east, riding out of town and circling for a mile or so before angling back to the main road. No one tried to stop him as he trailed south toward the Rocking T.

A low-voiced challenge came from the grove of cottonwoods beside the road. "Hold it right there, hombre," a man called. Frank couldn't see him in the darkness, but the tone of menace in the voice told him that the words were backed up by a gun.

Something about the voice was familiar, too, and as Frank reined in, he cast his mind back and tried to figure out who it belonged to. The answer came to him, and he said, "Nick? Nick Holmes?"

This time the voice sounded surprised. "Who's there?"

"It's Frank Morgan."

Cecil Tolliver's younger son-in-law stepped out from the trees. "Mr. Morgan!" he exclaimed. "What are you doin' out here in the middle of the night? Ben said he'd heard a rumor you were still in Mexico."

So that was how Ben had explained it,

Frank thought with a grin. The youngster couldn't come right out and say that he'd seen Frank at the Almanzar hacienda, because then he would have had to explain what *he* was doing there. And it was likely Ben wanted to keep his romance with Carmen a secret just like she did.

"I've been south of the border, all right," Frank said. He thumbed back the sombrero. "That's where I picked up this big hat. But I'm back now, and I need to see Cecil."

"Well, come ahead," Nick told him. "Just ride a mite easy when you get to the house, so nobody gets trigger-happy."

"What's going on, Nick?" Frank asked. "Has there been more trouble while I was gone?"

"Hell, there's been nothin' but trouble! I don't know if it's Almanzar's gunnies or the Black Scorpion's bunch, but rustlers have hit us nearly every night. And the Rangers don't do a damned thing to stop it! That Captain Wedge treats us like *we're* the lawbreakers!"

That didn't surprise Frank. He could have told Nick that neither Don Felipe Almanzar nor the Black Scorpion were to blame for the problems plaguing the Rocking T and the rest of the border country. If he'd had to guess, Frank would have said that the so-called Rangers under Nathan Wedge were responsible for the rustling. That would explain why they couldn't catch the wide-loopers: They would have had to chase themselves in order to do that.

It was a nice setup for the Rangers-turned-outlaws . . . as long as they didn't mind betraying everything that their badges were supposed to stand for.

"That's why your father-in-law has extra guards out?" Frank said to Nick.

"Yes, sir. Every trail in and out of the ranch has men posted on it around the clock. There were a couple of rifles besides mine trained on you when you rode up."

"Well, keep a sharp eye out for trouble," Frank told him. "It's liable to come calling any time."

With that, he rode on, heading for the ranch headquarters. He had known that he was getting close to the Rocking T boundary line, and the presence of Nick Holmes and the other guards had confirmed that Frank was now riding on the Tolliver range.

Quite a few lights were burning in the ranch house when he came within sight of it. Dogs began to bark when they heard

Stormy's hoofbeats. Several men emerged from the barn and walked out to meet Frank. He saw the rifles in their hands.

"Take it easy, fellas," he called to them. "It's Frank Morgan."

The front door of the house opened and a stocky figure stepped out onto the porch in time to hear Frank identify himself. "Frank!" Cecil Tolliver said. He came to the edge of the porch as Frank rode up to the steps. Waving the rifle-toting cowboys back to the barn, Tolliver went on. "Good Lord, where did you come from? I didn't know if you'd ever get back this way. We heard you were down in mañana-land."

Frank swung down from the saddle and looped Stormy's reins around the hitching post beside the porch. As he came up the steps, he said, "That's right, I've been in Mexico for a while. They have the same sort of trouble down there that you do up here, Cecil."

Tolliver snorted. "How can that be? All our trouble *comes* from Mexico!"

"That's where you're wrong," Frank insisted. "We need to have a long talk."

"Sounds fine to me. Come on inside. Peg will be glad to see you." The rancher looked askance at the sombrero on Frank's head. "Where'd you get that Mexican hat?"

"Mexico," Frank said. He was really starting to miss his old Stetson.

Tolliver ushered him inside. "The womenfolk have gone on to bed, but Ben and Darrell and I were chewin' the fat in the kitchen. You're welcome to join us."

They went down the hall to the kitchen, where Ben Tolliver and Darrell Forrest were sitting at the heavy, butcher-block table. Ben looked especially surprised to see Frank — and none too happy about it, either. Frank nodded to the young man and said, "Ben, how are you?"

"I'm fine," Ben said warily. He had to be wondering if Frank was about to spill his secret.

Frank thought about it. It might be better to get everything out in the open right here and now. But he decided to hold off and see what Cecil Tolliver had to say first.

The men had cups of coffee in front of them, and as Tolliver motioned for Frank to sit down at the table, he got another cup and filled it from the pot on the stove. Before this night was over, Frank thought wryly, he was going to have drunk enough coffee to keep him awake for a week. But that was all right, because there was a lot to talk about.

"First of all, tell us about the Black Scorpion," Tolliver requested when all four men were sitting down. "We know the Rangers caught up to his bunch but let him get away. Captain Wedge said he thought you'd been killed in the ruckus, Frank."

"Came close," Frank said with a smile. "I even tangled with the Black Scorpion himself."

Tolliver slapped a hand on the table. "By God, I hope you gave him a wallop for me!"

"I'm the one who got walloped," Frank said ruefully. "The Scorpion got away from me . . . that time."

"You met him again?" Darrell asked eagerly.

Frank nodded. "I did. And I found out something about him. He's not a *bandido* at all."

"Not a *bandido!*" Tolliver burst out. "That's crazy!"

"Ask the farmers and the other common folks on the other side of the Rio Grande about the Black Scorpion," Frank said. "They'll tell you that he and his men were just trying to fight a bunch of brutal, corrupt Rurales. They're the real *bandidos*."

Stubbornly, Tolliver said, "That doesn't make any sense. I know for a fact that the Black Scorpion and his men have raided on this side of the river."

Frank nodded. "That's right. They were trying to break up a smuggling operation that the captain of the Rurales runs on both sides of the border."

Quickly, Frank filled them in on everything he had learned about Captain Estancia and the Rurales. He didn't mention that he knew the Black Scorpion's true identity. Revealing that now wouldn't serve any purpose.

When Frank was finished, Tolliver said reluctantly, "I suppose there could be something to that. I can believe that a company of Rurales would go bad. From all I've ever heard about them, they've always been sort of a shady bunch."

"I think you've got something of the same sort going on up here," Frank said.

"What do you mean by that?"

"I mean the way the Rangers under Nathan Wedge have taken control of everything around here and are running things with an iron fist."

Tolliver frowned darkly. "We were just talkin' about that."

He might have said more, but at that moment footsteps sounded on the porch and one of the cowboys called from outside, "Somebody else comin', Boss."

31

The four men stood up and moved quickly to the front of the house. They stepped outside as a buggy rolled to a stop beside the porch. Frank recognized the lean figure of Doc Ervin at the reins. His son Bob sat beside him, a chunky boy with a scowl on his face.

"Hello, Doc," Tolliver greeted the medico. "What brings you out here?"

"I thought you might like to know what happened to Howard Longwell, Cecil," Ervin said as he handed the reins to his son. He started to climb down from the vehicle, but paused in surprise when he saw Frank. "Well, I didn't expect to run into you again so soon."

"You two know each other?" Tolliver asked.

Ervin nodded toward Frank. "This fellow brought me the news that Howard Longwell had been shot."

"Shot!"

"That's right. However, he didn't mention that Howard was gunned down by some of Wedge's erstwhile Rangers."

Frank tensed. "I told you Longwell accidentally shot himself, Doc."

"Yes, and under the circumstances I forgive you for lying to me," Ervin said crisply as he came up onto the porch. "I suppose you weren't sure who you could trust and who you couldn't in San Rosa."

"That's about the size of it," Frank drawled.

"Howard, however, knew he could trust me, so he and Doris told me what really happened. You saved their lives, sir." Ervin put out his hand. "Thank you. The Longwells are good people."

Frank shook hands with the doctor as Darrell Forrest said, "I don't know what the hell's goin' on here."

"Just what we were afraid of," Ervin went on. "The Rangers have crossed the line. They've gone renegade, damn them."

Tolliver turned to look at Frank. "So you already knew about Wedge and his men?"

"I got a pretty good idea, pretty fast, once I rode up to the Longwell place earlier this evening and found three of Wedge's men trying to steal Longwell's horses after putting a bullet through his shoulder."

Tolliver cursed in a low, heartfelt voice. "Let's all go back inside," he said. "We've got a lot to talk about."

For the next half hour, Frank heard more about how the Rangers had tightened their grip on the area in the past couple of weeks. No massacres such as the one in the Mexican village had been carried out, but other than that the parallels between the situations above and below the border were uncanny. They were so similar, in fact, that Frank began to wonder if there might be some connection. Nathan Wedge and Domingo Estancia knew each other; maybe they had hatched their schemes together. It was something to ponder.

In the meantime, though, there were more pressing problems. Cecil Tolliver thumped a fist on the table and declared, "We've got to do something about this. We can't just let Wedge buffalo us."

"No one man is any match for the Rangers," Frank pointed out. "Even with all your crew, Cecil, you'd be outnumbered."

Doc Ervin said, "That's why we need to get together, all you ranchers and some of the men from town who aren't afraid to stand up to Wedge, and figure out a way to act in concert."

"That's a good idea, Doc," Tolliver said enthusiastically. "We can have a meeting here. You'll spread the word, won't you?"

Ervin nodded. "I reckon I can do that. I travel all over the area tending to the sick and injured. Wedge won't be suspicious of me."

"You'd better send a rider to Austin, too," Frank suggested to Tolliver. "Write a letter to the governor and ask him to send some honest Rangers down here. That would be a better way to break Wedge's stranglehold than if you try to fight him yourself. That would just make you and your friends look like criminals."

"Mr. Morgan has a point," Doc Ervin agreed.

Tolliver scowled. "Maybe so, and I'll write that letter, but if Wedge gets any more high-handed before the real Rangers can get here, there's liable to be trouble." He looked at Frank. "You'll stand with us if there is?"

"I reckon you know the answer to that," Frank replied quietly.

"Yeah, I reckon I do, and I'm sorry I asked it." Tolliver pushed his chair back.

"We've talked a lot, and now we got a lot to think about. I'm gonna turn in. Doc, you and Bob will stay the night since it's so late?"

"Yes, and we're much obliged."

"Frank, you can have the same room you did before," Tolliver went on.

Frank came to his feet. "Thanks. I'll admit that I'm a mite tired. I'll turn in as soon as I've seen to my horse."

"Some of the boys could do that," Tolliver offered.

"No, thanks. I want to handle it myself."

Tolliver nodded, and Frank went out to take Stormy over to the barn and find an empty stall.

He was unsaddling the Appaloosa when a footstep made him turn, his hand dropping to the butt of his gun. Ben Tolliver stepped forward in the shadowy barn, his hands held out empty to show that he wasn't a threat.

"It's just me, Mr. Morgan," the young man said. "I wanted to talk to you."

Frank grunted. "About Carmen, I'll bet."

"Is she all right?" Ben asked anxiously, keeping his voice pitched low so their conversation wouldn't be overheard.

"She was fine when I left the hacienda,"

Frank assured him. "As far as I know she still is."

Ben heaved a sigh of relief. "Thank you for not saying anything to my pa. He just wouldn't understand."

"Pretty soon he may have to," Frank said bluntly. "I don't think you're going to be able to keep your secret much longer."

"Why not?"

"Because I've got a letter for him from Don Felipe Almanzar asking for a meeting between the two of them six days from now in San Rosa, so that they can hash everything out and put an end to their feud."

Ben's eyes widened in surprise. "That's impossible! Don Felipe would never agree to such a thing. Neither would Pa."

"It was my idea," Frank said, "but Don Felipe came around to my way of thinking."

Ben shook his head, obviously unable to comprehend what he was hearing. "I don't believe it. I just don't believe it."

Frank put a hand on his shoulder and said, "This could be just what you and Carmen need, Ben. If your fathers agree to get along again, or at least to not hate each other, there's no reason the two of you can't admit how you feel. There wouldn't be any reason to keep it secret anymore."

"That would be . . . wonderful," Ben said, his voice a little awed now. "But they've hated each other for so long —"

"For no good reason, just a prideful misunderstanding," Frank pointed out.

"Yeah, but it's hard to believe it could ever happen. Did you say anything about it to my pa?"

Frank shook his head. "Not yet. He had enough to do tonight, what with this problem with the Rangers. Maybe we can get that settled, and then we'll see about patching things up between him and Don Felipe."

"That might be best," Ben agreed. "But there are those rustlers, too, and the Black Scorpion. . . ."

"The Black Scorpion never was your enemy, Ben. You might as well get that through your head. And I'm convinced the Rangers are behind all the rustling, although I can't prove it yet."

"Those men who jumped me and Pa, that evening when we first met you . . . do you know who they were?"

"I know who they *weren't*," Frank said with conviction. "They weren't working for Don Felipe, and they weren't the Black Scorpion's bunch."

"Then who . . . ?"

"Maybe some of Wedge's friends," Frank suggested. "With some recruits from below the border to make it look good, so either Almanzar or the Black Scorpion would get the blame."

That idea had slipped fully formed into Frank's brain, but he saw that it made sense and tied right back in with his speculation that there was a connection between Wedge and Estancia.

"Tell me," he went on, "had your father had any trouble with Wedge before that evening?"

"Well, sure," Ben said. "In fact, Pa was the first one around here to start talking about how Wedge was coming down on folks too hard, like he was trying to take over or something."

"So Wedge might have gotten the idea that your father was starting to stir up trouble for him. He wouldn't have wanted Cecil to rouse the whole border country against him."

"Like we're trying to do now."

Frank nodded. "Exactly. What Wedge was worried about is starting to come true. But a couple of weeks ago, he thought he could nip the problem in the bud by getting rid of your pa and laying the blame for it on either Almanzar or the Black Scorpion."

"It would have worked, too, if you hadn't come along when you did."

Frank smiled thinly, thinking of the attempt on his life earlier in the night. "If our theory is true," he said, "then I reckon I've been a thorn in Wedge's side right from the start."

"You're lucky he didn't just kill you when you went across the border with him after the Black Scorpion."

"I reckon he was just biding his time. If I hadn't gotten separated from him and his bunch of gunnies, I doubt if I'd have made it back across the Rio Grande alive."

Ben sighed. "It's sure a complicated state of affairs, isn't it?"

"It is, at that," Frank agreed.

But he knew that sooner or later there would be a showdown, and nothing untangled a mess of knots like gun smoke and hot lead.

Though an air of tension hung over the border country for the next couple of days, there were no outbreaks of violence. It was a lull, like the eye of a hurricane, but Frank knew that such respites never lasted. Trouble seldom if ever went away on its own.

As Cecil Tolliver had predicted, his wife

Pegeen was happy to see Frank. Visitors were always welcome on the Rocking T, and Pegeen was the sort to seize any excuse for some extra cooking and baking, happily bustling around the ranch house kitchen with her daughters Jessie and Debra.

Frank didn't say anything to Cecil Tolliver about the proposed meeting between him and Don Felipe Almanzar, and neither did Ben. Frank had found more trouble here on this side of the Rio Grande than he had anticipated, and he hoped to be able to wait for a better time before springing the idea of a truce on Tolliver.

During those two days, according to the plan worked out with Doc Ervin, the physician was traveling around the area, ostensibly on medical calls, but actually he was telling the other ranchers to come to the Rocking T after dark on the second night, so they could try to figure out what to do about Nathan Wedge and the renegade Texas Rangers. Some of the men from San Rosa would probably attend the meeting, too.

Tolliver had chosen one of the cowhands, a fresh-faced youngster named Hardy, to ride downriver to Laredo and send the letter that Tolliver had written to the governor of Texas, outlining the situation and asking for help. Frank had helped Tolliver with the letter and was convinced it would draw the results they wanted. The question was whether or not help would arrive in time to keep Wedge from taking over completely. Hardy had set out at night, on a fast horse, hoping to escape notice in case Wedge was having the ranch watched.

So all they could do was to bide their time and wait for the meeting. Around noon on the second day, Frank sought out Cecil Tolliver and made a suggestion.

"Why don't you see if Pegeen and the girls would be willing to go into San Rosa and visit Roanne for a few days?" Frank said as the two men stood beside one of the corrals.

Tolliver frowned. "You really think that's necessary?"

"I'm convinced Wedge has already tried to kill you once, Cecil. If he got wind of this meeting, he might see it as a chance to wipe out all his opposition at the same time."

"I trust Doc," Tolliver said stubbornly. "He's a sly old bird. He won't let Wedge know what's going on."

"I trust Doc, too, but there are other

people who know about the meeting now, and I don't know how careful all of them will be. It's just a precaution, but I think it's a good idea."

Tolliver sighed. "What you say makes sense, Frank, but you don't know that woman of mine. If she thinks I'm tryin' to get her out of harm's way, that'll just make her more bound and determined to stay."

"Maybe you can tell her that she needs to go in order to get your daughters to go. Appeal to her maternal instinct."

Tolliver scratched at his close-cropped beard. "Aye, could be you're right. But I still think Pegeen will outsmart me somehow. She always does."

To his surprise, Pegeen agreed to go into San Rosa with Jessie and Debra and put up no argument about it. She didn't allow any protests from the young women, either. By the middle of the afternoon they had one of the ranch buckboards loaded with enough bags for a visit of several days. The women kissed their husbands good-bye and then drove away, trailed by a couple of well-armed cowboys who would escort them to the settlement and then return to the Rocking T. Frank had considered going along himself, so that he could see Roanne again and check on Dog, but decided against it. If there was any trouble at the meeting that night, he didn't want to risk finding himself cut off from it.

With that taken care of, the men settled down to wait again. Frank suggested that they do something useful to pass the time.

They cleaned their guns.

32

High, patchy clouds blew in with the twilight, obscuring some of the stars and
forming streaks across the brilliant orange
moon as it climbed into the sky. An hour
after dark, wearing a Stetson he had bor-
rowed from Darrell Forrest, Frank Morgan
stood in front of the largest barn on the
Rocking T and looked up at that moon,
feeling its pull on him. Tidal forces were at
play within him, forces that urged him to
move on. They were part of the restless nature that had given him his nickname, and
they were at odds with the part of him that
longed for a respite from all the trouble in
his life, for a peaceful place to settle down
and grow old. . . .

But he no longer truly believed that he
would ever find such a place, and he had
already lived for more years than he had
any right to expect, given his reputation.
He looked around at the men gathering to-

night at the Rocking T and knew that there was a fundamental difference between them and him. They were the ones who had homes and families and lives that really meant something. They were the bedrock, the stuff that lasts.

He was the lightning bolt, the flash that was there and then gone, but with tremendous destructive force that was sometimes needed to start a cleansing fire and sweep away all the deadwood, so that new life could grow and continue the endless cycle.

Frank smiled faintly, telling himself he wasn't really the sort to wax poetical. Then he turned and went into the barn, which was lit by lanterns hung at intervals along the walls.

Between thirty and forty men were in there: all the ranchers from up and down the river, including Howard Longwell, his arm in a sling, who had gotten out of bed over his wife's objections to come here tonight; Doc Ervin and half-a-dozen men from San Rosa, one of them the former marshal Walt Duncan, who had been relieved of his position by the Rangers; and several *tejanos,* Mexican by heritage but whose families had lived and farmed on the Texas side of the river for generations. At times in the past there had been friction between the gringos and those of Mexican ancestry, but tonight they were all Texans and they all wanted to find a solution to the threat represented by the Rangers who had gone bad.

The Rocking T punchers had piled some bales of hay at the front of the barn to form a platform. Cecil Tolliver climbed up onto it and raised his hands for quiet, calling, "Settle down now, boys. Settle down."

The room had been filled with talk, but it quieted in response to Tolliver. The men all looked up at him, waiting to hear what he was going to say. At the rear of the group, Frank propped a shoulder against one of the beams that held up the barn roof and listened as well.

"Y'all know why you're here tonight," Tolliver began. "For weeks now, ever since the Rangers under Captain Nathan Wedge rode into the area supposedly to enforce the law, things have been getting worse along the border. All of us cattlemen have lost stock to rustlers. Gangs of gunmen ride unmolested through the night, shooting and terrorizing. *Bandidos* from below the Rio Grande have raided our ranches and our settlements. Smugglers bring across opium and gold and take back guns, and nobody bothers them. And if anybody says a word about it to the Rangers, trouble comes down hard on his head!"

Shouts of agreement came from the men.

"Lately, though," Tolliver continued, "things have gotten even worse. Walt Duncan, who's done a good job for years as the marshal in San Rosa, got his badge taken away from him by Captain Wedge. Accordin' to the Rangers, Walt just ain't needed anymore. And Heck Carmichael at the telegraph office isn't allowed to send a wire unless the Rangers approve it first. Likewise, he can't deliver any message that comes in until Wedge or one of the other Rangers has seen it. Buckshot Roberts, at the San Rosa *Sun*, can't print his newspapers any more without the Rangers lookin' over his shoulder to see what he's gonna say. That just ain't right!"

Again, shouts rose to the barn rafters.

"Now, though, they've gone too far. You all know Howard Longwell."

The men in the crowd murmured in agreement and looked at Longwell, who stepped forward beside the hay bales.

"Three nights ago," Tolliver said, "some of Wedge's men rode out to Howard's ranch to take some of his horses. When Howard told them they couldn't do it, one of the bastards shot him!"

Angry shouts, now.

Tolliver leveled an arm and pointed at Frank, still standing at the back of the crowd. "If our friend Frank Morgan hadn't come along when he did and ventilated those so-called Rangers, the buzzards likely would have killed Howard and Doris and stole all their horses."

Well, his involvement in that affair was out in the open now, Frank thought with a grim smile. But things had gone so far that there was no longer any point in trying to conceal what had happened.

"Howard's gonna be all right," Tolliver said, "but who knows what sort of deviltry the Rangers will try next?"

Despite the general mood of agreement in the room, one of the men spoke up, saying, "It sure pains me to hear you talkin' about the Rangers like they're outlaws or somethin', Cecil."

Tolliver nodded solemnly. "I know it. It pains me to say such things, Sam. All of us remember what it was like in Texas after the war, when the Yankee carpetbaggers came in and took over and tried to force their way of livin' on us. They had their damned State Police, and they were the worst bunch of crooks to ever call themselves lawmen! It wasn't until the carpet-baggers were booted out and the State Police dissolved that the Rangers could come back and be real lawmen again. I know all that."

Despite the coolness of the night, Tolliver was sweating. He pulled a bandanna from his pocket and mopped his face before going on.

"But just because the Rangers, by and large, are an honorable, straight-shootin' bunch, that don't mean that some of 'em can't go bad from time to time. I blame Wedge. He must've decided a long time ago to cross over to the owlhoot side, and he took his time drawin' men who felt the same way to him and gettin' them into the Rangers, too. And when they were ready, they rode down here with badges pinned to their chests, knowing that we'd never suspect just what polecats they really are. It took us some time to figure that out, but by God, we know it now!"

Another man yelled from the crowd, "But what are we gonna *do* about it?"

"Hang Nathan Wedge from the nearest tree!" came an answering shout. Several men roared their approval of that suggestion.

Cecil Tolliver raised his hands over his

head again. "Hold on, hold on!" he rumbled. When relative quiet had settled in, he said, "I know that most of us lived through a time when the only real law was what a man packed on his hip and the only justice was a hang rope! I ain't sayin' that it's always been for the better, but things have changed since then. If we fight the Rangers, it's likely to look to everybody else in the state like *we're* the outlaws, not Wedge and his bunch! What we need is some real law in here, and that's what I've asked the governor to send us. There's a letter on the way to him right now, tellin' him just how bad things are down here."

"How long is that gonna take?" a man demanded.

"Yeah, what if Wedge has wiped us all out before the governor gets around to doin' anything?" another rancher added.

"That's why we're havin' this meeting tonight," Tolliver said. "For the time bein', I think we should all send our womenfolk into San Rosa. Wedge is less likely to try anything really bad as long as there are a lot of people around. You little ranchers, fellas who run one-man layouts, maybe you ought to think about gatherin' all together at one of your spreads and fortin' up there."

"I can't do that!" one of the men protested. "I can't just abandon my ranch!"

"It wouldn't be permanentlike," Tolliver pointed out. "Just until Wedge is dealt with."

"Yeah, well, that sounds fine and dandy, but what if he burns down my house and barn and rustles all my stock while I'm gone? What then, Tolliver? You gonna stake me to start over?"

"Now hold on," Tolliver said, and Frank could tell that he was trying to keep the meeting from getting out of hand. Frustration was an insidious thing. These men knew the situation was bad but they didn't know what to do about it, and that might lead them to do the wrong thing, just so they could take action of some sort.

"I still say we gotta fight!" a man yelled.

"Dadgummit, hush up!" Tolliver bellowed. "This ain't gonna solve anything —"

Frank lifted his head as he heard a faint popping sound over the angry hubbub in the barn. He frowned and straightened from his casual pose, turning toward the wide-open barn doors. As he moved closer the sounds became clearer, and he recognized them for what they were.

Gunshots.

Frank knew that Rocking T cowhands

were guarding the approaches to the ranch tonight, as they had been for the past several nights. A ragged volley sounded in the distance, telling Frank that those sentries were under attack.

That could mean only one thing. Somehow, Nathan Wedge had found out about the meeting tonight. That was the possibility that had worried Frank the most, because he suspected Wedge would be unable to resist the temptation to strike at all his enemies at once. Now, as the shots came closer, that seemed to be exactly what was happening.

The men in the barn were still wrangling over their best course of action. What they didn't realize was that the choice had been taken out of their hands. Within minutes, they would be faced with a situation where the only thing they could do was fight for their lives.

Frank whirled toward them and shouted, "Shut up! *Listen!*"

His deep, powerful voice cut through all the arguing and made the men fall silent. As they did so, all of them heard what Frank's keen ears had already detected. The rattle of gunfire shattered the night and came steadily closer as the Rocking T cowboys retreated, fighting a delaying action against the evil horde that had swept out of the darkness against the ranch.

Every man in the barn was armed. Some of them were seasoned frontiersmen who had fought Indians and outlaws in the past, while others had never fired a gun in anger. But even though Frank saw fear on some of their faces, he saw determination on every face.

"Get as many of the horses as you can inside the barn, then spread out and hunt some good cover!" he barked, instinctively taking charge at this moment of crisis. "They'll be here in a few minutes, and we'll give them a warm welcome."

Counting all the men who had come to the meeting, plus the few Rocking T cowboys who were also on hand, Frank figured they had a fighting force of at least forty men. Wedge had no more than thirty men in his command, so the renegade Ranger was in for a surprise.

Frank's forehead creased in a frown as he hurried toward the house with Tolliver, Ben, Darrell, and Nick. Something was wrong. Wedge might be an outlaw, but he wasn't a fool. He had to know there was a good-sized group of fighting men at the ranch tonight. Would he attack anyway, even knowing that he would be outnumbered?

Maybe Wedge *wasn't* outnumbered, Frank thought. Maybe he had rounded up some more gunmen somewhere.

They would know shortly, because the fighting was close enough now so that Frank could see muzzle flashes in the darkness as he and the others bounded up onto the porch. All around the ranch, in the barns, the corrals, and the bunkhouse, men were finding good spots to put up a fight. Frank cupped his hands around his mouth and shouted, "Blow out all the lanterns!"

Instantly, lights began going out around the ranch. The house was plunged into darkness, too, as the lamps were blown out. Cecil Tolliver opened up the gun rack in his parlor and pressed Winchesters into the hands of Frank, Ben, and his sons-in-law. Frank stepped back out onto the porch and dropped to one knee, waiting to see what was going to happen.

He heard hoofbeats in the night, and then as horsemen raced toward the house, they shouted, "Rocking T! Rocking T!" They were the surviving guards, identifying themselves so that the ranch's defenders wouldn't shoot them down. In the moonlight, Frank saw that there were only three of them. His mouth tightened into a grim line. The other sentries must have been killed in the attack.

He stood up and waved to the riders. "Rocking T, over here!" he shouted, and the cowboys veered their mounts toward the house. They flung themselves out of their saddles while the horses were still moving and stumbled up the steps to the porch. One of them gasped, "It's Wedge! Wedge and the Range —"

Muzzle flame lanced from a rifle barrel about fifty yards away, accompanied by a sharp crack. The cowboy who had been delivering the warning cried out and stumbled, then pitched forward on his face, his hat flying off. Frank saw the dark stain already spreading on the back of the waddy's shirt where the bullet had struck him. Snapping the Winchester to his shoulder, Frank fired at the muzzle flash he had seen just before the young cowboy was hit. He didn't know if his bullet found its mark or not, but as he worked the rifle's lever and threw another cartridge into the chamber, he knew one thing.

The battle for the Rocking T was on.

33

Frank bent and grabbed the cowboy who had been shot. "Give me a hand with him!" he snapped at the other punchers, and one of them got hold of the wounded man under the other arm. Together they dragged him inside the house as Tolliver, Ben, Darrell, and Nick opened fire from the windows they had thrown open. They slammed lead at the dark area near one of the barns where the shot had come from.

Defenders opened up from the barns and the corrals, too, and as Frank stepped back to the doorway he saw several men on horseback fleeing from that deadly storm of bullets. The moonlight revealed something that sent a shock through him.

A couple of the fleeing gunmen wore high-crowned sombreros.

Just like the ones the Rurales wore.

Frank bit back a curse as he realized what that meant. There was a connection between Wedge and Estancia, all right. And now the two outlaws had probably joined forces in an effort to wipe out their opposition on this side of the border. Antonio Almanzar had mentioned that Estancia had partners in his smuggling operation. What better partner than Wedge, who was supposed to be in charge of enforcing the law in this area? It was as neat a setup as Frank had ever encountered, two "lawmen" who were really the bosses of a burgeoning owlhoot empire.

The presence of the Rurales also meant that the ranch's defenders no longer outnumbered the attackers. Estancia would be able to throw at least twenty men into the fray on Wedge's side, maybe even more than that if he'd already gotten some of his reinforcements from Mexico City. The position of the honest Texans had changed abruptly from perilous but tenable to downright precarious.

And once all the opposition north of the Rio Grande had been put down, the Rangers would lend a hand below the border as well and help Estancia take over there. If the power grab wasn't stopped here, ultimately hell would break loose on both sides of the border.

Those thoughts flashed through Frank's

mind in a matter of seconds. No more shots came from the attackers, but he knew better than to think Wedge and Estancia had withdrawn their forces.

Those two bastards were just getting started.

That hunch was confirmed a few moments later. With a pounding of hoofbeats like rolling thunder, a large group of riders charged the house and the barns, blazing away as they galloped forward. "Let 'em have it!" Frank bellowed over the gun blasts. He stood at the edge of the doorway, partially shielded by the jamb, and played a deadly tune on the Winchester, crashing out the shots as fast as he could work the lever and squeeze the trigger.

The moonlight made accurate shooting difficult. Silver shadows shifted and darted in the yard between the house and the barns. The raiders spread out, too, instead of bunching up, which made them harder to hit. Frank saw a couple of the gunmen pitch from their saddles, but most of them survived the charge unscathed and continued spraying the house and barns with lead.

Sparks flew in the air as something tumbled end over end through the night. Frank heard it hit the porch and saw the sparks roll against the wall of the house. "Dynamite!" he yelled, but the blast of the explosive swallowed up the warning.

That end of the porch and part of the wall disappeared in a burst of flame and noise that shook the earth. The concussion slammed Frank off his feet. As he lay there for a moment, half in and half out of the door, stunned by the explosion, he heard several more blasts like the first one. The raiders had brought plenty of dynamite with them.

Frank pushed himself to his knees, shaking his head to try to get rid of some of the cobwebs clogging his brain. Somehow he had managed to hang on to the rifle. He saw one of the raiders veer his mount toward the house. The man was one of the sombrero-wearing Rurales, and he had another stick of dynamite in his hand, the fuse sputtering and throwing off sparks as it burned.

Without really aiming, Frank jerked the Winchester to his shoulder and fired. The Rurale flipped backward off his horse, and the stick of dynamite went straight up in the air. It fell among some of the raiders, who shouted in terror and tried to rein their horses away from it.

The dynamite blew, sending men and horses pinwheeling through the air. That was finally enough to blunt the charge and make some of the attackers fall back. Frank scrambled to his feet and turned toward the parlor. That was the room closest to the explosion that had rocked the house.

Flames flickered up one of the walls, casting a hellish glare into the room. Everything was in disarray. Windows were shattered, pictures had been knocked off the walls, furniture was overturned. Ben Tolliver and Nick Holmes were trying to drag the unconscious forms of Cecil Tolliver and Darrell Forrest out of the room before the fire spread to them.

"Ben!" Frank shouted. "How bad are they hurt?"

"Just knocked out, I think!" Ben's face was grimy with powder smoke and taut with strain. "They were the closest to that dynamite when it went off."

Darrell was hurt worse than that, Frank saw in the glare of the flames. The young man's left arm was bent at an unnatural angle and had to be broken. Right now, though, getting out of the burning house was more important than tending to a busted arm.

The thud of rapid footsteps made Frank

whirl around and bring up the Winchester. One of the men who had just run into the parlor yelped, "Don't shoot! It's just us!"

Frank recognized the cowboys who had ridden in a few minutes earlier. "Give Ben and Nick a hand," he snapped at them. "Get Mr. Tolliver and Darrell out the front door and head for the main barn. We'll try to fort up there."

Gunfire still roared outside as the attacking force probed at the ranch's defenses. Getting from the house to the barn was going to be like running a gauntlet of flying lead. But Frank knew they had no choice. The fire started by the explosion was burning fiercely. If they hadn't been under attack, they might have been able to put it out and save the house. As it was, all they could do was abandon the ranch house to the flames.

That was a bitter pill to swallow, but it was going to get worse, Frank thought as he snapped a shot, through the gaping aperture of the blown-out wall, at one of the Rurales who flashed past outside. The men who had gathered here tonight were outnumbered, and the raiders had dynamite, too. This fracas had turned into an unwinnable fight for the defenders. If they stayed and fought, they would take a heavy toll on the attackers, but in the end they would be slaughtered to the last man.

Like it or not, they had to cut and run, in hopes of fighting — and winning — another day.

Frank turned and hurried after the others. They had reached the porch and lifted the half-conscious Tolliver and Darrell to their feet. Frank knelt for a second beside the cowboy who had been shot, and checked for a pulse without finding one. The young man was dead.

Straightening, Frank said grimly, "I'll cover you. Head for the barn."

Ben, Nick, and the two punchers started across the open ground, half-carrying, half-dragging Tolliver and Darrell. Frank paced after them, snapping shots at every target he picked out from the moonlit chaos. Bullets whined around their heads and kicked up dust around their feet. Nick yelled in pain as a slug burned a path across his back. He stumbled but kept his feet.

Frank looked around and saw that the bunkhouse and the blacksmith shop were burning, too. As he watched, flames reached the hay barn, and it went up like a torch, throwing a red glare that stretched for hundreds of yards around it. Now the whole battlefield that the Rocking T had become was lit up like the middle of the day in Hell.

Something slammed hard into Frank's hip and nearly knocked him off his feet. He reached down and felt a rip in the leather of his gun belt. A spent slug had struck him a glancing blow, but the thick leather had stopped it from penetrating. That had been a close call.

The men inside the barn had seen them coming. The doors swung open far enough to let Ben and the others stagger through. Frank hustled after them, his hip still smarting from the blow and making him limp a little. As he ran into the barn, the defenders slammed the doors behind him.

"What'll we do, Morgan?" one of the men asked him, a note of desperation in the question. "There's too damned many of 'em!"

"How many men do we have left?" Frank asked.

The man shook his head. "I don't know! Some of 'em must've got blowed up by all that dynamite!"

A tall, lean figure strode forward. Enough light from the fires came into the barn through cracks between the boards for Frank to be able to make out the strained features of Doc Ervin.

"There are about thirty of us in here now, Morgan, counting you fellows who just got here," the medico from San Rosa said. "That leaves eight or ten unaccounted for. I'm afraid they must have been killed in the fighting. When those explosions went off in the bunkhouse and the blacksmith shop, the men who had sought cover there abandoned the buildings and fought their way over here."

Just like he and his companions had done, Frank thought. He nodded and said, "We can't stay here. They probably saw us converging on the barn, and this is where they'll concentrate their next attack. If they've got any dynamite left, they'll try to blow us to Kingdom Come!"

Ervin jerked his head in a nod. "So we've got to get out of here."

"That's how I see it," Frank agreed.

Ben Tolliver spoke up, saying, "We can't do that! We can't run!"

"It's run or die, Ben," Frank told him.

An old-timer with a jutting gray brush of a beard said, "When I was in the army durin' the war, we'd call it a strategic retreat. Ain't no shame in it."

"But this is my home!" Ben protested.

Nick put a hand on his shoulder. "Mine,

426

too, Ben, but Mr. Morgan and the others are right. If we stay and fight, we'll all be killed. We need to get out, split up, and regroup later."

Frank nodded. "That's right, Nick. See about getting the horses ready. Ben, you help him."

Ben looked like he wanted to argue some more, but the tone of command in Frank's voice allowed no argument.

"We'll go out the back," Frank went on to Ervin. "I'm sure they've got it covered, but at least it'll be darker that way, and they might not be able to shoot quite as well."

"The battle is over," Ervin said, "but the war isn't. That's right, isn't it?"

"Damned right," Frank said curtly. "We're not going to let Wedge and his friends get away with this. But when we tangle with them again, it'll be at a time and place of our choosing."

"Very well. I —"

What else the doctor was going to say remained a mystery, because at that moment one of the men who was up in the loft yelled, "Here they come again!" The riflemen up there had been trading potshots with the raiders, but now another concerted attack was on the way. The firing increased, and some of the bullets tore through the heavy planks of the barn to whine like bees among the defenders.

"Mount up!" Frank shouted. "Mount up and bust out the back! Don't stop firing until you're well away from the barn!"

Some of them wouldn't make it, he thought bleakly. But some of them would, and the survivors would live to fight again.

He spotted Stormy on the other side of the barn and started toward the Appaloosa. Ervin caught his arm to stop him for a moment.

"About five miles north of here there's a big coulee where a creek used to cut through a ridge," the sawbones said. "It would be easily defended, and we could rendezvous there tomorrow."

Frank jerked his head in a nod. "Sounds good to me. Spread the word as best you can, and I'll do the same."

Ervin agreed and then hurried off to find a horse. Not all of the mounts had been brought into the barn before the fighting started, but Frank thought there were enough for everyone who was left. He reached Stormy, slid the Winchester into the saddle boot, and swung up onto the Appaloosa's back. Most of the men were mounted, Frank saw, and as he looked around, the last of the defenders from the loft dropped down the ladders and hit leather.

"Go!" Frank shouted.

The bar securing the rear doors had been removed. The horses surged against the doors, throwing them open. Six-guns blazing, the men poured out of the barn.

As Frank expected, they ran into heavy fire from gunmen posted to watch the back of the barn. But the riders were moving quickly and the shadows were thick back here. Up front, a dynamite blast blew in part of the barn wall. The explosion came too late to catch any of the men inside, however.

A glance to the side showed Frank that Ben and Nick had managed to get Tolliver and Darrell onto a couple of horses. They had regained their senses, at least to a certain extent, and were hanging onto the reins themselves, even though neither man was shooting. Ben and Nick were staying close by in case either of them got dizzy and started to fall out of the saddle.

Frank's Peacemaker was in his hand as he rode. He triggered at the muzzle flashes dotting the darkness around the ranch. One of the Rurales suddenly loomed up beside him, on foot, reaching up in an attempt to grab him and drag him off Stormy. Frank kicked the man in the chest and sent him flying backward. Another man charged him on horseback, firing wildly. One of the bogus Rangers, Frank judged as he snapped a shot that sent the man flying off the back of his horse.

As he rode up alongside Ben Tolliver, Frank holstered the Colt and leaned over to catch the young man's arm. "Coulee five miles north!" he shouted over the tumult of gunshots and hoofbeats. "Meet there tomorrow!"

"Got it!" Ben called back to him.

"Spread the word!"

With that, Frank galloped on, pulling away from Ben and the others. He told several more of the fleeing cattlemen about the rendezvous. With luck, the word would get around to most of the survivors.

Of course, they hadn't survived yet, he reminded himself when a bullet screamed past his left ear, only inches away. Twisting in the saddle, he saw a Rurale coming up fast behind him. Frank ducked as the Mexican fired again. His hand flickered to the Colt, palmed it out of the holster, and fired it in one smooth move. The Rurale rocked back as Frank's bullet slammed into him.

Then, with almost shocking suddenness,

Stormy was in the clear and running freely through the night. Guns still barked and roared, but none of them seemed to be near Frank. He looked around, saw darting shadows here and there that he recognized as men riding hell-bent-for-leather. The ranchers and the men from San Rosa had broken through the screen of renegade Rangers and Rurales, and now they were scattering across the south Texas plains, spreading out as widely as possible so that even if the enemy caught up to a few of them, the rest would get away.

There was a bitter taste in Frank's mouth. Running away from trouble went against everything in his being. All through his long, eventful life, he had made a habit of standing straight up against whatever danger came his way.

But tonight he wasn't the only one involved. There were dozens of other men who had to be thought of. Not only them, but their families, too, back on the other ranches and in the settlement. Doc Ervin had summed it up when he said that this battle might be over, but the war would continue.

And it was a war that Frank Morgan intended to win.

34

Frank rode long and hard that night, circling far to the east and then riding north, steering his course by the stars. By morning he estimated that he was a good fifteen miles from the Rocking T. He hadn't seen any of the other men, but hoped that most of them had gotten away.

As the sun rose he angled southwest, figuring that would bring him by midday to the vicinity of the coulee Doc Ervin had mentioned. He didn't push Stormy, but let the Appaloosa set his own pace after the hard run during the night.

When he spotted another rider ahead of him, he reined in and pulled the Winchester from its sheath. The man's path was converging with Frank's. They approached each other warily, but then Frank relaxed as he recognized one of the men who had been at the meeting in Cecil Tolliver's barn the night before. The man raised a hand in greeting.

Frank returned the rifle to the saddle boot and rode forward. "Howdy," he said. "Good to see somebody else made it through."

"Damn right," the man said. "You're Morgan, aren't you? I'm Pete Carson."

"Glad to meet you, Pete," Frank said as he reached over to shake hands with the cattleman. "Seen any of the others yet?"

Carson shook his head. "Nope, but Doc Ervin told me we were supposed to meet at Grant's Coulee. I'm headed there now."

"I didn't know the place had a name," Frank said with a tired grin, "but that's where I'm headed, too."

The two men rode on together, and about an hour later they came in sight of a long, shallow ridge that ran east and west as far as the eye could see. Pete Carson pointed out a notch in the higher ground.

"That's the coulee," he said. "A long time back a creek must have run through there, but it's been dry as far back as I can remember."

Doc Ervin had said that the coulee would be easy to defend, but as Frank and Carson approached, Frank decided he didn't much like the looks of the place. True, both ends of the coulee were relatively narrow and could be held by a small number of defenders, but if riflemen were able to get on the rims of the slash in the earth, they could fire down into it and the coulee might become a death trap. If this war against Wedge and Estancia turned into a long struggle, the Texans would have to find a better location for their headquarters.

Maybe it wouldn't come to that, Frank thought. If Hardy had gotten through to Laredo and mailed that letter to Austin, help might soon be on the way.

When they were within a few hundred yards of the northern end of the coulee, Frank saw sunlight flash on something inside the cut. They were probably being watched through field glasses. A minute later, several riders emerged from the coulee and trotted toward them. Frank recognized the tall, hatless figure of Doc Ervin. When the men came closer he saw that one of them was Cecil Tolliver, seemingly recovered from being knocked out by the dynamite blast the night before.

"Frank, it's good to see you," Tolliver said as he and the others came up to Frank and Carson. "You, too, Pete. Are you fellas all right?"

"Made it through without a scratch," Frank said.

434

"I wish we could say the same for everyone," Doc said. "Come on in. Welcome to our new home."

There was a bitter edge to the physician's voice, and as he rode into the coulee, Frank saw why. There were barely a dozen men there, and several of them were wounded, with crude, bloodstained bandages wrapped around heads, arms, and legs. Darrell Forrest's broken arm had been roughly splinted with mesquite branches.

"We're hoping more of the boys will show up later," Tolliver said as he saw the bleak expression on Frank's face. "After all, you and Pete just got here, Frank."

"That's true," Frank said with a nod. "We'll hope for the best."

A few patches of grass dotted the floor of the coulee, but there was no water. They would definitely have to relocate, Frank thought. As soon as everyone had shown up that they could reasonably expect to, they would have to start scouting for a better place to lick their wounds and figure out what to do next.

When Frank said as much, Doc Ervin nodded in agreement. "I'm afraid I'm not much of a tactician when it comes to warfare," the sawbones said. "This was just the first place I thought of that everyone might know."

"That's fine, Doc," Frank assured him. "We had to have a place to regroup, and this is as good as any."

As the day went on, men continued to show up at the coulee, some of them wounded, a lucky few having come through the fighting unscathed. Doc tended to the ones who were hurt.

Late in the afternoon, Walt Duncan rode in. The former marshal had a bullet crease on his upper left arm, and a slug had bitten a chunk out of his left thigh. His face was deeply trenched with lines of pain. Frank and Ben helped him down out of the saddle.

"Thank God you made it, Walt," Cecil Tolliver said as Duncan sat down on a rock and Doc Ervin knelt beside him to examine the leg wound.

"You may not be so glad to see me once you hear what I've got to say," Duncan responded. "I've been to town."

Frank asked sharply, "You went back to San Rosa?"

"That's right." Duncan winced as Doc probed the bullet hole. "I wanted to see what was going on there. Once I got close, though, I realized I couldn't go all the way into the settlement." Duncan swept his grim gaze around the group of men who had gathered to listen to his report. "Wedge has taken over the town."

"What do you mean by that?" Tolliver asked, his voice taut with worry.

"I guess he's declared martial law. Those so-called Rangers of his are all over the settlement, standing guard with rifles and shotguns. All the citizens are staying off the streets, and the road in and out of town is closed."

"He doesn't have enough men to do that, does he?" one of the ranchers asked.

Duncan said, "He does when you count all the Rurales he's got helping him. They're right in there with the Rangers, working side by side with them." The former marshal added bitterly. "Just like this was Mexico, not Texas!"

Frank nodded. "I saw enough Rurales at the Rocking T last night to know that Wedge has to be working with Captain Estancia of the Rurales. They're both as crooked as they can be, and they've gone partners in trying to take over the border country."

"They've damned near done it, if you ask me," Duncan said. "You ain't heard the worst of it, though."

Tolliver groaned. "It gets worse?"

"It does, for a fact. While I was watching, Wedge and some of his men brought in some prisoners. I had my field glasses, and I got a good enough look to recognize them. Three of 'em were ranchers who were at the meeting last night: Finn, Andrews, and Gruber. I guess they got rounded up after we busted out of the barn."

"Who was the fourth man?" Frank asked.

Duncan looked at him and said, "That young cowpuncher named Hardy. The one who was carrying the letter to the governor."

Frank's jaw tightened. "They must have been holding him prisoner for a couple of days. No way of knowing if they caught him while he was on his way back from Laredo . . . or if he never got there."

In a hushed voice, one of the men asked, "You mean there may not be any help comin' from Austin?"

"There's no way of knowing whether there will be or not." Frank looked around at the group, now about two dozen strong. "We may be all that's left to fight Wedge and Estancia."

"A handful of men, and some of them

shot up," Tolliver muttered. "Not very good odds."

Frank turned back to Walt Duncan. "What did they do with the prisoners?"

"Remember I said you hadn't heard the worst yet? The bastards hung them."

"What?" Doc Ervin exploded, his head jerking up from his examination of Duncan's wounded leg.

"They strung those poor boys up," Duncan said. "They didn't go to the time or trouble to build a gallows, just threw some ropes over the second-floor railing on the false front of the Border Palace and hauled 'em up in the air." Duncan's voice trembled a little as he went on. "Took 'em a long time to die that way, choking and kicking. And then Wedge left their bodies hanging there, I guess as a warning to everybody else in town that they'd better cooperate with him."

Thinking about Roanne Williamson and the Tolliver women, Frank asked, "Did you see them bothering any of the townspeople?"

Duncan shook his head. "No, like I said, everybody is staying off the streets. Maybe Wedge ordered 'em to, I don't know. All I know is that he's got San Rosa locked down tighter'n a drum."

Frank wasn't the only one concerned, of course. Doc Ervin was worried about his wife and son, and the other men from San Rosa who had survived the attack at the Rocking T also had families in the settlement. One of the townsmen said, "We've got to get in there and run Wedge out!"

Walt Duncan shook his head solemnly. "I hear you, Luther, but I don't hardly see how we can do it. Wedge has at least thirty men guarding the town, and if we ride in shooting, some of our loved ones are bound to get hurt."

"Marshal Duncan is right," Frank said. "When it comes to a fight, we'll have to figure out some way of drawing the Rangers and the Rurales out of San Rosa so that things can be settled away from innocent folks."

"I wish you'd quit callin' those sons o' bitches Rangers," Tolliver groused. "They don't deserve the name anymore."

Frank nodded. "You're absolutely right, Cecil. They're outlaws, and we all know it."

Doc said, "All right, we've heard the news from San Rosa, bad as it is." He looked at Duncan. "That *was* all of it, wasn't it, Walt?"

"Yeah, I reckon."

"Everybody move on and let me get these bullet holes patched up," Doc ordered.

The men spread out across the coulee floor again. Frank gathered with Tolliver, Ben, Nick, and Darrell near one of the walls of the coulee. "I've been thinking about what happened to Hardy," he said.

"I know it," Tolliver grated. "Hangin's too good for Wedge and his bunch after what they did to our boys."

Frank shook his head. "That's not what I mean. We can't assume that Hardy got through to Laredo and sent that letter. It's entirely possible that no one outside of this area knows what's really going on in these parts."

"What are you gettin' at, Frank?"

"I think I need to see if I can get out and send word to Austin."

"You mean you're gonna run?" Darrell said.

Frank frowned, but Tolliver burst out, "Damn it, boy, you know better'n that! Frank Morgan is no coward. Hell, he'd be takin' a big chance just tryin' to get past Wedge's men. That son of a bitch has probably got patrols out all over."

"Yes, but they're bound to be spread pretty thin," Frank said. "I've got a fast horse, and I think I'd have a chance."

"There's a telegraph office in Laredo," Nick pointed out.

Frank nodded. "Yes, if I send wires to the governor and to some other influential men I know, I think I can stir up enough of a hornet's nest to get either the army or some real Rangers down here."

"It'd have to be pretty quicklike to do us any good," Tolliver pointed out.

"I know. That's why I'm leaving tonight. If I can make it through and back, where will I find you?"

Tolliver scratched his beard and frowned in thought. "There's a place north of here called Sand Mountain. More of a big hill, really. But there are some springs at the foot of it, and a little canyon where we can fort up if we need to. I reckon we'll move up there tonight, when it's dark and Wedge's patrols won't be able to spot us as easily."

"Sounds good," Frank said with a nod. "I reckon I can find the place."

"You mean to say that if you make it to Laredo, you're gonna come back?" Darrell asked.

"That's right," Frank said quietly.

The young man with the broken arm looked embarrassed. "I'm sorry about

442

what I said earlier, Mr. Morgan. I should have known better."

Tolliver snorted and said, "You damn sure should have."

"Don't worry, Darrell," Frank said with a smile. "No offense taken."

"When are you leaving?" Ben asked.

"As soon as it's good and dark, before the moon rises. Stormy's had all afternoon to rest, so he ought to be ready to go."

"Good luck to you, Frank," Tolliver said as he held out a hand. Frank clasped it, and the rancher added, "Could be the fate of each and every one of us will be ridin' with you."

Frank didn't need Tolliver to tell him that. He already knew it.

35

Once he had made up his mind what he was going to do, the time for action couldn't come soon enough to suit Frank Morgan. Impatience grew inside him as he waited for the sun to go down and darkness to settle over the plains. He told himself he was too old to be feeling like that, but he knew it really didn't matter.

He gnawed on some jerky. That was all anybody had to eat. If the men had to stay out here for very long, they would have to hunt for food. There were deer in the area, along with prairie chickens and wild boars. But they didn't have any ammunition to waste, either, so anybody who went hunting would have to be very efficient with their bullets.

The sun dipped below the horizon and the sky deepened in color from blue to purple to black. Stars glittered from horizon to horizon, but the moon was still down. Frank shook hands all around and then swung up into the saddle, ready to ride.

He headed east, using the stars to guide him. He planned to follow an easterly course for most of the night and then cut due south for Laredo.

As he rode, thoughts of Roanne Williamson went through his mind. He recalled that Nathan Wedge had seemed interested in Roanne. Now that Wedge was running San Rosa like his own little kingdom, would he decide to force himself on Roanne? That possibility made Frank's jaw tighten with anger, and his hand on the reins clenched into a fist. It would have felt mighty good, he thought, to smash that fist right into the middle of Wedge's face.

Roanne was smart, Frank told himself. She would figure out a way to keep Wedge at bay without infuriating him to the point that he lost control. But Frank's instincts told him that Roanne would only be able to dodge trouble for so long, and then Wedge would take what he wanted.

With any luck the showdown would come before that time. Frank was going to do everything in his power to see that it did.

He kept Stormy moving at a fast, steady

pace, stopping only to let the Appaloosa drink from a puddle in a mostly dry streambed. Frank estimated that he had covered more than ten miles by the time the moon began to rise. It was orange, what folks up in Parker County had called a harvest moon when he was a kid. The night air now had enough of a chill to it that Frank was glad for the denim jacket he was wearing.

The moon was pretty, but it also represented an added risk. Frank thought he was far enough away from San Rosa that he was beyond the range of any patrols Wedge might have sent out. But he couldn't know that for sure, and as the moon rose higher and the orb faded to a paler shade of orange, he suddenly caught sight of some dust in the air, revealed by the moon glow. Frank reined in to study it.

He figured at least half-a-dozen riders would be necessary to kick up that much dust. Tonight, the chances were good that meant an outlaw patrol. Frank turned Stormy and looked to the south. That way appeared clear. He hadn't intended to turn south just yet, but the enemy was right in front of him and he didn't have much choice in the matter.

Frank kept casting glances over his left

shoulder at the dust as he rode toward the Rio Grande. He didn't think Stormy's hooves were kicking up enough dust so that the patrol would spot it, even in the bright moonlight, but there was always a chance they would notice. If the outlaws swung toward him, he would have to make a run for it. If need be, he could try crossing the river and working his way toward Laredo on the Mexican side of the border.

Suddenly, so close at hand that it was shocking, somebody yelled, *"Madre de Dios!"* Frank jerked back on the Appaloosa's reins as dark figures seemingly began to rise up out of the ground itself right in front of him, like dead souls leaving their graves.

These hombres weren't dead, though, just mad and well armed. Muzzle flashes split the darkness as somebody yelled commands in Spanish.

Rurales!

Frank bit back a curse as he whirled Stormy. Bullets sang past his ears. From the looks of it, luck had deserted him and he had ridden right into the middle of a Rurale camp. He had avoided the patrol he had seen earlier, only to find himself in an even worse spot.

He jabbed his boot heels into Stormy's flanks, sending the Appaloosa leaping forward into a gallop. A sombrero-wearing figure jumped in front of them, only to go down screaming as Stormy trampled right over him. Frank didn't know if the Rurale had meant to get in the way of the charging horse or if it had been an accident. Either way, it was fatal.

He drew his Peacemaker and sprayed bullets into a line of Rurales. A couple of the Mexicans went down. Stormy jumped, and Frank knew that a bullet must have burned across the big horse's hide. Stormy settled back down instantly into a smooth stride, however, so Frank knew the Appaloosa wasn't seriously wounded.

He holstered his Colt and leaned forward over Stormy's neck, making himself a smaller target. Moonlight was better than no light at all, but it still made for poor shooting conditions. If he could just bust through, he thought, then Stormy could outrun any of the Rurales' horses. He still had a chance to get away.

But then once again Lady Luck turned her back on Frank Morgan. Stormy stumbled and went down with shocking suddenness, whinnying shrilly as he fell. Instinct made Frank kick his feet free of the stirrups and throw himself out of the saddle. He slammed hard into the ground, the impact knocking all the air out of his body. He rolled over several times and came to a stop on his back. All he could do was lie there stunned and breathless.

Babbling excitedly, the Rurales surrounded him, looming over him in the moonlight. Frank expected them to use their bayonets to make a pincushion out of him, and they might have done just that if a commanding voice had not started barking orders at them.

Most of the Rurales drew back a little, but several of them bent over, grabbed Frank, and jerked him roughly to his feet. He was starting to catch his breath now, and his wits came back to him. He had dropped his gun when he fell, so he couldn't fight back. He stood there, willing himself to remain calm, and waited to see what was going to happen next.

The Rurale who had been shouting orders strode up in front of Frank and glared at him. "You!" he practically spat. "Morgan!"

"Do we know each other, hombre?" Frank drawled.

"I am Sergeant Lopez. I replaced the sergeant who was killed at the village." The man backhanded Frank across the face to punctuate the introduction. The Rurales holding Frank didn't let him fall or even stagger. Sergeant Lopez smiled and went on. "Capitán Estancia is going to be very glad to see you, gringo."

Frank tasted blood at the corner of his mouth. "I don't reckon the feeling will be mutual."

"Tie him up!" Lopez snapped at his men. "*Andale!* We ride tonight!"

Frank felt hollow inside. If indeed he was the last chance for Cecil Tolliver and the other honest Texans to get help from outside, then they might well be doomed.

But he couldn't give up yet. There were still cards to be played in this game. Stormy was all right; Frank had already seen the big Appaloosa up and walking around, limping slightly but not enough to indicate a serious injury. Stormy must have stepped in a prairie-dog hole while Frank was trying to break through the Rurales. That was the only explanation for his sudden fall. But such a mishap could have easily broken the horse's leg. Shoot, thought Frank, a fall like that could have broken *his* neck.

But instead, both of them were still alive and relatively intact. Maybe luck hadn't completely deserted them.

Sergeant Lopez had Frank's wrists tied together in front of him. Some of the Rurales tried to catch Stormy and bring him over so that Frank could mount up, but Stormy shied away and reared up, making the Rurales jump to avoid his slashing hooves. Lopez drew a pistol and aimed it at Stormy's head, saying, "Get that devil horse of yours under control, Morgan, or I'll kill him and make you walk where we're going!"

Frank whistled softly and said, "Stormy! Take it easy, boy. Come here."

Stormy came over to him and nudged him with his nose. Frank talked to him for a moment in a quiet, calming tone, then grasped the saddle horn with his bound hands, put his left foot in the stirrup, and pulled himself up onto the Appaloosa's back. The Rurales began to mount up as well. Following Lopez's orders, several of them kept their rifles trained on Frank at all times.

From what Lopez had said, it was obvious that they were going to take him to wherever Estancia was. Frank had no idea where that might be, but his hope was that somewhere along the way he would have a chance to make a break for freedom. If that opportunity came along, he would seize it.

Lopez was a careful man, though. He kept Frank surrounded and under the gun as the group rode through the night.

One of the Rurales asked the sergeant, "Were not our orders to remain in this area and patrol to make sure none of the gringos escape?"

Lopez turned in the saddle and backhanded the man as he had done to Frank. "Stupid! Is not this man Morgan one of the greatest prizes among the gringos? There are other patrols, but only *we* have captured the famous gunfighter! Capitán Estancia will surely reward us."

That put to rest any grumbling that the other men might do. The idea of a reward was appealing to all of them.

The Rurales rode most of the night with their prisoner. Lopez didn't set a very fast pace, though, so Frank wasn't sure how far they actually went. He knew they had not yet reached the Rio Grande when they came in sight of an adobe ranch house. Frank didn't recognize the place. He figured it was the home of one of Cecil Tolliver's neighbors.

At the moment, though, the Rurales had taken it over. In the graying dawn light, Frank saw that the corral was full of their mounts, and several of the Rurales lounged around the door of the bunkhouse. Smoke rose from the chimney of the cookshack. The day was getting started.

Sergeant Lopez hailed one of the men and said to him in Spanish, "Tell Captain Estancia that we have captured the man named Frank Morgan!"

Wide-eyed, the Rurale stared at Frank for a second before turning and hurrying into the ranch house to carry out the sergeant's order. Lopez, Frank, and the men surrounding him all came to a halt in front of the house as Captain Domingo Estancia strode outside a moment later, a look of arrogant hatred on his hawklike face.

As nattily uniformed as ever, despite the early hour, Estancia glared up at Frank and said, "Ah, Señor Morgan! I was afraid that we might never cross paths again."

"So was I," Frank said.

Estancia frowned and asked, "Why is that?"

"I was afraid I might never get the chance to line you up in my gunsights."

The officer's face darkened with rage, but after a moment he brought himself under control and forced a cold smile onto his face. "Tell me where the rest of the Texans who escaped may be found, and perhaps I will give you the gift of a quick death."

"Go to hell," Frank said.

He knew he was taking a chance. Estancia might kill him out of hand. But Frank thought there was a good chance the captain would want to keep him alive for the time being. Estancia might believe that he could torture valuable information out of Frank. There had to be a rivalry of sorts between Estancia and Wedge, even though they were partners. Such a thing would be only natural between two such ambitious men. Estancia might think that having Frank as his prisoner would give him a slight advantage over the renegade Texas Ranger.

For a long moment Estancia looked like he wanted to whip out his pistol and blow Frank out of the saddle. But finally he said to Lopez, "Sergeant, take Señor Morgan to the smokehouse over there and lock him up. We will see if he feels more like talking later."

"*Sí, Capitán.*"

Frank was dragged out of the saddle, taken across the ranch yard to a sturdy little log structure near the cookshack, and thrown inside. There was only one door. It slammed shut behind him as he lost his balance and fell to his knees. Darkness closed in around him.

Frank moved over and sat against the wall in a more comfortable position. If Estancia thought that locking him up in a small, confined space was suddenly going to make him start cooperating, the captain was bound to be disappointed. If it had been mid-summer, the heat in the smoke-house might have been enough to cook a man's brain. Now, in late autumn, it wasn't all that unpleasant in here, even as the sun rose higher in the sky and the temperature grew warmer.

Without even thinking about it, Frank fell asleep, his head propped against the log wall behind him.

36

The Rurales left Frank in the smokehouse all day. Hunger gnawed at his belly and thirst parched his throat. Worse than any physical discomfort, however, was the knowledge that he had let his friends down. Worry over what might be happening to them plagued his thoughts.

Finally, that evening, the bar over the smokehouse door was removed and the door was opened. Even though the sun was down, the twilight seemed bright enough to make Frank squint. Several burly Rurales entered and hauled him outside. He was set on his feet and marched across to the ranch house.

Captain Estancia was waiting for him in the parlor, hands clasped behind his back as he stood ramrod-straight beside the fireplace. "Señor Morgan," Estancia said with a curt nod. "I trust you enjoyed your day."

Frank was a little dizzy from hunger and

thirst, but he didn't let Estancia see that as he put a faint smile on his face and said, "Mighty pleasant. I appreciate the chance to get in some good rest. Been a mite busy lately."

Estancia's lips thinned in anger, but he remained in control. "Now that you have had time to think," he said, "perhaps you would reconsider telling me what I want to know."

"Nope," Frank said with a shake of his head. "I can't help you."

"You realize I can force the information out of you?"

"Correction," Frank said. "You can try."

Estancia looked past Frank and nodded. Frank had an idea of what was coming and tried to prepare himself, but there was no way to get ready for a rifle butt slammed into the small of his back. Sergeant Lopez, who was standing behind Frank, struck the blow, grunting with effort as he thrust it home.

Pain exploded up Frank's spine. His legs went numb and he would have fallen if two of the Rurales hadn't caught hold of his arms and held him up. He sagged in their grip, breathing hard. But he hadn't cried out. His mouth had remained tightly closed.

"Señor Morgan, there is no need to

make things so difficult for both of us," Estancia said. "Tell me where to find those troublesome Texans, and your pain will all be over."

Through clenched teeth, Frank said, "Because you'll kill me, right?"

Estancia shrugged. "Sometimes a bullet in the head can be a merciful thing."

He nodded again, and Lopez struck a second blow, this time on the point of Frank's left shoulder blade. Agony flooded through Frank's body. He wondered if the bone was broken.

"Señor Morgan?"

"Go . . . to . . . hell!" It was the same answer he had given Estancia early that morning, but Frank didn't see how he could improve on it.

While Estancia stood there watching impassively, Sergeant Lopez and the other Rurales beat Frank mercilessly, striking him with rifle butts and fists. Somewhere along the way, his feet were kicked out from under him, and as he lay huddled on the floor of the parlor, their boots thudded relentlessly into his ribs and stomach. There was no telling what damage they were doing to him inside. And there was nothing he could do except lie there and endure it.

Finally, Estancia called a halt to the beating. Frank heard the words only vaguely. He held on stubbornly to the few shreds of consciousness remaining to him. He tasted blood in his mouth as somebody took hold of his hair and jerked his head up so that Estancia could look down into his face.

Frank's lips curled in a snarl as he gazed blearily up at the officer. Estancia just straightened and shook his head.

"I can still see the defiance in his eyes. Take him back to the smokehouse and lock him up again."

Lopez asked, "Should we send word to Capitán Wedge that Morgan is our prisoner?"

"Fool!" Estancia snapped. "I am in command here, not Wedge."

"Of course, Capitán," Lopez said hastily. "I meant no disrespect."

Estancia flicked a hand, signaling for them to drag Frank's bloody, half-conscious form out of the room.

Frank drifted in and out of awareness. It was dark where he was, pitch black. He didn't know if that was because it was night, or because he was back in the smokehouse, or because he was blind. All three of those things might be true. He lay

459

on something hard — the ground? — and concentrated on breathing deeply and slowly. His ribs were sore, but he didn't feel the sharp pain that would have told him some of them were broken. He moved his fingers, wiggled his toes. Everything still worked. At last he pushed himself into a sitting position. A wave of dizziness went through him. He felt sick, but there was nothing in his stomach to come up. Reaching out in the darkness, he touched the rough surface of the log wall. He shifted around until he was leaning against it again. He saw a faint glow of starlight filtering in around the door and knew that he wasn't blind after all. He was locked up and it was night, but he was still alive.

He began to laugh softly. He was alive. Sooner or later, Captain Domingo Estancia was sure going to regret that.

Frank didn't know if he passed out or merely fell asleep. Somehow, though, the night passed, and when the cracks around the smokehouse door began to turn gray with the approach of dawn, he was alert. In pain, certainly, but he was able to push that out of his brain and not think about it. He put his hands against the wall and braced himself as he struggled to his feet.

After a long moment, he was able to stand up on his own.

He took stock of himself. His belly was so empty his backbone was gnawing on his belt buckle. His tongue was swollen from lack of water and his throat was as dry as Death Valley. He didn't know if he could talk or not. When he tried to take a step, he stumbled and almost fell. But he caught himself with his hands against the wall and tried again, and this time he was steadier. Slowly, stubbornly, he began to make his way around the empty interior of the smokehouse. Stiff, sore muscles loosened slightly, so that after a while he was actually walking, rather than hobbling. Even though his wrists were still tied, he swung his arms back and forth, loosening those muscles as well.

A grim smile tugged at Frank's mouth. He was in no shape for a fight, but at least he could move around a little. If a chance to strike back at his captors somehow presented itself, he could at least try to seize it. Estancia and the Rurales might still be in for a surprise or two. . . .

He heard footsteps approaching the door. When it was opened, the dawn light made his eyes narrow. Sergeant Lopez started to step into the smokehouse, but stopped short when he saw that Frank was on his feet, waiting for him.

"Ah, Morgan, you are a tough gringo," Lopez said with a mean grin. "*Muy malo.* You want to jump me, try to take my gun away from me?" Lopez raised both hands and beckoned Frank forward. "Go ahead, try. I dare you."

Frank ignored the challenge. "Did Estancia send you to fetch me, or did he give you some other errand?"

The note of contempt in Frank's voice made the grin disappear from Lopez's face. He snapped an order in Spanish to the men with him, who came into the smokehouse and reached for Frank's arms to pull him out. He avoided their grip and stepped forward on his own, walking out of the makeshift prison without any help. Rifle-toting Rurales fell in around him and escorted him to the ranch house.

Estancia waited just outside the front door, wearing his gray sombrero this morning. He said, "I did not expect to see you so hale and healthy-looking, Señor Morgan. You must be a very strong man."

"Strong enough," Frank said.

"Enough to be an annoyance." Estancia gave a jerk of his head. "I have grown tired of dealing with you. My patrols are searching this part of the country, and I am confident they will find the pitiful remnants of the band of Texans who foolishly thought to oppose us. So I have decided that I no longer require your assistance."

"Going to let me go, are you?"

Estancia snapped his fingers and said, "Take him."

The Rurales closed in, grabbing Frank from both sides. He writhed and tried to pull free, but there were too many of them. They dragged him around the ranch house toward an adobe barn. Frank saw half-a-dozen more Rurales waiting there, lined up facing the wall of the barn. Each man held a rifle.

A firing squad. Frank had never seen one before, but he recognized it for what it was anyway.

When he looked past the barn he saw several mounds of freshly turned earth. New graves, he thought, probably where the owners of this ranch were buried. Estancia had moved in and taken the place over as his headquarters, brutally murdering the unfortunate Texans who had lived here. Now Frank was destined to join them.

The Rurales dragged Frank over to the barn and slammed him against the wall, standing him up there with his back against the adobe. They moved out of the way, leaving him to face the firing squad.

Estancia strolled up, looking pleased with himself. "I suppose I should give you one last chance to cooperate and tell me what I want to know, Morgan," he said. "You will die in the next few minutes regardless, but perhaps you have had a change of heart."

"There's a fiery place I've been telling you to go to for the past couple of days, Estancia. You don't seem to be able to get that idea through your head."

The Rurale officer's face darkened with anger. "Very well." He turned to Sergeant Lopez. "Proceed."

"One thing," Frank said quickly before Lopez could start giving the orders for the execution. He held out his bound wrists. "You reckon somebody could cut these thongs? I'd rather die with my hands free."

"How unfortunate," Estancia said, "but I am not in the mood to do any favors for you, Señor. You will die bound like the animal you are."

Frank's jaw tightened. Fear made his heart hammer in his chest. Despite the cool nerves with which he had been blessed, the nerves that had helped him to

464

survive this long in a hazardous time and a perilous land, he was as human as the next man, and he couldn't stare death in the face without feeling something. He had never been afraid of the mere act of dying. Hell, anybody could do that. Everybody did, sooner or later. And even though he had broken his share of commandments along the way, he wasn't that worried about what the afterlife might hold in store for him, either. What he hated, what his heart and soul and brain raged against even though he showed none of the turmoil going through him, was the fact that he would never see his friends and his loved ones again. Tyler Beaumont and old Luke Perkins, Mercy and Victoria, even his son Conrad, who had no real use for him . . . At a time like this, it would have meant so much to see them again, if only for a moment. . . .

And then there were the things left undone, the true regrets in life. He would have liked to help set things straight here in the border country, to restore justice and see to it that hydrophobic skunks like Wedge and Estancia didn't escape what they had coming to them. All his life Frank Morgan had stood up to evil wherever he found it. He wasn't ready to give up that fight.

But Sergeant Lopez shouted out, "Ready . . ." and the firing squad lifted their rifles. "Aim!" the sergeant said, and the Rurales nestled their cheeks against the smooth wooden stocks of their weapons and squinted over the barrels as they settled their sights on the chest of the man who stood with his back pressed against the adobe wall. As Lopez paused with a Latin flair for the dramatic, Frank's eyes darted to Estancia's face and saw the smug satisfaction there.

It couldn't happen like this, Frank thought. By God, it just *couldn't!*

Sergeant Lopez opened his mouth to shout, "Fire!"

But before the word could escape, a shot rang out and Lopez's head jerked backward as a bullet hole appeared in the center of his forehead. His black sombrero flew up in the air. The sergeant's body hit the ground first, dead as it could be.

Just like that, all hell broke loose. Shots roared and blasted and men yelled and cursed. Hoofbeats thundered as mounted men swept around the corner of the barn and charged through the ranks of the Rurales, laying waste to them.

Frank saw Estancia turn and sprint toward the house, trying desperately to escape. Billowing clouds of dust and powder smoke rolled between Frank and the officer, and he couldn't see Estancia anymore.

The rapid barking of a six-gun somewhere above him made Frank lift his head and peer upward. He saw that a wooden door set in the wall of the barn to allow access to the hayloft had been swung open, and someone in there thrust a revolver out and squeezed off several shots, dropping a couple of Rurales who ran toward Frank, evidently intent on gutting him with their bayonets. As Frank's somewhat stunned brain thought back over the events of the past few moments, he realized that the shot that had killed Sergeant Lopez had come from the hayloft, too. That had been the signal for the attack that now drove the Rurales into a full-scale retreat.

A thick wooden beam stuck out from the wall above the hayloft door. A rope and block-and-tackle arrangement was fastened to it so that bales of hay could be lifted to the loft that way. As Frank watched, a black-clad figure leaned out, grasped that rope, and swung down to land lightly in front of him. Frank found himself staring into dark eyes above a black silk bandanna pulled up to serve as a mask over the lower half of his rescuer's face.

Then a knife flashed in the hands of the Black Scorpion, cutting the bonds around Frank's wrists, and he was free.

37

"Carmen!" Frank exclaimed, recognizing those dark, long-lashed eyes. "What the hell — !"

"No time for explanations, Señor Morgan," the disguised young woman said. "We must get you out of here."

She turned and waved an arm, and a large figure hurried toward her and Frank, leading three horses. Frank recognized Lupe, who had been Antonio Almanzar's second in command in the band of revolutionaries led by the Black Scorpion. Lupe had the reins of Stormy, El Rey, and a big chestnut stallion that evidently was his mount.

"Can you ride?" Carmen asked Frank.

"Just you watch me," was his reply.

He took the reins that Lupe pressed into his hands and swung up lithely onto Stormy's back. It hurt to move like that, but Frank didn't care. Lupe gave him a pistol, too, and Frank slid the Colt into the empty holster he still wore. The weight of the gun on his hip felt mighty good.

Carmen practically sprang onto El Rey, and Lupe mounted up as well. The three of them wheeled the horses and Carmen took the lead, galloping away from the ranch that had come so close to being Frank's final resting place.

Scattered gunfire still sounded around the ranch buildings, but Frank had seen enough to know that the Rurales had been routed. He wished he knew whether or not Estancia had been killed in the fighting. It certainly wasn't too much to hope for . . . but Frank wasn't going to be surprised if the captain had escaped somehow. Evil men tended to be slippery men, able to duck away from trouble even when the odds were against them.

Frank let Carmen stay out in front. She probably knew where she was going better than he did. Lupe brought up the rear. Frank was glad to see that the big *segundo* had survived the battle with the Rurales below the border. From the looks of things, enough of the revolutionaries had lived through that fracas to regroup into a sizable band. It was possible that the bunch had recruited some new members, too.

As that thought passed through his head, he suddenly understood why Carmen was wearing the Black Scorpion getup. Any cause had to have a leader, or else it was doomed to fail. Antonio was still laid up from his bullet wound, so the burden had fallen on Carmen. With Lupe to do the talking . . . It was possible that the new members in the band didn't even know Carmen was a woman. The blousy black shirt concealed the curves of her slender figure, and her long hair was tucked securely under the black hat.

Yes, it could have been that way, Frank thought. The Black Scorpion rode again.

Frank wondered whether Antonio had revealed his masquerade to his sister and asked for her help, or if she had been aware of his double life all along. She might have taken it on herself to assume the role of the Black Scorpion after her brother was wounded. Antonio might not even know what she was doing.

Carmen didn't slow El Rey to a stop until they were a couple of miles away from the ranch. Frank and Lupe halted, too, and when Frank looked behind them he saw a cloud of dust rising into the early morning air.

"That will be our men," Lupe said. "The

Rurales all fled the other direction, the ones who lived through our attack."

Frank looked at Carmen and smiled. "Your timing was almost a mite too slow, but you showed up just when I needed you. I'm much obliged for my life."

Carmen pulled down the bandanna and said, "How do you gringos say it? We are even now, Señor Morgan. We have each saved the other's life." She paused and then added, "But I still owe you for my brother's life, and that is a debt I will perhaps never be able to repay."

"Antonio's doing all right?"

She nodded and laughed despite the seriousness of their situation. "Yes, but he will be very angry when he discovers what I have done."

"You didn't tell him you were taking over as the Black Scorpion," Frank guessed.

"He would have forbidden me to do such a thing," Carmen said. "But our people need the Black Scorpion. Men will follow him into battle, men who would pay no attention to . . . a little girl."

"Who knows your secret?"

"Just you and Lupe and a few of the men who were with Antonio. The few who lived through the terrible battle that almost cost my brother his life."

Lupe said, "After Señorita Carmen approached me with her idea and I saw I could not talk her out of it, I went to all the villages up and down this part of the Rio Grande and appealed for men to join us. When they heard that they could ride with the famous Black Scorpion, many men took up their guns and left their homes and came with me to help us restore freedom to our land."

"How many?" Frank asked bluntly.

"There are fifteen of us," Carmen said.

Frank raised his eyebrows in surprise. The revolutionaries had been considerably outnumbered when they attacked the Rurales. But the element of surprise had been on their side, and the Rurales must have cut and run before they realized their superior numbers. Frank recalled a certain fracas at San Jacinto, nearly sixty years earlier, where a much larger Mexican army had been defeated by a small force of determined Texans who had taken them by surprise.

"We have been on Estancia's trail for several days," Carmen went on. "Early this morning, before dawn, we came up to the ranch where you were being held prisoner. It took a while for us to slip in and get ready for the attack. I managed to get into the barn along with several of our men. We opened fire as soon as we could."

"Soon enough to pull my bacon out of the fire," Frank said.

Lupe waved a big hand toward the approaching riders. "Señorita, you should pull your mask up. The men will be here soon."

Carmen did as he suggested, adjusting the black bandanna and pulling down the brim of her hat so that only her eyes were visible.

"What do we do now?" Lupe asked. "The Rurales will regroup and come after us."

Since he had been given an unexpected lease on life, Frank had been asking himself the same question. Now he said, "Do you know what's going on over here in Texas?"

Her voice slightly muffled by the bandanna, Carmen said, "Estancia and his men seem to be looking for someone. It surprised us when his trail led us to the north of the Rio Grande, but we followed it anyway."

"Estancia can die just as well north of the border as south of it," Lupe said gruffly.

474

"Estancia is working with a renegade Texas Ranger captain named Nathan Wedge," Frank explained. "Wedge and his men have turned lobo just like Estancia and the Rurales. They may have even hatched the scheme together. Now they're after nothing less than completely taking over the border country, on both sides of the river."

"Madre de Dios," Lupe muttered. "They must be mad."

"No, saying they're crazy lets them off too easy," Frank replied. "They're ruthless and just downright evil. They'll do anything to get what they want, no matter who gets hurt."

"We must stop them," Carmen said.

Frank thought swiftly as the rest of the revolutionary band approached. "You have fifteen men," he said. "All the ranchers in this area, along with some of the men from the town of San Rosa, have had to take to the hills to hide out from Wedge. There are around twenty of them left alive and able to fight. If Wedge and Estancia join forces, they can muster between fifty and sixty men, maybe even more depending on how many Estancia brought across the border with him."

"The odds are long, but right is on our

side," Carmen said. "We will prevail."

"We'll have a lot better chance if we can even the odds some. What day is it?"

Carmen and Lupe both frowned at Frank as he asked the question. Carmen said, "It is . . . I think . . . Friday. Yes, it is Friday."

"Tomorrow your father planned to meet with Cecil Tolliver in San Rosa."

Carmen's dark eyes widened. "*Dios mio!* You are right, Señor Morgan. I had forgotten about that."

"Was he still planning to be there?"

She nodded. "Yes, as far as I know. He said that if he heard nothing from you to the contrary, he would trust you and go to San Rosa. In fact, he was going to ride across and make camp outside the settlement tonight, so that he could meet with Señor Tolliver tomorrow. Now he will ride right into danger!"

"Not if we intercept him on the way," Frank pointed out. "Will he be bringing some of his vaqueros with him?"

"*Sí,* perhaps a dozen men."

Frank sighed. "Well, it's not enough to make the odds even, but every fighting man we can get on our side gives us a better chance."

"I can ride to the border, circling around

San Rosa, and meet him before he gets there," Carmen said. She smiled. "No doubt he will be shocked to see me —"

"Especially in that getup," Frank said.

"*Sí*. But when I tell him what is going on, I am sure he will help you, Señor Morgan." Suddenly she frowned as a thought occurred to her. "But that will mean fighting alongside Señor Tolliver as well."

"Your father and Cecil Tolliver will have to put their feud aside, at least for now," Frank said, "or else the Rio Grande is liable to run red with blood before Wedge and Estancia are through."

Carmen nodded slowly. "Yes. I must make Papa see reason." She gave a hollow laugh. "That is not always an easy task."

"You know Don Felipe better than I do, but he struck me as an honorable man. Tolliver is an honorable man, too. They ought to be able to fight side by side to rid the world of a couple of polecats like Wedge and Estancia."

"Yes. I will make him understand," Carmen vowed.

The rest of the band was almost there. Frank said quickly, "Northwest of here there's a big hill called Sand Mountain. It's probably the highest point for quite a ways on this side of the border. That's where Tolliver and the other Texans are supposed to be holed up."

"We can find it," Lupe said. "We will meet Don Felipe and bring him there tonight. Is this not right, Señorita?"

"Yes," Carmen said, her voice strong and determined. "Do you go now to this Sand Mountain, Señor Morgan?"

Frank nodded. "I reckon that would be the best thing to do."

"Then look for us there, and together we will crush the wicked!"

Frank lifted a hand in farewell and heeled Stormy into a trot. His muscles and bones ached, he still hadn't had anything to eat or drink, and he wasn't exactly sure where he was going.

But he had been given a reprieve from almost certain death, and now he had a chance to strike once more at the men who were trying to establish their own little evil empire here along the Rio Grande.

Life was pretty good, he thought with a smile as he rode through the morning. It would be even better if he got another shot at Wedge and Estancia.

A search through the saddlebags turned up a single strip of jerky. Frank chewed it for a long while, making it last, and by the time he finished it, he and Stormy had come to a narrow creek. Frank dismounted, cupped some of the water in his hand, and tasted it. It didn't taste very good, but it was fit to drink. He and Stormy both slaked their thirst.

Feeling a little better, Frank pushed on, angling northwest. He didn't know how big Sand Mountain really was, but he hoped he would be able to pick it out from the plains surrounding it. As he rode, he kept a lookout for Rurale patrols. If there were any in the area, he wanted to spot them before they spotted him. To that end, he kept Stormy moving at a fairly slow pace so that the Appaloosa wouldn't kick up too much dust.

By early afternoon, Frank had spotted a low, humplike shape on the horizon ahead of him and steered toward it. It was the only sort of elevation he had seen all day, and he hoped it was Sand Mountain. As he drew closer, he was able to make out more of the details. A sandy ridge dotted with brush stretched for about a mile, rising a hundred feet from the surrounding terrain. Some of the slopes were gradual, but in other places the earth had been worn away so that the ridge jutted up sharply. This seemed to be the only thing even remotely resembling a mountain for miles around, so Frank hoped he was headed in the right direction.

Tolliver had mentioned some springs being located at the base of the mountain. Frank saw a few areas of thicker brush along the bottom of the ridge and figured the vegetation might be a sign of those springs. As he rode toward them, he saw what at first he took to be the shadow of a cloud on the slope. When he came closer, he saw it was actually the mouth of a canyon. That jibed with what Tolliver had said, too.

A couple of horsemen appeared at the foot of the ridge and rode toward him. Relief washed through Frank as he recognized the stocky figure of Cecil Tolliver and the taller, leaner shape of Doc Ervin. They had seen him coming and were riding out to meet him.

When they were close enough, Tolliver raised a hand in greeting and called, "Frank! Did you make it to Laredo?"

Frank reined in and shook his head as Tolliver and Doc brought their mounts to a halt as well. "One of the Rurale patrols grabbed me," Frank explained. "I barely got away with my life."

"Son of a bitch!" Tolliver exploded. "So we still don't know if help is on the way or not. What are we going to do now?"

"Well, we've got *some* help on the way," Frank said. "I don't know if it'll be enough, but it's better than nothing. Thing is, it's going to require something out of you, Cecil."

"Me?" Tolliver said in surprise. "What do I have to do?"

"You have to agree to get along with Don Felipe Almanzar."

"What?" Tolliver's face purpled with anger. "That damned Mex —"

Frank raised a hand to forestall the rancher's protest and said, "That's not all. We've got another ally you probably wouldn't expect."

"Who's that?" Doc Ervin asked.

"The Black Scorpion," Frank said.

38

That surprised Tolliver and Doc even more. "The Black Scorpion is an outlaw!" Tolliver argued.

Frank shook his head. "Like I told you before, he and his men just want to break Estancia's grip on the territory across the Rio Grande. They followed the Rurales across the river and had a skirmish with them at a ranch southeast of here. That happened to be where I was being held prisoner, and that's how I was able to get away."

He didn't mention that the Black Scorpion was no longer a "he." Carmen could reveal that or not reveal it at the time and place of her choosing.

Tolliver scrubbed a weary hand over his face. "This is all gettin' too mixed up for me. We're fightin' the Rangers, and we've got a bunch of Mex *bandidos* on our side. The whole damn world's got turned upside down."

"That happens sometimes when men get too greedy," Frank said. "Come on. Let's ride on into your camp and I'll fill you in on everything that's happened. There's still more you don't know about," he added, thinking of the impending arrival of Don Felipe Almanzar on the scene.

"Lord help us," Tolliver muttered as he turned his horse and led the way back to Sand Mountain.

Frank and Doc followed, and the physician said quietly, "You look like you've been through the wringer, Frank."

"Estancia tried to get me to tell him where he could find you fellas."

"Torture?" Doc asked in a hushed, angry tone.

"Nothing fancy. His sergeant and some of the men tried to beat it out of me."

Doc looked intently at him and said, "But I'll bet they didn't succeed, did they?"

Frank smiled thinly and shook his head. "Nope."

The three men rode past the springs and into the narrow canyon that cut deeply into Sand Mountain. The canyon made a bend and widened slightly, and Frank saw that that was where the fugitive Texans had made their camp. As he looked around he made a quick head count and came up with thirty men, including himself, Tolliver, and Doc. A few stragglers had shown up after he'd left on his ill-fated mission to Laredo.

That raised Frank's spirits even more. They probably still couldn't match the number of men Wedge and Estancia had at their disposal, but at least the Texans were no longer outnumbered by nearly two to one.

Just a fair fight . . . that was all Frank wanted now.

And a chance to settle things with Domingo Estancia and Nathan Wedge.

The men gathered around Frank to hear about what had happened to him. Somewhere they had come up with some coffee, and as Frank sipped a tin cup of the strong black brew, he thought he had never tasted anything better in his life. As the men listened raptly, he told them how he had been caught by the Rurales, taken before Estancia, and tortured.

"When they figured out I wasn't going to talk, they put me up against a wall in front of a firing squad," he related. "I thought I was a goner."

"What happened?" Ben Tolliver asked eagerly. "How'd you get away?"

"I had some help," Frank said. "That was when the Black Scorpion showed up." He didn't mention that in this case, the Black Scorpion was actually Carmen Almanzar, the woman Ben loved. The young fella would have been a mite shocked, Frank thought wryly.

To most of these men, the Black Scorpion was nothing but a bandit. Frank had to explain that he had been with the band of revolutionaries for their first battle with the corrupt Rurales under Captain Estancia, and he added that his own life would have been forfeit without the lightning raid on the ranch just as he was about to be executed.

"I give you my word," he said forcefully, "the Black Scorpion is no outlaw. All his raids on this side of the border were carried out against people who were part of the smuggling operation set up by Wedge and Estancia."

"You're sure about all this, Morgan?" one of the men asked.

Frank nodded. "I'm as certain as I can be. The Black Scorpion is on the same side we are."

Doc asked, "What happened to these so-called revolutionaries, Frank? Where did they go after they helped you get away from the Rurales?"

Now things got even trickier, Frank thought with a glance at Cecil Tolliver. "They went to get some more help for us," he said. "A week ago, while I was down in Mexico at the Almanzar hacienda, I decided it was time that all the trouble between Don Felipe and Cecil here got patched up."

"What?" Tolliver burst out. "You up and decided that on your own, did you?"

Frank reached into his pocket. The letter from Don Felipe was considerably crumpled and creased, but it was still there. He took it out and extended it toward Tolliver.

"Don Felipe agreed to a meeting with you in San Rosa tomorrow," Frank said. "He wants to hash everything out, and I reckon he says as much in this letter. But when he agreed to that, it was before we knew that Wedge and Estancia were going to bring everything out in the open and declare war on all the law-abiding folks in the border country. Don Felipe is on his way up here today with some of his vaqueros, and the Black Scorpion has gone to meet them and bring them here."

"Almanzar's comin' here?" Tolliver grated.

"That's right," Frank said. "With Don

Felipe, the Black Scorpion, and all the men the two of them have added to our numbers, we'll make up a big enough force to take on Wedge and Estancia." Frank's voice rose a little as he went on. "We don't have to wait for help from outside. We're strong enough to take on those bastards ourselves . . . and beat them."

Even though the men were uncertain, Frank saw hope spring to life on their tired, dirty faces in response to his words. Men just naturally liked to have their destinies in their own hands, and these rugged Texans were no exception. Given the chance, they would fight for what was rightfully theirs, would fight to defeat the usurpers and the evil-doers, to their last breath and the last drop of their blood.

"Almanzar," Cecil Tolliver muttered. "I . . . I just don't know I can bring myself to trust him, to fight alongside him."

Ben reached out to grasp his father's arm. "Pa, you can trust him and you can fight beside him."

"How would you know?" Tolliver demanded with a frown.

"I . . . I just know," Ben answered, unwilling to reveal the relationship he had with Carmen. His voice strengthened a little, though, as he went on. "If we don't trust the Mexicans and let them help us, sooner or later we'll be wiped out, and you know it, Pa."

Tolliver rubbed his bearded jaw. "A couple dozen good fightin' men sure would come in handy, that's for damned sure," he mused. "And Felipe, blast his eyes, was always a tough hombre."

Frank tried not to smile as he saw that Tolliver was getting used to the idea. The rest of the men looked to Tolliver as a leader. If he went along with the idea of teaming up with Don Felipe Almanzar and the Black Scorpion, then the others would accept it, too.

"You say they're comin' here tonight?" Tolliver said to Frank.

"Unless they run into trouble or something else happens to prevent it."

"Well, I reckon we can wait and talk it over, at least." Tolliver's fingers clenched on the letter from Almanzar he still held in his hand, unread. "If we call a truce, though, it'll be just that. I ain't sayin' that the war between us is over."

"Let's take care of Wedge and Estancia first," Frank said. "One war at a time."

The afternoon dragged in the Texans' camp as they waited for the fall of night

488

and the hoped-for arrival of the reinforcements from south of the border. There was another worry that Frank wasn't aware of until after he had been in the camp for a while. Nick Holmes and one of the other men had ridden out early that morning to scout the ranches around San Rosa and had not returned. Many of the men were worried, naturally enough, about their families. Frank didn't think Wedge would move against the women and children who had been left behind when their menfolk went to the Rocking T several nights earlier for that fateful meeting. But when a man turned renegade like Wedge, it was hard to be sure just what he might do. Worry about Roanne Williamson still lurked in the back of Frank's mind. The fact that Nick and the other scout had not returned was just one more concern.

Night finally fell, bringing a chilly wind with it. A short time after darkness settled down, the sound of hoofbeats approaching the camp could be heard. The tiny cook fire had been extinguished before nightfall, so the canyon was lit only by the stars. Orders were whispered, and the Texans spread out, hunting whatever cover they could find in case they were in for a fight. Frank, Tolliver, Ben, and Doc Ervin went to the mouth of the canyon, all of them holding rifles. The horses were closer now, and Frank could hear the clink and rattle of their harness as well as their hoofbeats. The sounds stopped as the riders came to a halt about fifty yards from the canyon mouth.

A shout came through the darkness. "Señor Morgan! Señor Morgan, are you there?"

Frank felt relief wash through him as he recognized the deep, powerful tones of Don Felipe Almanzar. He glanced over at Tolliver and Doc, and they nodded at him, urging him to answer the call.

"Don Felipe!" Frank said as he stepped forward. "Come ahead! We've been waiting for you."

The riders moved toward the canyon. Don Felipe's tall figure was in the lead, but someone else rode beside and just behind him. Frank was willing to bet that was Carmen.

As the newcomers moved past him, Frank counted them and came up with twenty-five. The Texans and their allies from below the border were now roughly equal to the combined forces of Wedge and Estancia. And since it was possible that the Rangers and the Rurales might be somewhat split up and scattered, Frank and his friends might actually hold a numerical advantage when it came to a fight. They couldn't know that for sure yet, however.

A small fire was kindled again, so that the leaders of the groups could see each other. Don Felipe and the Black Scorpion dismounted and came up to the fire. Frank was a little surprised to see that Carmen still had the bandanna over the lower half of her face. He had assumed that her masquerade would be over by now.

Tolliver and Don Felipe regarded each other warily for a moment before Tolliver finally said, "Felipe. It's good to see you again."

Don Felipe's eyes were narrow with distrust, but he nodded and said, "And you, Cecil. It has been a long time."

"Too long, if you ask me," Doc Ervin put in. "I've been around the border a long time, and I remember when you two were friends."

"That was a different time, Doctor," Don Felipe said. "Señor Tolliver and I were different men then."

"Well, right now we need you to be the men you used to be," Doc said. "We need you to stand together with the rest of us against the men who are trying to take over this country, lock, stock, and barrel."

Tolliver took out the letter Frank had given him earlier. "I'm ready to bury the hatchet for a while, Felipe," he said. "From the sound of this letter, you are, too."

Almanzar nodded. "For the good of all, I will put aside my honor and stand with you."

"Your honor never had any reason to be offended," Tolliver snapped. "If you'd just listened to reason when I tried to talk to you years ago —"

Frank stepped in, saying, "Maybe you two had better save this part of the discussion for later."

"No!"

The clear, high-pitched voice made most of the men around the campfire stiffen in surprise. Obviously, it belonged to a woman, and none of the Texans except Frank had known that there was a female anywhere around here. But the slender, black-clad figure stepped forward, pulled down the mask, and took off the black, flat-crowned hat to shake her hair free. The long, straight, sable mane tumbled down her back.

"Carmen!" Ben Tolliver yelped like he had just been stuck with a knife.

Don Felipe sighed. "Carmen, you promised me you would not reveal yourself to these men."

She tossed her head with the defiance that Frank had come to recognize was second nature with her. "If we are to fight side by side, they deserve to know who I am."

"You will *not* fight," Don Felipe insisted. "It was foolish enough of me to allow you to come along with us."

"You knew if you tried to send me back to the rancho, I would ignore you," she said.

Ben still stared at her in disbelief as he said, "Carmen, you . . . I never dreamed. . . . Damn it, this just isn't possible! You can't be the Black Scorpion!"

She stepped over to him, holding the black hat in her left hand while she reached up with her right to caress his cheek. "When this is over, I will tell you all about it," she said quietly. She came up on her toes to brush her lips against his.

"Ben!" Cecil Tolliver exclaimed.

"Carmen!" Don Felipe Almanzar roared.

Frank tried not to grin at the looks of amazement and shock on the weathered faces of the two men as Carmen turned to face them and Ben put his arm around her shoulders. "Papa, Señor Tolliver, you see with your own eyes why the feud between you must end. Ben and I love each other, and when all this trouble is over, we will be married."

"Hold on," Ben said. "We were gonna wait until the time was right to say anything —"

"What better time than now?" Carmen asked. "Your father is here, my father is here, and they are about to forge an alliance." She faced Don Felipe and Tolliver. "Is this not true?"

"We said we'd fight them damned renegades together," Tolliver said. "I never figured my own son would . . . would go crazy like this —"

Don Felipe cut in. "You mean to say it is crazy for a young man to fall in love with such a wonderful — if headstrong — young woman such as my daughter?"

"Hell, that's not what I mean, and you know it. I always thought Carmen was a fine young lady."

"And Benjamin is a fine young man," Don Felipe snapped back.

Grinning, Doc Ervin stepped forward and said, "Will you two old pelicans just stop and listen to yourselves? Everybody here can tell that you want to shake hands and put the past behind you. You're just too blasted stubborn to admit it."

"Stubborn, am I?" Tolliver blazed. "Well, we'll just see about that!" He took a step toward Almanzar and held out his hand. "Felipe, I tell you this flat out, as square as I can make it: Whatever you thought there might be between me and your wife, you were wrong. I never did anything to insult your honor, and neither did she, God rest her soul. But I know it was a mighty bad time for you, and I reckon I can see why you felt like you did. I'm willing to call it all quits and put it behind us. What do you say?"

For a long moment, Don Felipe didn't say anything. His face was as hard and unreadable as an Aztec carving.

But then the stern lines softened a little, and slowly, his hand came up. He reached out and clasped Tolliver's hand. "Men fight together better when they are amigos," he said hoarsely.

"Damn right . . . pard," Tolliver said.

Frank felt a surge of satisfaction. Old habits were hard to break, and there might still be some friction between Tolliver and Don Felipe in the future, but Frank was willing to bet that they would work it out and solve any problems as they came up.

They would never again be bitter enemies as they had been.

All that assumed, of course, that they would live through the battle to come.

That thought had just gone through Frank's brain when one of the sentries called from the mouth of the canyon, "Riders comin'! Comin' fast!"

39

Dirt was quickly thrown over the fire, extin-guishing the flames, and the fifty or so men in the canyon spread out, drawing their guns and getting ready for trouble. But a moment later a familiar voice shouted, "Hello to the camp! We're comin' in!"

"That's Nick!" Tolliver exclaimed. "He's back!"

Sure enough, a moment later Nick Holmes and the man who had gone with him on the scouting expedition rode in. Frank and the other leaders of the group gathered around them as they dismounted.

Tolliver clasped Nick's shoulder and said, "How are you, boy? What did you find out?"

The weariness that Nick felt could be heard in the young man's voice as he said, "I'm all right, I reckon. And we've got a little good news, too. Jack and me have been to all the ranches hereabouts, and they're all quiet. We didn't go right up to 'em, of course, since there could have been outlaws there waitin' to set a trap for anybody who came scoutin', but we checked them out from a distance and didn't see any signs of trouble, no buildings burned or folks shot up or anything like that."

"Same thing was true of San Rosa," the other scout put in. "We looked the settlement over with field glasses, and it seemed peaceful enough."

Murmurs of relief went through the crowd gathered around the scouts.

"But there's one place that wasn't true," Nick added grimly. "The Rocking T."

Tolliver stiffened. "What's going on there?"

"A council of war, looked like. Late this afternoon, Estancia and a bunch of Rurales rode in. Wedge came out to meet them, and him and Estancia were talkin' when they went back into the bunkhouse." Nick shook his head regretfully. "The main house is gone, burned down."

Tolliver sighed and nodded. "I figured as much after that dynamite started such a big fire."

Nick grew excited again as he went on. "I think the whole bunch is there, Cecil. Could be they're tryin' to decide what to do next." Nick paused and looked around, frowning in the light of the rising moon as he saw all the sombrero-wearing figures. "What in blazes is goin' on here? Who are all these folks?"

Don Felipe stepped forward. "My men and I have come to help, Señor Holmes."

"And my followers as well," Carmen put in.

Nick jumped a little in surprise. Obviously he hadn't noticed Carmen until now. "What the hell!"

"It's a long story, Nick," Ben said. "This is Carmen Almanzar . . . sometimes known as the Black Scorpion, I guess." Ben shook his head. "It was news to me, too."

Frank had listened with great interest to the scouts' report. Now he asked Nick, "Are you sure that most of the Rangers and the Rurales are at the Rocking T?"

"Judging by the number of horses in the corral, I'd say they are," Nick replied with a nod. "We stayed close by until after dark, just to make sure, and it didn't look like they were going anywhere."

"The Rangers aren't in San Rosa anymore?"

"There may be a few still around there, but not many," Nick said.

Frank looked at Tolliver, Don Felipe,

and Doc Ervin. "This is our chance," he said. "We can hit them while they're all gathered at the Rocking T, just like they did to us."

"How do we know this is not some sort of trap?" Don Felipe asked.

"We don't," Frank said bluntly. "But Wedge thinks he's got us on the run, and Estancia doesn't even know you and your men are on this side of the river, Don Felipe."

"He knows the Black Scorpion is here," Carmen pointed out.

"Yes, but he doesn't know that you've teamed up with the Texans. He shouldn't have any idea that our force is now almost as big as his and Estancia's. My guess is that they've gotten together to figure out how to carve up the border country between themselves, now that they think no one is strong enough to challenge them anymore."

"I say we prove 'em wrong!" Tolliver declared, punching the air with a clenched fist.

After a second, Don Felipe nodded as well. "We should strike while we can. We may not get another chance."

"I'll go along with that," Doc Ervin said.

"And I," Carmen added.

Ben Tolliver and Don Felipe said at the same time, "You're not going along."

Carmen didn't know which of them to glare at first. "I am part of this now," she insisted. "You cannot keep me out of it." She waved at some of the men. "These are my followers."

Lupe stepped up and said, "They will ride with me into battle, Señorita. I am sorry, but your father and Señor Ben are right. What is coming tonight will be no place for a woman."

"Oh!" Carmen exclaimed furiously.

"I'll hogtie you and leave you here if I have to," Ben warned.

Don Felipe nodded. "Yes, you should learn now that you will have to take a firm hand with this one, Benjamin."

Carmen fumed and fussed, but Ben and her father ignored her.

"Let's get mounted up," Frank suggested. "It'll take some time to reach the Rocking T, but that's all right. We'll hit them right after the moon sets, not long before dawn."

Don Felipe was unwilling to leave Carmen at Sand Mountain by herself. He picked one vaquero to go with her to San Rosa and wait there in the vicinity of the settlement, well hidden until they knew for sure that the Texans and their Mexican allies had been victorious in their attack on the renegades. Then the rest of the group, led by Frank, Cecil Tolliver, Don Felipe Almanzar, and Doc Ervin, set out for the Rocking T.

As Frank had said, the ride took most of the night. The eastern sky was gray, a harbinger of the approaching dawn, when the men neared the ranch. Along the way, the leaders had discussed strategy, so they knew what to do when they got there. Splitting into four groups of twelve to fifteen men each, the men spread out to the compass points. They would attack not in unison but in a slightly staggered maneuver, each group waiting thirty seconds before charging. The northern group would strike first, led by Frank. He had insisted on that, even though Doc Ervin had seemed to think he was too banged up to even be part of this fight. Just try keeping him out of it, Frank had replied with a grin, but he meant every word of it.

After that, the attack would proceed in a counterclockwise rotation. Frank had suggested staggering the charges just in case this really was some sort of trap. He believed that they would take Wedge and

Estancia by surprise, but it wouldn't hurt to be a little cautious. This way, if it was a trap, not all the men would be caught in it.

Just before they split up, Frank shook hands with the other leaders. "See you when the fight is over," he said with a smile.

Then he checked the Colt, slid it back into the holster, and led his men into position.

Waiting for the battle to start reminded Frank of similar experiences during the War of Northern Aggression. As harrowing as combat could be, often waiting was worse.

Finally, enough time had passed so that Frank knew the others were in position. He drew the Winchester from the sheath lashed to Stormy's saddle and worked the lever. "Let's go," he said quietly to the men with him.

They rode forward, slowly at first and then picking up speed. Ahead of them Frank could see scattered lights that indicated a few lamps were already burning at the Rocking T, despite the early hour. Normally by this time the ranch hands would be getting ready for another day's work, but the outlaws and killers who inhabited the place now weren't that industrious.

Wedge and Estancia weren't careless, though. They had guards posted, and those men couldn't fail to hear the hoofbeats of the approaching horses. As Frank and his men swept toward the ranch, he heard shouts of alarm and saw gouts of flame spurting from gun muzzles. The guards were firing blindly, though; the moon had set, and the darkest hour of the night was upon them.

Frank guided Stormy with his knees and brought the Winchester to his shoulder. He targeted one of the muzzle flashes and squeezed the trigger. The whip-crack of the rifle's report split the night. Frank worked the lever, shifted his aim, and fired again. All around him, the rifles and six-guns of the men with him began to sing a deadly song as well.

To the west, the men in the next group would be counting off the seconds after that opening volley, and when they reached thirty they would charge. After that the other two groups would attack in order, and in less than two minutes, the entire force would be engaged.

That was the way it played out. Frank and his men galloped past the corrals and sprayed the barns with lead as startled Rangers and Rurales hurried outside to see what was going on. They ran right into a storm of lead that scythed them off their feet.

When the rifle was empty, Frank rammed it back in its sheath and drew the revolver that Lupe had given him. It was a Peacemaker just like the one he usually carried, and it had been well cared for. The gun leaped in Frank's hand as he triggered at running Rurales, the bullets sending a couple of them spinning limply to the ground in death.

All over the sprawling ranch headquarters the battle raged. Frank could tell that the renegades had been taken completely by surprise, and the tide was turning swiftly against them. With a tug on the reins, Frank veered the Appaloosa past the burned-out hulk of the main house toward the bunkhouse. Nick had said that was where Wedge and Estancia had gone. Frank didn't want either of those killers to get away.

Gunsmoke and dust clogged the air, but Frank caught a glimpse of a familiar figure running toward a corral where horses milled around in a frenzy, spooked by all the shooting. Estancia! Frank sent Stormy lunging after the Rurale officer. He didn't think Estancia would be able to control any of those crazed horses enough to mount up and make a getaway, but he didn't want to risk it. Estancia had made a habit of slipping out of trouble.

Not this time, Frank vowed as he holstered the Colt. Not this time.

As Stormy closed the distance in a couple of long strides, Frank kicked his feet out of the stirrups and launched himself in a diving tackle. He slammed into Estancia from behind, wrapping his arms around the officer's waist as he knocked Estancia off his feet. Both men rolled through the dust near the corral.

Frank came up first and swung a fist, crashing it into Estancia's jaw and stretching the man out on the ground. Pouncing, Frank landed on top of Estancia. He smashed a right and a left into Estancia's face, bouncing his head off the hard-packed dirt. Frank Morgan had never been a vindictive man, but as he struck the blows he couldn't help but think about the beating he had suffered at the hands of Estancia's minions.

Estancia was stunned, only half-conscious. Frank pushed himself up and got to his feet. As he did so, a strident yell from behind warned him. He whirled around and saw one of the Rurales charging him, bayonet thrust out to impale him. There was no time to get out of the way.

But there was time for Morgan's amazing gun speed to come into play. Frank's hand flickered to his holster and the Colt came up roaring, spitting fire and lead. The bullet drove deep into the Rurale's chest and flung him backward. The tip of the bayonet had been only inches from Frank's stomach when he fired.

Suddenly, Estancia kicked out and knocked Frank's legs from under him. The officer had been shamming to a certain extent, Frank realized as he fell. He tried to roll away, but Estancia landed on top of him and knocked the Peacemaker out of Frank's hand. The gun slid away. Estancia went after it, desperation giving him added speed. His hand closed around the butt of the gun and he brought it up and around, swinging it toward Frank.

Another gun roared and Estancia staggered. He was already crouching. Now he bent over even more and dropped the gun to paw feebly at his chest where the bullet had gone through him. He opened his mouth and blood poured out. Slowly, he crumpled forward and landed on his elbows and knees. His head drooped. After a second he fell over on his side and lay motionless in death.

Frank looked around and saw Don Felipe Almanzar sitting there on his horse, a smoking gun in his hand. Frank lifted a hand in acknowledgment, and Don Felipe nodded. Then the don wheeled his mount and plunged back into the fight that was still swirling around the ranch.

The firing was beginning to die away, however, and Frank knew the battle was almost over. As he picked up his Colt, opened the cylinder, and began to thumb fresh cartridges into it, he looked around and saw the bodies of Rurales and renegade Rangers lying everywhere. He snapped the Colt's cylinder shut and strode toward the bunkhouse, becoming aware as he did so that the dawn had arrived. The eastern sky was rosy now, casting the first light of a new day over the Rocking T.

Frank was looking for Nathan Wedge. So far, he hadn't caught even a glimpse of the Ranger captain. Wedge had to be here somewhere. . . .

Or maybe not. Cecil Tolliver came riding up and called urgently, "Frank! Doc told me he spotted Wedge on horseback, heading hell-bent-for-leather toward San Rosa!"

Alarm went through Frank. Wedge might have a few men left in the settlement. He could intend to rally them, or he might be just trying to escape.

But would he go alone? Or would he grab Roanne Williamson and take her with him?

Frank gave a shrill whistle, summoning Stormy. "Thanks, Cecil," he said to Tolliver. "If you and Don Felipe can handle the mopping up here, I'm going after Wedge!"

The rancher's bearded face split in a grin. "That's what I was hopin' you'd say. Go get the son of a bitch and give him a bullet for me! I got a burned-down house he's partly to blame for, the hydrophobic skunk!"

Frank grabbed the saddle horn as Stormy trotted up. In a flash, he was in the saddle again and had heeled the Appaloosa into a run.

Leaving the Rocking T behind, Frank galloped toward San Rosa and what he hoped would be the final showdown with Nathan Wedge.

40

San Rosa appeared quiet and peaceful in the early morning light as Frank rode toward the settlement. The street was deserted. That right there told Frank something was still wrong in this town. If Wedge and the other Rangers who had been left here to keep the citizens under control were gone, folks would have flocked outside to celebrate. Storekeepers would be sweeping off the walks in front of their places of business. Wagons would be rolling through the street. San Rosa would start getting back to normal.

Instead, the silence and emptiness meant that everyone was still lying low. Frank would have to draw the enemy out.

He did so by riding right down the middle of the street, inviting their fire. They didn't disappoint him. In the eerie stillness, he suddenly heard the scrape of boot leather on boards and swiveled his head toward the false front of the Border Palace Saloon. When he spotted the rifle butt protruding through the window opening, his hand dipped to the Colt on his hip and brought it up blazing.

Frank fired twice, the bullets punching through the boards of the false front and knocking the hidden gunman backward. The rifle in his hands discharged, but the bullet screamed off harmlessly into the air. The dead man rolled down the sloping roof of the building and fell with a thud in the alley next to the saloon.

Stormy shied to the left, whinnying angrily, and Frank twisted to the right in time to see another outlaw leap out the door of a hardware store brandishing a shotgun. As the scattergun roared, Frank left the saddle in a dive. The twin loads of buckshot hadn't had time to spread out much as they tore through the space where Frank had been a heartbeat earlier. Landing lithely in the road in a crouch, Frank fired up at the shotgunner. His slug caught the man in the body and threw him back against the window behind him. The glass shattered into a million pieces as the gunman fell through it. The broken window lay in glittering shards around his unmoving body.

Frank surged up and darted across the street as a rifle barked at him, the bullets kicking up dust around his feet. The rifleman was on the roof of the blacksmith shop. Frank snapped a couple of shots at him and saw the man clutch his leg and fall. He slid off the roof and dropped hard to the ground, wounded badly enough to be out of the fight.

Ducking into an alcove at the entrance of a closed café, Frank pressed his back against the wall and watched the street closely as he reloaded. His experienced fingers could handle that chore by feel. This time he thumbed six bullets into the Colt, instead of leaving one chamber empty for the hammer to rest on.

He didn't know how many of the enemy were left, and he still hadn't seen Nathan Wedge. But as the echoes of the shots rolled across the Texas plains and faded away, Frank heard the planks of the boardwalk creak a little, first to his right and then to his left.

Men were closing in on the alcove from both directions. If he waited, they would have a chance to catch him in a cross fire.

He wasn't going to give them that chance.

Frank took a deep breath and charged out of the alcove, diving into the street.

Guns blasted behind him as nervous trigger fingers spasmed. He landed, rolled, and came up firing to his left, blasting two shots into the man who had been sneaking up on him from that direction. The bullets slammed the outlaw into the wall of the building. He bounced off, leaving a bloody smear on the boards, and collapsed on the walk.

Even before that man fell, Frank pivoted smoothly toward the second would-be killer. He didn't fire, though, because he saw that the man had already dropped his gun and had his hands pressed to his belly as he bent over. Blood welled between his fingers. He looked at the man Frank had just shot and grated, "Leo, you . . . idiot . . . you done shot . . . me . . ."

The idea of a cross fire had backfired on this gunman. His own partner had ventilated him while trying to hit Frank. The gut-shot man fell to his knees and pitched forward on his face.

"Morgan!"

Frank sprang to his feet and turned toward the sound of the shout. Once again he had to stop his finger from pulling the trigger, because Nathan Wedge had just come out of the building that housed Roanne's dress shop and her living quarters. He had Roanne in front of him, an arm looped around her neck holding her in position as a shield. Wedge's other hand pressed a revolver to her head.

Wedge forced Roanne toward Frank. "You've ruined everything, Morgan," the renegade Ranger said bitterly. "I should've killed you in Mexico instead of figuring the Black Scorpion would do it."

"Yeah, you should have," Frank said, "especially since the Black Scorpion is on the side of the honest Texans now. Estancia's dead, and so is the plan you hatched with him."

"I didn't hatch anything with Estancia," Wedge snapped. "The whole thing was my idea. When he'd helped me get what I wanted, I would have double-crossed the dirty greaser and killed him, too."

"Well, it's over now. You might as well drop that gun and let Miss Williamson go."

"The hell I will! I'm getting out of here, and she's going with me."

Frank shook his head. "Nope. You're not going anywhere."

Wedge sneered at him. "You can't stop me, you dumb son of a bitch."

"Actually," Frank said as he lifted the Colt, "I can."

He fired.

The bullet hit the cylinder of Wedge's gun, knocking it straight backward away from Roanne and driving it into Wedge's throat before he could pull the trigger. The impact smashed his larynx and left him gasping for air. His grip on Roanne slipped, and she pulled away from him and flung herself to the side. Frank waited to see if Wedge was going to surrender now, but instead the renegade Ranger fumbled behind his back and brought out another gun that had been tucked behind his belt. Frank sighed and fired again. This time the bullet hit Wedge in the midsection and doubled him over. He dropped the second gun and staggered a couple of steps to the side. When he lifted his head to stare at Frank, his face had already started to turn blue and purple. He was literally choking to death, and it was a good question: What would kill him first, the crushed throat or the bullet in his vitals?

Frank rendered the question moot by firing a third time, putting this bullet through Wedge's forehead. Wedge went over backward and landed in a loose sprawl. Blood began to puddle under his head and his body.

Frank let out the breath he had been holding and slowly lowered his gun.

Hoofbeats behind him made him turn swiftly and raise it again.

The half-dozen men entering San Rosa from the eastern end of Main Street reined in, coming to an abrupt halt. One of them walked his horse forward. He was a tall, ruggedly handsome man, and Frank had never seen him before.

Pinned to the breast of his butternut shirt was a Texas Ranger badge.

He brought his horse, a magnificent golden sorrel, to a halt a few yards from Frank. His wide mouth quirked in a grin as he said, "Take it easy, hombre. In case you didn't know it, I'm a Texas Ranger, and we don't take kindly to havin' guns pointed at us."

Frank leaned his head toward the sprawled body of Nathan Wedge and said, "He was a Texas Ranger, too."

The stranger looked at Wedge, and his gray-green eyes seemed to change color, turning to ice as the smile disappeared from his face. "Wedge?" he asked.

"That's right."

"Then he wasn't a Ranger, mister. Hasn't been since the first day he stepped over the line to the owlhoot side." The man cuffed his wide-brimmed Stetson back on his thick black hair. "My name's Hatfield. The governor and Cap'n

516

McDowell sent me and a few pards down here after they got word from a rancher named Tolliver about what was goin' on." Grim humor edged into Hatfield's voice as he went on. "We were supposed to clean up a mess, but it looks like you've already done it, Mister . . . ?"

"Morgan. Frank Morgan." Frank finally lowered his gun again and holstered it this time. The young cowhand called Hardy had gotten through to Laredo before he was captured, but as it turned out, the fighting Texans hadn't needed the help after all.

"The Drifter," Hatfield said.

"That's right."

"Wedge didn't know what he was lettin' himself in for, did he?"

"He wouldn't have cared if he did," Frank said with a shake of his head. "All he could see was the power he wanted, and he was willing to do anything to get it."

"Any more of the varmints left?"

"I don't think so. Some friends have rounded up what's left of them, out at a ranch called the Rocking T."

"We know where that is. We'll ride out there and see if your friends need a hand." Hatfield paused. "That is, if you can take care of everything here, Morgan."

Frank turned and looked at Roanne, who now stood in front of her shop waiting for him. She still looked a little shaken, but as her eyes met Frank's, a warm smile spread over her face.

"You go on ahead, Hatfield," Frank said. "I reckon everything here is just fine."

It was a beautiful evening, cool and clear, and guitar music floated through the air from one of the cantinas that catered to San Rosa's Mexican population. Frank and Roanne strolled along the street, Dog trailing behind them. The big cur still seemed disappointed that he had not been able to take part in the final showdown with Wedge. The renegade had managed to shut him up in one of the rooms in Roanne's house when he showed up early that morning.

Now Roanne had a shawl around her shoulders against the chill, and Frank wore his denim jacket. They had eaten dinner in the café, and he was walking her home.

"It's nice to see the town getting back to normal so quickly," she said. "It was really horrible, having the men we trusted at first to maintain law and order turn out to be the worst outlaws this part of the country has ever seen."

Frank nodded. "You're right. To be honest, across the border they're used to the Rurales being a pretty low-down bunch, but the Rangers have always been above that."

"Well, with Ranger Hatfield and his friends here now, we shouldn't have to worry about any of the renegades who got away."

"There were only a few, according to Cecil Tolliver, and I imagine they've all taken off for the tall and uncut by now. Likely they won't ever show their faces in this part of Texas again."

Roanne stopped and looked up at him. "What about you, Frank?" she asked. "Are you going to stay around here for a while?"

"Why, sure," he said. "I plan to be on hand for the wedding when Ben Tolliver and Carmen Almanzar get hitched. That may be a while, though, since Don Felipe insisted that Ben has to court Carmen properly for a while first."

Roanne laughed softly. "I can't believe she was really the Black Scorpion."

"Only for a little while," Frank said. The whole story was out in the open now, and everyone knew about the way Antonio Almanzar had gathered a band of daring followers to try to break Estancia's brutal hold on the border country south of the Rio Grande. "With Wedge and Estancia and their men all gone, I don't reckon there'll be any need for the Black Scorpion to ride again."

But you never knew, he thought. Out here in the West, darned near anything was possible. . . .

Footsteps on the boardwalk made them turn. Doc Ervin's lanky figure approached. The sawbones paused and tipped his hat to Roanne. "Miss Williamson," he greeted her. "Good to see you again. How are you, Frank?"

"Just fine, Doc. Where have you been?"

"Making the rounds of my patients. A doctor's work is never done, you know." Doc chuckled. "About the same as a gunfighter's, I guess."

"That's where you're wrong, Doc," Frank said. "My work is over and done with."

"I wish that was true, my friend . . . for your sake."

Doc said his good-nights and moved on, and when he was gone, Roanne asked quietly, "Was Doc right, Frank? Will there ever truly be peace for you?"

"Maybe someday," Frank said. "Right now, there's peace in San Rosa, and that's good enough for me."

"Me, too," she said, smiling up at him. She linked her arm with his and leaned her head on his shoulder, and together they strolled on into the night.

Frank Morgan had come to the border country looking for a warm place to spend the winter.

He reckoned he had found it.

Afterword

Notes from the Old West

In the small town where I grew up, there were two movie theaters. The Pavilion was one of those old-timey movie show palaces, built in the heyday of Mary Pickford and Charlie Chaplin — the silent era of the 1920s. By the 1950s, when I was a kid, the Pavilion was a little worn around the edges, but it was still the premier theater in town. They played all those big Technicolor biblical Cecil B. DeMille epics and corny MGM musicals. In Cinemascope, of course.

On the other side of town was the Gem, a somewhat shabby and run-down grind house with sticky floors and torn seats. Admission was a quarter. The Gem booked low-budget "B" pictures (remember the Bowery Boys?), war movies, horror flicks, and Westerns. I liked the Westerns best. I could usually be found every Saturday at the Gem, along with my best friend,

Newton Trout, watching Westerns from 10 a.m. until my father came looking for me around suppertime. (Sometimes Newton's dad was dispatched to come fetch us.) One time, my dad came to get me right in the middle of *Abilene Trail*, which featured the now-forgotten Whip Wilson. My father became so engrossed in the action he sat down and watched the rest of it with us. We didn't get home until after dark, and my mother's meat loaf was a pan of gray ashes by the time we did. Though my father and I were both in the doghouse the next day, this remains one of my fondest childhood memories. There was Wild Bill Elliot, and Gene Autry, and Roy Rogers, and Tim Holt, and, a little later, Rod Cameron and Audie Murphy. Of these newcomers, I never missed an Audie Murphy Western, because Audie was sort of an antihero. Sure, he stood for law and order and was an honest man, but sometimes he had to go around the law to uphold it. If he didn't play fair, it was only because he felt hamstrung by the laws of the land. Whatever it took to get the bad guys, Audie did it. There were no finer points of law, no splitting of legal hairs. It was instant justice, devoid of long-winded lawyers, bored or biased jurors, or black-robed, often corrupt judges.

Steal a man's horse and you were the guest of honor at a necktie party.

Molest a good woman and you got a bullet in the heart or a rope around the gullet. Or at the very least, got the crap beat out of you. Rob a bank and face a hail of bullets or the hangman's noose.

Saved a lot of time and money, did frontier justice.

That's all gone now, I'm sad to say. Now you hear, "Oh, but he had a bad childhood" or "His mother didn't give him enough love" or "The homecoming queen wouldn't give him a second look and he has an inferiority complex." Or "cultural rage," as the politically correct bright boys refer to it. How many times have you heard some self-important defense attorney moan, "The poor kids were only venting their hostilities toward an uncaring society?"

Mule fritters, I say. Nowadays, you can't even call a punk a punk anymore. But don't get me started.

It was, "Howdy, ma'am" time too. The good guys, antihero or not, were always respectful to the ladies. They might shoot a bad guy five seconds after tipping their hat to a woman, but the code of the West demanded you be respectful to a lady.

Lots of things have changed since the heyday of the Wild West, haven't they? Some for the good, some for the bad.

I didn't have any idea at the time that I would someday write about the West. I just knew that I was captivated by the Old West.

When I first got the itch to write, back in the early 1970s, I didn't write Westerns. I started by writing horror and action adventure novels. After more than two dozen novels, I began thinking about developing a Western character. From those initial musings came the novel *The Last Mountain Man: Smoke Jensen*. That was followed by *Preacher: The First Mountain Man*. A few years later, I began developing the Last Gunfighter series. Frank Morgan is a legend in his own time, the fastest gun west of the Mississippi . . . a title and a reputation he never wanted, but can't get rid of.

The Gunfighter series is set in the waning days of the Wild West. Frank Morgan is out of time and place, but still, he is pursued by men who want to earn a reputation as the man who killed the legendary gunfighter. All Frank wants to do is live in peace. But he knows in his heart that dream will always be just that: a dream, fog and smoke and mirrors, something elusive that will never really come to fruition. He will be forced to wander the West, alone, until one day his luck runs out.

For me, and for thousands — probably millions — of other people (although many will never publicly admit it), the old Wild West will always be a magic, mysterious place: a place we love to visit through the pages of books; characters we would like to know . . . from a safe distance; events we would love to take part in, again, from a safe distance. For the old Wild West was not a place for the faint of heart. It was a hard, tough, physically demanding time. There were no police to call if one faced adversity. One faced trouble alone, and handled it alone. It was rugged individualism: something that appeals to many of us.

I am certain that is something that appeals to most readers of Westerns.

I still do on-site research (whenever possible) before starting a Western novel. I have wandered over much of the West, prowling what is left of ghost towns. Stand in the midst of the ruins of these old towns, use a little bit of imagination, and one can conjure up life as it used to be in the Wild West. The rowdy Saturday nights, the tinkling of a piano in a saloon, the laughter of cowboys and miners letting off steam after a week of hard work. Use a little more imagination and one can envision two men standing in the street, facing one another, seconds before the hook and draw of a gunfight. A moment later, one is dead and the other rides away.

The old wild untamed West.

There are still some ghost towns to visit, but they are rapidly vanishing as time and the elements take their toll. If you want to see them, make plans to do so as soon as possible, for in a few years, they will all be gone.

And so will we.

Stand in what is left of the Big Thicket country of east Texas and try to imagine how in the world the pioneers managed to get through that wild tangle. I have wondered about that many times and marveled at the courage of the men and women who slowly pushed westward, facing dangers that we can only imagine.

Let me touch briefly on a subject that is very close to me: firearms. There are some so-called historians who are now claiming that firearms played only a very insignificant part in the settlers' lives. They claim that only a few were armed. What utter, stupid nonsense! What do these so-called historians think the pioneers did for food? Do they think the early settlers rode down to the nearest supermarket and bought their meat? Or maybe they think the settlers chased down deer or buffalo on foot and beat the animals to death with a club. I have a news flash for you so-called historians: The settlers used guns to shoot their game. They used guns to defend hearth and home against Indians on the warpath. They used guns to protect themselves from outlaws. Guns are a part of Americana. And always will be.

The mountains of the West and the remains of the ghost towns that dot those areas are some of my favorite subjects to write about. I have done extensive research on the various mountain ranges of the West and go back whenever time permits. I sometimes stand surrounded by the towering mountains and wonder how in the world the pioneers ever made it through. As hard as I try and as often as I try, I simply cannot imagine the hardships those men and women endured over the hard months of their incredible journey. None of us can. It is said that on the Oregon

Trail alone, there are at least two bodies in lonely, unmarked graves for every mile of that journey. Some students of the West say the number of dead is at least twice that. And nobody knows the exact number of wagons that impatiently started out alone and simply vanished on the way, along with their occupants, never to be seen or heard from again.

Just vanished.

The one-hundred-and-fifty-year-old ruts of the wagon wheels can still be seen in various places along the Oregon Trail. But if you plan to visit those places, do so quickly, for they are slowly disappearing. And when they are gone, they will be lost forever, except in the words of Western writers.

As long as I can peck away at a keyboard and find a company to publish my work, I will not let the Old West die. That I promise you.

As The Drifter in the Last Gunfighter series, Frank Morgan has struck a responsive chord among the readers of frontier fiction. Perhaps it's because he is a human man, with all of the human frailties. He is not a superhero. He likes horses and dogs and treats them well. He has feelings and isn't afraid to show them or admit that he has them. He longs for a permanent home, a place to hang his hat and sit on the porch in the late afternoon and watch the day slowly fade into night . . . and a woman to share those simple pleasures with him. But Frank also knows he can never relax his vigil and probably will never have that long-wished-for hearth and home. That is why he is called The Drifter. Frank Morgan knows there are men who will risk their lives to face him in a hook and draw, slap leather, pull that big iron, in the hopes of killing the West's most famous gunfighter, so they can claim the title of the man who killed Frank Morgan, The Drifter. Frank would gladly, willingly, give them that title, but not at the expense of his own life.

So Frank Morgan must constantly drift, staying on the lonely trails, those out-of-the-way paths through the timber, the mountains, the deserts that are sometimes called the hoot-owl trail. His companions are the sighing winds, the howling of wolves, the yapping of coyotes, and a few, very few, precious memories. And his six-gun. Always, his six-gun.

Frank is also pursued by something else: progress. The towns are connected by telegraph wires. Frank is recognized wherever he goes and can be tracked by telegraphers. There is no escape for him. Reporters for various newspapers are always on his trail, wanting to interview Frank Morgan, as are authors, wanting to do more books about the legendary gunfighter. Photographers want to take his picture, if possible with the body of a man Frank has just killed. Frank is disgusted by the whole thing and wants no part of it. There is no real rest for The Drifter. Frank travels on, always on the move. He tries to stay off the more heavily traveled roads, sticking to lesser-known trails, sometimes making his own route of travel, across the mountains or deserts.

Someday perhaps Frank will find some peace. Maybe. But if he does, that is many books from now.

The West will live on as long as there are writers willing to write about it, and publishers willing to publish it. Writing about the West is wide open, just like the old Wild West. Characters abound, as plentiful as the wide-open spaces, as colorful as a sunset on the Painted Desert, as restless as the ever-sighing winds. All one has to do is use a bit of imagination. Take a stroll through the cemetery at Tombstone, Arizona; read the inscriptions. Then walk the main street of that once-infamous town around midnight and you might catch a glimpse of the ghosts that still wander the town. They really do. Just ask anyone who lives there. But don't be afraid of the apparitions, they won't hurt you. They're just out for a quiet stroll.

The West lives on. And as long as I am alive, it always will.

William Johnstone

The employees of Thorndike Press hope you have enjoyed this Large Print book. All our Thorndike and Wheeler Large Print titles are designed for easy reading, and all our books are made to last. Other Thorndike Press Large Print books are available at your library, through selected bookstores, or directly from us.

For information about titles, please call:

(800) 223-1244

or visit our Web site at:

www.gale.com/thorndike
www.gale.com/wheeler

To share your comments, please write:

Publisher
Thorndike Press
295 Kennedy Memorial Drive
Waterville, ME   04901